Mike Gardiner

EX LIBRIS

Ross King was born in Canada in 1962. His first
novel, *Domino*, was published to critical acclaim in
1995 and has since been translated into six languages.
Ex Libris is his second novel. He lives with his wife
near Oxford.

D1043273

ALSO BY ROSS KING

Domino

Ross King

EX LIBRIS

V

VINTAGE

I am grateful to Dr Bryan King for his assistance with
matters alchemical and astronomical.

Published by Vintage 1999

2 4 6 8 10 9 7 5 3 1

Copyright © Ross King 1998

The right of Ross King to be identified as the author of
this work has been asserted by him in accordance with
the Copyright, Designs and Patents Act, 1988

This book is sold subject to the condition that it shall not
by way of trade or otherwise, be lent, resold, hired out,
or otherwise circulated without the publisher's prior
consent in any form of binding or cover other than that in
which it is published and without a similar condition
including this condition being imposed on the subsequent purchaser

First published in Great Britain by
Chatto & Windus in 1998

Vintage
Random House, 20 Vauxhall Bridge Road,
London SW1V 2SA

Random House Australia (Pty) Limited
20 Alfred Street, Milsons Point, Sydney
New South Wales 2061, Australia

Random House New Zealand Limited
18 Poland Road, Glenfield,
Auckland 10, New Zealand

Random House South Africa (Pty) Limited
Endulini, 5A Jubilee Road, Parktown 2193, South Africa

Random House UK Limited Reg. No. 954009

A CIP catalogue record for this book
is available from the British Library

ISBN   0 7493 9585 0

Papers used by Random House UK Ltd are natural,
recyclable products made from wood grown in sustain-
able forests. The manufacturing processes conform to the
environmental regulations of the country of origin

Printed and bound in Great Britain by
Cox & Wyman, Reading, Berkshire

For Lynn

Me, poor man, my library
Was dukedom large enough . . .

Shakespeare, *The Tempest*

I

The Library

Chapter One

Anyone wishing to purchase a book in London in the year 1660 had a choice of four areas. Ecclesiastical works could be bought from the booksellers in St Paul's Churchyard, while the shops and stalls of Little Britain specialised in Greek and Latin volumes, and those on the western edge of Fleet Street stocked legal texts for the city's barristers and magistrates. The fourth place to look for a book – and by far the best – would have been on London Bridge.

In those days the gabled buildings on the ancient bridge housed a motley assortment of shops. Here were found two glovers, a swordmaker, two milliners, a tea merchant, a book-binder, several shoemakers, as well as a manufacturer of silk parasols, an invention that had lately come into fashion. There was also, on the north end, the shop of a *plummassier* who sold brightly coloured feathers for the crowns of beaver hats like that worn by the new king. Most of all, though, the bridge was home to fine booksellers – six of them in all by 1660. Because these shops were not stocked to suit the needs of vicars or lawyers, or anyone else in particular, they were more varied than those in the other three districts, so that almost everything ever scratched on to a parchment or printed and bound between covers could be found on their shelves. And the shop on London Bridge whose wares were the most varied of all stood halfway across, in Nonsuch House, where, above a green door and two sets of polished window-plates, hung a signboard whose weather-worn inscription read:

NONSUCH BOOKS
All Volumes Bought & Sold
Isaac Inchbold, Proprietor

I am Isaac Inchbold, Proprietor. By the summer of 1660 I had owned Nonsuch Books for some eighteen years. The bookshop itself, with its copiously furnished shelves on the ground floor and its cramped lodgings one twist of a turnpike stair above those, had resided on London Bridge – and in a corner of Nonsuch House, the most handsome of its buildings – for much longer: almost forty years. I had been apprenticed there in 1635, at the age of fourteen, after my father died during an outburst of plague and my mother, confronted shortly afterwards with his debts, helped herself to a cup of poison. The death of Mr Smallpace, my master – also from the plague – coincided with the end of my apprenticeship and my entry as a freeman into the Company of Stationers. And so on that momentous day I became proprietor of Nonsuch Books, where I have lived ever since in the disorder of several thousand morocco- and buckram-bound companions.

Mine was a quiet and contemplative life among my walnut shelves. It was made up of a series of undisturbed routines modestly pursued. I was a man of wisdom and learning – or so I liked to think – but of dwarfish worldly experience. I knew everything about books, but little, I admit, of the world that bustled past outside my green door. I ventured into this alien sphere of churning wheels and puffing smoke and scurrying feet as seldom as circumstances permitted. By 1660 I had travelled barely more than two dozen leagues beyond the gates of London, and I rarely travelled much within London either, not if I could avoid it. While running simple errands I often became hopelessly confused in the maze of crowded, filthy streets that began twenty paces beyond the north gate of the bridge, and as I limped back to my shelves of books I would feel as if I were returning from exile. All of which – combined with near-sightedness, asthma and a club foot that lent me a lopsided gait – makes me, I suppose, an improbable agent in the events that are to follow.

What else must you know about me? I was unduly comfortable and content. I was entering my fortieth year with almost everything a man of my inclinations could ask for. Besides a prospering business, I had all of my teeth, most of my hair, very little grey in my beard, and a handsome, well-tended paunch on which I could balance a book while I sat hour after hour every evening in my favourite horsehair armchair. Each night an old woman named Margaret cooked my supper, and twice a week another poor wretch, Jane, scrubbed my dirty stockings. I had no wife. I had married as a young man, but my wife, Arabella, had died some years ago, five days after scratching her finger on a door-latch. Our world was a dangerous place. I had no children either. I had dutifully sired my share – four in all – but they too had died from one affliction or another and now lay buried alongside their mother in the outer churchyard of St Magnus-the-Martyr, to which I still made weekly excursions with a bouquet from the stall of a flower-seller. I had neither hopes nor expectations of remarriage. My circumstances suited me uncommonly well.

What else? I lived alone except for my apprentice, Tom Monk, who was confined after the conclusion of business hours to the top floor of Nonsuch House, where he ate and slept in a chamber that was not much bigger than a cubby-hole. But Monk never complained. Nor, of course, did I. I was luckier than most of the 400,000 other souls crammed inside the walls of London or outside in the Liberties. My business provided me with £150 per year – a handsome sum in those days, especially for a man without either a family or tastes for the sensual pleasures so readily available in London. And no doubt my quiet and bookish idyll would have continued, no doubt my comfortable life would have remained intact and blissfully undisturbed until I took my place in the small rectangular plot reserved for me next to Arabella, had it not been for a peculiar summons delivered to my shop one day in the summer of 1660.

On that warm morning in July the door to an intricate and singular house creaked invitingly ajar. I who considered myself so wise and sceptical was then to proceed in ignorance along its dark arteries, stumbling through blind passages and secret chambers in which, these many years later, I still find myself searching in vain for a clue. It is easier to find a labyrinth, writes Comenius, than a guiding path. Yet every labyrinth is a circle that begins where it ends, as Boethius tells us, and ends where it begins. So it is that I must double back, retrace my false turns and, by unspooling this thread of words behind me, arrive once again at the place where, for me, the story of Sir Ambrose Plessington began.

The event to which I refer took place on a Tuesday morning in the first week of July. I well remember the date, for it was only a short time after King Charles II had returned from his exile in France to take the throne left empty when his father was beheaded by Cromwell and his cronies eleven years earlier. The day began like any other. I unbarred my wooden shutters, lowered my green awning into a soft breeze, and sent Tom Monk to the General Letter Office in Clock Lane. It was Monk's duty each morning to carry out the ashes from the grate, brush the floors, empty the chamber-pots, cleanse the sink and fetch the coal. But before he performed any of these tasks I sent him into Dowgate to call for my letters. I was most particular about my post, especially on Tuesdays, which was when the mail-bag from Paris arrived by packet-boat. When he finally returned, having dallied, as usual, along Thames Street on the way back, a copy of Shelton's translation of *Don Quixote*, the 1652 edition, was propped on my paunch. I looked up from the page and, adjusting my spectacles, squinted at the shape in the doorway. No spectacle-maker has ever been able to grind a pair of lenses thick enough to remedy my squinch-eyed stare. I marked my place with a forefinger and yawned.

'Anything for us?'

'One letter, sir.'

'Well? Let us have it, then.'

'He made me pay tuppence for it.'

'Pardon me?'

'The clerk.' He extended his hand. 'He said it was undertaxed, sir. Not a paid letter, he said. So I had to pay tuppence.'

'Very well.' I set *Don Quixote* aside, remunerated Monk with a show of irritation, then seized the letter. 'Now off with you. Go fetch the coal.'

I was expecting to hear from Monsieur Grimaud, my factor

in Paris, who had been instructed to bid on my behalf for a copy of Vignon's edition of the *Odyssey*. But I saw immediately that the letter, a single sheet tied with string and embossed with a seal, bore the green stamp of the Inland Office rather than the red one of the Foreign Office. This was peculiar, because domestic mail arrived at the General Letter Office on Mondays, Wednesdays and Fridays. For the moment, however, I thought little of this oddity. The Post Office was in a state of upheaval like everything else. Already many of the old postmasters – Cromwell's busiest spies, so the rumours went – had been relieved of their positions, and the Postmaster-General, John Thurloe, was clapped up in the Tower.

I turned the letter over in my hand. In the top, right-hand corner a stamped mark read '1st July', which meant that the letter had arrived in the General Letter Office two days earlier. My name and address were inscribed across it in a secretary hand, slantwise and hectic. The writing was blotched in some places and faint in others, as if the ink was old and powdery or the goose quill splayed at the nib or worn to a stump. The oblong impression of a signet ring on the reverse bore a coat of arms with the legend 'Marchamont'. I cut the frayed string with my penknife, broke the seal with my thumb and unfolded the sheet.

I still possess this strange letter, my summons, the first of the many texts that led me towards the ever-receding figure of Sir Ambrose Plessington, and I reproduce it here, word for word:

28th June
Pontifex Hall
Crampton Magna
Dorsetshire

My good Sir:

I trust you will forgive the impertinence of a Lady writing to a stranger to make what will seem, I have no doubt, a peculiar request; but circumstances force the expediency upon me. These melancholy affairs are of a pressing nature, but I believe you can play no small part in their resolution. I dare not enumerate further details until I have your more private attentions, and must therefore, with regret, depend entirely on your trust.

My request is for your presence at Pontifex Hall at the earliest possible convenience. To this end a coach driven by Mr Phineas Greenleaf will be waiting for you beneath the sign of the Three Pigeons in High Holborn, at 8 o'clock in the morning of the 5th of July. You have nothing to apprehend from this journey, which I promise shall be made worth your while.

Here I must break off, with the assurance that I am, dear Sir, with gratitude,

Your most obliging servant,
Alethea Greatorex

Postscriptum: Let this caution regulate your actions: neither mention to anyone your receipt of this letter, nor disclose to them your destination or purpose.

That was all, nothing more. The strange communication offered no further information, no further inducements. After reading it through once more, my first response was to crumple it into a ball. I had no doubt that the 'melancholy' and 'pressing' business of Alethea Greatorex involved disposing of a crumbling estate entailed upon her by a late indigent husband. The sorry appearance of the unpaid letter suggested the impecunious condition of its author. No doubt Pontifex Hall comprised among its meagre charms a library with whose modest contents she hoped to appease her creditors. Requests of this variety were not unusual, of course. The sad business of assigning values to the dire remains of bankrupt estates – mostly those of old Royalist families whose fortunes had tumbled low during Cromwell's time – had three or four times fallen within the compass of my duties. Usually I purchased the better editions myself, then sent the rest of the worm-eaten lot to auction, or else to Mr Hopcroft, the rag-and-bone man. But never in the course of my duties had I been engaged under such secretive terms or required to travel as far as Dorsetshire.

And yet I didn't discard the letter. One of the more cryptic phrases – 'I dare not enumerate further details' – had snagged my imagination, as did the plea in the postscript for secrecy. I pushed my spectacles further up the bridge of my nose and once again fixed the letter with a myopic squint. I wondered why I should feel I had something to 'apprehend' from the journey and how the vague promise that it would be worth my time might fulfil itself. The profit to which the words alluded seemed at once grander and vaguer than any vulgar financial transaction. Or was this simply my imagination, anxious as usual to weave and then unpick a mystery?

Monk had disposed of the rubbish in the ash-can and was now returning through the door with a few lumps of sea coal clattering in his pail. He set it on the floor, sighed, picked up his broom and brushed apathetically at a beam of sunlight. I laid the letter aside, but a second later took it up to study more closely the secretary hand, an old-fashioned style even for those days. I read the letter again, slowly, and this time its text seemed less explicable, less certainly the appeal of a financially embarrassed widow. I spread it on the counter and studied the crested seal more closely, regretting the haste with which I broke it, for the legend was no longer decipherable.

And it was at this point that I noticed something peculiar about the letter, one more of its strange and, for the moment, inexplicable traits. As I held the paper to the light I realised that the author had folded the paper twice and sealed it not with wax but a rust-coloured shellac. This was not unusual in itself, of course: most people, myself included, sealed their letters by melting a stick of shellac. But as I gathered the flakes and tried to reconstruct the image impressed by the matrix I noticed how the shellac was mingled with a substance of a slightly different colour and composition: something darker and less adherent.

I moved the letter into the beam of light falling across my counter. Monk's broom rasped slowly across the floorboards, and I became aware of his curious gaze. I prised at the seal with the blade of my penknife as gently as an apothecary slicing the seed pod of a rare plant. The compound crumbled and then sprinkled over the counter. A beeswax was clearly distinguishable from the shellac into which, for whatever reason, it was mingled. I carefully separated a few of the grains, puzzled that my hand seemed to be trembling.

'Is there something wrong, Mr Inchbold?'

'No, Monk. Nothing at all. Back to work with you now.'

I straightened and gazed over his head, out of the window. The narrow street was busy with its morning commerce of bobbing heads and revolving wheels. Dust was raised from the carriageway and, caught in the slats of morning sunlight, turned to gold. I lowered my eyes to the flakes on the counter. What, if anything, might the mixture mean? That Lady Marchamont's matrix bore a residue of wax? That she had closed another letter with a beeswax only moments before sealing mine with shellac? It hardly made sense. But then neither did the alternative: that someone had moulded her original wax seal, broken it, then closed it with shellac impressed by a counterfeit seal.

My pulses quickened. Yes, it seemed most likely that the seal had been tampered with. But by whom? Someone in the General Letter Office? That might explain the delay in its delivery – why it was available on a Tuesday instead of a Monday. There were rumours that letter-openers and copyists worked out of the top floor of the General Letter Office. But to what purpose? So far as I knew, my correspondence had never been opened before – not even the packets sent by my factors in Paris and Oxford, those two bastions of Royalist exiles and malcontents.

It was more plausible, of course, that my correspondent was the true object of this scrutiny. Still, I was struck with the oddity of the situation. Why, if she had something to fear, should Lady Marchamont have entrusted her correspondence to a means of conveyance as famously unscrupulous as the Post Office? Why not send the summons with Mr Phineas Greenleaf or some other messenger?

As I folded the letter along its creases and tucked it in my pocket I felt no uneasiness, as perhaps I should have done. Instead I felt only a mild interest. I was curious, that was all. I felt as if the peculiar letter and its seal were merely parts of a difficult but by no means incomprehensible puzzle to be solved by an application of the powers of reason — and I had tremendous faith in the powers of reason, especially my own. The letter was just one more text awaiting its decipherment.

And so on a sudden impulse I arranged for an incredulous Monk to tend to the shop while I, like Don Quixote, prepared to leave my shelves of books and venture into the country — into the world that, so far, I had managed to avoid. For the rest of the day I served my usual customers, helping them, as always, to find editions of this work or commentaries on that one. But today the ritual had been altered, because all the while I felt the letter rustling quietly in my pocket with soft, anonymous whispers of conspiracy. As instructed, I showed it to no one, nor did I tell anyone, not even Monk, where I would be travelling or to whom I proposed to pay my visit.

Chapter Two

One day after the receipt of my summons, in the hour before dawn, three horsemen entered London from the east. They came in sight of the spires and chimney stacks as the stars paled and the clouds were mantled here and there with light: a trio of black-clad riders galloping along the riverside towards Ratcliff. Their journey must have been a long one, though little of it is known to me except those few leagues at the end.

They had landed on the Kent coast, in Romney Marsh, two days earlier, after crossing the Channel in a fishing smack. Even with calm weather and a level sea the crossing must have taken a good eight hours, but the landing would have been carefully timed. The boat's master, Calfhill, had been under scrupulous instructions and knew every shoal, cove and customs official along fifty-mile stretches of either coast. They put in to shore in darkness, at high tide, with the prow bouncing in the swell, the sail struck low as Calfhill stood in the bows grasping a long pole. At that hour the customs sheds further along the line of beach would have stood empty, but only for another hour, perhaps less, so they were forced to work quickly. Calfhill dropped anchor and, when the flukes bit, stepped over the gunwales and into the knee-deep water, which must have been icy even at that time of year. They disembarked without a torch or flare and scraped the boat across the shingle to the high-water line, where three black stallions had been tethered among the screen of osiers. The horses, snickering and stamping in the darkness, were already saddled and bridled. The beach was otherwise empty.

For the next few minutes Calfhill hovered, anxious and suspicious, as the men tiptoed back into the waves and scrubbed the pitch from their faces and hands. Overhead a skein of plovers sailed inland. Smells of thyme and pastured sheep blew out to sea. Only a few minutes remained before daylight, but Calfhill's passengers worked as punctiliously as if making their morning toilets. One of them even paused to polish a few of the gold buttons on his coat – some kind of black livery – with a wetted handkerchief; then, stooping, the toes of his boots. His efforts were fastidious.

'For heaven's sake,' Calfhill murmured under his breath. He understood the risks, of course, even if his passengers did not. He was an 'owler', a smuggler whose usual freight was the sacks of wool he shipped to France or the crates of wine and brandy he transported back. Nor was he averse to smuggling passengers – an even more profitable trade. Huguenots and Roman Catholics, like the hogsheads of brandy, came to England, while Royalists went the other way, into France. And now it was the Puritans who were fleeing England, of course; Holland was their destination. In the past six weeks he had smuggled at least a dozen of them out of Dover or the Romney Marsh and across to Zeeland or on to pinks anchored near the North Foreland; a few others he smuggled off the pinks and into England to act as spies against King Charles. It was dangerous work, but he calculated that if all of this distrust and deception held out (as he knew it would, human nature being what it was) he would be able to retire to a sugar plantation in Jamaica within four years.

But this latest assignment was a peculiar one, even for an owler of Calfhill's experience. Two days earlier in Calais, in a tavern in the *basse ville* where he normally received information about his consignments of brandy, a man named Fontenay approached him, paid half of an agreed sum – ten gold pistoles – and gave him patient instructions. It would be another good night's work. Fontenay had since disappeared, but then, at dusk the previous day, the strangers met him, as promised, in the sheltered reach from which, disguised as a fisherman, he normally set out with his hogsheads and – so far as he could ever determine their identities – the occasional Royalist agent or Romish priest. His new passengers had been puffing heavily as they clambered aboard. He caught a good view of one of them in the moonlight: a corpulent figure, red-faced as an innkeeper's wife, with hooded eyes, a sensuous mouth, and a gross, well-fed belly that would have done credit to a London alderman. Hardly a seafaring man. Would he take ill in the smack, as so many of them did, and retch over the gunwales? Amazingly, he did not. But throughout the ensuing voyage the three men spoke not a word, neither to Calfhill nor to each other, even though Calfhill – something of a linguist, as his trade required – attempted to draw them in English, French, Dutch, Italian and Spanish.

Now, still in silence, they were staggering towards the snorting stallions, the dry osiers crackling underfoot. Calfhill found himself wondering for the dozenth time which country – or which party within which country – they represented. All three seemed to be gentlemen, which was unusual, because in Calfhill's experience spying was not exactly a gentleman's occupation. Most of the men he smuggled were a foul-mouthed bunch of villains – bravos, bungs, cutpurses, nose-slitters, ruffians of every description, all of them recruited in the worst bawdy-houses and taverns of London or Paris and then paid a slave's wages to betray their friends and countries, which most were only too eager to do. But these fellows? They looked too soft for such rough-and-tumble recreations. The palms of the fat one, as he handed over the remaining coins, had been smooth and plump as those of a lady. Before he applied the pitch, a measure at which he baulked at first, his smooth chops had smelled of shaving soap and perfume. And their black livery, their coats, waistcoats, breeches and doublets, all were of a fine cut, even decorated, a bit ostentatiously, with a few gold frogs and ribbons. So what desperate mission could have tumbled them from their wine-cellars and dinner-tables and sent them to venture life and limb in England?

The three of them were now, at long last, ready to depart. The fat one swung clumsily on to the horse at his fourth attempt – he was accustomed to the aid of a mounting-block, Calfhill supposed – and then, without so much as a nod or a wave, guided the Percheron up a steep knoll. He was an abysmally poor rider, Calfhill could see that right away. He swayed from side to side, head bobbing, fat legs limply bouncing at every step. A man more familiar with carriages and sedan-chairs, Calfhill guessed. The unfortunate horse strained towards the cornice of grass, cleared it with a desperate surge, and began making his way inland at a canter.

His duties at an end, Calfhill turned and began bumping the boat back into the water. He was in a hurry because in that same *auberge* in Calais he had been approached by a second man besides Fontenay, and now six tods of the finest Cotswold wool were waiting for him in a cove two miles further down the coast. He would be met among the reeds by three men and paid five pistoles to smuggle the wool to the French coast, where he would be paid five more. But now as the keel scraped across the beach he heard a sound behind him. Turning, he saw that one of the three riders was still on the beach, his horse facing the water.

'Yes?' Calfhill straightened and took a few clattering steps over the shingle. 'Forgot something, have you?'

The black-clad rider said nothing. He merely tugged at the

reins and swung his horse round towards the hill. Almost as an afterthought, he twisted in his saddle and with a flash of gold brocade produced from the folds of his cloak a firelock pistol.

Calfhill gaped as if at a cunning trick, then took a step backwards. 'What the devil – ?'

The man discharged the weapon without ceremony. There was a surprisingly soft explosion and a small puff of smoke. The lead ball struck Calfhill square in the chest. He staggered backwards like a clumsy dancer, then lowered his head and blinked curiously at the wound, from which blood spurted as if from the bung-hole of a wine cask. He raised his hands to staunch it, but the front of his doublet had already darkened and his face was as white as a goose. His mouth opened and closed as if forming one last outraged objection. It never came, for with a smooth, almost balletic manoeuvre he executed a half turn and crumpled into the reeds at the water's edge.

The man tucked the pistol away and, five minutes later, reached his two companions, who were waiting for him beyond the crest of the rise. For a mile the three of them followed one of the sheep tracks on the downlands. Then they swung inland on to a narrow post-road. By this time a half-dozen sand crabs were scuttling across the shingle towards Calfhill's body, over which the tallest osiers were bent like mourners. His corpse would not be discovered for several more days, by which time the trio of riders had entered the gates of London.

Chapter Three

The only way to reach Crampton Magna in those days was to follow the road from London to Plymouth as far as Shaftesbury and then turn south along an ill-defined and seldom-used network of trackways leading towards the distant coast. On its way to Dorchester, one of the most rustic of these passed round the edge of a village of ten or twelve timber-built houses with sooty, moss-dripping thatches, all crouched in a snug fold of low hills. Crampton Magna – for this, at last, was it – also contained a decrepit mill with broken sluices, a single inn, a church with an octagonal spire, and a shrunken, peat-coloured stream that was forded in one spot and crossed in another, some hundred yards below, by a narrow stone bridge.

The sun was declining into the hills when the coach in which I was travelling came in sight of the village and then scraped and jostled across the bridge. Five days had passed since I received my summons. I leaned through the open door-window and looked back at the houses and church. There was a faint smell of woodsmoke on the air, but in the failing light and stretching umber shadows the village appeared unnaturally empty. All day the laneways from Shaftesbury had been deserted except for the occasional herd of black-faced sheep, and I felt by now as if I had arrived on the verge of a desolate precipice.

'Have we much further to go before Pontifex Hall?'

My driver, Phineas Greenleaf, emitted the same low, bovine grunt which had greeted most of my enquiries. I wondered for the dozenth time if he was deaf. He was an old man, lethargic of movement and lugubrious of manner. As we rode I found myself staring not at the passing countryside but, rather, the wen on his neck and the withered left arm that protruded from its foreshortened coat-sleeve. Three days earlier he had been waiting for me, as promised, at the Three Pigeons in High Holborn. The coach had been by far the most impressive vehicle in the tavern's stable-yard, a commodious four-seater with a covered box-seat and a lacquered exterior in which I could see my undulant reflection. A fussy coat of arms was painted on the door. I had been forced to revise my impression of the impecuniosity of my prospective hostess.

'Am I to see Lady Marchamont?' I had asked Greenleaf as we cleared the stable-yard's narrow coachway. I received his noncommittal grunt in reply but, undaunted for the moment, ventured another question: 'Does Lady Marchamont wish to buy some of my books?'

This enquiry had met with better luck. 'Buy your books? No, sir,' he said after a pause, squinting fiercely at the road ahead. His head was thrust forward beneath his shoulders, giving him the appearance of a vulture. 'I should think Lady Marchamont has quite enough books already.'

'So she wishes to sell her books, then?'

'*Sell* her books?' There was another baffled, ruminative pause. His frown deepened the wrinkles cut like cuneiforms across his brow and cheeks. He removed his hat, a low-crowned beaver, and wiped at his brow, exposing a naked skull that was spotted like a quail's egg. At length, replacing the hat with his shrunken child's hand, he allowed himself a grave chuckle. 'I shouldn't imagine so, sir. Lady Marchamont is most fond of her books.'

That was more or less the extent of our conversation for the next three days. Further questions were either ignored or else answered with the customary grunt. His only other articulations proved to be the sepulchral snores that hindered my sleep on our first night in Bagshot and our second in Shaftesbury.

Our progress had been maddeningly slow. I was a creature of the city – of its smoke and speed, its pushing crowds and whirling iron wheels – and so our leisurely advance through the countryside, across its vacant heaths and through its tiny, nameless villages, was almost more than I could bear. But the saturnine Greenleaf was in no hurry. For mile after mile he sat erect in the box-seat with the reins loose in his hands and the whip dangling between his knees like an angler's rod above a trout stream. And now, after Crampton Magna, the trackway deteriorated badly. The last leg of our journey, though only a mile or two, lasted another hour. No one, it seemed, had passed this way in years. In places the road was overcome by vegetation and all but disappeared; in others the left rut stood at a greater height than the right, or vice versa, or both were littered with sizeable stones. The branches of unpruned trees scored the coach's top, unkempt hedges of beech and quickthorn its doors. We were in constant danger of tipping over. But at long last, after the coach squeezed across another stone bridge, Greenleaf pulled at the reins and laid aside his whip.

'Pontifex Hall,' he growled as if to himself.

I thrust my head through the window and was blinded for a second by the lurid brushstrokes painted across the low shoulder of the sky. At first I saw nothing but a monumental arch and, at its top, a keystone upon which, squinting, I could read a few letters of an inscription: L T E A S RI T M N T.

I raised my right hand to shield my eyes from the sun. Greenleaf clucked his tongue at the horses, who lowered their heads and advanced wearily, tails switching, hoofs crunching the gravel that, a few yards before, had replaced the dirt lane. The carved writing – cast in shadow, pleached with ivy and spotted mustard-and-black with moss – was still illegible but for a few letters: L TTE A S RIPT M NET.

One of the horses snorted and drifted a step sideways, as if refusing the gate, then reared in its traces. Greenleaf jerked at the reins and shouted opprobriously. An enormous house hove suddenly into view as we entered the shadow of the arch. I dropped my hand and thrust my head further through the quarter-light.

For the past few days I had been trying to form a mental picture of Pontifex Hall, but none of my fantasies measured up to the building framed like a painting between the heavy piers of the arch. It was set on a long green sward split by an ochre sweep of carriageway flanked on either side by a row of lime trees. The sward dipped and rose until it reached an enormous façade of rubbed brickwork divided by four giant pilasters and a symmetrical arrangement of eight windows. Above, the low sun picked out a brass weathercock and six circular chimney shafts.

The coach shunted forward a few more paces, traces jingling. As promptly as it appeared, the vision now transformed itself. The sun, all but lost behind the hipped roof, suddenly cast the scene in a different light. The sward, I now saw, was rank and overgrown, pitted here and there, like the carriageway, with old excavations and heaped with pyramids of earth. Many of the lime trees were diseased and leafless, while others had even been reduced to short stumps. The house, whose long shadow stretched towards us, fared no better. Its façade was pockmarked, its mullions splintered, its dripstones snapped off. Some broken window-panes had been replaced in makeshift fashion by straw and strips of cloth; one of them had even been invaded by a thick stem of ivy. A broken sundial, a dry fountain, a stagnant pond, a rank parterre – all completed the portrait of ruin. The weathercock as we trotted forward flashed a minatory glint. My anticipation, roused a moment before, drained abruptly away.

One of the horses whinnied again and shied sideways. Greenleaf jerked the rein sharply and uttered another guttural command. Two more halting steps on the gravelled carriageway; then we were swallowed by the arch. At the last second before it closed over our heads I glanced upwards to the wedge-shaped voussoirs and, above them, the keystone: LITTERA SCRIPTA MANET.

Ten minutes later I found myself standing in the middle of an enormous chamber whose only light fell through a single broken window giving on to the scrubby parterre, which in turn gave on to the fractured fountain and sundial.

'If you would be good enough to wait here, sir,' said Greenleaf.

His bootfalls resounded through the cavernous building, up a creaking flight of stairs, then across a floor above my head. I thought I heard the intonation of voices and another, lighter step.

A moment passed. Slowly my eyes adjusted to the dim light. There seemed to be no place to sit. I wondered if I was being slighted or if this strange hospitality – being left alone in a darkened room – was simply the way of noble folk. I had already decided from its dilapidated condition that Pontifex Hall was one of those unfortunate estates overrun by Cromwell's army during the Civil Wars. I had no love of Cromwell and the Puritans – a gang of iconoclasts and book-burners. But I had no special love of our puffed-up noblemen either, so I had been quietly amused by accounts in our newssheets of rampaging London apprentices showering these grand old homes with cannon-balls and grape-shot, then turning their pampered inhabitants into the fields before liberating the wine from their cellars and the gold leaf from the doors of their carriages. The once stately Pontifex Hall must, I supposed, have suffered this undignified fate along with so many others.

A board creaked under my boot as I turned round. Then the toe of my crippled foot struck something. I looked down and saw a thick folio spreadeagled below me, its pages fluttering in the light breeze from the broken window. Beside it, in similar states of disarray, lay a quadrant, a small telescope in a corroded case, and several other instruments of less discernible function. Scattered among them, badly creased, corners furling, were a half-dozen old maps. In the poor light their coastlines and speculative outlines of continents were unrecognisable.

But then ... something familiar. An old smell was permeating the room, I realised: one I knew better, and loved more, than any perfume. I turned round again and, looking up, saw rows of book-lined shelves covering what seemed to be every inch of the walls, which were girdled halfway up by a railed gallery, above which more books pressed upwards to an invisible ceiling.

A library. So, I thought, face upturned: Greenleaf had been right about one thing at least – Lady Marchamont possessed plenty of books. What light there was cast itself across hundreds of shelved volumes of every shape, size and thickness. Some of the volumes I could see were massive, like quarried slabs, and were attached to the shelves by long chains that hung down like necklaces from their wooden bindings, while others, tiny sextodecimos, were no larger than snuff-boxes, small enough to fit in the palm of the hand, their pasteboard covers tied with faded ribbons or locked with tiny clasps. But that was not all. The overspill from the shelves – two hundred volumes or more – had been stacked on the floor or was colonising adjacent corridors and rooms; an overflow that began in soldierly ranks only to scatter, after a few paces, into wild disorder.

I looked about in amazement before stepping over one of

the advancing columns and kneeling carefully beside it. Here the smell – of damp and rot, like that of mulch – was not so pleasant. My nostrils were offended, as were my professional instincts. The soft throb and glow roused in my breast by the gilt letters of four or five different languages winking at me from scores of handsomely tooled bindings – the sight of so much knowledge so beautifully presented – swiftly flamed out. It seemed that, like everything else about Pontifex Hall, these books were doomed. This wasn't a library so much as a charnel-house. My sense of outrage mounted.

But so, too, did my curiosity. I picked one of the books at random from its collapsing rank and opened the battered cover. The engraved title-page was barely legible. I turned another crackling page. No better. The rag-paper had cockled so badly because of water damage that, viewed side-on, the pages resembled the gills on the underside of a mushroom. The volume disgraced its owner. I flipped through the stiffened leaves, most of which had been bored through by worms; entire paragraphs were now unintelligible, turned to fluff and powder. I replaced the book in disgust and took up another, then another, both of which were likewise of use to no one but the rag-and-bone man. The next looked as though it had been burned, while a fifth had been faded and jaundiced by the rays of some long-ago sun. I sighed and replaced them, hoping that Lady Marchamont had no expectations of restoring the fortunes of Pontifex Hall by means of a sale of scraps like these.

But not all of the books were in such a sorry state. As I moved towards the shelves I could see that many of the volumes – or their bindings at least – were of considerable value. Here were fine morocco leathers of every colour, some gold-tooled or embroidered, others decorated with jewels and precious metals. A number of the vellums had buckled, it was true, and the morocco had lost a little of its lustre, but there were no defects that a little cedarwood oil and lanolin couldn't mend. And the jewels alone – what looked to my inexpert eye like rubies, moonstones and lapis lazuli – must have been worth a small fortune.

The shelves along the south wall, nearest the window, had been devoted to Greek and Roman authors, with an entire two shelves weighed down by various collections and editions of Plato. The library's owner must have possessed both a scholar's eye and a deep purse, because the best editions and translations had obviously been hunted down. Not only was there the five-volume second edition of Marsilio Ficino's Latin translation of Plato – the great *Platonis opera omni* printed in Venice and including Ficino's corrections to the first edition commissioned by Cosimo de' Medici – but also the more authoritative translation published in Geneva by Henri Etienne. Aristotle, meanwhile, was represented not only by the two-volume Basel edition of 1539, but by the 1550 edition with its emendations by Victorius and Flacius, and finally by the *Aristotelis opera* edited by the great Isaac Casaubon and published in Geneva. All were in reasonable condition, give or take the odd nick or scrape, and would fetch a fair price.

The other classical authors were done equal justice. Standing on tiptoe or squatting on my haunches, I removed volume after volume from the shelf and inspected each one before carefully replacing it. Here was Plamerius's edition of Pliny's *Naturalis historia*, bound in red calfskin, and the Aldine edition of Livy, along with the *Historiarum* of Tacitus, edited by Vindelinus and wrapped in a delicate chemise. There was also the Basel edition of Cicero's *De natura deorum*, bound in olive morocco with a pretty repoussé design . . . Dionysus Lambinus's edition of *De rerum natura* . . . and, most amazing of all, a copy of the *Confessiones* of St Augustine in the blind-tooled brown calfskin I recognised as that of the Caxton binder. There were, besides, dozens of thinner volumes, commentaries and expositions such as Porphyry on Horace, Ficino on Plotinus, Donatus on Virgil, Proclus on Plato's *Republic* . . .

I was walking and gazing now, my errant hostess completely forgotten. Not only was the wisdom of the ancients represented, but so were the advancements in learning made earlier in our century. There were books on navigation, agriculture, architecture, medicine, horticulture, theology, education, natural philosophy, astronomy, astrology, mathematics, geometry and steganography or 'secret writing'. There were even quite a number of volumes containing poetry, plays and *nouvelles*. English, French, Italian, German, Bohemian, Persian, it didn't seem to matter. The authors and titles scrolled past, a roll-call of fame. I stopped and ran my fingers across a shelf of quarto editions of Shakespeare's plays; nineteen of them in all, bound in buckram. But there was not, I noticed, a collection of the folio edition of his plays that, as any bookseller knew, William Jaggard had printed in 1623. This struck me as out of keeping with the exhaustive urge for assimilation, for completeness, elsewhere so evident. Nor did there appear to be anything else printed after 1620. In the large collection of herbals, for example, there were copies of *De historia plantarum* by Theophrastos, Agricola's *Medicinae herbariae*, and Gerard's *Generall Historie of Plants*, but not any of the more recent works such as Culpeper's *Pharmacopoeia Londinensis*, Langham's *Garden of Health*, or even Thomas Johnson's enlarged and far superior 1633 edition of Gerard. What did this mean? That the collector had died before 1620, his ambitious dreams unfulfilled? That for forty years or more the magnificent collection had lain undisturbed, unsupplemented, unread?

By now I was standing before the north wall, and here the collection grew even more remarkable. I reached up to touch a few of the wobbly bindings. The light from the window was fading quickly. A large section on the left appeared to be devoted to the art of metallurgy. At first there were the sort of works I would have expected to see, such as Biringuccio's *Pirotechnia* and Ercker's *Beschreibung allerfürnemisten Mineralischen Ertzt*, bound in pigskin and featuring beautiful woodcuts. A little out-of-date, but respectable books none the less. But what was I to make of many of the others interspersed among them – Jakob Böhme's *Metallurgia*, Isaac of Holland's *Mineralia opera*, a translation of Denis Zachaire's *True Natural Philosophy of Metals* – books that were almost manuals of devilry, the products of inferior and superstitious minds?

Other inferior and superstitious minds were found further along the shelf. The wisdom and good taste governing the selection now deteriorated into an indiscriminate and omniverous consumption of authors of scurrilous reputation, men who placed their faith too readily – and somewhat impiously – in the occult operations of nature. The faded ribbon-pulls protruded from the gilt backs like impudent pink tongues. Squinting in the poor light, I pulled down a French translation of the works of Artephius. Next to it was Alain de Lisle's commentary on the prophecies of Merlin. Soon matters grew even worse. Roger Bacon's *Mirror of Alchymy*, George Ripley's *Compound of Alchymy*, Cornelius Agrippa's *De occulta philosophia*, Paul Skalich's *Occulta occultum occulta* . . . All of these volumes were the work of jugglers, charlatans and mystery-men who had nothing to do, as far as I could see, with the pursuit of true knowledge. On the shelves below were dozens of books on various forms of divination. Piromancy. Chiromancy. Astromancy. Sciomancy.

Sciomancy? I propped my thorn-stick against a shelf and reached for the book. Ah, 'divination by shadows'. I clapped it shut. Such nonsense seemed wholly out of place in a library otherwise dedicated to more noble subjects of learning. I replaced the book and, without looking at it, drew down another by its ribbon-pull. Too bad the worms hadn't feasted themselves on *these* pages, I thought as I opened it. But before I could read the title-page, a voice from behind suddenly interrupted me.

'Lefèvre's edition of Ficino's translation of the *Pimander*. An excellent edition, Mr Inchbold. No doubt you own a copy yourself?'

I started and, looking up, saw two dark shapes in the doorway to the library. I had the uneasy impression, all of a sudden, that I had been watched for some time. One of the shapes, that of a lady, had advanced a few steps and now, turning round, lit the wick of a fish-oil lamp perched on one of the shelves. Her shadow feinted towards me.

'Allow me to apologise.' I was hastily restoring the book to its place. 'I should not have presumed—'

'Lefèvre's edition,' she continued as she turned round and blew out the taper-stick, 'marks the first time the *Corpus hermeticum* was gathered together between two covers since it was collected in Constantinople by Michael Psellos. It even contains the *Asclepius*, of which Ficino possessed no manuscript copy so was unable to include it in the edition prepared for Cosimo de' Medici.' She paused for only the briefest of moments. 'Will you take some wine, Mr Inchbold?'

'No – I mean, yes,' I replied, making an awkward bow. 'I mean . . . wine would be—'

'And some food? Phineas tells me you've not eaten tonight. Bridget?' She turned to the other figure, a serving-maid still hovering in the doorway.

'Yes, Lady Marchamont?'

'Fetch the goblets, will you.'

'Yes, m'lady.'

'The Hungarian wine, I think. And tell Mary to prepare a meal for Mr Inchbold.'

'Yes, m'lady.'

'Quickly now, Bridget. Mr Inchbold has made a long journey.'

'Yes, m'lady,' murmured the girl before scurrying away.

'Bridget is new to Pontifex Hall,' Lady Marchamont explained in an oddly confidential tone, slowly crossing the library with the lantern squeaking on its hinges and turning her eye-sockets to dark hollows. She seemed disinclined to perform introductions, as if she had known me for ages and considered it perfectly ordinary to discover me crouched in the darkness like a housebreaker, thumbing greedily through these shelves of books. Was this, too, the way of aristocrats? 'One of the servants,' she added, 'from the family of my late husband.'

I fumbled for a reply, failed, and instead watched in stupefied silence as she approached in her muted flourish of lamplight, the thin drift of taper smoke rising ceilingward behind her. Oh, how precisely I remember this moment! For this is how, and where, everything began . . . and where it would end such a short time later. Through the broken panes of window had come the sounds of a watch of nightingales in the overgrown garden and the scratching of a dead branch at one of the mullions. The library itself was silent but for her slow footfalls – she was wearing a pair of leather buskins – and then a loud slap as one of the books piled on the floor toppled from its rank, knocked sideways by her skirts.

'Tell me, Mr Inchbold, how was your journey?' She had drawn to a stop at last, her half-visible expression apparently vague and vexed. 'No, no. We must not begin our acquaintance with a lie. It was terrible, was it not? Yes, I know it was, and I do apologise. Phineas is dependable enough as a driver,' she said with a sigh, 'but, yes, a dreadful companion. Poor fellow hasn't read a book in his entire life.'

'The journey was pleasant,' I murmured weakly. Yes: our association was a series of lies, despite what she said. Lies from beginning to end.

'I regret I cannot offer you a place to sit,' she was continuing, gesturing at the library with a sweep of her arm. 'Oliver Cromwell's soldiers burned all of my furniture to cook their dinners and warm their feet.'

I blinked in surprise. 'A regiment was quartered here?'

'Fourteen or fifteen years ago. The estate was forfeited for acts of treason against Parliament. The soldiers even burned my best bed. Twelve feet high, Mr Inchbold. Four beech-framed posts, with yards and yards of hanging taffeta.' She paused to offer me a wry smile. 'I should think that must have kept them warm for a time, don't you?'

She was standing before me, or nearly so, and I could see her more clearly in the sallow lamp glow. I was to meet her on only three short occasions, and my first impression – it now surprises me to recall – was not especially favourable. She must have been roughly my own age, and though she was pleasing enough, even noble, in appearance, with a flawless brow, a sharp aquiline nose, and a pair of dark eyes that suggested a strong determination of will, these advantages had been eroded by negligence or poverty. Her dark hair was thick and, unlike mine, had not yet begun to grey, but it was worn loose and rose upwards from her crown in an unruly and unbecoming nimbus. Her gown had been made from a good enough material, but the nap had long since worn off, and it was of an obsolete cut and, even worse, stained like an old sail. She was wearing some sort of calash or hooded mantle, which might have been silk, though it was not one of those pretty bird's-eye hoods such as one sees on the heads of fashionable ladies promenading through St James's Park, for it was black as jet-stone, like her dress, and in poor repair. She looked, from its lugubrious colour, and from the pair of black gloves that stretched halfway up her forearms, to be in mourning. All of which together served to lend her the same air of distressed splendour, I decided, as Pontifex Hall itself.

'The Puritans burned all of your furnishings?'

'Not all,' she replied. 'No. I presume some of them, the more valuable items, were sold.'

'I'm so sorry.' Suddenly the image of Cromwell's ragtag band of soldiers did not seem quite so amusing after all.

A half smile had appeared on her face. 'Please, Mr Inchbold. No need to apologise on their behalf. Beds can be replaced, unlike other things.'

'Your husband,' I murmured sympathetically.

'Even husbands can be replaced,' she said. 'Even a man like Lord Marchamont. You knew of him?' I shook my head. 'He was an Irishman,' she said simply. 'He died two years ago in France.'

'He was of the Royal party?'

'Of course.'

She had turned from me and now strode slowly round the room, examining the books and shelves like a steward examining a prize herd or a particularly satisfactory crop of corn. I was already wondering if they belonged to her. It seemed unlikely. Books were not, in my experience, a woman's business. But how, in that case, had she known about Ficino and Lefèvre d'Étaples and Michael Psellos? I felt a wary excitement shudder softly and cautiously engage.

'These are all I have left,' she said as if to herself. She had begun running her gloved fingertips across the spines, much as I had done a few minutes earlier. 'Everything I own. These and the house itself. Though I may not own Pontifex Hall for so very much longer.'

'Was it Lord Marchamont's?'

'No, his estate was in Ireland, and there's also a house in

Hertfordshire. Dreadful places. Pontifex Hall was my father's, but after our marriage Lord Marchamont was named heir presumptive. We had no children, and it was entailed upon me in his will. There . . .' She was pointing to the window, from which the light had all but drained. The parterre outside was lost in shadow and our two reflections. 'Four leather-covered chairs sat there, next to a table and the beautiful old walnut scriptor where my father used to write his letters. And a hand-knotted turkey carpet on the floor, with monkeys and peacocks and all sorts of oriental designs woven into it.' Slowly her gaze returned to me. 'Now I wonder what could possibly have become of that? Sold as booty, I shouldn't wonder.'

I cleared my throat and voiced the thought that had occurred to me a moment earlier. 'Quite a miracle your books have survived.'

'Oh, but they did not survive,' came her swift reply. 'Not all of them. A number were missing when I returned. Others, as you can see, have been badly damaged. But, yes, quite a miracle. The soldiers would have burned the lot of them, and not only because of the cold winters. Some would have been considered popish, or diabolical, or both.' She nodded at the shelf behind me. 'Ficino's translation of the *Pimander*, for example. Fortunately they were hidden away.'

'What do you mean?'

'By my father. A long story, Mr Inchbold. All in due time. You see, each one of these books has its own history. Many of them survived a shipwreck.'

'A shipwreck?'

'And others,' she continued, 'are refugees. Do you see these chains?' She was pointing to a group of volumes tethered by their bindings to the shelves. The loops of chain reflected dully in the gloom. I nodded. 'These books were already rescued once before, that time from the colleges in Oxford. From the chain libraries,' she explained, sliding one of them, a folio, from the shelf. She ran a gloved hand over its vellum cover – a loving gesture. The chain rattled thinly in protest. 'That was during the last century.'

'They were rescued from Edward VI?'

'From his commissioners. They were smuggled out of the college libraries and escaped the bonfires.' She had opened the enormous volume and began riffling idly through the pages. 'Quite amazing how determined kings and emperors have been to destroy books. But civilisation is built on such desecrations, is it not? Justinian the Great burned all of the Greek scrolls in Constantinople after he codified the Roman law and drove the Ostrogoths from Italy. And Shih Huang Ti, the first Emperor of China, the man who unified the five kingdoms and built the Great Wall, decreed that every book written before he was born should be destroyed.' She clapped the volume shut and replaced it with a firm push. 'These books,' she said, 'my father acquired much later.'

'Ah,' I said, hoping we were at last reaching the heart of the matter. 'So all of these are *his* books? And you wish to sell them.'

'Were,' she said. 'They *were* his books. Yes, he assembled the collection.' She paused for a second and regarded me gravely. 'No, Mr Inchbold, I do not wish to sell them. Most definitely not. Ah,' she said, turning, 'here is Bridget. Shall we withdraw to the dining-room? I think I will be able to offer you a seat in there.'

A short time later I was sitting before a duck which Mrs Winter, the cook-maid, had roasted on a bed of green shallots and served on a large plate. In lieu of a dining-table – another casualty of the wars, evidently – the plate was balanced precariously on my lap. I ate self-consciously, without appetite, aware of the penetrating eyes of my hostess, who sat opposite. For a second her frank gaze had taken in my shrunken and inward-turning foot that looks, I have always thought, like the miserable appendage of some villainous dwarf from a German storybook. I felt myself blush with resentment, but by then Lady Marchamont had already glanced away.

'I must apologise for the wine,' she said as she nodded at Bridget to fill my glass for a third time. 'Once upon a time my father grew his own vines. In the valley.' She gestured vaguely in the direction of one of the broken windows. 'On the slopes above the river, sheltered from the wind. They produced some excellent wines, or so I have been told. I was too young to enjoy them at the time, and the vines have since been uprooted.'

'By the soldiers, I suppose?'

She shook her head. 'No, by a different breed of vandal, a more indigenous one. The villagers.'

'The villagers?' I thought of the eerily empty village through which the coach had passed. 'Crampton Magna?'

'There and elsewhere. Yes.'

I shrugged. 'But why would anyone do that?'

She raised her goblet and gazed thoughtfully into the dark liquid. She had already explained, in the boggling and somewhat gratuitous manner that was becoming familiar, how the goblets were manufactured. Her father had been granted some form of patent for the process, which involved mixing gold and quicksilver in a crucible, then evaporating the quicksilver and gilding the glass with a thin film of the extracted gold. He had owned many patents, she explained. A true Daedalus. Now she seemed to be studying the cypher at the bottom of the cup – an entwined 'AP' – which I had myself already noticed.

'Tell me, Mr Inchbold,' she began after a pause, 'did you by any chance see the excavations on the lawn and carriageway as you approached Pontifex Hall?'

I nodded, remembering the haphazard trenches and the black hillocks of earth beside them. 'I took them for some sort of earthworks.' She shook her great dark nimbus at me. 'Cannon-fire?'

'Nothing as drastic as that. No siege took place here. The immediate area was deemed unimportant by the armies of either side. Fortunately for us, Mr Inchbold, or I don't expect we should be having this conversation.'

I resisted the urge to ask her why it was the two of us were having this conversation. I still had no idea why I had been summoned here, or why she was offering me a history of her peculiar and, frankly, inhospitable house. Was this another example of the strange ways of aristocrats? If she did not wish me to appraise or auction her books, then what on earth was my task to be? Surely she had no desire – no need – to purchase any more? It would be bringing owls to Athens. All at once I felt more exhausted than ever.

But it seemed I was not to discover my task soon, for she now launched into an account of the recent history of Pontifex Hall. As I clumsily dismembered the duck, she explained how after the regiment of troops departed, having chopped up the orchard and the furniture for firewood and stripped the wrought-iron railings to make their muskets and cannons, the house stood empty for a number of months. The estate had been placed in the hands of a trust which, authorised by an Act of Parliament in 1651, eventually sold it to the local Member of Parliament, a man named Standfast Osborne.

'Lord Marchamont and I were in France at the time, in exile. I moved back to England some two months ago, when the house was restored to me under the terms of the Act of Indemnity and Oblivion. Osborne has now been gone for almost a year. Fled to Holland. Quite prudent of him, as he was one of the regicides. When I returned from France I did not expect to be welcomed back to Pontifex Hall, because the people of this area supported the Parliamentarians. Nor was I welcomed. Already the good people of Crampton Magna look upon me, I believe, as a witch.' Her half smile reappeared as her shoulders flexed in an indifferent shrug. 'Yes, strange as it may sound to you, a Londoner, an educated man, but true none the less. In these parts any woman who can read is fancied for a witch. And a woman who lives by herself, in a ruined house, surrounded by books and scientific instruments, without a husband or father or children to guide or control her . . . well, that is even worse, is it not?'

She paused, watching me carefully with her intense, close-set eyes, which, in the better light of the dining-room, I saw were a pale grey-blue. I was chewing slowly and awkwardly, a cow with its cud. My foot had been thrust under the chair, out of sight. She turned and motioned for Bridget to fill my cup.

'You may go now,' she said to her when the task was accomplished. Only when the maid's footfalls disappeared, swallowed up by the immense, echoing house, did she continue.

'I experienced great difficulties hiring servants from the area,' she said in a confidential tone. 'That is why I was forced to recruit from among Lord Marchamont's domestics.'

'But why should you have difficulties? Because of Lord Marchamont? Or because of your . . . politics?'

She shook her head. 'No, because of my father. You may have heard of him – he was famous enough in his day. His name was Sir Ambrose Plessington,' she added after a short pause.

This name, strange as it now seems, then meant nothing to me, nothing at all. But in my recollection the moment now seems accompanied by a ringing silence, a kind of terrible poise in which a long shadow crept forward, darkening the room, throwing its heavy pall slantwise across me. But in fact I only shook my head, wondering to myself how I could not have known of someone capable of amassing such a formidable collection.

'No, I've not heard of him,' I replied. 'Who was he?'

For a moment she said nothing. She was sitting perfectly still, hands folded in her lap. The fish-oil lamp threw her shadow on to the buckling wall behind her. I thought idly of the book on 'sciomancy' in the library and wondered what clues its author might divine in the shifting shadow of Lady Marchamont.

'Drink your wine, Mr Inchbold,' she said at last. She had leaned forward into the jaundiced light of the lamp, and her eyes were searching my face again, as if looking for signs that I might be trusted. Perhaps I was, at this moment, almost as unfathomable to her as she was to me. 'I have something I wish to show you. Something you may well find of interest.'

In what respect? By now my curiosity was being eclipsed by impatience. But what was there for me to do? I gulped my wine and hastily wiped my hands on my breeches. Then, holding back a half-dozen exasperated questions, I followed her from the dining-room.

Chapter Four

S o it was that my first confrontation with Sir Ambrose
Plessington took place in a vault or crypt beneath
Pontifex Hall.

After leaving the dining-room, we went back down the
wide staircase, then took a number of left turns through an
interconnecting series of corridors, antechambers and deserted
rooms before descending another, much narrower set of steps.
Lady Marchamont was holding the fish-oil lamp aloft like
a constable of the watch as I flumped along behind her.
The inadequate light fell on to a scarred wall across which
our shadows loomed in fantastic, threatening postures. Our
feet scuffed the steps that proceeded downwards into what
looked like some sort of undercroft. Cobwebs tickled my scalp
and lips. I brushed them aside and then hastily placed my
handkerchief to my mouth and nose. With every step the
stink of decay seemed to increase twofold. Lady Marchamont,
however, appeared as oblivious of the stench as of the cold and
darkness.

'The pantry, the buttery,' she was saying, 'all were down here,
along with the footmen's chambers. We had three footmen, I
remember. Phineas is the last of them. He was in my father's
service more than forty years ago. It was a godsend that I was
able to find him again. Or, rather, that he found me after my
return. He is, you understand, very devoted to me . . .'

As we descended I had been expecting to enter a maze of
passageways and chambers reflecting the one above the stairs.
But on reaching the bottom at last we found ourselves in a
low-ceilinged corridor that ran ahead in a straight line for as far
as the lamp's shrunken halo of light extended. We proceeded
slowly along it, picking our way over fragments of furniture, the

staves of broken casks, and other less identifiable obstructions. The floor didn't seem quite level; we were descending still, proceeding down a gentle slope. Down here the walls dripped, and faint sounds of running water came to us, followed by an acrid smell. The floor seemed to be covered in grit. There was still no end to the passage. Perhaps we were in a labyrinth after all, I thought: some sort of *mundus cereris* like those the Romans built beneath their cities – all dark vaults and twisting tunnels – in order to converse with the inhabitants of the lower world.

Suddenly Lady Marchamont tapped one of the walls with her gloved knuckles. It reverberated like a kettledrum. 'Copper,' she explained. 'Cromwell's men stored their powder down here, so the walls and door were sheathed with copper. Not exactly the driest place in the house, I shouldn't have thought.'

'Gunpowder?'

At once I knew the identity of the acrid smell and the grit beneath my feet. I began to fret about the lamp, which Lady Marchamont was swinging to and fro with little regard. Its light now illuminated a number of sealed doors and smaller recesses on either side. I shuddered again in the cool dankness, wondering if behind these doors the skulls and shin-bones of a hundred Plessingtons were heaped promiscuously together in crumbling ossuaries. We hurried along the corridor, whose terminus – if there was one – was lost in blackness.

At last we reached our destination. Lady Marchamont stopped before one of the doors and, after struggling with a set of keys, forced it open. A pair of rusted hinges creaked portentously.

'Please,' she said, turning to me with a smile, 'do step through, Mr Inchbold. Inside you will find the mortal remains of Sir Ambrose Plessington.'

'Remains . . . ?' I made to retreat, but it was too late for resistance. Lady Marchamont had my wrist and was tugging me across the threshold.

'There . . .'

She was pointing to a corner of the tiny room, where a battered oak coffin sat on a low trestle-table. I recoiled, trying to free my arm, but then saw to my relief that her father's 'remains' were textual, not corporeal; for the coffin, whose lid had been propped open, was filled not with bones but rather with piles of documents, great sheaves of which threatened to spill over.

'Everything is here.' Her tone was reverential as she picked her way carefully forward. 'Everything about my father. About Pontifex Hall. Rather, very nearly everything . . .'

She had hung the lamp on a wall sconce and now knelt before the coffin on a bed of rushes that had been strewn across the dirt before the trestle-table. The coffin, I now saw, was caked with dirt. She began withdrawing the documents one by one, riffling through and then replacing them. The mantle hung over her shoulders like a pair of folded wings. Some sort of archive, I supposed, hanging back in the doorway until she beckoned me forward.

'The estate papers,' she explained. 'The inventories, the indentures, the conveyances.' She might have been delving her gloved hands in a trunk filled with moonstones and amethysts instead of these heaps of yellowed documents. 'It was for these that Standfast Osborne purchased the estate, you see.' Her voice echoed harshly against the bare walls. 'For its muniments. He cared nothing for the house, as you can see all too plainly. But the coffin was hidden safely away. Lord Marchamont saw to that.'

The room was airless and cramped, its walls encrusted with what I took to be deposits of saltpetre. The flame, glowing feebly now, lit generations of cobwebs, all of them thick with dirt. I have been troubled all my life with asthma – the upshot of having my lungs kippered by the coal smoke of London. Now, standing in the doorway to this strange vault, I felt a familiar gurgle beneath my breastbone.

'They were kept here, in this room,' I managed to ask, leaning on my thorn-stick, 'for all those years?'

'Of course not.' Her winged back was still turned to me. 'They would have been found in an hour. No, they were buried in a plot in the churchyard at Crampton Magna. In this coffin. Ingenious, no? Beneath a headstone inscribed with the name of one of the footmen. Here . . .' She turned, extending a single sheet in her gloved hand. 'This is the order that sealed our fate.'

The paper was of heavy linen, its edges curling and faintly seared. I took it and, tipping it into the light of the lamp and bringing it to within two inches of my nose, saw the impression of a Parliamentary seal and, below, the inscription, slightly faded, in a thick chancery hand:

Be it therefore enacted, That all the Manors, Lands, Tene-ments and Hereditaments, with every of their Appurten-ances whatsoever, of he the said Henry Greatorex, Baron Marchamont, were seized or possessed of, in Possession, Reversion or Remainder, on the 20th day of May, in the year of our Lord 1651, and all rights of entry into the said Manors, Lands, Tenements or Hereditaments . . .

'The order for the seizure of the estate,' she explained. She handed me another paper, or, rather, a small sheaf. This gathering, tied with a faded and fraying ribbon, was less obviously official and inscribed in a formal secretary hand which, though I didn't know it at the time, was that of Sir Ambrose Plessington himself, who first appeared to me, therefore, between the lines of a lengthy text, a list of his accoutrements: *'An Inventorie taken of all the Cattelse and Chatteles moveable and unmoveable of Ambrose Plessington, Kn*^{t}*, of Pontifex Hall, in the Parish of St Peter's, valued and prized in the presence of four Bailies . . .'*

I set my stick aside and untied the ribbon. The remain-der, six pages in all, inscribed on both sides, consisted of a formidably long list of Sir Ambrose's possessions, of his furniture, paintings, draperies, silver and plate, along with more esoteric items such as telescopes, quadrants, calipers, compasses and several cabinets whose contents − preserved animals, shells and corals, coins, arrowheads, fragments of urns, *objets d'art* of all kinds, and even two automata − had been enumerated individually. One of the most valuable of all was a *'Kunstschrank'* whose surface was inlaid with diamonds and emeralds, though what might have been inside this glittering ark – valued at an astonishing £10,000 – the inventory declined to report. The entire contents of the house were valued on the last page at £155,000; an incredible sum that was enormous enough in 1660, and one that in June of 1622, the date of the inventory, must have been well and truly boggling. Not even the treasures of the late King Charles, that great connoisseur, had fetched so high a price when Cromwell stripped them from the royal palaces and then sold them to the ravening princes of Europe.

Lady Marchamont had caught my astonished gaze. 'Of all of these items,' she said in a quiet voice, 'you can see that almost nothing now remains. All were taken from us or were destroyed by the troops. Only this trunk and these papers bear witness to what Pontifex Hall used to be. To everything my father built.'

'But the library . . .' I had returned to the front of the list and was now scrolling slowly through it for a second time. 'I see no mention of your father's books.'

'No.' She took the paper from me and, after tying the ribbon, replaced it in the coffin. 'This particular inventory does not include the contents of the library. A separate one was compiled for that.' She turned round and, after further riffling, disinterred a larger sheaf. 'Extremely detailed, as you can see. It contains the price paid for every book, along with the bookseller or agent from whom each was purchased. An interesting record, but there's no time to study it now. For the moment . . .' She set it aside and delved carefully into the coffin, turning over heavy sediments of paper. 'For the moment, Mr Inchbold, you must read something else. During his lifetime my father received letters patent in a number of countries, from several kings and emperors. But these ones may be of particular importance.'

Importance to what? What had my presence at Pontifex Hall to do with this foul subterranean vault and its scraps of old paper? With kings and emperors? Lady Marchamont had already turned round and handed me three or four documents. The first was a parchment and at its foot bore in cracked red wax the impression of an enormous seal whose circumference read, in characters that were barely perceptible,

Romanum Imperatores Rudolphus II
Caesarum Maximus Imp : Rex
SALVTI PUBLICAE

I held the paper closer to the light. Above the seal, inscribed in heavy gothic script, were several paragraphs in German, what my limited knowlege of that language told me amounted to a commission to search for books and manuscripts in the regions of Bohemia, Moravia, Silesia and Glatz. It was dated 1610. For a few seconds I rubbed the cockled edge of the document between my finger and thumb, enjoying the furry texture of the membrane, as soft and smooth as a lady's cheek. Then I turned it over, carefully, with a quiet, satisfying crackle, and jabbed with a thumb at the nose-piece of my spectacles.

The next document, dated a year later and impressed with the same seal, was of similar import but extended the commission beyond the Czech lands to include Austria, Styria, Mainz and both the Upper and the Lower Palatinate, as well as – most remarkable of all – the lands of the Ottoman Sultan. The final three pages granted, respectively, a patent of Imperial nobility, a pension of 500 thalers per annum, and a doctorate in philosophy from the Carolinum. This last document was inscribed in Latin and embossed with a coat of arms. I looked up to see Lady Marchamont's eyebrows knit together as if in close attentiveness to my reaction. The light from the lamp spluttered and, to my alarm, nearly extinguished itself.

'It's in Prague.'

'Prague?' My questioning gaze had returned to the skins, which my hands were shuffling nervously.

'The Carolinum,' she said in a clipped tone, as though repeating a simple lesson to an obtuse child. 'It's in Prague. Bohemia. My father spent a number of years there.'

'In the Carolinum?'

'No. In Bohemia. After Rudolf moved the Imperial Court from Vienna to Prague.'

I was still studying the parchments. 'Sir Ambrose was in the service of the Holy Roman Emperor?'

She nodded, apparently pleased at the note of awe inflecting my voice. 'At first, yes. As one of the agents hired to procure books for the Imperial Library. Afterwards he was in the service of the Elector Palatine, furnishing the Bibliotheca Palatina in Heidelberg.'

She stooped and once more began to sift through the papers in the coffin. For the next ten minutes I was obliged to wheeze over and fumble through a dozen-odd other documents, all of them patents for various monopolies and inventions – new methods of essaying gold or rigging ships – together with the title-deeds for freehold properties scattered across England, Ireland and Virginia. More dog-eared pages of Sir Ambrose's busy life. I was barely paying attention as Lady Marchamont thrust each one into my hands with the zeal of a street-corner Quaker. But soon I found myself squinting at a document of a different sort, another letter patent with the Great Seal of England embossed at its foot, but one whose designs were grander than the others:

This Indenture, made the 30th day of August, in Anno Domini 1616, the Fourteenth Year of the Reign of our Sovereign Lord James, by the Grace of God, King of England, Scotland and Ireland, Defender of the Faith, between our said Sovereign Lord of one Party, and Ambrose Plessington, Knight of the Garter, of the other Party, to build, rig, provision, and otherwise fit, and thereafter to captain and sail, the Ship known as the Philip Sidney, *from the Port of London, to the Cittie of Manoa, in the Empire of Guiana . . .*

I blinked, rubbed at my eyes with a knuckle, then continued reading. The document was a commission of £3,000 for Sir Ambrose to make a voyage in search not of books and manuscripts – as in the days of the Emperor Rudolf – but rather the headwaters of the Orinoco River and a gold mine near a city called Manoa in the Empire of Guiana. I knew something of the expedition, if it was the same one, for I was well aware of how Sir Walter Raleigh went to the scaffold one year after his disastrous expedition set off for Guiana in 1617. So had the *Philip Sidney* ascended the Orinoco with Raleigh's doomed fleet? And, if so, what became of the ship and her captain?

I could read no more. The letters of the patent were swimming before my tired eyes, and now my chest felt even tighter. I removed my spectacles and rubbed at my eyes with the balls of my fingers. I coughed, trying to clear my lungs of the stale air and motes of dust. Again I could hear the gentle rush of water, which now seemed to originate behind the wall of the tiny archive. I replaced my spectacles, but the letters on the page still feinted and shrank before my smarting gaze.

'I'm sorry but I . . .'

'Yes, of course.'

Lady Marchamont took the papers from me and returned them to the coffin. But before she slammed shut its lid I caught a glimpse of what looked like a newer document, another indenture of some sort. The top edge of the parchment was jagged, while the bottom had been folded over and fixed with a seal suspended on a parchment tag. Did she grant me on purpose, I would later wonder, this briefest of visions, this most subtle of clues? The signature beside the seal was illegible, but I was able to make out a few words inscribed at the top: '*Sciant presentes et futuri quod ego . . .*'

But then the lid was banged shut forcefully and a second later I started at the light touch of the gloved hand on my forearm. When I turned my head she was giving me the most curious and unsettling smile.

'Shall we return upstairs, Mr Inchbold? The air in these vaults is poor. Enough for two people to breathe for no more than thirty minutes at a time.'

I nodded gratefully and fumbled for my thorn-stick. The air suddenly seemed denser than ever, and for the first time I realised that she too was breathing heavily. Removing the lamp from its sconce she turned towards the door.

'My father ventilated the vaults with an atmospheric pump,' she continued, 'but of course the pump was stolen along with everything else.'

The hinges squealed again as she shut the door and there was a jangle of keys and silver chatelaine as she locked it. I followed the black gown along the corridor.

Sciant presentes et futuri . . .

I sculled through the darkness on my stick, brow drawn in puzzled concentration. Let all men present and future know *what*? As we climbed the stairs I found myself thinking not so much about the dozens of documents that had been thrust under my nose, but instead about the mysteriously new parchment half hidden among the other papers in the coffin, the indenture with its serried edge waiting to fit like a piece of a jigsaw puzzle into its counterpart, the twin parchment from which it had been carefully severed. Did I guess then that it might fit into a larger puzzle whose other pieces were as yet unknown and undiscovered? Or is it only now, in retrospect, that I remember it so clearly?

My chest was whistling like a tea-kettle as we climbed, my crippled foot noisily scuffing and thumping. I winced with shame, glad of the darkness. But Lady Marchamont, two steps ahead, her face half turned towards me, appeared to notice none of these commotions. As we made our way upwards she described some of her father's services for Rudolf II, the great 'Wizard Emperor' whose palace in Prague was filled with astrologers, alchemists, bizarre inventions and, above all, tens of thousands of books. A good many of the Emperor's possessions came courtesy of Sir Ambrose, she claimed. For whenever a nobleman or scholar of means died anywhere within the borders of the Empire – from Tuscany in the south, to Cleves in the west, to Lusatia or Silesia in the east – her father had been despatched across the fraying quilt of principalities and fiefdoms to secure for the Emperor the most important and impressive items from the legacy: paintings, marbles, clocks, precious stones, new inventions of any sort, and of course the library, especially if its collection held volumes on alchemy and other occult arts, which had been Rudolf's particular favourites. In these missions, she boasted, her father had rarely disappointed.

'In one year alone he negotiated the acquisition of the libraries of Benedikt of Richnov and the Austrian nobleman Anton Schwarz von Steiner.' She paused for breath and turned to face me. 'You must have heard of these collections?'

I shook my head. We had reached the top of the steps. The tiled floor seemed to sway beneath my feet like the deck of a foundering ship. She pushed open the door for me, and I stumbled through after my shadow. Benedikt of Richnov? Anton Schwarz? There was much, apparently, that I didn't know.

'Each library contained more than ten thousand volumes,' came her voice from the darkness behind me. 'Among other treasures they included Rupescissa's work on alchemy and Fine's edition of Roger Bacon. Even manuscripts on astrology by Albamazar and Sacrobosco. Most were sent to the Imperial Library in Vienna to be catalogued by Hugo Blotius, the *Hofbibliothekar*, but some were taken to Prague for inspection by His Excellency. No simple task. They were transported across mountains and through the Böhmerwald in special mule-carts and wagons with sprung wheels, a new invention in those days. The wooden boxes in which they were packed had been caulked at the seams with oakum and pitch, like the hull of a warship. These in turn were wrapped in two layers of tanned canvas. It must have been an amazing sight. From front to rear the convoys were almost a mile long, with all of the books still in alphabetical order.'

Her voice echoed against the bare, unmarked walls. The words seemed rehearsed, as if she had told the story many times before. I remembered the copious shelves of occult works in her father's library and wondered if these books had some connection with either Benedikt of Richnov or Anton Schwarz, or possibly even with the 'Wizard Emperor' himself.

We were walking abreast now, quickly, winding our way back in the direction – so far as I could tell – of the library. It was impossible to determine if we had passed this same way earlier. The servants, even Phineas, seemed to have vanished.

It occurred to me that two people, even a half-dozen, could easily go about their business in Pontifex Hall for days on end without so much as setting eyes on one another.

Abruptly the narration ended. 'My dear Mr Inchbold . . .'

I had been hurrying to keep pace, wheezing and blowing like a grampus. Now I almost collided with her as she halted in the middle of the corridor.

'My dear Mr Inchbold, I have imposed too long on your good nature. You must wonder why I have told you all of these things. Why I have shown you the library, the inventory, the patents . . .'

I straightened and found I couldn't meet her eyes. 'Well, Lady Marchamont, I must confess—'

'Oh, please.' She interrupted me with a raised hand. 'Alethea. We have no need of formalities, I hope.'

A command rather than a request. I acquiesced: she was my superior in rank, after all, whether or not her title was used. A name – a word – changes nothing.

'Alethea.' I pronounced the strange name with caution, like a man sampling an exotic new dish.

She resumed walking, though more slowly now, the thick soles of her buskins scuffing the tiles. We turned left into another, longer corridor.

'The fact is that I wished you to see something of what Pontifex Hall used to be. Can you imagine it yet? The frescos, the tapestries . . .' Her free hand gestured like a conjuror's at the bare walls, at the expanse of vacant corridor before us. I blinked stupidly into the darkness, able to imagine none of it. 'But even more,' she resumed in a lower voice, 'I wanted you to know what manner of man my father was.'

We had reached the library, whose darkness was now complete. I was startled once more by the touch of her hand. Turning, I saw two tiny flames, reflections from the lamp, dancing in the pupils of her close-set eyes. I looked nervously away. Sir Ambrose was, at this point, even more unimaginable than his plundered possessions.

'I have no husband, no children, no living relations.' Her voice had dropped to a whisper. 'Very little now remains for me. But I *am* left with one thing, one ambition. You see, Mr Inchbold, I wish to restore Pontifex Hall to its former condition. To render it exactly the same in every last detail.' She released my arm to gesture again at the empty darkness. 'Every last detail,' she repeated with a peculiar emphasis. 'The furniture, the paintings, the gardens, the orangery . . .'

'And the library,' I finished, thinking of the books eroding to rags and dust on the floor.

'Yes. The library as well.' She had taken my forearm again. The lamp swung in short arcs. Our shadows wavered to and fro like dancers. Here in the vacant house with its bare walls and falling plaster her ambition seemed outlandish and impossible. 'All precisely as my father left them. And I shall do it, too. Though I expect no easy time of it.'

'No,' I replied, hoping to sound sympathetic. I was thinking of the quartered troops, of the house's devastated façade, of the great branch of ivy insinuating itself through a second-floor window . . . of the whole dreadful picture of ruin I had seen through the archway. No easy time of it indeed.

'I shall be frank.' She had raised the lamp as if to illuminate our faces. It was burning more brightly now, but the flame served only to deepen the shadows. 'Difficulties with the hall's restoration will arise not simply because of the desecrations, and not simply because, yes, if you must know, I am, shall we say, embarrassed for funds. They will arise also because certain other stakes are involved.' Her voice was casual but her eyes, grown obsidian in the dark with their expanded pupils, maintained their intense, searching gaze. 'Certain other interests. You see, Mr Inchbold, I, like my father, have accumulated more than my share of enemies.' The pressure on my arm grew almost painful. 'You've seen from the inventory that Sir Ambrose was a man of enormous wealth.'

I nodded obediently. For a second I could see the bailies passing along this corridor and through the rest of the house, through chambers as rich as Aladdin's cave; the four of them touching vases, clocks, tapestries, secretaires, jewels of unimaginable price; their eyes growing wide; item after fabulous item added to the incredible inventory. All now vanished.

'Wealth attracts its enemies,' she said, then added in the same casual tone: 'Sir Ambrose was murdered. As was Lord Marchamont.'

'Murdered?' The word possessed its due resonance against the bare walls of the corridor. 'But by whom? Cromwell's men?'

She shook her head. 'That I cannot say for certain. But I have my doubts. The fact is that I do not know. I had hoped the muniments would offer some clue. Lord Marchamont thought he might have discovered something, but . . .' She shook her head again and lowered her eyes. Raising them a second later, she must have seen what she interpreted as an alarmed look on my face, for she added quickly: 'Oh, but there's no need to worry. There's nothing to fear, Mr Inchbold. Do let me reassure you of that. Please understand. You will be quite safe. I promise you that.'

This reassurance opened a small crevice of doubt. Why should I *not* be safe? But I had no time to contemplate the question, for now she released my forearm and plucked up a bell. Its sound was harsh and plaintive, like an alarm.

'Never fear,' she said, turning back to me as the echoes died away. 'Your task will be a simple one. One that will bring you into no danger at all.'

Ah, I thought. At last. 'My task?'

'Yes.' Phineas had appeared at the end of the corridor. Lady Marchamont turned to face him. 'But I have talked too much already. Do forgive me. All of this must wait for tomorrow. You should rest now, Mr Inchbold. You have come such a long way. Phineas?' The footman's lugubrious face hove into the yellow track of the fish-oil lamp. 'Please show Mr Inchbold to his chamber.'

Yes, I thought, as I followed Phineas up the staircase: I had come a long way. Further, perhaps, than I knew.

I was accommodated for the night in a bedchamber at the top of the stairs, along a broad corridor lined at regular intervals with closed doors. The quarters were large but, as I expected, inadequately furnished. There was a straw pallet, a three-legged stool, an empty fireplace festooned with skeins of dirty cobwebs, and a small table, on which sat a quill, a book, a few other items. I was too exhausted to look at any of them.

For a moment I was also too exhausted to move. I stood in the centre of the room and gazed dully at its emptiness. I reflected that the peasant cottages through which I had passed on the road to Crampton Magna were probably better appointed. I thought for a second of the inventory locked in the tiny room two floors below; of its endless catalogue of carpets, tapestries, long-case clocks, wainscot chairs. In another lifetime this room – the 'Velvet Bedchamber', Alethea had called it – must have been spectacularly furnished; perhaps it was that of Sir Ambrose himself. Even now traces of its former life betrayed themselves, such as the chipped, peeling overmantel or the triangular patch of crimson flock paper high on the wall. Scraps of the glory that once was Pontifex Hall. For half-starved Puritan soldiers in their black homespun it must have made an obscene spectacle. And for someone else, apparently, a motive for murder.

I undressed slowly. Phineas, or someone, had carried my trunk into the room and placed it beside the pallet. I pawed through it for my nightshirt, which I slipped over my head. Then, using my moistened forefinger and thumb, I snuffed the tallow candle that Phineas had placed on the table, and an instant later the bedchamber was flooded through its cracked casement with deep billows of night. I closed my eyes, and sleep, with its heavy die, pressed its seal across their lids.

Chapter Five

P rague Castle, seen from a distance, was an irregular diadem that perched on the craggy brow of a rock overlooking the wattled rooftops of the Old Town across the river. At dawn its windows glinted in the morning sun, and at dusk its shadow crept across the river like the hand of a giant, then inched into the narrow streets of the Old Town to gather up the spires and squares. Seen from within, it was even more imposing, a multitude of archways, courtyards, chapels and palaces, even several convents and taverns. All were enclosed within fortified walls whose shape, from above, suggested a coffin. The Cathedral of St Vitus occupied the castle's centre, and to the south of the cathedral stood the Královsky Palace, which was home in the year 1620 to Frederick and Elizabeth, the new King and Queen of Bohemia. Two hundred yards as the crow flies from the Královsky Palace, but through a succession of courtyards, then past a well-house, a fountain and a garden, stood what in 1620 would have been the newest and most remarkable of the castle's buildings, a set of galleries known as the Spanish Rooms. These rooms were found in the northwest corner, a short distance from where the Mathematics Tower rose above the moat. They had been built some fifteen years earlier to house the thousands of books and copious other treasures of the Emperor Rudolf II, a bronze statue of whom, ruffed and bearded, hook-nosed and melancholic, was erected outside the south front. By 1620 Rudolf had been dead for almost ten years, but his treasures remained. The books and manuscripts, among the most precious in Europe, were housed in the library of the Spanish Rooms, and at that time the castle's librarian was a man named Vilém Jirásek.

Vilém was in his middle thirties, a shy and modest man, ill-shod and unkempt, with a patched coat and a pair of spectacles behind whose lenses his pale eyes flitted and swam. Despite the coaxings of Jirí, his lone servant, he remained indifferent to his humble appearance. He was equally indifferent to the affairs of the world beyond the walls of the Spanish Rooms. Much had happened in Prague during the ten years he had worked in the library, including the rebellion of 1619 in which the Protestant noblemen of Prague had deposed the Catholic Emperor Ferdinand from the throne of Bohemia. Yet no event, however turbulent, had disturbed his scholarly labours. Each morning he shuffled out of his tiny house in Golden Lane and, exactly seventeen minutes later, arrived before his cluttered desk as the hundreds of mechanical clocks in the Spanish Rooms were tolling eight o'clock. Each evening, red-eyed and weary, he began his shuffle back to Golden Lane at the moment when the clocks struck six. In ten years he had never been known to deviate from this orbit by missing a day of work or even arriving so much as a minute late.

Vilém's post demanded such precision, of course. For the past ten years, with the help of two assistants, Otakar and István, he had been cataloguing and shelving each volume in the Spanish Rooms. The task was immense and doomed to failure, for Rudolf had been an insatiable collector. His books on the occult sciences alone numbered in their thousands. One entire room was stuffed with volumes on 'holy alchemy', another with books on magic, including the *Picatrix*, which Rudolf had used to cast spells on his enemies. As if these tons of books were not enough, hundreds were still arriving in the library each week, along with scores of maps and other engravings, all of which had to be catalogued and then shelved in one of the overcrowded and interconnecting rooms in which sometimes even Vilém himself got lost. To make matters worse, crates of volumes and other valuable documents were now being shipped to Prague from the Imperial Library in Vienna for safekeeping from both the Turks and the Transylvanians. So it was that the edition of Cornelius Agrippa's *Magische Werke* sitting on Vilém's desk on his first morning of work in 1610 still sat there ten years later, uncatalogued and unshelved, buried ever deeper beneath growing piles of books.

Or that, at least, had been the situation in the library until the spring of 1620, when it seemed that a period of respite had arrived. The river of incoming books had slowed to a trickle after the revolt against the Emperor and the coronation of Frederick and Elizabeth. A few of Frederick's crates of books had arrived the previous autumn from Heidelberg, from the great Bibliotheca Palatina, and most of these still had not been unpacked, let alone catalogued or shelved. But the other sources – monasteries, the estates of bankrupt or deceased noblemen –

seemed to have dried up altogether. There were even alarming rumours that some of the most valuable manuscripts would be sold off by Frederick to finance the shabby and ill-equipped Bohemian army in what a related rumour claimed was the forthcoming war against the Emperor. Many other books and manuscripts from the Spanish Rooms would be sent for safekeeping either to Heidelberg or, in the event that Heidelberg fell, to London.

Safekeeping? The three librarians had been baffled by such stories. Safekeeping from what? From whom? They could only shrug at each other and return to work, unable to believe that their quiet routine could be disturbed by events as far-flung and incomprehensible as wars and dethronements. If the world outside was, from the little that Vilém understood of it, disordered and confused, here at least, in these rooms, a beautiful order and harmony prevailed. But in the year 1620 this delicate balance was to be upset for ever, and for Vilém Jirásek, cloistered among his stacks of beloved books, the first hint of the approaching disaster was the reappearance in Prague of the Englishman Sir Ambrose Plessington.

Sir Ambrose must have returned to Prague Castle, after a long absence, during either the winter or spring of 1620. At the time he, like Vilém, was in his middle thirties, though unlike Vilém he looked not even remotely studious. He was as thick in the middle as a butcher or a blacksmith and stood tall despite a pair of bandy legs that suggested he spent more time sitting in the saddle than at a desk. Both his brow and his beard were dark, and the latter was sculpted into the new V-shape that, like his millstone ruff, had lately come into fashion. Vilém would have known him by reputation since Sir Ambrose was responsible for a good many of the books and artefacts in the Spanish Rooms. Ten years earlier he had been Rudolf's most celebrated agent, criss-crossing every duchy, *Erbgut*, fiefdom and *Reichsfreistadt* in the Holy Roman Empire in order to bring back to Prague ever more books, paintings and curiosities for the obsessive and demented Emperor. He had even travelled as far as Constantinople, from which he returned not only with sacks of tulip bulbs (a particular favourite of Rudolf's) but also dozens of ancient manuscripts that were among the greatest prizes in the Spanish Rooms. Quite what brought him back to Bohemia in 1620, however, was no doubt a mystery to the few people in Prague – Vilém among them – who knew of his presence.

Of course, Sir Ambrose was not the only Englishman who arrived in Prague at this particular time; the city was bursting with them. Elizabeth, the new Queen, was daughter to King James of England, and the Královsky Palace had become home to her cumbersome entourage; to her hordes of hosiers, milliners and physicians, the dozens of deckhands who struggled to keep her afloat from one day to the next. Among these legions were six ladies-in-waiting, and among these ladies-in-waiting was a young woman named Emilia Molyneux, the daughter of an Anglo-Irish nobleman who had been dead for some years. Emilia was twenty-four years old at the time, the same age as her royal mistress. In appearance, too, she resembled the Queen – who was prim, pale and slight – except for a thick mass of black hair and a near-sighted squint.

How Emilia first encountered Vilém is a matter for speculation. It may have been at one of the numerous masques of which the young Queen was so fond, at a late hour when the punctilio of the court was lapsing amid the frenzy of music and drink. Or perhaps the meeting was a more sober affair. The Queen was a dedicated reader – one of her more endearing traits – and therefore might have sent Emilia to the Spanish Rooms to fetch a favourite book. Or possibly Emilia went to the Spanish Rooms on a mission of her own: she had been taught, among her other accomplishments, how to read. Whatever the case, their subsequent meetings would have been kept a secret. Vilém was a Roman Catholic, and the Queen, a devout Calvinist, detested Roman Catholics almost as much as she detested Lutherans. So devout was she, in fact, that she had refused to cross the bridge over the Vltava because of the wooden statue of the Holy Mother at its far end, and at her command all statues and crucifixes were being prised loose from the chapels of the Old Town. Even the curiosities in the Spanish Rooms had been inspected by her chaplain lest any of the shrivelled fragments should prove the bones of saints or other such popish relics. And so for Emilia to be discovered in the company of a Roman Catholic – a Roman Catholic educated by the Jesuits in the Clementinum – would have meant expulsion from Prague and an immediate return to England.

The two of them would therefore have met in Vilém's house in Golden Lane. On those evenings when her services were not required until late, Emilia would have slipped out of the Královsky Palace at eight o'clock, by the back stairs, and made her way through the courtyards without a torch or lantern, feeling her way along the walls. Golden Lane, a row of lowly cottages, lay on the far side of the castle, and Vilém's house, one of the smallest, was at the far end, cowering under the arches of the castle's north wall. But there was always a light in the window, smoke from the chimney, and Vilém to embrace her.

And he was always waiting to open the door each time she made her dark excursion, until the cold night in November when she found the window dark and the chimney smokeless. She hurried back to the palace that evening but returned the following night, then the night after that. On the fourth night, when there was still no response, she went to the Spanish Rooms, and there she discovered not Vilém, nor even Otakar or István, but someone else, an immense man in spurred boots whose long shadow, cast by an oil-lamp, was writhing on the floorboards behind him. Later she would remember the evening not so much because that was when she first met Sir Ambrose Plessington, but because that was the night when the war began.

It had been a Sunday. There were flakes of snow in the air and a skin of ice on the river. Another winter was arriving. The servants had trudged into churches whose steeples were lost in fog, then afterwards played skittles in the frost-rimed courtyards or chitter-chattered in the corridors and back stair-wells. The stables and dung-heaps steamed. A herd of scrawny cows was driven, bells jingling, through the steep streets of the

Lesser Town. Faggots of wood and bags of fodder were carted up to the castle along with the casks of alewife and Pilsener unloaded from the barges floating along the river. The ice had crackled against the hulls of the boats, sounding like thunder or, to the more nervous, gun-fire.

Emilia had been dreading another winter in Prague, for the castle was a hard place when the weather turned. The doors in the Královsky Palace shrank in the cold and banged in the draughts, and snow blew underneath them, silting inches-deep against the furniture. Water in the well-houses froze and had to be broken by soldiers brandishing pikes. At night the wind howled through the courtyards, in reply, it seemed, to the starving wolves on the hills outside. Sometimes the wolves would slink into the Lesser Town and attack the almsfolk foraging for scraps in the middens, and sometimes an almsman would be discovered dead in the snow, half naked and frozen stiff, still clutching his staff, looking like a statue toppled from its pedestal.

But if the poor starved in the cold, the rich gorged themselves, for winter was the season when the Queen of Bohemia held her dozens of banquets. At these ceremonies the six ladies-in-waiting were expected to remain on their feet for hours on end, without food or drink, without speaking, without coughing or sneezing, as the Queen and her guests – princes, dukes, margraves, ambassadors – stuffed themselves on steaming plates of peacock or venison or wild boar, all washed down with kegs of Pilsener or bottles of wine. The topics of discussion were always the same. Did the guests support Frederick's claim to the throne of Bohemia? How much money would they send to defend it? How many troops? When might the troops arrive? Only long afterwards, when the royal party had finally eaten its fill, did the ladies-in-waiting fight the cook-maids and footmen for the greasy scraps.

It was to one of these feasts that, after the churches had emptied, Emilia and the other ladies-in-waiting were summoned. Yet another banquet had been laid in Vladislav Hall, this time in honour of two ambassadors from England. Emilia had been in bed at the time and was roused from her reading by the fierce chiming of the bell suspended on a hook beside her bed. Reading was one of her few pleasures in those years, one she indulged in bed, swaddled in blankets and propped on her pillows with a candle burning on the nightstand and the book held three inches from her nose. She had devoured hundreds of volumes since leaving London for Heidelberg in 1613 – mostly tales of Arthurian romance such as *Sir Gawain and the Green Knight* and Malory's *Le Morte d'Arthur*, or stories of love and adventure like Torquemada's *Olivante de Laura* and Lofraso's *The Fortune of Love*. But she had also read Whetstone's biography of Sir Philip Sidney, and many of Sidney's sonnets she had reread so often that she knew them by heart, as she did those of Shakespeare, whose plays she read in dog-eared quarto editions. So passionate a reader was she that many times over the past seven years she had been chosen to read to the Queen herself – one of the few tasks in the Královsky Palace that she ever enjoyed. As Elizabeth was being put to bed after a banquet or masque, or even confined for one of her pregnancies, Emilia would take her place in a chair at the royal bedside and read a chapter or two of some chosen volume until her royal mistress fell asleep. The Queen asked to hear such soporific fare as *The Chronicles of England* by Holinshed or sober works of religious faith.

But her duties today would be nothing quite so agreeable as whiling away an hour or two with a fat volume on her lap. She arrived in Vladislav Hall to find the table heaped with meat and the walls lined with casks of wine. The Queen did not stint herself or her guests even though prices in the market had risen and there was talk of famine. The ambassadors must have heard the rumours, for they gorged themselves on whole chickens and knuckles of pork as if it was to be their last meal. The Queen's pet monkey, a stranger to decorum, leapt from chair to chair, chattering shrilly and accepting hand-outs. Emilia stood still and silent the whole time, barely listening as the ambassadors told their news of King James's bold plans for sending troops to defend Bohemia and rescue his daughter from the clutches of the papists. Only after two hours, growing faint, did she dare nibble at a piece of bread slipped into her pocket by one of the maidservants. The bread had gone greenish-grey with mould. It was the kind of bread she imagined people were reduced to eating during a siege – the kind of bread that, if half of the reports were true, everyone in Prague Castle would soon be eating. The crumbs were thick and pasty in her mouth. It was like chewing birdlime.

But there would be no siege, the ambassadors were assuring the Queen, nor even a war. Prague was safe. The Imperial Army was still eight miles away and Frederick's troops, all twenty-five thousand of them, were poised to block their advance. English troops were on their way, as were the Dutch, and Buckingham, the Lord High Admiral, was outfitting a fleet of ships to attack the Spaniards. Besides, winter was arriving, one of them observed as he leaned forward on his elbows and picked at his teeth with the tines of a fork. No general would be so uncivilised as to fight a war in winter, especially in Bohemia. Not even the papists, he assured the company, would be so barbaric.

But of course the ambassadors had been wrong about the Catholic armies, just as they would be wrong about King James and Buckingham's fleet of ships. The dirty plates had not even been cleared from the table and the scraps fought over by the servants before the first cannon-ball soared over the crest of the Summer Palace, just five miles distant, and skidded into the woods. The Imperial artillery had come within range of the White Mountain. The first barrage rattled the frosty air, crackling and bursting like an oncoming storm, startling the horses in their stables and sending the townsfolk scurrying home.

By that time Emilia had returned to her room on the top floor of the palace and begun tying her hood over her head, preparing for her last desperate foray into Golden Lane. Her thoughts had not been about the Imperial soldiers, those vast armies supposedly on their way to humble Bohemia and reclaim for Ferdinand the throne stolen by Frederick and Elizabeth. She was thinking about Vilém instead, and so it had taken several more explosions before she realised the sound was not that of thunder or ice breaking apart on the Vltava.

What happened next she was able to watch through the lens of a telescope, an instrument from the Spanish Rooms that Vilém had taught her to use only a fortnight earlier. The battle had begun at the Summer Palace, where the Bohemian soldiers were entrenched behind earthworks. Fog was creeping upwards from the hollows and into the game park so that only one of the palace's outbuildings could be seen, alight with petals of flame. Her hands trembled as she held the instrument to the window. Smoke was lolling upwards through the collapsed roof of the building, an exotic flower coloured mallow and orange with each burst of cannon-fire. Then one of the explosions lit the Bohemian soldiers as they fled downwards, zigzagging through the trees, leaving behind their tumbrels and gun-carriages. Further above, the first of the enemy troops – a squadron of pikemen and musketeers – reached the breastworks.

She left the palace by the back stairs less than an hour later. On the landings she pushed past clutches of kitchen-maids wailing about the invading Cossacks, then made her way into the courtyard. By this time dusk had fallen and the first of the fleeing Bohemian soldiers reached the gates. From the palace courtyard she heard their angry shouts as they pleaded with the sentries, then the sound of the gates scraping open. Some of the men had discarded their weapons – flails and sickles – others were dragging them like exhausted workers returning from a day in the fields. They were ill-fed and, with their grubby buff-coats and dented breastplates, looked more like tinkers than soldiers. She dodged between them as they stumbled in their dozens across the cobbles. Then she hitched up her skirts and ran north towards Golden Lane, her path lit by explosions.

The houses in Golden Lane were dark at that hour, every last one of them. Their occupants must have fled along with dozens of others from the castle. A few days earlier, when the Imperial Army reached Rakovník, the English and Palatine counsellors had decamped with their families and possessions. Had Vilém fled with them? Had he abandoned her? She knocked again on the door, this time more forcefully, but still there was no reply. Had he even abandoned his books?

The sky was still on fire a few minutes later when, after she could see no sign even of Jiří, she made her way back towards the Královsky Palace. By this time the gates to the Powder Bridge were swinging shut amid much shouting. The Queen's coach had been summoned and now stood at the ready in the palace courtyard. The drum-fire had drawn closer, and she could hear the bark of guns as the musketeers gave fire, then fell back in their ranks to reload for another bloody enfilade. Teams of horses were dragging long culverins and stubby mortars across the brow of the mountain, pulling their carriages into place for the next bombardment. She ducked her head and ran towards the Spanish Rooms, frost crunching underfoot.

The library stood in the line of fire, the windows on its west side overlooking the dark hulk of the White Mountain, which in the twilight resembled a huge crouching beast. The thousands of books were housed in the deepest recesses of the Spanish Rooms, so she first had to pick her way through the labyrinth of galleries devoted to Rudolf's other treasures, dozens of bejewelled, glass-faced cabinets that with their bizarre curiosities – the horns of unicorns, the teeth and jawbones of dragons – looked like the reliquaries of a mad priest. Except that in the past few days most of the rooms had been emptied of their cabinets, or else the cabinets of their contents. Only a few stuffed animals and reptiles could be seen hunched in lifelike postures behind their panes of glass. But the scores of mechanical clocks were missing, as were the priceless scientific instruments – the astrolabes, the pendulums, the telescopes – that Vilém had demonstrated for her a few weeks earlier. As were the paintings, the urns, the suits of armour . . .

She was not surprised by this desolation, having tiptoed into the Spanish Rooms two nights earlier and seen the rooms emptied of their contents. There had been no sign of Vilém then either; he seemed to have vanished along with everything else. Only Otakar remained. She had discovered him sitting on a half-filled crate of books, a bottle of wine overturned on the floor beside him. He had been weeping and was so drunk he could barely keep his head erect or his eyes open. Most of the treasures, he explained through his hiccups, were being sent away.

'For safekeeping,' he told her, rising unsteadily to his feet and sloppily refilling his cup from a second bottle, which had also been purloined from the royal wine cellar. 'Lock, stock and barrel. The King is worried that his treasures will fall into the soldiers' hands or, even worse, into those of the Emperor Ferdinand.'

'What do you mean? Where have they been sent?'

The two of them had been standing beside Vilém's desk, which for once had been cleared of its huge stack of un-catalogued books. The shelves, to her astonishment, had also been cleared of most of their books. Otakar's voice echoed against the bare walls as he spoke. He had no idea where the crates had been sent but was full of gloomy prophecies that the wine prompted him to impart. He appeared to regard the invasion of Bohemia as a personal affront, its purpose nothing other than the desecration of the library. Did she know, he asked, that in the year 1600, when Ferdinand was Archduke of Styria, he had burned all of the Protestant books in his domains, including more than 10,000 volumes in the city of Graz alone? And so now that he was Emperor he would make it his business to incinerate all of the books in Prague as well. Because every ruler celebrated his conquests by setting torch to the nearest library. Did not Julius Caesar incinerate the scrolls in the great library at Alexandria during his campaign against the republicans in Africa? Or General Stilicho, leader of the Vandals, order the burning of the Sibylline prophecies in Rome? His slurred syllables had reverberated in the empty room. Emilia had made to go, but a clumsy hand grasping at her forearm stayed her. There was nothing so dangerous to a king or an emperor, he went on, as a book. Yes, a great library – a library as magnificent as this one – was a dangerous arsenal, one that kings and emperors feared more than the greatest army or magazine. Not a single volume from the Spanish Rooms would survive, he swore, sniffling into his cup. No, no, not a single scrap would escape the holocaust!

But tonight, as the guns blazed outside, there was no sign

even of Otakar. She wove her way between the naked shelves until she reached the tiny room where Vilém worked. Though the door was closed, she could see a crack of light underneath, but the room was empty except for an oil-lamp and Otakar's two exhausted wine bottles. Vilém's desk stood in its usual place before the fireplace, and the oil-lamp, trimmed low, sat beside it, almost empty of fuel. She was about to withdraw when she noticed the faintly astringent scent in the air and then saw a clutter of objects on the desk: ink bottles and goose quills, along with a book – a parchment – bound in leather. She remembered none of these things from two nights earlier. Was this Otakar's handiwork? Or had Vilém returned? Perhaps the book belonged to him. Perhaps it was one of the works of philosophy – something by Plato or Aristotle – with which he had been trying to wean her from her diet of poetry and romance.

She tiptoed to the desk to examine the litter. There was also, she saw, a pumice-stone and a piece of chalk, as if the desk were that of a scrivener. She knew all about such things, about scribes and their parchments, which were rubbed with pumice-stones and then chalked to absorb the animal fats and keep the ink from running. Two weeks ago Vilém had shown her, besides the telescopes and astrolabes, a number of ancient manuscripts, ones copied, he said, by the scribes of Constantinople. The manuscripts were the most valuable documents in the whole of the Spanish Rooms, and the monks, he told her, the most exquisite artists the world had known. He had angled one of the documents into the lamplight to show her how not even the passage of a thousand years had faded the lettering – the reds made from ground-up cinnabar, the yellows from dirt excavated on the slopes of volcanoes. And some of the most beautiful and valuable parchments of all – the so-called 'golden books' made for the collections of the Byzantine emperors themselves – had been dyed purple and then inscribed with ink made from powdered gold. When Emilia closed their boards, which were as thick as the planks of a ship, her palms and fingers glittered as if she had been running them through a treasure chest.

But now the beautiful parchments from Constantinople had disappeared along with the rest of the books. Only the one on the desk remained. She moved aside the clutch of quills and studied it more carefully. The binding was exquisite. The front cover had been elaborately tooled, its leather stamped with symmetrical patterns of whorls, scrolls and interlacing leaves – intricate designs she recognised as those decorating some of the books from Constantinople. Yet when she opened the cover she saw how, far from being dyed purple or inscribed in gold, the pages were in a poor condition, stiff and wrinkled as if they had been submerged in water. The black ink was badly faded and smudged, though the words looked to be in Latin, a language she was unable to read.

Slowly she thumbed the pages, listening to the mortars echo and grumble outside the walls. One of the cannon-balls must have struck the battlements, because the floor seemed to tremble underfoot and the window-panes rattled in their fittings. A soft diffusion of light, the fire from the Summer Palace, lay lambent on the far wall. *'Fit deorum ab hominibus dolenda secessio,'* she saw at the top of one of the pages, *'soli nocentes angeli remanent . . .'*

Another piece of mortar struck the battlements, this time much closer, and a section of the wall collapsed into the moat with a crash. She looked up from the parchment, startled by the blast, and saw the tall figure and its black, sprawling shadow. It took a few seconds for her to absorb the sight of him – the beard, the sword, the pair of bowed legs that made him look like a bear standing upright. Later she would decide that he looked like Amadís of Gaul or Don Belianís, or even the Knight of Phoebus – one of the heroes from her tales of chivalry. How long he had been there, watching her from across the room, she had no idea.

'I'm sorry,' she stammered, dropping the book to the desk. 'I was only—'

Then another piece of mortar struck the wall and the window exploded in flames.

Chapter Six

I was awakened by the sound of hammering. For a moment, staring at the ceiling, at the ribs of oak laths and timber joists exposed beneath broken plaster, I could not recall where I was. I pushed myself on to my elbows, and a strip of sunlight fell like a bandolier across my chest. I was surprised to find myself on the right side of the pallet – on what, in another life, would have been Arabella's half. In my first year as a widower I had slept on her side of the bed, but then slowly – month by month, inch by inch – I had crept back to my own half, where I remained. Now I had the disturbing impression that I had dreamt of my wife for the first time in almost a year.

I rose from the bed and, pushing my spectacles on to my nose, trudged to the casement window, eager to take my first view of Pontifex Hall by daylight. Underfoot the bare boards were cool. Pushing open the casement and looking down, I saw that I was in one of the south-facing rooms. The window gave on to the parterre and, beyond it, an obelisk that corresponded to a ruined one I had seen the night before on the north side of the hall. Beyond the obelisk was another fountain and another ornamental pond, now stagnant and shrunken, each the twin of those on the north side. Or was I facing the north side? The entire grounds of the park seemed to have been composed symmetrically, as if Pontifex Hall, even in ruin, were a mirror of itself.

No, the sun was to the left, above a wall – barely visible through the branches and leaves – that marked the perimeter of the park. So, yes, I was facing south after all. Peering down through the open casement at the sorry remains of the parterre, I realised I must be directly above the library.

I stayed at the window for a minute; the air smelled fresh and green, a pleasant change from Nonsuch House, where the stench of the river at low tide is sometimes not to be borne. The hammers ceased their tattoos and were replaced, seconds later, by a sharp knock on my door. Phineas entered with a basin of steaming water.

'Breakfast served downstairs, sir.' He began clearing a space on the table with his right hand as the water slurped at the rim of the basin clutched in his wizened claw. 'In the breakfast parlour.'

'Thank you.'

'Whenever you are ready, sir.'

'Thank you, Phineas.' He had turned to go, but I stopped him. 'That knocking, what was it?'

'The plasterers, sir. Restoring the ceiling of the Great Room.' There was something unctuous and faintly unpleasant about his manner. He exposed a row of teeth that were sharp and gapped like a thatcher's rake. 'I do hope you were not disturbed, sir?'

'No, no. Not at all. Thank you, Phineas.'

I performed my ablutions quickly, scrubbing vigorously at my beard, and then began to dress, wondering about the 'interests' and 'enemies' Alethea had spoken of. Last night I had not been frightened by these revelations, as she assumed – merely puzzled. Now, in the light of day, with the fresh breeze stirring in the sunlit chamber, the idea seemed ridiculous. Possibly the townspeople were right. Poor Alethea, I thought as I struggled with my braces. Perhaps she was stricken with lunacy after all. Possibly the deaths of her father and husband – by murder or not – had unhinged her mind. This business of restoring the hall to its former condition was without doubt an eccentric pursuit.

At last I was ready to go downstairs. Closing behind me the door to the Velvet Bedchamber, I started along the corridor. There were two doors on either side, both closed; then a third, also closed, directly ahead of me. I passed through this and into an antechamber, then into a length of corridor. Two closed doors stood on either side of the corridor, which eventually intersected with a second, also lined with closed doors.

I was confused for a second. Which turn to take? I thought I could hear the creak of a banister and Phineas's footfalls rising up as if from the bottom of a well. I considered calling out to him, but something in his manner – his banked-down insolence, his carnivorous smile – warned against it. Phineas was not my friend. So I kept to a straight line, following the corridor, club foot noisily clumping. Should I turn back, I wondered, and try one of the other doors? But I kept walking. A short distance beyond the intersection the corridor terminated at a locked door.

I turned round and retraced my steps. By now Phineas's footfalls had disappeared and all was silent but for my own hesitant steps and the occasional squeal of a naked floorboard. I realised with dismay that the doors and passageways must repeat the maze on the ground floor. The symmetry operated on a vertical as well as a horizontal axis.

I stood for a moment at the intersection before choosing the new corridor. I turned left into it and, after a dozen paces, left again. I remembered having read somewhere that one conquered labyrinths by turning always to the left. This policy seemed to be rewarded, for after a few more steps the corridor widened perceptibly and I found myself in a long gallery. On the walls I could make out dark rectangles, like shadows – the after-images of framed portraits that I supposed had been smashed or stolen by the Puritans. But there was no sign of the staircase.

I continued along the gallery, tapping my thorn-stick like a blind beggar. Soon the passage narrowed and the doors and niches disappeared. This corridor now seemed as perplexing and treacherous as the other. Should I backtrack, I wondered, and return to the Velvet Bedchamber? But could I find even that now? I was completely disoriented. But then the corridor took another left turn and at last, twenty paces ahead, came to an abrupt halt before two doors, one on either side. Both stood invitingly ajar, their brass knobs winking conspiratorially in the gloom. I paused for only a second before nudging open the one on the right and stepping inside.

I was struck immediately by the pungent smell. The acrid

air tickled my nose like the stink in an apothecary's, the worst-smelling shop in London. And as my eyes adapted to the gloom I saw to my surprise that the room actually looked like that of an apothecary: every inch of its work-table and shelves was laden with alembics, blowpipes, funnels, burners, several pestles and mortars, as well as dozens of bottles and flasks filled with chemicals and powders of every colour. I had stumbled upon some sort of laboratory. Except these were not the potions of an apothecary, it appeared, but those of an alchemist. Remembering a few of the books on the library's shelves – the twaddle by charlatans such as Roger Bacon and George Ripley – I decided that Alethea must dabble in alchemy, that eccentric art supposedly invented by Hermes Trismegistus, the Egyptian priest and magician whose works, translated by Ficino, were also to be found on her shelves.

I felt a slight tweak of regret as I crept forward to the table. Was Lady Marchamont one of those seekers after the so-called *elixir vitae*, the miraculous potion that was supposed to grant eternal life? Or perhaps she hoped to discover the elusive philosopher's stone that would turn lumps of coal or clay into nuggets of gold. I had a sudden image of her bent over bubbling flasks and alembics, muttering spells in dog Latin as the bat-wings of her black cape drooped about her shoulders. Little wonder that the good people of Crampton Magna thought her a witch.

It must have been another few seconds before I saw the telescope on the window-sill. A handsome instrument, two feet in length, with vellum casing and brass ferrules, it was perched on a wooden tripod at a 45-degree angle to the floor, like a long finger pointed at the heavens. I leaned forward and tried to squint through the convex eye-lens, wondering if Alethea was an astrologer as well as an alchemist. I thought once again of the volumes of superstitious nonsense, along with the half-dozen star-atlases I had also spotted on the shelves. Or had the telescope and chemicals belonged to her father and was he the necromancer and stargazer? Perhaps Alethea was restoring his laboratory, like all else, to its original condition, one more side-chapel in the great shrine to Sir Ambrose Plessington.

But the room was not merely a shrine. The telescope was new – I could still smell its vellum – and someone had recently mixed the chemicals, for there was a powdery residue in one of the mortars and spillage on the table. A number of the vials, including one marked 'potassium cyanide', were half empty.

Cyanide? I set the vial, filled with crystals, back on its shelf, feeling as though I had blundered across some forbidden secret. Was Alethea concocting some deadly sort of poison to deal with her mysterious adversaries? The thought was not so outlandish as it sounds. After all, in those days our newssheets teemed with alarming reports of how beautiful Parisiennes kept their poison bottles on their dressing-tables next to their perfume and powder. And in Rome priests were reporting to the Pope that young ladies had described in the confessional how they murdered their wealthy husbands with arsenic and cantharides bought from an ancient fortune-teller named Hieronyma Spara. So did Lord Marchamont meet his end in this hideous fashion – by poison? By his own wife's hand? Or was Alethea involved in some other activity, something slightly more innocent? Because from what little I understood of alchemy I knew that cyanide, a poison found in laurel leaves and the stones of cherries and peaches, was used in the extraction of gold and silver.

A wave of goose-flesh rose on my forearms. The chamber seemed chilly all of a sudden. From somewhere beyond the open window came the whinny of a horse and, below it, a clicking sound, sharp and silvery, like the clash of falchions. I turned round slowly, telling myself that my task, whatever it was, had nothing to do with this dreadful little room. The library and not the laboratory was my domain. But then I noticed something else amid the clutter.

The two volumes were almost hidden among the dozens of flasks and instruments. I reached for the one on top, expecting to see yet another alchemical treatise. But the volume turned out to be an atlas of the world, the *Theatrum orbis terrarum* by Abraham Ortelius. This edition had been printed in Prague in the year 1600, a few years after Ortelius's death, if I recalled. The pages were badly water-damaged but had been expertly rebound in buckram. Franked on the pastedown was an elaborate ex-libris with the motto *Littera Scripta Manet*.

For a moment I flipped through the ruckled pages, through dozens of beautifully engraved maps. I was familiar enough with the atlas, though this particular edition was unknown to me. This was not so unusual, however, because the work had gone through dozens of editions since its first publication in 1570. I wondered how it had migrated from the library. Perhaps the great Ortelius, once the Royal Cosmographer to Philip II of Spain, had been reduced to a doorstop or a step-stool?

I set the atlas back on the table and picked up the second volume, which was newer and in considerably better condition. It was, I found, an equally distinguished work: Thomas Salusbury's translation of Galileo's *Dialogo sopra i due massimi sistemi del mondo*. Entitled *The Systeme of the World: in Four Dialogues*, it had been printed in London only a month or two earlier. I had ordered two dozen copies from the printer, all of which were sold in a matter of hours. Now I had scores of other orders from all over the country – and from Holland, France and Germany as well. The whole of Europe, it seemed, was clamouring to read this philosophical masterpiece, which was by far the most important and controversial book of its time, one the Jesuit priests in the Collegio Romano claimed would do more harm to Rome than Luther and Calvin combined.

I had only just finished reading the book myself. It contains a series of dialogues that pit a supporter of the Ptolemaic system, named Simplicius, against a more astute supporter of Copernicus. What happened to Galileo following its publication in 1632 is known well enough. Despite diplomatic support for Ptolemy and an enthusiastic reception across Europe, the book ran foul of the Church authorities. Pope Urban VIII, a friend of Galileo, ordered a prosecution, and so the old astronomer was summoned to Rome to stand trial before the Inquisition, charged with propagating Copernicanism, the theory holding that, contrary to the Holy Writ, the sun rather than the earth is the centre of the universe. In 1633 he was found guilty as charged, marched into the dungeons of the

Inquisition to be shown the instruments of torture at the disposal of the Pope, then marched to church and made to recant his views. He was placed under house arrest for the rest of his life, while the *Dialogo* was placed on the *Index librorum prohibitorum*, the Vatican's list of forbidden books.

Snick-snick-snick . . .

The peculiar champing sound outside the window had grown louder. I shivered again and replaced the book, wondering what interest Alethea might have in this masterpiece of Europe's greatest astronomer. The volume seemed strangely out of place in the laboratory, for Galileo had been an enemy of the hocus-pocus and superstition bred by alchemists, occultists and other followers of the ancient shaman Hermes Trismegistus. So what connection could lie between the book and the chemicals ranged about it? Or even between Ortelius and Galileo, between the map-maker and the astronomer?

I had decided that there was no connection, that their presence in the laboratory was merely adventitious, when suddenly I spotted something else. The breeze from the window, riffling the pages of the *Theatrum*, exposed a strange insertion, a slip of paper, halfway through the text. The paper seemed to have been imprinted with a meaningless jumble of letters, what appeared to be some barbaric language:

> FUWXU KHW HZO IKEQ LVIL EPX ZSCDWP YWGG
> FMCEMV ZN FRWKEJA RVS LHMPQW NYJHKR
> KHSV JXXE FHR QTCJEX JIO KKA EEIZTU
> AGO EKXEKHWY VYM QEOADL PTMGKBRKH

At first I thought the garbled inscription was a drastic mistake of the printer or bookbinder. Yet an error of this magnitude hardly seemed possible.

I turned the page. The verso was blank, but one of Ortelius's maps – that of the Pacific Ocean and its sprinkling of islands – continued on the following recto. Could it be that the leaf insertion was a deliberate but concealed interruption of the text? No doubt it wasn't part of the original gathering at all but had been stitched inside, for whatever reason, when the book was rebound. And the planed edges of the leaves told me that the book had indeed been rebound. So had it been an accident by the bookbinder? Had a page from another work – a page whose watermark was, I noted, different from the others – found its way into the loose quire and then into the binder's sewing-frame? Tom Monk, who was all thumbs when it came to binding books, often made errors of this sort. But I doubted that incompetence was at work in this case. Some effort had gone into its production, for it seemed no ordinary scrap of paper. I thumbed quickly through the rest of the maps and, finding no more anomalies, turned back to the mysterious leaf.

If its inclusion was no accident, there was one possible explanation, of course. For the past ten years rumours had abounded about how wealthy Royalist families had concealed their valuables in the grounds of their estates before fleeing into exile, hoping to reclaim them when they returned in happier times. Such rumours were probably the cause of the excavations I had seen beside the carriageway, the ones Alethea blamed on some misguided zeal of the villagers. I put little stock in such stories but now found myself wondering if the letters comprised not a foreign language but some sort of cipher, one that had been inscribed on the page and then hidden in the copy of Ortelius's *Theatrum* at the start of the Civil War. Perhaps the paper held a clue as to the whereabouts of Sir Ambrose's wealth of paintings and artefacts, all of which, as Alethea claimed, had disappeared. Perhaps the cipher was, like the book's beautiful engravings, a map of some sort.

I felt as if I had been conducted from one maze – the lengths of corridor – into an even more perplexing one. There seemed no way out . . . unless, of course, I took the book with me or, better yet, cut out the mysterious page with the penknife I now saw on the table. But was it, under any circumstances, excusable for me, a bibliophile, to mutilate a book?

The shameful deed was completed in two or three seconds. I pressed on the book's binding with my palm and drew the point of the instrument downwards along the hinge of the leaf, close to the stitching, as if opening the belly of a fish with a gutting knife. The page came away with a soft rip. I folded it twice and, placing it in my breast-pocket, was surprised to discover how swiftly my heart was beating. Then I drew a deep breath and stepped back into the corridor.

Snick. Snick. Snick-snick-snick . . .

The sound was brisk and penetrating, like the champing of teeth or the cry of some peculiar bird. I turned round, the morning sun warm on my back. No, not a bird. The top half of a man's head, its brow sunburnt, had appeared through a gap in the hedge. I squinted at the curved wall of foliage and caught, below the head, the swift glint of metal.

Snick, snick, snick . . .

The rhythm gathered pace, each sharp syllable answered a second later by the house's brickwork. The gap in the hedge was widening as I watched. Leaves and branches tumbled away. The hedge, like the parterre, was badly overgrown or, where not overgrown, either uprooted or chopped down – a hopeless tangle of hornbeam, whitethorn, privet and holly. The head ducked and the champing beak vanished from sight.

'The springs rise over there,' Alethea said, 'to our left. Just past the orangery.'

I turned my attention from the hedge. The two of us were standing to the west of Pontifex Hall, a few yards beyond the reach of its great quadrangular shadow, which stretched towards us across the sward. Alethea was pointing past a shallow pit, clogged with debris, above which a few miserable spars rose like ancient, idolatrous forms. Heaped about them were shards of old masonry. Beyond, on higher ground, a scattering of rocks had been arranged in broken geometric patterns.

'You can still see the remains of the dip-well.'

She nodded in the direction of the concentric rings. Once again her hand had grasped my forearm, this time in a gesture of intimacy. In the fresh light her soiled gown now proved not black after all but a mallard green. The hooded mantle, still draped over her shoulders despite the heat, looked to be embroidered with tiny faded flowers.

'The springs pour out of the rocks,' she continued, 'and into the dip-well and cress-pond, both devised by my father. From there the water disappears down a drain and runs towards the wings of the hall in a network of channels. The water was tamed and used in fountains and waterfalls. Even a giant waterwheel. It stood over there,' she said, turning to point vaguely to the south of the hall.

'All built by Sir Ambrose.'

'Of course. He was granted a number of patents for water pumps and windmills.'

She fell silent. At times this morning she seemed distracted, absorbed in some private, melancholy reverie that manifested itself in silence and oblique, unfathomable glances. We skirted the devastated orangery and now stood at the edge of the stone-lined cress-pond. It was infested with duckweed, and even at this hour its surface was thick with clouds of gnats.

When her silence promised to endure, I turned to look back at the gaunt hulk of Pontifex Hall, trying unsuccessfully to imagine the fountains and waterworks in place of the weed-choked sward and overgrown hedge now confronting us. A single magpie was swaggering across it, coming in our direction. A bad omen, my mother would have said: one for sorrow, two for joy. Instinctively I looked for a second bird but, shading my eyes, saw only the leavings of the workmen hired to restore the house, a careless litter of chisels, brick hammers, bullnose planes, handsaws. Several tarpaulins, their corners pinned by bricks, shrouded thick sheets of marble. For the fireplaces, Alethea had explained. A half-finished wooden scaffold clambered awkwardly up the scarred wall of the north wing. Beneath it lounged one of the plasterers, smoking a tobacco-pipe and throwing us the occasional glance.

By now an hour had passed since I fled the chamber with the torn page tucked in my pocket, next to my original summons. On my second attempt I had negotiated the passages unerringly; the door that originally impeded my progress had proved not to be locked, but merely stiff, and I found my way downstairs in a few minutes. It was as if the alien leaf had been some sort of key or passport – a golden skein – without which I was doomed to endless wanderings above stairs. Phineas had been awaiting my arrival in the breakfast parlour. Lady Marchamont, he explained, had already eaten and was outside in the park. If I would be so good as to take a seat, then Miss Bridget would be pleased to serve me. Then Lady Marchamont was most anxious that I should join her for a walk.

The paper was crackling softly in my pocket as the two of us returned to the house, walking side by side and passing the dozens of stunted, limbless trunks that rose through the overgrowth of what was once an orchard. I had already decided that it was a cipher, some kind of encrypted message. But encrypted by whom?

The sound of the shears grew louder as we approached the ravaged hedge, and the gardener's disembodied head bobbed and floated along the irregular green parapet. A complex pattern was defining itself as more and more branches fell away. It seemed not just one hedge, but rather a dozen, all interconnected. The lines of the plantation appeared to imitate the angles of bastions, half-moons, scarps, counter-scarps, like the model of a fortress – a series of concentric rings like those of the drip-well. What was the purpose? A puzzle maze? I was shading my eyes, studying the row of unpruned hornbeam; the dark patches of yew; the newly gravelled pathway imperfectly penetrating the wall.

Yes, a hedge-maze: an 'infernal garden' like those I had read about at the castles in Heidelberg and Prague. Through the arched entrance I could see the intricate windings beginning to take shape. The plan, I supposed, had been destroyed or lost, so that now the fractured outlines of the garden formed an impossible, patternless labyrinth. The gardener had bent his head and the shears were snapping furiously. Did a premonition nudge me as we passed, or is it merely the warping eyepiece of memory – the memory of those events that were so shortly to follow – that now gives horrible resonance to the sight of that overgrown maze and the gardener with his murderous blades?

'The pipes have become blocked.' Roused from her reverie, Alethea was continuing her account. 'They were made of the hollowed trunks of elm trees, which underground have a life expectancy of only twenty-five, perhaps thirty, years. After that, they tend to collapse or clog or leak. Then the water flows everywhere.' She pulled up short and gazed across at the scaffolded wing of Pontifex Hall. 'The foundations of the house are being undermined, you see. Water is pooling underneath, more of it every day. I am told that in a few months the entire house might collapse.'

'Collapse?' I had turned from the hedge-maze and was shielding my eyes as I peered up at the tragic spectacle of Pontifex Hall. I thought suddenly of the sounds last night in the crypt, the steady rush of unseen waters. 'Can the waters not be dammed at the source? Or conducted away?'

'The sources are too numerous for a dam. The springs rise at five or six points at least. Some of them haven't even been found. The whole building is being undermined by an underground river. So, yes, the water must be conducted away. I have an engineer in London working on plans for a new set of pipes.' She gave an exhausted sigh, then tugged my arm as she had at the door to the muniment room. 'Come.'

As we walked through the grounds Alethea described something more of the house's history. It was a replacement, she said, for one built in the time of Queen Elizabeth, which in turn was a replacement for Pontifex Abbey, an ancient foundation confiscated by Henry VIII from its little band of Carmelite friars after the Act of Dissolution in 1536. The history of the house seemed to be one of growth and destruction, of one building rising from the ashes – sometimes literally – of another; a cycle of oblivion and renewal. She indicated where the vineyard and herb garden of the dissolved abbey had extended; where its confiscated library had stood; where cupolas, bell-towers and turrets once reared high above surrounding crofts and wastes. All were now long vanished except for the odd earthwork or cairn of shattered masonry – so many scars and old bones. I was reminded, suddenly, of what she had said earlier about civilisation being founded by acts of desecration. But how in that case, I wondered, did one tell the difference between them, between acts of civilisation and those of barbarism?

'The Elizabethan house burned down some fifty years ago, killing its inhabitants, an ancient family named de Courtenay.

Quite impoverished, I believe. A year after the fire, my father purchased the freehold from the family's even more impoverished heir, a cheesemonger in Dorchester. Over the course of the next five or so years he raised the current house. He designed it himself, you understand. Every last detail of its construction, both inside and out.'

So Sir Ambrose himself was the architect, the one obsessed with mazes and symmetries. Yes, a true Daedalus – as Alethea had called him – for was not Daedalus the architect of, among other things, the Labyrinth in Crete? But I was at a loss to explain the fixation with these peculiar repetitions and echoes. Mere vagary, or was there an ulterior consideration? I felt that, despite Alethea's anecdotes and the 'remains' I had seen in the underground vault, I knew almost nothing about Sir Ambrose. The seared leaves and cockled animal skins stacked in the disinterred coffin told some strange and possibly tragic tale, as did his collection of books. But at that point I could not even begin to guess what obscure thread might hold them all together. He seemed to show one face, then another, so that it was impossible to form a picture of this strange chimera. Was he a collector? An inventor? An architect? A sea captain? An alchemist? I resolved that when I returned to London I would make a few enquiries.

I realised too that I hardly knew more about Alethea. Her every account – of the library, of the house, of her father – seemed to withhold as much as it gave out. I wondered how far I should trust her. As we approached the house I deliberated whether or not I might safely confide in her, if it would be wise to tell her about my experience in the maze of corridors above the stairs, or even to ask about the copy of Ortelius. Or was silence still the most prudent course?

Before I had made up my mind, she steered me towards the door as one does a blind man.

'The library awaits us, Mr Inchbold. The time arrives for you to learn your task.'

Chapter Seven

My task, it transpired, was to be, at least on first impression, relatively straightforward, if not exactly easy.

It had to do with Sir Ambrose's books. What else? After leading me back inside the library – which was even more spectacularly voluminous lit by the band of light streaming through its casement window – Alethea produced a list of books, a dozen in all. It had been discovered on her return, she said, that these particular volumes were missing from the library. And since she wished to complete the collection and restore the library to the condition in which Sir Ambrose had left it at his death, it was imperative that all of them be found.

'So you wish me to find replacement copies . . .' I was trying to read the upside-down names inscribed on the page. I felt relief – mingled, perhaps, with disappointment – that at last everything was becoming clear. Such an enormous fuss for twelve books. Craning my neck slightly I was able to make out one of the titles: Girolamo Benzoli's *Historia del Mondo Nuovo*. 'I see. Very well. I should be able to find copies—'

I was interrupted by Alethea, who seemed strangely nettled at my assumption.

'No, Mr Inchbold. You do not understand. I said it was imperative that these books were returned to the library.' She rapped her finger smartly against the page, which rattled like stage thunder. '*These* copies exactly, the originals. Each is identified by its ex-libris, which shows my father's arms. Here . . .'

Pulling a book at random from the shelf, she opened it to the inside cover, on which a black-and-white shield had been embossed. She then handed me the volume, an edition of Leonzio Pilato's Latin translation of the *Iliad*, whose insignia I studied more closely for fear of disturbing her temper further. The shield, I saw, was divided by a chevron and adorned at its base by a single charge, an open book with two seals and two clasps. Very appropriate, I thought. I noticed further that the device also betrayed Sir Ambrose's peculiar fondness for symmetries, because the left side of the shield – the sinister half – perfectly matched the dexter. Rather, they matched perfectly except for their colours, since the shield had been counterchanged: the sinister half was white wherever the dexter was black, and vice versa, so that the left half of the chevron was black and the right half white, while the left half of the charge was white and the right black, and so forth. The effect was a peculiar one of both reflection and contrast, of symmetry together with variation or difference. The only exception to the regime was the scroll unfurling beneath, on which was inscribed Sir Ambrose's now familiar motto: *Littera Scripta Manet*. 'The written word abides.' It was a motto that seemed at once a promise and a threat.

I closed the book and looked up to find Alethea studying me with a strangely nervous *empressement*. Gone were the melancholy reveries of a few moments earlier; she was now alert and anxious. I handed back the book, which she carefully replaced on the shelf, before returning her attention to me.

'You wish me to find twelve books owned by your father,' I ventured. 'Twelve books with his ex-libris.' I was giving the upside-down list a dubious frown. By now I could make out several more of the titles. One appeared to be the *Elegías de varones ilustres de las Indias* of Juan de Castellanos, and another was Pedro de Léon's *Primera parte de la crónica del Perú* – both of them, like the edition of Benzoli, chronicles of the Spanish explorations of the New World. 'But that may be difficult,' I added, adopting my most professional tone, 'even impossible. A thousand things might have become of them. They could be anywhere. Or nowhere. What if they were burned by the troops in the garrison?'

A vertical line appeared between the two dark arches of her eyebrows. She shook her head and gave me the hopeless, wearied look of one forced to explain recondite matters to a difficult child. I felt myself flush – from anger, but also from something more subtle, for I noticed how the change in her appearance went beyond her obvious frustration with me. This morning her face had been powdered, her lips lightly painted, and the great crop of hair subdued, partially at least, by a coif of black lace. She was still Junoesque in both stature and demeanour – I might even say Amazonian – but none the less she looked . . . well . . . rather beguiling. I even thought I smelled some kind of sweet oil that reminded me, with dreadful incongruity, of Arabella's orangeflower perfume. Still, Alethea's charms were so contrary to those of Arabella – my quiet, modest Arabella – that I found them difficult to recognise and appreciate, face powder and crimson paint or not. I swiftly averted my gaze, catching a glimpse as I did so of a fourth title inscribed on the page: Edward Wright's *Certaine Errors in Navigation*.

'Please, Mr Inchbold. You must listen very closely.' Her voice was more earnest and insistent than the case seemed to demand, with none of the patience and propriety I had so far associated with women. 'I wish to engage you to find one book. One book only. The eleven other volumes, I am happy to say, have been located. But this last, the twelfth book, has not – though not for want of trying.'

So much fuss, then, for a single book. I sighed inwardly. 'And so it is on account of this one, the twelfth, that you wish to engage me.' I was attempting to keep an edge of resignation from my voice. I had no wish to see her temper ruffle again.

'Precisely. For, you see, much depends on your finding it.'

'It seems like a great deal of trouble to bring someone all the way from London for a single book.'

'A very valuable book.'

'Even for a valuable one.'

The vertical line on her dark brow deepened. 'Mr Inchbold, I wish to emphasise the importance of your task.'

'And so you have.'

But there was more, much more, that she had not 'emphasised'; I was certain of that. Everything she told me seemed meticulously selected from a larger, unexposed story, some intrigue at which she only hinted. Her father's enemies, for example, these 'other interests'. Did they, too, wish to claim this mysterious twelfth book? But I wondered also how much of what she said – about her father, about her husband – I should let myself believe.

I had turned my back to her and for a few calculated seconds glowered blindly through the window, past the shards of glass hanging precariously in their decrepit lead fittings. I cleared my throat softly and asked: 'And if I should refuse?'

'Then we both shall lose,' she replied evenly. 'Then my situation becomes most unfortunate.'

'There are other booksellers.'

'That's as may be. But none, I think, possesses your resources.'

That was true, or at least I liked to tell myself it was. But appeals to my vanity were no good. Nor was the appeal to my greed that followed.

'I shall pay you very well.' Her voice was coming from a few feet behind me, chiming with a note I'd not heard before. 'One hundred pounds. Will that be sufficient? Plus expenses, of course. I expect you will be required to travel.'

'Travel?' The idea appalled me. I had no wish to travel anywhere except back to Nonsuch House. A hundred pounds was a good deal of money, true enough. But what did I want with more money? I was perfectly happy as I was, with my handsome £150 a year; with my tobacco-pipe, my armchair, my books.

'One hundred pounds, mind you, simply to *accept* the task,' she was continuing. I could feel her eyes boring into my back. 'Then, should you find the book . . . as I am certain you will . . . one hundred more. Two hundred pounds, Mr Inchbold' – she had adopted a tone whose levity belied the magnitude of the offer – 'two hundred pounds simply to hunt down a book. My only condition is, of course, your complete discretion.'

Two hundred pounds for a book? Removing my spectacles I began polishing their lenses vigorously on the hem of my coat. My curiosity began to wriggle free from the strict tethers with which I had bound it. Two hundred pounds for a *single* book? Unheard of. Ridiculous. Half my entire stock could be had for that price. What sort of volume could possibly be worth such a sum? Even the Caxton binder's edition of St Augustine's *Confessiones* – the edition I had glimpsed last night – could not possibly fetch a price as grand as that.

I replaced my spectacles and for a moment said nothing. Alethea had remained silent, awaiting my reply. Well . . . what did I really have to lose? It was possible I wouldn't be required to travel after all. I had all of my factors, of course: good men in Oxford, Paris, Amsterdam, Frankfurt. And Monk could be counted on to scour the bookstalls in Paternoster Row and Westminster Hall, or anywhere else I might see fit to send him. And for all I knew the book might even be on my walnut shelves at this very minute. Well? Stranger things did happen. After all, I knew for a fact that I had a copy on my shelves of Sir Walter Raleigh's *Discoverie of the large, rich, and beautifull Empire of Guiana* – a fifth title that I had made out on the upside-down page a minute earlier.

I turned round to face her. Almost despite myself I extended my hand.

'Well? What, may I ask, is the name of this valuable book?'

That afternoon I was slumped back in the seat of the carriage for the return journey to London. For the first time in hours – in *days* – I felt myself relax. Phineas cracked his whip, the horses plunged forward, the stunted trees flew past the quarter-lights. But then as we approached the archway we came within inches of colliding with a lone horseman riding full pelt towards the house.

'Sir Richard!'

'Bloody old fool! Out of my path!'

'*Yes*, Sir Richard!'

Phineas jerked the reins violently sideways. The carriage lurched towards the grassy verge, where the right front wheel jarred over a rock and then slipped into a trench. I was flung forward on to the floor of the box, twisting my hip. The rider spurred his mount, a big chestnut roan, and flew past my window with a rook-like caw.

By the time I righted myself we had climbed out of the trench and were passing beneath the archway. Grimacing, I twisted round in the seat and raised the leather flap on the tiny oval rear-window. I watched the rider dismount and then bow before Alethea, who curtsied and offered her hand. She had already changed into a riding-habit in expectation of his arrival. Her visitor was a big fellow in an old-fashioned millstone ruff and a high-crowned hat with a purple ribbon that twitched in the breeze. They were framed for a second by the wings of Pontifex Hall, two figures in an oil painting. Then we turned a corner and the painting was riven by a length of broken wall and unkempt hedgerow.

'Sir Richard Overstreet,' shouted Phineas, for once volunteering some information. 'A neighbour. Betrothed to marry Lady Marchamont.'

'Is that so?'

'Before the year is out, I shouldn't wonder. A scoundrel, sir, if you ask me,' he finished with uncharacteristic passion.

'Oh?'

But Phineas had said his piece. There were to be no further divulgations. We rode on, for three more days, in gloomy silence.

But the incident left a strange effect on me. My anger and impatience had drained away to be replaced by something else. For at some point during the previous day a small breach had been prised open. Certain images of Alethea filtered back along the irregular sluices of memory. As I closed my eyes these trickling channels carried past me images of her bent over the volumes, blowing dust from their bindings or tracing her fingertips across their surfaces like someone exploring the curve of a lover's face. Once she had even raised one of the books to her lips and, closing her eyes, sniffed at it as one would at a rose.

And so as the road twisted before us and untwisted behind I felt the first twinges of a confusing and unexpected distemper, the timid quivering of a stunted and vestigial organ for which, as with an appendix, I no longer had a use; something that, like a tail-bone or wisdom tooth, had been carried over from an extinct life, quiescent and forgotten. All at once I remembered how she looked at me in the crypt, as well as the dozens of books on sorcery crammed on to the shelves of the library, and for a moment I wondered if during my stay she might not have magicked me like a witch or a wisewoman – if some heathen spell was the source of these strange quavers. But before I could contemplate this foolish notion any longer, the leaky flood-hatches had been closed by the pain in my hip. Still, the event was no less worrying for its brevity. I would remain on the alert for further symptoms.

As my seat tipped back and forth I watched the combes open and dip, the hills and trees rise to meet us, then fall away. A few clouds hung overhead, grey as gun-smoke. Again I felt myself relax. Soon I would see the golden cupolas and brass weathercocks of Nonsuch House rising into the smoke-filled London sky. Soon I would be back inside my thick walls of books, sealed off from the alarming conundrums of the world. The events of the past day would seem nothing but a strange dream from which I had gratefully awakened, unsure of where I had travelled or what might have transpired.

But I would still possess a memento of my journey, a garbled testament of its strange purpose. As we reached Crampton Magna I withdrew a piece of paper from my pocket and stared hard at the smudged words inscribed in Alethea's old-fashioned secretary hand: *Labyrinthus mundi*, or *The Labyrinth of the World*.

Rattling about in my seat, I frowned at the paper as I had when Alethea first placed it into my hands. The name sounded vaguely familiar, though I was far from certain where I might have heard of it. It was the name of a work quite different from the other errant volumes, those treatises on navigation and remote explorations of the Spanish Americas. It was a parchment that dated, she claimed, from early in the fifteenth century, when it had been copied from a papyrus original – now lost – and translated into Latin by a scribe in Constantinople: a fragment of perhaps ten or twelve vellum leaves in the ornate oriental blind-tooled binding known as *rebesque* or *arabesco*. She would say nothing more except that it was a Hermetic text, an obscure one that had never been published. But how such a parchment could be worth two hundred pounds, and how it had become the mysterious index of Lady Marchamont's fortunes, such riddles I did not wish, at this point, to consider.

How much did I know, at that time, about the so-called *Corpus hermeticum*? No more, I suppose, than anyone else. I was aware, naturally, of how the manuscripts first appeared in Florence some two hundred years ago, after Cosimo de' Medici sent forth bands of his agents with orders to bring back to his magnificent library whatever parchments they could lay their hands on in every church and monastery that would let them past their doors. And I knew how these explorers – mostly monks from the San Marco in Florence – had recovered scores of lost masterpieces in the fusty libraries and scriptoria of the far-flung monasteries of Monte Cassino, Langres, Corvey and St Gall, works by such esteemed authors as Cicero, Seneca, Livy and Quintilian, and dozens more besides, all of which were quickly edited, translated and placed for study and safekeeping with the other treasures in the Medici Library. The thought of these scholar-explorers, these intrepid friars on muleback, I had always found appealing. Theirs were the humblest and yet most noble voyages of discovery, dangerous trips made decades before the sailing of Columbus and Cabot, before the mania for navigating the world took over, perilous journeys whose object was not gold or spices or trade routes but ancient manuscripts, a few dried-out animal skins whose secret worlds were brought back to life only after weeks of plodding along overgrown, bandit-infested mountain tracks.

And I knew, finally, how the greatest of all these discoveries was made in or about the year 1460, less than ten years after the fall of Constantinople to the Turks, when one of Cosimo's fearless monks brought back to Florence the first fourteen books of the *Corpus hermeticum*. The treasure uncovered in Macedonia was as valuable – or so Cosimo believed – as the spices of India or the gold of Peru, and worth all of the other manuscripts in the Medici Library combined. The parchments reached Florence soon after the untranslated dialogues of Plato, which had been brought out of Macedonia by Giovanni Aurispa. But Cosimo ordered Marsilio Ficino, the greatest scholar in Florence, and therefore the greatest scholar in the entire world, to translate the works of Hermès first, because he believed, like everyone else, the great Ficino included, that Plato had received all of his wisdom from none other than the ancient Egyptian priest Hermes Trismegistus. For, after all, had not ancient scholars like Iamblichus of Apamea described how Plato drank down the revered knowledge of Hermes Trismegistus while visiting Egypt? So why should Cosimo read copies by this upstart Plato if he owned their originals, the works of Hermes Trismegistus himself?

As Ficino busily translated the fourteen books from Greek into Latin there arose in Florence and then throughout the rest of Europe dozens of rumours about the existence of more Hermetic manuscripts, in Macedonia and elsewhere, all still awaiting discovery. Some twenty more parchments were eventually recovered, after much bribing of priests and ransacking of temples, but all were versions or fragments of the same fourteen books, and three more besides, so that the total number of Hermetic texts in existence stood at seventeen. A century after Cosimo's death, the Greek text of the Macedonian parchments was published in Paris, and afterwards both copies of the *Corpus hermeticum* – the one Latin, the other Greek – went through many editions and emendations, all of which Sir Ambrose had, it seemed, dutifully collected: as many editions and translations as were printed throughout Europe in the past two hundred years.

Alethea had beckoned me forward to the shelves to show how her father owned the editions prepared by Lefèvre d'Étaples, Turnebus, Flussas, Patrizzi, Rosseli, even Trincavelli's edition of Johannes Stobaeus, a Macedonian pagan who had collected together some of the Hermetic works more than a millennium earlier. But none of these collections, she claimed, contained the eighteenth manuscript, *The Labyrinth of the World*, the first Hermetic text discovered in almost two hundred years.

I had watched sceptically as she stood beside the shelf and ticked them off one by one, thinking what a pity it was that, on these volumes at least, Sir Ambrose had wasted so much money. All were handsomely bound, it was true, and I could have sold most of them in a matter of days to any one of a dozen collectors. But fifty years ago the great Isaac Casaubon had demonstrated how the entire *Corpus hermeticum* – this supposed fountainhead of the world's most ancient magic and wisdom – was nothing more than a fraud, the invention of a handful of Greek scholars living in Alexandria at some time in the century after Christ. So of what possible value or interest for anyone was one more book, one more of these fakes?

The coach forded the thin stream, its wheels tossing curtains of water to either side. The downpayment gold sovereigns – an even dozen of them – chimed softly in my pockets. I closed my eyes and didn't open them, for all I remember, until we reached the smoke of London, which I swear had never smelled so good.

Chapter Eight

The battle for Prague lasted less than an hour. Frederick's soldiers and their feeble earthworks were no match for the Imperial hordes with their 24-pound cannon-balls and flintlock muskets. The artillery ripped apart the trenches in front of the Summer Palace, then the musketeers went to work, balancing their weapons on forked rests and firing on the Bohemian infantry skidding and tumbling down the hillside. Those who escaped the musket-balls were cut down by the sabres of the cavalry who came sweeping through the game park on their war-horses a few minutes later. Those who escaped the cavalry spilled through the gates and into the castle or, failing that, leapt into the Vltava. They tried to swim the river at its bend, hoping to reach the Jewish Quarter or the Old Town, to put water between themselves and the rampaging enemy.

Others too were trying to escape across the Vltava. A convoy of overloaded coaches drawn by mules and dray-horses was jostling three abreast on the bridge, stretching all the way across the river and filling Charles Street as it wound its narrow channel through the rows of houses and towards the Old Town Square. The Queen herself was in the middle of the turbid flow, her bags hastily packed and then piled atop the roof like those of a gypsy or a tinker. A few minutes earlier she had been wrapped in a furred cape and bundled into the royal coach. Now the brocaded window-curtains did a sad shuffle as the coach teetered along the bridge, its wheels grinding against those of tumbrels and handcarts pulled or pushed by her fleeing subjects. The statues of saints wavered slowly past. They had been decapitated on her orders a few months earlier and now made an eerie sight. Then the wooden statue of the Virgin lurched into view, another wavering ghost. But the driver shouted and showed the whip to his horses. The Queen would cross into the Old Town after all, Holy Mother or not.

Emilia was also crossing into the Old Town. She had fled through the Spanish Rooms with Sir Ambrose, then through the castle, which was empty by then except for a few servants who were trundling hand-barrows piled with furs and casks of wine across the courtyards, claiming what they could before the Imperial troops breached the gates and the looting began in earnest. There would be little enough for them in the library, though. Two of its rooms were ablaze; the flames had filled the corridors with clouds of black smoke and then cast a gaudy, flickering light across the bastion garden and the onion-shaped dome of the cathedral. The cannon-ball had been heated on a brazier and so flames leapt through the wreckage of the wall seconds after it struck. Sir Ambrose had flailed at them with his cape, his enormous shadow vaulting on the wall behind him, but he was beaten back as the flames rose upwards, blackening the plastered ceiling, then the air itself. Spinning round, he had thrust out a black-gloved hand.

'Come! This way!'

In the courtyard outside he had caught the reins of a riderless horse, then leapt astride and pulled her up behind him. It was an old hackney horse, a beast more used to carts than riders, but Sir Ambrose rode it hard, spurring it down the steep descent into the Lesser Town. Emilia clung to the hind-bow of the saddle as they scrabbled along the steps, horseshoes sparking. Before them lay the Lesser Town Square, where the river of mule-carts split into two arms at the plague column, then merged together, thicker than ever. Already she could see the pinnacled bridge tower shifting against the irregular ground of spires and vanes crowded together in the Old Town.

Where were they headed? Sir Ambrose had said little since leaving the library, merely issuing terse commands to follow him, to hold tight, to duck her head as the horse passed under each keystone. He had not even bothered to introduce himself – he had the manners of a Turk, she would discover, even at the best of times. But already she could guess who he was. She knew that the tall Englishman was the agent who had brought the Golden Books to Prague along with dozens of other parchments from Constantinople – those ancient works that Vilém claimed had not seen the light of day since the Sultan Mehmet captured the city in the year 1453. But Vilém had told her nothing of the Englishman's return to Bohemia. Evidently his visit was *sub rosa*, or 'under the rose', as the ambassadors termed it. She knew of his presence only because gossip in the Královksy Palace claimed he had come to Prague not to buy books for the Spanish Rooms, as of old, but to sell them, to trade them for soldiers and musket-balls.

The horse overtook the ragtag procession on the bridge, barrelling past the carts and dray-horses and cantering into Charles Street. Here on the opposite side of the river their route suddenly became more circuitous and involved, their pace even quicker. Sir Ambrose split away from the herd, kicking the horse to a gallop and guiding it through a succession of darker and narrower streets that wound deeper into the Old Town. Emilia, a poor rider, teetered out of her balance and had to grasp handfuls of his cloak to keep from tumbling into the street. The hilt of his sword pressed against her hip. It was one of those curved blades, wide at the tip, that she knew from her reading was called a scimitar – something else that Sir Ambrose must have brought back from Constantinople. She could also see a pistol tucked into a holster on his belt and another in his boot. She closed her eyes and tightened her grip.

The artillery on the mountain had fallen silent, its task complete. Now there was only the rattle of iron shoes on stone and, far in the distance, the odd bark of a musket. When she dared to open her eyes she saw the castle shunting in and out of view beneath a single volute of smoke. Much closer, scrawled on the side of one of the buildings across the street, barely legible, she glimpsed something else, a single hieroglyphic chalked on to the sooty nogging:

The image looked familiar. She had seen it quite recently but couldn't think where. On another wall? Or in a book? She turned her head as they passed it, then quickly ducked as they flew under an arch.

They rode for the next quarter of an hour, back and forth through the streets, bowling north along by-roads parallel to others down which the horse had pelted south a minute earlier. The gutters were frozen, the muck and mud hard with frost. She wondered if they were lost. They seemed to be travelling in circles, doubling back on themselves. She had never crossed the bridge before, never entered the Old Town or the Jewish Quarter, through whose deserted streets they also galloped, passing prayer-schools and synagogues.

At some point on the edge of the Jewish Quarter there came from the street behind them a loud burst of gun-fire. The horse reared at the report, then lunged forward into the next street. Emilia, too, started at the sound. Had the Emperor's soldiers breached the gates and reached the Old Town so soon? There was another burst and a wasp buzzed past their heads, striking an alms-box in the wall of a synagogue and rattling its coins. By now she could smell the acrid stink of gunpowder on the wind. As the horse bolted forward she turned her head to see three horsemen in the street behind.

At first she thought they were Cossacks, the fiercest and most brutal warriors in Europe, the subject of dozens of fearful rumours in the palace's sculleries and kitchens. But the trio was not in the dress of Cossacks – the long coats and the tall astrakhan hats. They wore livery instead, cloaks and breeches as black as a Puritan preacher's but trimmed on the sleeves with a gold brocade that glinted as they flew past a rushlit tavern. She had never seen such garb before, neither in Prague nor Heidelberg. Nor had she seen such hideous faces. Swarthy and bearded, they were twisted like gargoyles' with murderous intent. Gold brocade flashed as one of them raised his pistol. But Sir Ambrose had already pulled his own pistol from his boot and twisted round to return fire. There was a brief hiss before the match smouldered and sparked, then flashed barely six inches from her nose. Another acrid stink. Blinded, she cried out in alarm. Sir Ambrose fumbled for the pistol in his holster, spurring the horse into the next street.

She closed her eyes again, clinging desperately to Sir Ambrose. But there were no more pistol shots. A few minutes and many turns later their pursuers on their faster mounts were somehow shaken loose. When she opened her eyes the foam-flecked horse was clattering into a wide courtyard with a twin-towered church and a clocktower. They had reached the Old Town Square. Dozens of horses and pack-mules were milling about on the cobbles. Men in uniform were shouting instructions in English, German and Bohemian, while others scrambled about like dock workers.

Sir Ambrose drove the horse into their midst, cutting diagonally across the cobbles before reaching a row of arcaded houses with skinny bay windows ablaze with light. There he reined in the winded animal in front of one of the larger houses and swiftly dismounted before handing Emilia down and seizing her elbow. As she landed on the cobbles, his face, grimacing, suffused with shades of carmine and orange, looked less like that of Amadís of Gaul or the Knight of Phoebus and more like those of the black-clad pursuers. Had she been rescued, she wondered, or captured?

The house with its prettily painted façade was a confusion of swooping flambeaux and darting figures. Sir Ambrose led her to the arcade through archipelagos of dung and heaps of baggage that seemed to have been washed against the columns by a forceful tide. Donkeys were braying and flames ruffling through the air. Where was he taking her? She felt like the game-bird caught in the jaws of the retriever. She struggled briefly – her first show of resistance. Then, as they passed by an upheld torch, she saw how he was clutching something in his other hand. The gauntlet had been removed and his fingers were stained with ink. It took her another second to recognise the object as a book, the one from the library: the lone, leather-bound parchment that had been sitting on Vilém's desk. Again she tried to twist free, but then the door swung open and she was swept inside.

II

The Interpreter of
Secrets

Chapter One

Nonsuch Books was not in the chaos I expected it to be in when I returned home, exhausted, after the arduous journey from Crampton Magna. As Phineas deposited me on London Bridge I caught a glimpse of Monk through one of the polished windows. He was bent over the counter, and behind his bowed head the books were ranged in soldierly ranks along their shelves, the afternoon sunlight lambent on their bindings. Everything was in its proper place – including, at last, me. My exile had ended.

On disembarking from the coach, I stamped my boots on the tiny cobblestones as if ridding them of the dirt and decay of Pontifex Hall. I paused to wipe my brow and inhale several lungfuls of the acrid breeze from the river. It was nearing six o'clock in the afternoon. Crowds were returning from the markets with their suppers, passing over the bridge and into Southwark. Shins of beef, wrapped in brown paper, and silver-finned fishes with wide, sardonic grins protruded from baskets as wives and servants pushed past me along the footway. I stepped forward and opened the green door with a grateful sigh and a promise to myself – soon violated – never to leave London again.

'Sir! Good afternoon!' Monk leapt from his seat like a singed cat, then helped me scrape the trunk across the threshold. 'How was your journey, Mr Inchbold? Did you enjoy the country?' He was giving the trunk a peculiar look, I suppose because he expected it to be filled to bursting with books, which he rightly supposed were the only possible inducements to my departure. 'Was the weather fine and dry, sir?'

I patiently answered these questions and a half-dozen excited others. By the time I had finished, the bells of St Magnus-the-Martyr were striking six o'clock, so I raised the awning, fastened the shutters and locked the door. I performed these operations with a certain reluctance, because I was eager to immerse myself in the waters of beautiful routine; to see my regular customers streaming through my door; to have the familiar sight of their faces and sound of their voices dilute the disturbing memories of the past week. Monk saw me spot my mail in a neat pile on the counter. The letter from Monsieur Grimaud, he explained, had at last arrived from Paris.

'Come, Monk.' I was reading the letter as I climbed the turnpike stair. Vignon's edition of Homer had eluded us after all, but not even this disappointment could dampen my reviving spirits, for by now I had caught a reassuring smell of food and heard the familiar clatter of pots and pans in the scullery. 'Shall we see what Margaret has prepared for our supper?'

But of course I knew that, today being Wednesday, a rabbit from the market in Cheapside would, as usual, be roasting on the spit, next to a boiling pot of sweet potatoes purchased in Covent Garden. And, also as usual, Margaret would have uncorked a bottle of Navarre wine, from which I would allow myself three purple inches as I sat in my upholstered armchair and smoked my two bowls of tobacco.

My immediate task, as I then saw it, was to solve the riddle of the cipher. The copy of the manuscript could wait, at least for a day or two. I cannot say why I felt this to be the order of priority. Possibly I thought the two mysterious texts – the one I possessed and the one I sought – were in some way connected, and that the former, unriddled, might lead to a solution for the latter. Since Sir Ambrose was himself a cipher – to me, at least – I reasoned that by decoding the piece of paper I might learn something more about him than the paltry information vouchsafed by Alethea. The opposite would prove the case, of course, for the cipher was not, as I believed, my golden thread, and instead it was to lead me ever outward from the centre of the labyrinth. But I could know nothing of this at the time, and so it was that as I finished my supper I was resolved to take a stab at the cipher, using for my assistance the books on steganography, or 'covered writing', found among my shelves. I had further decided to write a letter to my cousin Erasmus Inchbold, a mathematician at Wadham College in Oxford.

I climbed the steps to my study and lit a tallow candle. By this time Monk had retired to his garret and Margaret to her hovel in Southwark. Outside, the bridge had fallen silent except for the outgoing tide chuckling between its piers. Inside, the last light of the day lit the casement, whose prospect of the river had long ago been blocked by piles of books. The study was a tiny affair, the first of the rooms above the turnpike stair to suffer the encroachments from below. Every horizontal surface was now aswarm with books, a pile of which I had to clear from the bureau before there was room enough for my candlestick.

Before studying the cipher I looked for a moment at the other slip of paper from Pontifex Hall, the one Alethea had given me: *The Labyrinth of the World*. A Hermetic text? I was more puzzled than ever by my task. Ours was an age of reason and scientific discovery, not of the so-called secret wisdom of the *Corpus hermeticum*. Nowadays we read Galileo and Descartes instead of wizards such as Hermes Trismegistus and Cornelius Agrippa. We performed blood transfusions and wrote treatises on the composition of Saturn's rings. We admired and sought to imitate the beautiful forms of the ancient marble statues shipped back from Greece by Lord Arundel. We fought wars not for religious reasons but in the interests of trade and commerce. We had founded a university in New England and, in London, a 'Royal Society for Improving Natural Knowledge'. No longer did we burn witches or perform exorcisms. No longer did we think that an affliction such as a goitre might be cured by the touch of a hanged man's hand, or the pox by prayers to St Job. We were, above all, a civilised people. And so of what concern to any of us was the obscure learning, the bogus wisdom, of the *Corpus hermeticum*?

After a minute I set the paper aside and took up the cipher. This was even more mysterious. I held it to the light of the candle to study the watermark. Those imprinted on the pages of Ortelius's *Theatrum orbis terrarum* had been fool's-caps, the symbol used by the Bohemian papermaker in 1600. However, the cipher was printed on paper whose manufacturer had marked it with the motif of a cornucopia, on either side of which was an initial: a J to the left, a T to the right.

My heart lifted. I recognised the motif, of course, just as I knew the monogram. Both were those of John Thimbleby, a papermaker whose factory stood east along the river, in Shadwell. This meant that the leaf must have been inserted into the *Theatrum* at a much later date than 1600. But this was my only clue to the paper's identity and probably a useless one at that, since Thimbleby was one of the biggest suppliers of paper in the country and had been in business for more than a quarter of a century. Still, it would be worth paying him a visit to find out which printers he supplied, Royalists or Puritans, and whether he had ever sent any consignments to Dorsetshire.

I turned the leaf over, sniffed at it, then touched it with the tip of my tongue to discover if it had been marked in any other way. I knew that even the most amateur cryptographers had a half-dozen ingenious methods of concealing messages by means of what was called 'sympathetic ink'. Onions, wine, aqua fortis, the distilled juice of insects – it seemed that almost anything could be used. I was surprised that Alethea with her strange concern for secrecy had not resorted to the tactic. But I supposed it was just as well. I had no wish to tinker in my study like an alchemist or an apothecary, fiddling with pans of water and coal-dust from the scuttle. Because that's what it took to decipher one of these secret messages. Letters written in a special ink made, for instance, from dissolved alum – a substance more usually used to stop bleeding, make glue or taw leather – couldn't be read until the paper was submerged in water, which caused crystals to form on the page. Others written in inks made from goat's milk or goose fat were invisible unless the page was first sprinkled with mill-dust, which magically brought the letters back from oblivion. Another devious method was to use an ink distilled from a putrefied willow tree – a kind that was visible only in pitch-black chambers, much like that made from another recipe that involved, I seemed to recall, the juice of the glow-worm. I had even read somewhere of a batch made from a mixture of sal ammoniac and rotten wine. Letters written with this foul-smelling concoction supposedly remained invisible unless the recipient had wits enough to hold the paper to a candle flame.

But I could find no evidence of any such tampering on my scrap of paper, so I set aside the leaf and took up the first of my books on decipherment.

Well, perhaps our age with its scientific spirit was not quite rid of the old trickeries after all. I sold an alarming number of books on decipherment, most of which titles were also on the shelves at Pontifex Hall. Indeed, had not a whole shelf been devoted to the art of steganography? Now, as I sat with a pile of the books spread before me like braces of grouse ready for plucking, I saw that many of them had been reprinted in London during the past twenty years. Yes, ours was evidently an age that prized the preservation – and the revelation – of secrets. And who could blame us, I suppose, after so many years of war and intrigue?

I had discovered on my shelves the *Steganographia* of Johann von Heidenberg, alias John Trithemius, a Benedictine monk who had supposedly raised the spirit of the dead wife of the Emperor Maximilian I. There was also the *Magia naturalis* of the occultist Gian Battista della Porta, who had founded an 'Academy of Secrets' in Naples, along with *De cifris*, written by Leon Alberti, whose greatest invention was a 'cipher disk', two copper wheels, one inside the other, that rotated forwards and backwards. I owned also the work of an English author, John Wilkins, whose wife was Oliver Cromwell's sister. And I had a copy of the most famous cryptographer's manual of all, Blaise de Vigenère's 600-page *Traicté des chiffres, ou secretes manières d'escrire*, first published in Paris in the year 1586. A copy of this particular work, I recalled, was likewise on the shelves at Pontifex Hall.

For two whole hours I sat hunched over the paper, shaking my head in dismay as I tried to make sense, first of the volumes, then of the cipher, to which I applied their obscure precepts. The concept of a cipher is simple enough. It consists of a series of masqueraders: a number of characters beneath which others, the true characters, hide their faces. The faces of these hidden characters have been changed according to some arbitrary and prearranged convention called a code, the 'language' in which the cipher is written. Like any language, a code consists of a network of connections governed by its own particular rules and conventions. Deciphering therefore involves knowing or else discovering these rules and conventions in order to reveal the true identities of the impostors occupying their places. The problem, naturally, is through what method these masqueraders should be unmasked. Ordinarily the recipient solves the mystery by means of a key, a sort of grammar explaining the language in which it is written. The key might stipulate, for instance, that the true characters are replaced by those two places down the alphabet, thus:

A B C D E F G H I J K L M N O P Q R S T U V W X Y Z
C D E F G H I J K L M N O P Q R S T U V W X Y Z A B

In this case – a two-letter shift to the right – the cryptographer simply replaces the letters in the top line with those below, while the decipherer moves two letters backwards instead of two letters forward. This fairly crude system is known as the 'Caesar Alphabet', since it was first used by Julius Caesar in his communications with his troops in Spain and Syria. Such a system may be cracked, the books on my desk explained, by a little guesswork. For example, according to type-founders' bills the most common letter in the English alphabet is E, while the second most common is A, then O, then N, and so forth. The most common word is, of course, the definite article, 'the'. Now, given this small bit of information, the decipherer should first determine whether one particular letter occurs more than the others. Presumably the letter will not be E, because, like the other letters, the E will have been occulted beneath its impostor. Should he find one – the letter X, shall we say – it will become his candidate for the letter E. And should this letter frequently occur in conjunction with two others, he will have reason to suspect the trio together represents the definite article – and he will moreover have solved the identities of two more letters.

Or so he hopes. But he must proceed carefully. Snares may have been laid for him as he blunders along. The word may be spelled backwards or otherwise transposed. Or perhaps nulls – letters of no value – will have been inserted to throw him off the scent. The key might stipulate, for example, that the letter Y is a null and therefore is paired with nothing whatsoever in the plain-text. Or else the key might stipulate that every fifth letter in the cipher should be ignored, or that only the second letter in each line should be accounted. Or perhaps the definite article, or even the letter E itself, will have been omitted from the cipher altogether.

My mind was beginning to spin at the thought of these duplicities, so I turned from the books on covered writing to the cipher itself. By this time the sun had turned bullfinch orange in the casement and the watchman was passing up and down the carriageway, ringing his bell. The most common letter in the text, I discovered, was K, of which I counted eleven. I made substitutions based on the assumption that K represented E, which meant, therefore, that the cipher alphabet would consist of a six-letter shift to the right of the plain-text alphabet. But after I made these simple changes the cipher was no clearer than before. It appeared that my cryptographer was a subtler creature than Julius Caesar.

I therefore decided that he must have used what was known to cryptographers as *le système Vigenère*, a more complex method in which a keyword is used to occult and then expose the letters in the plain-text. According to Vigenère, the keyword was the clue to the labyrinth of letters: the golden skein the decipherer unspools as he winds his way backwards and forwards. Its purpose is to explain which cipher alphabets – often as many as six or seven – have been substituted for the plain-text one. Usually it will be a single word, but occasionally two or three, or possibly even an entire phrase. Vigenère himself recommends a phrase, because the longer the keyword, the harder the cipher will be to solve.

Once more I felt daunted by the task confronting me. I had creaked open Vigenère's *Traicté* and was stumbling through passages of archaic French, trying to make sense of the long columns and tables of letters that filled page after page. Without the keyword it seemed that the cipher would be all but impossible to crack, since as many as a dozen codes might have to be solved in a single cipher.

At length, though, I discovered that *le système Vigenère* was really not as mysterious as all that, at least not in conception, and as a method of enciphering texts it was ingenious, not to mention dismayingly effective. As I studied the *Traicté* I came to see the great Vigenère as a wizard or conjuror whose medium was words and letters rather than chemicals or flames – words and letters whose shapes he transformed with the incantation of a spell or the gesture of a wand.

His method consists, like Caesar's, of polyalphabetic substitutions, but substitutions of a more complex variety, ones whereby the plain-text letters can be replaced by those in any one of twenty-five cipher alphabets. The plain-text letter A might be replaced in the cipher alphabet by C, as in the Caesar Alphabet. But it does not therefore follow that plain-text B will then be replaced in the cipher by the letter D: it could be replaced with equal probability by any one of the twenty-four other letters. Neither does it mean that when C reappears in the cipher it will once again represent the plain-text letter A, because A, too, might have changed its value. For in Vigenère's substitution table, any plain-text letter along the horizontal axis may be replaced by any one below it in the vertical or left-hand one, which becomes its cipher:

```
A B C D E F G H I J K L M N O P Q R S T U V W X Y Z
B C D E F G H I J K L M N O P Q R S T U V W X Y Z A
C D E F G H I J K L M N O P Q R S T U V W X Y Z A B
D E F G H I J K L M N O P Q R S T U V W X Y Z A B C
E F G H I J K L M N O P Q R S T U V W X Y Z A B C D
F G H I J K L M N O P Q R S T U V W X Y Z A B C D E
G H I J K L M N O P Q R S T U V W X Y Z A B C D E F
H I J K L M N O P Q R S T U V W X Y Z A B C D E F G
I J K L M N O P Q R S T U V W X Y Z A B C D E F G H
J K L M N O P Q R S T U V W X Y Z A B C D E F G H I
K L M N O P Q R S T U V W X Y Z A B C D E F G H I J
L M N O P Q R S T U V W X Y Z A B C D E F G H I J K
M N O P Q R S T U V W X Y Z A B C D E F G H I J K L
N O P Q R S T U V W X Y Z A B C D E F G H I J K L M
O P Q R S T U V W X Y Z A B C D E F G H I J K L M N
P Q R S T U V W X Y Z A B C D E F G H I J K L M N O
Q R S T U V W X Y Z A B C D E F G H I J K L M N O P
R S T U V W X Y Z A B C D E F G H I J K L M N O P Q
S T U V W X Y Z A B C D E F G H I J K L M N O P Q R
T U V W X Y Z A B C D E F G H I J K L M N O P Q R S
U V W X Y Z A B C D E F G H I J K L M N O P Q R S T
V W X Y Z A B C D E F G H I J K L M N O P Q R S T U
W X Y Z A B C D E F G H I J K L M N O P Q R S T U V
X Y Z A B C D E F G H I J K L M N O P Q R S T U V W
Y Z A B C D E F G H I J K L M N O P Q R S T U V W X
Z A B C D E F G H I J K L M N O P Q R S T U V W X Y
A B C D E F G H I J K L M N O P Q R S T U V W X Y Z
```

Thus the plain-text letter B in the top, horizontal, line could be replaced by any one of the twenty-five characters arranged vertically beneath it in the twenty-five possible cipher alphabets. The decipherer knows which of these cipher alphabets to choose only by means of the keyword, those few letters whose structure is logical but whose effect is nothing short of magical, like a spell chanted over a base metal which then miraculously transmutes itself into ingots of gold. The spell works when the letters of the keyword are superimposed on those of the cipher in a series of repetitions, so that each letter of the keyword is paired, on each of its repetitions, with one in the cipher-text. Then, the transmutation. The values of the letters in the cipher change according to which alphabet the letters in the keyword instruct the decipherer to employ. What follows is a smooth, steady interchange of letters, a textual metamorphosis in which the hidden inscription crystallises like alum immersed in water, reassembling its structure according to an ordained pattern. The act of decipherment becomes as simple and certain as flipping over playing-cards to read their values, or removing the satin mask to expose the villain's face.

I found something deeply appealing about this idea of a key that can be used to unlock the most complex secrets, this word or phrase that, almost like a divine fiat, turns the random and chaotic into an ordered pattern. Vigenère was not a magician after all. No – his system belonged to our new age, that of Kepler, Galileo and Francis Bacon, one in which outer husks were cast off and the kernel of truth exposed for all to see. His system confirmed my faith in the powers of human reason to penetrate the depths of any mystery. And so was it any wonder that I believed my scrap of paper, combined with a few secret syllables, might penetrate that of Sir Ambrose Plessington?

Except that I did not yet know the keyword. Feeling overwhelmed, I set the books aside as the watchman was calling ten o'clock. My cousin Erasmus still seemed my best policy. Over the years, I had sold him many books on the subject of decipherment and I had even heard a rumour that he had deciphered papers for Cromwell. So I decided that he, of all people, would know what to make of the scrambled letters. But I would tell him nothing of my suspicions that it was a cryptogram devised in order to conceal the location of Sir Ambrose's fortune. 'My dear Erasmus,' I began, surprised by the slight tremor in my hand.

Darkness was complete by the time I finished the letter, and the bells of St Magnus were announcing eleven o'clock. I would have to hurry, I realised, if I was to catch the night mail-coach. I reached for my coat, struck by a peculiar sense of urgency. But then I was struck, just as suddenly, by something else just as urgent.

There's nothing to fear, Mr Inchbold. You will be quite safe. I promise . . .

As I shrugged into my coat and stared at the cipher on the bureau, the tiny crevice of doubt that had opened on the first night at Pontifex Hall now widened, and on a sudden impulse I knelt beside the bureau and prised up two loose floorboards, then tucked the slip of paper between the scantlings. After a moment's thought I added the inventory of missing books and the summons from Alethea, along with my downpayment of twelve sovereigns – everything that could connect me with Pontifex Hall. Then I carefully replaced the boards, covered them with two stacks of books, and picked my way around other piles of books to the turnpike stair.

'Sir?'

I was halfway down the steps. Monk's face had appeared at the top, half hidden by his nightcap. He had given me a dreadful start.

'I shall be taking a turn in the street,' I called to him. Even in the gloom I could see his eyebrows rise in surprise. I rarely ventured outside after dark, and then usually only as far as the Jolly Waterman. If London was frightening by day, at night it was, from my limited experience, something else entirely. My resolve nearly deserted me. 'Only a short one,' I added. 'I have a letter to post.'

'Allow me, sir.' He started down the twisting steps. Posting letters was one of his many duties.

'No, no.' I shied a hand at him. 'All that sitting on the coach,' I explained, flexing my legs and patting my rump for his benefit. 'A walk will be just the thing for me. Now, please, Monk, to bed with you.'

The nightcap disappeared. A minute later I was stepping outside and on to the footway. The streets beyond the gate were empty and dark. The intermittent bull's-eye lanterns – a series of yellow haloes against the buildings – barely lit my way. From the distance came the sound of the bellman. I ducked my head and hurried after my shadow, moving as tentatively as if treading on eggshells.

The nearest receiving station to Nonsuch House was in

Tower Street, near Botolph Lane. I found it without difficulty and, after dropping the letter through the posting-hole (a strong-box attached to the wall by means of a chain), I hurried back down Fish Street Hill to the sound of the curfew tolling. At its funereal call two sentries had stirred to life and were preparing to scrape shut the gates of the bridge. The portcullis had begun its descent. I scurried beneath in the nick of time, grateful once again to see the black-and-white hulk of Nonsuch House rising against the sky to meet me.

Thirty minutes later the letter was collected from the strong-box and delivered to the Inland Office, which occupied the upper floor of the General Letter Office in Clock Lane. There, by the light of a candle stub, among a litter of labels and hand stamps, the string was cut with a penknife, the wafer seal carefully broken, and the letter copied out word for word by a clerk. The clerk then carried the copy downstairs and into a larger room where a man sat behind a desk, thrumming the fingers of his right hand on its surface. His back was to the door.

'Sir Valentine,' murmured the clerk, whose name was Ottermole.

'What is it?'

'Another letter, sir. From Nonsuch House.'

The leather squeaked as Sir Valentine turned in his chair. The clerk placed the copy on the desk and, after climbing the stairs, folded the letter along its creases and carefully resealed it with a drop of wax. This, too, was delivered downstairs. A half-dozen brass-bound satchels sat by the doorway. By this time Sir Valentine had disappeared. Outside in the small coach-yard a team of horses was being hitched to the waiting mail-coach, due to arrive in Oxford some fifteen hours and five posts later.

Ottermole returned up the staircase to the Inland Office. A new pile of letters, folded and sealed, had been placed on the desk during his short absence. Sighing, he sat down before his candle stub and took up his penknife to cut the strings of another letter. As usual, it was going to be a long night.

Chapter Two

From across the river, hemmed in by a November fog, Prague Castle looked poised and at peace. Snow had fallen heavily during the night. The fountains in the courtyards were still, their tumbling waters frozen solid, and the new snow stood inches deep on the arches and gateways. Beneath the ramparts the outlines of the gardens and their pollarded alleys could just be made out, their patterns broken by irregular clefts of shadow. The fire in the Spanish Rooms had died hours ago, for there was little left in the library to burn, but a ghost of black smoke hung motionless on the air. The entire castle seemed to have slipped into hushed suspension, as if holding its breath in wait. Then it came, the slow roll of gun-fire, still far in the distance but drawing steadily closer. It could not be long now, a day at most, before the soldiers crossed the river and breached the gates of the Old Town. Then the Cossacks – the subject of so many frightened rumours – would make their appearance.

Standing on the balcony of the house in the Old Town Square, Emilia eased out a wisp of breath and listened to the clamour welling up from below. The exodus was about to proceed. Small armies of men were struggling to strap panniers to the pack-mules, or to lash sheets of canvas to top-heavy carts and wagons whose wheels had carved chaotic paths through the snow. The men had worked through the night. There were more than fifty vehicles in all, most already loaded and hitched to draught-horses and yellow oxen that were swaying their heads from side to side in sleepy feints. The procession twisted all the way round the square and then lost itself in the mist-skeined streets. Liveried pages were scampering back and forth through the snow; a few outriders cantered alongside the baggage-wagons, cursing in English and German. Across the square, beneath the clock-tower of the town hall, a draught-horse was being shod. The muffled ring of the hammer reached the balcony a split-second after each swing of the blacksmith's arm, making the entire spectacle look false and deranged, like a painting come imperfectly to life.

Gripping the frosted rail, Emilia leaned into the cool air, peering westward across the snow-capped chimneys and wattled rooftops to where the White Mountain, five miles distant, stood lost in its pall of grey mist. The Summer Palace had been taken during the night. Soldiers and courtiers alike had been slain. Her gaze drifted back down the slope of the hill to the Vltava, a rusty blade flashing in odd glimpses between the gaps in the straw-and-plaster houses. She caught sight of a grisly ballet of bodies twisting downstream on the current, arms spread wide and coat-tails fanned like the wings of angels. The Moravian foot-soldiers. Last night they had tried, and failed, to swim across the river to the safety of the Old Town.

Safety? She averted her eyes and stepped back from the railing, wrapping her cloak more tightly about her shoulders. All night there had been rumours, each worse than the last. The Transylvanian soldiers had failed to make their appearance, as had the English troops, and the Magyar horsemen were either dead or had deserted to the Emperor. The first Cossacks were now making their way down the hill towards the bridge, whose gates could not be defended for long. The Catholics had triumphed. Prague was to be sacked, its citizens taken prisoner and tortured – if they weren't put to the sword first, that is, every last one of them, God save their souls.

King Frederick would not be captured, however. Already he had fled to his fortress at Glatz, or so another rumour claimed. But the Queen was here still, inside the house, making preparations of her own. All night Emilia had heard the shrill squawks of her monkey and the banging of doors as her ambassadors and advisers trooped in and out of the chamber. This was the hour when Emilia and the other ladies-in-waiting would be summoned by a page or a bell to participate in the hour-long ritual of draping the royal personage in layers of silk and damask, then fastening buttons, tying ribbons, stringing jewels, curling hair with heated tongs, completing the magical transformation of slight, frail Elizabeth into the Queen of Bohemia. But this morning no page had knocked and no bell had rung. Perhaps she was forgotten? Nor had there been any sign of Vilém, either inside the house or outside in the square, and no smoke rose from the chimneys in Golden Lane. So she stood on the balcony, with nothing to eat and nothing to read, and waited.

A shout rose from the square and she looked down to see Sir Ambrose Plessington tramping about in the snow. He at least was much in evidence. Last night he had escorted her upstairs to her room before disappearing, wordlessly, with the leather-bound parchment still tucked under his arm. This morning there was no sign of the parchment, though he was supervising the loading of crates of books on to one of the wagons, prising up their lids with his scimitar, then hammering them shut. There must have been a hundred crates in all. She wondered for the dozenth time what he had been doing in the library the previous night. Perhaps he was behind Vilém's disappearance? The two must know each other, she reasoned. Possibly Vilém was even part of whatever dark plot had brought the Englishman to Prague. From Vilém she knew that the library held, among its thousands of books, a secret archive, a locked subterranean chamber where the most valuable and even dangerous books were housed, those listed in the *Index librorum prohibitorum*, the Vatican's catalogue of forbidden books. Only a handful of men had access to this mysterious sanctum. Each year hundreds of scholars travelled to Prague to study in the library – scholars whose appearance, like swallows or cuckoos, heralded the arrival of spring. But none was ever allowed a glimpse of the books in the secret archive. Not even Vilém, their keeper, was permitted to read them. They included, he once explained, the works of religious reformers such as Huss and Luther, along with tracts by their followers and scores of other heretics besides. There were also works by renowned astronomers. Both Copernicus's *De revolutionibus orbium coelestium* and Galileo's disquisition on tides were lodged in the archives, as were various treatises on both the comet of 1577 and the new star that had appeared in the constellation Cygnus – works that supposedly contradicted the hallowed wisdom of Aristotle. Vilém had disapproved of such secrecy, especially where the scientific treatises were concerned. How many evenings in Golden Lane had she spent listening to him complain about the *Index librorum prohibitorum*? Books such as those of Galileo and Copernicus were meant to stir up debates among scholars and astronomers, he insisted, to challenge old prejudices and enlighten the ignorant, to work towards a great instauration of knowledge. Whatever wisdom they might possess became dangerous only when it was hidden away from the rest of the world – hidden away by the secretive few who, like the cardinals in the Holy Office, wished to rule like tyrants over the many.

Now as she watched Sir Ambrose inspect and then nail shut another crate she wondered whether the books from the secret archive had been removed from the library along with all the others. Perhaps the volume she had seen last night was one of them, some book feared and forbidden by Rome? For she knew from what little she understood of the treacherous morass of Bohemian politics that the Englishman was, like Frederick and Elizabeth, a champion of the Protestant religion and an enemy to both the Emperor Ferdinand and his brother-in-law, the King of Spain. Court gossips claimed that three years ago Sir Ambrose had taken part in the expedition of another daring Englishman and Protestant champion whose fleet sailed to Guiana in the hope of capturing a gold mine from the Spanish. Sir Walter Raleigh's voyage had been a disaster, of course. The mythical mine had not been found; nor had the sought-after route through the Orinoco to the South Seas. Nor had the Spaniards been trounced in battle and driven from the shores of Guiana. To cap it all, Sir Walter had lost his head for his troubles. But Sir Ambrose had survived – if, indeed, he took part in the voyage in the first place. Now she wondered whether his unexplained reappearance in Prague was for the same type of mission, yet another strike against the detested Catholics. If so, had the men who pursued them through the streets of the Old Town the previous night been the agents of a cardinal or bishop?

'Mistress . . .'

The astronomical clock across the square was striking eight. She turned to see the serving-maid framed in the doorway, strangling a lace handkerchief in her hands. She looked as though she had been weeping. From outside in the corridor came the sound of the Queen's voice and from below the lowing of an ox, then Sir Ambrose's angered curse.

'Come,' the girl was whispering. 'A coach has been prepared.'

It was another hour before the convoy began its march through the streets of the Old Town, led by a troop of horse. A winding river of horse-carts, baggage-wagons, carriages, pack-mules with baskets and panniers: it was as if the entire contents of Prague Castle had been decanted into the ramshackle caravan. One by one the vehicles inched forward, two abreast, into the narrow streets, moving eastward, the axles ploughing through the snow and the oxen baulking in protest as if headed for the shambles. Thin panes of ice crunched under their hoofs as they were whipped along the street, their traces stiff with frost. Progress was slow and disorderly. For minutes at a stretch the caravan stood at a standstill as the horsemen struggled to clear snow from their path with their boots and the butts of muskets. Then the snow began to melt and the streets became a quagmire and passage even more difficult. In thirty minutes the front of the procession had rolled barely halfway down Celetná Street.

Emilia was squeezed inside one of the smaller coaches at the back of the caravan, riding bodkin between two of the other ladies-in-waiting. She was shivering inside a stable blanket, flexing her fingers, blowing on to them, rubbing her palms together, clapping her hands and then thrusting them deep into her covering of sheepskin in a series of frenetic but futile rituals. She also kept twisting round in the seat to peer through the quarter-light at the square and then up at the castle, not looking for the pursuing Cossacks, like the others, or even for the three black-clad horsemen. But it was too late, she realised, as they rolled past the untidy jumble of empty wooden stalls strung along the walls of the Hussite church. They were leaving Prague. Vilém would not find her now, even if he was still alive.

She clutched the sheepskin more tightly about her knees and turned to see the bleary sun hoisting itself above the steep roof of the Powder Tower, into whose shadow the head of the caravan had crept. Their chariot stuck fast in the mire and had to be jemmied free. The horsemen cursed the delays. Then the tower's gates yawned wide, swung open by soldiers, giving on to snow-covered fields through which the trackway was muddier still, the water in the ruts deeper. But the caravan serpentined forward, shunting and sliding more swiftly over the undulations as if even the mules and oxen knew they were beyond the walls and therefore exposed to enemy guns. Drumfire was still sounding from the direction of the castle, enfilades that grew fainter and more irregular as the procession drifted away and the last of the Bohemian rebels were captured or killed.

For the rest of the day the caravan followed the muddy road, passing through a succession of walled towns that looked to Emilia like shrunken versions of Prague, with their spired watch-towers, plague columns, small squares with town halls surmounted by weather-vanes and enormous clocks. Soldiers lurked in the gatehouses above which coats of arms had been inscribed in stone. The procession wound through the streets under the eyes of silent groups of townsfolk, then lurched through another gatehouse at the opposite end. After a few more hours the towns grew wider apart. Forests appeared, then thickened, and the snow on the roadsides deepened. Signs of human infringement disappeared except for a scattering of half-buried waymarks and a few distant castles crouched in valleys or outlined on hilltops against the sky.

Where was the caravan fleeing? All day rumours about their destination flew up and down its meandering length. Some claimed they were heading for Bautzen, though soon afterwards a rider appeared with the glum news that the Elector of Saxony – a boar-hunting drunkard, a Lutheran who hated

Calvinists even more than Catholics – had overrun Lusatia and laid siege to the town. A rumour then arose that it would make its way to Brünn . . . until another rumour claimed that the Moravian Estates had withdrawn from the Bohemian confederacy. Another claimed that letters had been despatched to the Queen's cousin, the Duke of Brunswick-Wolfenbüttel, at one time her suitor, in which permission was asked for refuge in his dominions. But the Duke was dithering ungallantly in his reply, explaining how he must first consult his mother, who unfortunately was absent from Wolfenbüttel. So speculation seized on the cities of the Hansa League, although it was soon recalled how Frederick had borrowed from merchants in Lübeck and Bremen large sums of money, money that he had, alas, neglected to repay. A return to Heidelberg was rumoured next – a desperate choice, because the Palatinate, as everyone knew, was occupied by Spanish troops. Equally implausible was Transylvania, since although its Prince, Bethlen Gábor, was a good Calvinist, the country was perilously close to the lands of the Great Turk, whose janissaries were said to be buckling on their swords at that very minute. So finally Brandenburg reached the top of this shrinking list of possibilities, for Brandenburg's Elector, George William of Hohenzollern, was not only a good Calvinist but also the Queen's brother-in-law, a man who therefore could not possibly refuse her. But Brandenburg lay almost two hundred miles distant on the far side of the Giant Mountains.

At nightfall the caravan straggled into a small, multi-steepled town barely a dozen miles beyond the gates of Prague. It was divided by a river that flowed under fortified walls, then along the backs of a soldier-straight row of merchants' houses, its banks hedged by snow and its shallows paned with ice and covered in white spits. The Elbe, someone said. The procession lumbered as far as a deserted square, where it crowded to a halt, the animals exhausted and lame. Emilia caught sight of the Queen's carriage in the poor light, a massive affair, curtained and upholstered, that had been slung on sets of leather braces. Six powerful horses were required to haul it. The Queen sat inside, swaddled in a fur-lined lap robe and surrounded by bales of clothing and, it appeared, dozens of books. She, like Emilia, never embarked on even the shortest journey without an enormous supply of reading material. But she had almost embarked from Prague without one of the princes, the youngest, Rupert. He had been discovered at the last minute by the King's chamberlain, it was said, and thrust into a carriage. Now the three princes were riding behind their mother, Prince Rupert in the arms of his wet-nurse. As her chariot turned into the square Emilia could also see Sir Ambrose. He was mounted on a big Percheron, from whose back he patrolled the length of the procession like an overlord, barking commands in English and Bohemian as his mount threw up divots of mud and snow.

After much confusion, the ladies-in-waiting were ordered by the *demoiselle d'honneur* to a forlorn-looking inn, the Golden Unicorn, that stood in a by-street and overlooked a Calvinist church. It was, they agreed, a sad decline from the days when travel with the Queen involved banquets and triumphal arches in every town, audiences with nobles, troops of burghers appearing to doff their hats and bend their knees.

Emilia was placed in a tiny room whose bare floor was littered with rat droppings. She shivered for a long time on the narrow pallet, exhausted but unable to sleep. Someone was weeping next door, a low, choking sound, spasmodic and laborious. From outside in the street came the occasional erratic chime of the church bell and the crunching of feet in the snow. After an hour she rose from the bed, swaddled in blankets, and sat before the begrimed casement. The sky had blown clear and a fat moon arisen. The unpacking of the convoy was not yet finished. She could see Sir Ambrose in the middle of the square, leaning on a riding-stick and giving orders to the soldiers as they distributed fodder among the horses and oxen. She narrowed her eyes and studied his broad form. The man was a riddle. He had not spoken so much as a word to her since leaving Prague. He had offered no explanations either for his presence in the library or for their perilous flight through the streets of the Old Town. There was no sign that anything had passed between them, or even that he remembered her. She wondered if she ought to be offended or relieved.

What was his plan? With nothing to read on the journey and little to see through the quarter-lights except expanses of rock and snow, she had had hours to puzzle over the parchment in the library and the three horsemen, even about the imponderable Sir Ambrose himself. Various plots had begun to suggest themselves. Throughout the spring and summer, she knew, dozens of strangers had arrived in Prague Castle. These were not the usual students and scholars, those humble pilgrims who travelled on mail-coaches or mangy mules. No, these had been visitors of a different sort, often liveried or else bearing sealed letters of introduction from dukes and bishops in every corner of the Empire, and from France, Spain and Italy as well. 'Turkey-buzzards', Vilém had called them. Rumours were a-buzz, he explained, that in order to finance his armies King Frederick was preparing to sell the treasures of the Spanish Rooms – hundreds of paintings, clocks, cabinets, even the telescopes and astrolabes made by Galileo himself. A 500-page catalogue had been drawn up in secret by the Bohemian nobility and then distributed among the potentates of Europe. Their agents arrived in Prague Castle soon afterwards, one step ahead of their marauding armies.

Of course, a good many books from the library had been included in the enormous catalogue. Frederick was planning to sell them like a costermonger hawking cabbages in the street, Vilém bitterly complained. And naturally there were as many buyers for the books as for everything else, especially for the most valuable ones, including the Golden Books from Constantinople. In Rome, Cardinal Baronius – the man who oversaw the gargantuan task of cataloguing the Vatican Library – was said to have interested the Pope in the collection. It must have been a difficult task, Vilém sneered, for Paul V was a vulgar man, a detestable philistine – the same man who had censored Galileo in 1616 and placed the work of Copernicus on the *Index*. But apparently His Holiness was now interested in acquiring not only the treasures of Prague but also Frederick's patrimony, the books in the

Bibliotheca Palatina – the finest collection of Protestant learning in the world.

And now it seemed that the books in the library had brought someone else to Prague, another agent who was equally mysterious. She shivered in the chill, watching as Sir Ambrose supervised the soldiers, who were now carrying a succession of crates and portmanteaux indoors for the night. The Queen's baggage had already been unloaded and the horses stabled. The remains of the convoy twisted around the square and into a dark side-street, where the oxen were coughing and lowing or else sticking their broad heads into nosebags. The soldiers wove their way among the vehicles, working silently and swiftly, until one of them, struggling to raise a crate from a wagon, stumbled in the snow. The crate tumbled to the ground with the sound of breaking glass.

'Oaf!'

Sir Ambrose struck the prone soldier sharply across the posteriors with the riding-stick, then drew his scimitar and violently prised the lid from the damaged crate. Emilia, still at the window, leaned forward. The crate appeared to be packed with straw and filled, not with books, like so many of the others, but, rather, with dozens of flasks and bottles, several of which had broken and were spilling their contents across the snow. Whatever the liquid, its stench must have been powerful, for the soldiers quickly retreated several steps, gagging and covering their noses. But Sir Ambrose knelt in the snow and carefully inspected the bottles before resealing the lid with a few blows of a mallet.

Emilia was puzzled by the sight. At first she thought the bottles must have come from the royal wine cellar: had Otakar not claimed that Frederick was shipping his wine collection from Prague along with everything else? But the bottles were too small; they looked more like flasks or vials. She decided they must have come instead from one of the castle's numerous laboratories. Prague Castle was honeycombed with such mysterious places; no one lived in Prague for a year without hearing tales about them. The Emperor Rudolf's dozens of alchemists and occultists had practised their secret arts, it was said, in special rooms tucked away in the Mathematics Tower. The library was crammed not only with their published works, Vilém once told her – with copies of Croll's *Basilica chymica*, Sendivogius's *Novum lumen chymicum* and Thurneysser's *Magna alchemia* – but also with their manuscripts, hundreds of documents inscribed in bizarre codes composed of astrological signs and other chicken-scratchings. She wondered if Sir Ambrose was transporting these dubious masterpieces across the snowy wastes along with the powders and potions from their hidden laboratories? Some strange business was afoot, of that she was certain. Perhaps Sir Ambrose had been, on top of all else, an alchemist, yet another of Rudolf's superstitious wizards?

She drew back the moth-eaten curtain a few more inches, pressed her brow against the frosted pane and searched for a last glimpse of Sir Ambrose. But he had already vanished into the darkness with the wooden crate clutched in his arms.

Chapter Three

Eight o'clock. Morning came seeping across London in pale-pink and pearl-grey veins of light. The city had been up for hours already: seething, clattering, belching, chiming, singing, sighing. But a darkness lingered in the sky despite the season. Gnarled strands of smoke rose upwards to filter and tease apart the morning light, like dozens of genies released from flanched bottles scattered from Smithfield to Ratcliff and for as far along the estuary as the eye could see. They returned to settle over the city in a fine black powder, tarnishing, coating and corroding, a steady dredging from which there was no escape. The gammons of bacon hanging in Leadenhall Market were already rimed with black, as was every collar, hat brim, awning and window-sill the city over. And matters would only get worse, because even at this early hour came the promise of heat, and with the heat would come the smell. Beside the Thames the stink of the silt mixed with the sweeter exhalations of the molasses, sugar and rum in the jumble of decrepit storehouses and manufactories that pressed up from the quays, together with the acrid tangs of the sea-wrack and snails exposed by the ebbing tide. The wind came from the east, unusual for that time of year, and guided the foul-smelling cloud up river, through the endless reticulations of brick streets, sunless courts and alleys, half-opened doorways and windows, into the city's every fold or recess.

The stench was already catching in my throat and stinging my lungs as I crossed under the north gate of London Bridge and headed into Fish Street Hill. From Nonsuch House it would take me some twenty minutes to reach Little Britain, which was to be the first of my stops this morning. From there I would walk south into St Paul's Churchyard and Paternoster Row. Then, if I still had not found what I sought, I would catch a hackney-coach to Westminster. Not that I really had expectations of finding anything in the clutter of second-hand bookstalls outside Westminster Hall, or even in the bookshops of St Paul's Churchyard or Little Britain for that matter. As I limped forward on my thorn-stick I was frowning into my collar, which I had drawn up over my nose in an unsuccessful attempt to keep out the foul stink. It promised to be a long day.

I had decided over breakfast an hour earlier that it was time to begin my search for Sir Ambrose's parchment. But now, even before I was halfway up Fish Street Hill, I regretted my earlier resolve. Not only were the streets crowded and foul-smelling, but yesterday a search of my shelves and catalogues for editions and copies of the *Corpus hermeticum* had failed to turn up a single reference to *The Labyrinth of the World*. Yes, a long day. I ducked my head and hurried past a throng of people gathered to watch a cart-horse wallowing on its back in the middle of the street, hoofs wildly flailing.

Was it any wonder that I generally avoided the streets of London? I pushed along the pavement, through an obstacle course of rickety stalls and market porters struggling under the flayed carcasses of goats. The path was also blocked by old men trundling oyster-carts and others bearing trays heaped with combs and ink-horns. I stepped aside to let a pair of them pass but, pushed from behind, thrust my foot into a fresh heap of turd in the gutter. Scraping my boot on the kerb, I nearly came to grief beneath the hoofs of a lumbering dray-horse. Amid a chorus of rough laughter I cursed aloud and leapt to safety.

Not even these familiar humiliations, however, could quite manage to dampen my spirits. I may even have begun to whistle. For the night before – or, rather, at four o'clock the next morning – I had discovered the keyword and decrypted the mysterious leaf from Ortelius's *Theatrum orbis terrarum*.

Not having received a reply from my cousin after four days, it occurred to me that he might be on his long vacation, which invariably he spent in the Somersetshire countryside, at Pudney Court, a venerable wreck that served as the ancestral seat of the much-depleted Inchbold clan. So after closing up shop the previous evening I had decided to take the task of decipherment upon myself. Once again I sat in my candle-lit study with the copy of Vigenère propped on one side of the desk, the leaf on the other, and a sheaf of paper in between. I had digested enough of the *Traicté* by the time the sentry was announcing one o'clock to satisfy myself about the operations of the substitution table, but also to appreciate that, ingenious as it was, without the keyword the table would be useless.

By two o'clock I had tried a great number of likely – and, increasingly, unlikely – words and phrases, beginning with Sir Ambrose's name and eventually even Alethea's, which I realised with a start must have been derived from αληθεια, or *a-letheia*, the Greek word for truth, a concept which for the Athenian philosophers meant a process of unveiling, of flushing something into the open from where it lies coiled in hidden crevices. Yet even this promising name revealed no hidden truths as far as the cipher was concerned, only further nonsense, and I barely stopped work long enough to contemplate the curious irony of its connotations when applied to Lady Marchamont, who was hardly one to unveil anything. Hour after hour I hunched over the desk, humming and cursing, doodling endless figures, lighting the wick of each new candle from the stump of its predecessor. This was impossible, I kept telling myself, absolutely impossible: all of these hair-pulling labours. The decipherment could take months, and even then the scrap of paper might not have anything intelligible to say.

At last I had leaned back in the chair, exhausted, and watched the latest candle expend itself, hissing and spitting like a kitten. A warm wind was gusting through the window, rattling the shutters and guttering the flame. All at once I felt more tired than ever. I closed my eyes and for an instant, half asleep, glimpsed rising before me the outline of Pontifex Hall framed in its monumental arch, the inscribed keystone above cast in shadow and maculated with moss and lichen, the words barely visible beneath. ITT. LITTE. LITTER . . .

In retrospect – in the days that were to follow – the keyword would strike me as almost too easy and obvious. After all, it seemed that almost every second stone at Pontifex Hall was carved with Sir Ambrose's peculiar motto, which had also been stamped on to his many thousands of books. But for the moment I was merely disappointed not to have discovered it hours or even days earlier. From that point onward, deciphering the paper became a simple process of filling in the blanks, of finding the intersections between the cipher-text and the keyword and then watching the plain-text – the hidden message – steadily emerge. I took the letters from the motto, that is, and superimposed them on those in the cipher-text, like so:

L I T T E R A S C R I P T A M A N E T L I T T E R A
F V W X V K H W H Z O I K E Q L V I L E P X Z S C D

And so forth, one letter of the epigraph for each one in the cipher-text. Using Vigenère's table, I then substituted the letters in the plain-text alphabets suggested by the legend for those in the cipher-text, converting the values of each of them until a pattern soon emerged – one so tantalising that, after the first few words appeared, I could barely hold my quill steady in order to continue the task:

```
L I T T E R A S C R I P T A M A N E T L I T T E R A
F V W X V K H W H Z O I K E Q L V I L E P X Z S C D
U N D E R T H E F I G T R E E L I E S T H E G O L D
```

'*Under the fig tree lies the gold.*' I stared at the words, incredulous, wondering if there was a fig tree at Pontifex Hall and if perhaps my first instincts had been right after all: that at the start of the Civil War Sir Ambrose had concealed his treasures somewhere on the estate, leaving behind only this piece of paper, carefully coded and hidden, as the indicator to their whereabouts. Well, if there was a fig tree at Pontifex Hall, then Alethea would undoubtedly know something about it.

But as I made further substitutions the clues grew less and less intelligible as a reference to a trove of buried gold. I worked quickly, feeling like Kepler or Tycho Brahe bent over his scribbled calculations, seeking through an endless series of mathematical combinations the universal laws of cosmic harmony. At the end of forty-five minutes the following four lines had appeared:

> UNDER THE FIG TREE LIES THE GOLDEN HORN
> FABRIC OF MYSTERY AND SHAPES UNBORN
> THAT SETS THE MARBLE ON ITS PLINTH
> AND UNTWISTS THE WORLDS LABYRINTH

My elation at the discovery of this peculiar verse was diminished only by the fact that – beyond the heart-stopping allusion to *The Labyrinth of the World* – it made little more sense than the group of scrambled letters from which it had been extracted. The fig tree, the golden horn and the labyrinth obviously constituted another code of sorts: a contextual one for which, alas, the great Vigenère had no methods or answers, and one which referred to the topography of Pontifex Hall, if at all, only in the most elliptical fashion. Before going to bed I spent another hour trying to make sense of the lines. At first I thought they might be from a poem or play and went scrambling for Jaggard's folio edition of Shakespeare and then Ovid's *Metamorphoses* with its story of the Labyrinth in Crete. I could not recall a golden horn, however, in the story of Theseus and the labyrinth. A golden thread, yes, but a horn? Still, the reference to the labyrinth made me suspect that the message had something to do with Sir Ambrose. The golden horn – the skein that the bizarre verse promised would 'untwist' the labyrinth – also seemed to strike a familiar chord. It appeared to be, like the fig tree, an allusion to some episode in classical history or mythology.

It was only the next morning, as I awoke from three hours of scratchy sleep, that I remembered where I had seen a reference to a golden horn. In a cursory search through various editions of the Hermetic texts I had come upon enough references to Constantinople – that magnificent centre of learning where the monk Michael Psellos had compiled from Syriac fragments most of what we now know as the *Corpus hermeticum* – to become curious about the city. I had begun rooting about on the shelves devoted to geography and travel, where at last I found what I was looking for, Strabo the Stoic's gargantuan *Geography*. I had leafed halfway through the enormous volume, as Monk prepared a breakfast of kippers, before I finally found the passage I was looking for. In Book VII, part of which describes the geography of the borderlands between Europe and Asia, Strabo alludes to the 'Horn of the Byzantines', a gulf of water shaped like a stag's horn, one whose topography and location he depicts with reference to another harbour called 'Under the Fig-tree'.

I read and reread the passage for a good five minutes. Surely these references were more than mere coincidence? If so, the horn in the decrypted verse referred to the harbour at Constantinople, to what was now called Istamboul: a harbour also known as the Golden Horn. And it did so especially when one took into account the other, wholly unexpected allusion to the harbour named 'Under the Fig-tree'.

But these discoveries, like the actual decipherment, led to no immediate answers, nor prompted any further ideas. The reference to ancient Byzantium did not exactly elucidate the four lines, much less untwist the labyrinth; nor did it explain why the Golden Horn – a body of water – was called a 'fabric', as if it were a tapestry or even possibly a building. I could only begin to guess why the intricately coded verse between the pages of an edition of Ortelius appeared to lead to a quotation describing the meeting-point of two continents, a harbour some fifteen hundred miles distant from Pontifex Hall. At the time I had no idea whether Sir Ambrose had travelled as far as Constantinople in his quest for books, though I seemed to remember how one of the patents granted by the Emperor Rudolf – one of the dozens of parchments in the coffin at Pontifex Hall – had been for a voyage into the lands of the Ottoman Sultan.

So, as I ate my kippers, I wondered if the cipher had something to do with Sir Ambrose's library, or even with the missing Hermetic manuscript itself. It was impossible to be certain on so little evidence. But I decided the manuscript might well elucidate the verse, and so before I had finished my breakfast I was resolved to venture outside in search of it.

But my elation soon disappeared, for my quest among the shops and stalls proved as unhelpful and unpleasant as I feared it would. In Smithfield the stench had become so overpowering that as the orphans in Christ's Hospital began their first lesson of the morning the sashes in their classrooms were lowered despite the heat. Beneath the Hospital's east wall the booksellers in Little Britain had draped their windows with curtains soaked in chloride of lime. As I arrived they were holding handkerchiefs to their noses and setting out stalls of books whose covers would have to be dusted of soot three times before the working day was over. But after three hours of poking round in these stacks I had succeeded only in tiring my feet, burning my nose and neck in the sunlight – which was scorchingly hot whenever the coal smoke cleared enough to admit it – and attracting blank stares from disinterested shopkeepers who claimed never to have heard of either a book or a manuscript called *The Labyrinth of the World*.

A pint of Lambeth ale at lunch revived me, and I caught a hackney-coach to Westminster Hall, where, of course, I had no better luck than in either Little Britain or Paternoster Row. Yet the day was not an utter loss, for I did manage to learn something about the Prague edition of Ortelius's *Theatrum orbis terrarum*, though nothing that seemed to chime with anything I had so far discovered about either Sir Ambrose Plessington or his missing parchment. All of the booksellers and stallholders stocked copies of the *Theatrum*, and one even held the rare 1590 edition printed in Antwerp by the great Plantinus. But none had ever heard of the Prague edition, much less sold it. They were as puzzled by the edition as I had been. I therefore decided I must have misread the tailpiece; either that, or the 1600 edition was a forgery. I was about to return home, when I spotted, beneath the arcade of the New Exchange in the Strand, the shop of a map-seller, Molitor & Barnacle. I knew the establishment well. As an apprentice I always found it the most intriguing shop in London, for in those days I still dreamed of travelling the world, not fleeing from it, as I do now. Despatched on an errand by Mr Smallpace, I sometimes used to duck inside and browse for hours among the maps and metal globes, my task completely forgotten until Mr Molitor, an indulgent old soul, would chase me from the premises at closing-time.

Now it was almost closing-time as I stepped through the door to see that most of the globes and astrolabes had disappeared, as had the maps of the world, beautifully engraved reproductions of Ptolemy and Mercator that Mr Molitor would pin to the walls like charts in the cabin of a ship. Eight or nine years must have passed since my last visit. Mr Molitor, alas, had also disappeared – dead of consumption in '56, I was told by Mr Barnacle. I was sorry to see that the shop had fallen on hard times and that Mr Barnacle, now an elderly gentleman, failed to recognise me. Seeing him stooped behind his counter, breathing heavily, I had a chastening vision of myself twenty or thirty years hence.

But Mr Barnacle knew his business as well as ever. He informed me that he knew of the Prague edition of the

Theatrum but had never actually seen a copy. They were, he explained, exceedingly rare and even more valuable than the editions published by Plantinus, for only a very few copies had ever been printed. But this scarcity was not the sole reason for their great value. The edition was the first posthumous one, since Ortelius had died a year or two before its appearance. He was Flemish, suspected of Protestantism, but for a quarter of a century he had been Royal Cosmographer to the King of Spain. After Philip's death in 1598 he travelled to Prague at the invitation of the Emperor Rudolf II, but died before he could take up his post as Imperial Geographer. Mr Barnacle alluded to a legend among map-makers, thoroughly unsubstantiated, that he had been poisoned. The Prague edition appeared a year or two later. The legend further suggested that it included some sort of variant, though Mr Barnacle could not say precisely what. But it was for the sake of this new detail that the great cartographer was murdered.

'A variant? What do you mean?'

'I mean that the 1600 edition was different from all of the other editions, including those printed by Plantinus. Mr Molitor had his own theory about it,' he said in a confidential tone, producing from his shelves a copy of the atlas. When he opened the cover I could see a plan of the Pacific Ocean and, inside a cartouche, the words NOVUS ORBIS. 'It involved the particular method of projection that Ortelius uses for the Prague edition.' He turned round again, suddenly spry, and reached down another text. 'The scale of latitude and longitude. All of the other editions use Mercator's projection. You know about the Mercator projection?'

'A little.' I was watching as he creaked open Mercator's famous atlas – an atlas whose maps I used to study with especial delight during my daydreaming apprenticeship. I am not mathematically inclined; far from it. Words, not numbers, are my *métier*. But I was able to appreciate a little of Gerardus Mercator's feat in representing a sphere, the earth, on a plane; in flattening the world and putting it in a book, its proportions more or less intact.

'His projection was created for the sake of navigators,' Mr

Barnacle was explaining as he tapped one of the sheets with a cracked yellow fingernail, then readjusted his spectacles – a pair with lenses almost as thick as my own – on the bridge of his nose. 'It was devised in 1569, during the great age of exploration and discovery. His scales of latitude and longitude form a grid of parallel lines and right angles that make it possible for mariners to plot compass courses along straight lines instead of curves. Most helpful, of course, for voyages across the ocean.'

He was tracing a thumbnail diagonally across the sheet, along a rhumb-line that stretched like a spider's web across a grid of squares. Then abruptly he pushed both atlases aside and reached for one of the globes, an enormous pasteboard model, some four feet in diameter, which he spun on its lacquered pedestal. Blue oceans and mottled landmasses flashed past beneath the brass horizon-ring on the equator.

'But a map is not a globe,' he continued, peering at me over the top of the great spinning ball. 'All maps entail distortion. Mercator makes his meridians run parallel to each other, but everyone knows that meridians are not parallels like latitudes are.'

'Of course,' I murmured, made dizzy by the sight of the globe, which was still revolving swiftly, its axle squeaking as seas and continents reeled past. 'Meridians converge at the poles. The distances between them shrink as the lines extend north or south of the equator.'

'But Mercator's meridians never converge.' He was pecking at the map once again. 'They remain parallel to each other, something that distorts east–west distances. So Mercator changes the distances between the latitudes as well, increasing them as they move away from the equator and towards the poles. We therefore speak of his "waxing latitudes". The result of these alterations is a distortion towards the poles. Landmasses in the far north and south are exaggerated in size because the parallels and meridians are distended so that the grid of parallel lines and right angles can be preserved. Mercator's projection is therefore well and good if one is sailing along the equator or in the lower latitudes but not much use to someone exploring the high latitudes.'

'Not much use,' I was nodding eagerly, 'to someone exploring the northwest passage to Cathay.' I was remembering how, as a boy, I used to trace the voyages of Frobisher, Davis and Hudson – those great English heroes – through the ice-ridden Arctic seas and labyrinths of islands represented at the top of Mr Molitor's globes.

'Or the sea route to the northeast through Archangel and Novaya Zemlya. Yes. Or the southwest passage to the South Seas through the Strait of Magellan or round Cape Horn.'

He was turning the sheets of the atlas and jabbing with a forefinger at the passages. When he raised his head and squinted at me I could smell his decaying teeth along with the fustiness of his threadbare garb. And for a second I thought I saw, reflected in one of his spectacle lenses, a shape in the bow-window behind me: a lone figure leaning forward as if to peer through the glass. But then Mr Barnacle lowered his head and the reflection was lost.

'You see, all of these new sea routes, if they exist, will be found in the high latitudes, near the poles, places where Mercator's projection is next to useless. For this reason mariners have never discovered them. It's also the reason why the Spaniards and the Dutch have been at work on new and better methods of map projection. In 1616 the Dutch discovered a new route into the Pacific between the Strait of Magellan and Cape Horn, the so-called Le Maire Strait' – he was licking his finger and fumbling to unfurl another sheet – 'which lies along the fifty-fifth parallel. Their fleets used the new passage to sail into the Pacific and attack the Spaniards at Guayaquil and Acapulco. So such routes were of obvious strategic importance,' he said, 'but a clue was needed to find them, something that would guide navigators through the labyrinths of islands and inlets.'

Such, then, was the legend that had been favoured by Mr Molitor: mathematicians and cartographers in Seville, in the service of Philip II, had, round about the year 1600, perfected a new method of map projection, one that preserved Mercator's grid while doing away with its distortions, so that navigation became easier in the higher latitudes. New and shorter routes to Cathay and India might thereby be discovered, along with the famous lost continent, *Terra australis incognita*, which was thought to lie somewhere in the South Seas, in the high latitudes south of the equator.

'And Ortelius?' I was studying the upside-down atlas, hoping to guide him back to the matter at hand. 'He would have known about this new projection?'

Mr Barnacle nodded vigorously. 'Of course he would have known about it. He was the Royal Cosmographer, after all. He may even have helped devise it. But when Philip died in 1598, Ortelius left Spain for Bohemia. Possibly he hoped to pass the secrets of the new method, for a price, to the Emperor Rudolf, or even to someone else. Prague was filled with fanatical Protestants in those days, enemies of Spain and the Habsburgs. And so perhaps he was murdered by Spanish agents as his reward.' He shrugged and clapped the volume shut. 'The rumour is compelling but impossible to verify as the plates have since disappeared. Some say they were stolen, but that cannot be verified either.' He smiled, thinly and helplessly, then shrugged again. 'Nor do any of the books themselves survive. The few copies ever printed are all thought to have been either lost or destroyed when Prague was pillaged during the Thirty Years War.'

No, I thought, shuffling through his doorway a few minutes later and back into the heat, thinking of the water-damaged volume in the queer little laboratory: not quite all of the copies had vanished. But as I wandered aimlessly back towards Charing Cross I wondered if I had not wasted my time after all. For what connections could exist between Ortelius's *Theatrum* and the Hermetic text I had been hired to locate? Between a new map of the world and a manuscript of ancient wisdom? But then I recalled what Mr Barnacle had said about the age of discovery and wondered if I had stumbled upon a connection, however remote, with Sir Ambrose's expedition to Guiana, if in fact the voyage ever took place.

I thrust the thought from my head. I decided that my

imagination, like my feet, had taken me too far afield. It was time to return home.

It must have been after six o'clock when I hailed a hackney-coach outside the Postman's Horn (in whose tiny garden I had consoled myself with another pint of ale under a mulberry tree) and began making my way back towards London Bridge through the knots and streams of evening traffic. I fell asleep after a few minutes but was roused, somewhere along Fleet Street, by the sound of shouting. The traffic must have been even thicker now, because for minutes on end the hack barely moved. I dozed again but found myself awakened once more, this time by the abrupt, two-toned bleat of a horn. I sat upright and drew back the curtain, expecting to see the Fleet Bridge with Ludgate beyond it. Only we were no longer in Fleet Street.

I thrust my head outside the window and peered up and down the street. We must have taken a wrong turn. I didn't recognise any of the taverns and alehouses overhanging the street, or even the street itself, a narrow, deserted channel darkened by billows of black smoke.

'Driver!' I rapped on the roof of the coach. Had the idiot lost his bearings?

'Sir?'

'Where the devil are you taking us, man?'

He had swivelled round in his seat, a big bear of a fellow with a thick neck and sun-peeled nose. He was grinning uneasily through a set of wooden dentures.

'An accident in Fleet Street. Cart-horse dropped down dead, sir. So I thought that if you pleased—'

I interrupted him. 'Where are we?'

'Whitefriars, sir,' he replied, teeth clicking. 'Alsatia. I thought I'd come back up to the Fleet Bridge from Water Lane, sir, and then—'

'Alsatia – ?'

The narrow passage had now assumed a more sinister aspect. I knew of Alsatia's unsavoury reputation. It was a dangerous hinterland beside the noxious sludge of the Fleet River: a dozen-odd streets and God only knew how many back courts and alleyways, all claiming exemption from the jurisdiction of the City's magistrates and justices by right of a charter granted earlier in the century by King James. The result of these privileges was that the quarter now gave sanctuary to criminals and villains of every description. Bailiffs and catchpoles entered at their peril, as did anyone else foolish enough to wander south of Fleet Street. The horn that awakened me must have been, I supposed, a signal from one of their look-outs, a warning to the others that strangers had arrived in their midst. Although the quarter now seemed innocent enough in its faint gilding of antique-gold sunlight, I was taking no chances.

'Take us out of here immediately,' I commanded the driver.

'Yes, sir.'

The hack shunted forward, negotiated a dog's-leg, rounded a bend, then crept through a tight street bordered on either side by decrepit buildings whose window-panes were filmed with grease and soot. The road was cratered with pot-holes, a few of which had been imperfectly repaired with brushwood. No one seemed to be about. The Thames lay to our right, parallaxing into view every now and then across vacant, rubble-littered lots, its front lined by a number of precarious-looking wharves. Black ghosts of coal dust hurried across our path. We kept a course parallel to the river, the hack swaying from side to side as the wooden-toothed Jehu on the box-seat picked our way recklessly round an obstacle course of desquamated roof-tiles, shattered bits of quern-stone and the iron hoops and broken staves of long-emptied kegs of ale. Soon I could smell the mud of the Fleet; then a minute later its bank cut us off, and we turned on to a path that did not, to my eyes, look like leading back up to Fleet Street.

'For God's sake, man!'

'Another minute, sir . . .'

But after another minute we were still bumping and swaying on the path, downwind of the constipated river, our wheels squelching in the mud. The Fleet's surface was scummed over and clouds of insects hung in the air. I covered my nose with a handkerchief and held my breath.

All at once, however, I caught sight through the window of something that looked familiar, a bit of graffito – the work of a child? – scrawled in chalk across a dead wall, thus:

I craned my neck as we lumbered slowly past. What did this peculiar hieroglyph mean? Was it the caricature of a man? A horned man? Perhaps the devil? I was certain I had seen the figure somewhere before. But where? In a book?

'Damn!'

I swung round and peered up at the box-seat. 'What is it?'

'Apologies, sir.' The hack had stopped moving. 'We seem to have reached a dead end.'

'A dead end – ?'

The graffito was forgotten. I flung open the door, stepped outside and immediately sank halfway to my ankles in some sort of ooze. The horses, too, stood fetlock-deep in sludge and the wheels of the hack were buried to their rims. I raised my eyes. I could see ahead of us the bell-tower of Bridewell Prison and the steeple of St Bride's, but little else other than a cluster of sheds in the gathering shadows. It was later than I had realised, for the sun was dipping behind the irregular serrulations of Whitehall Palace, and here and there among the buildings a few rushlights had begun to flicker. Alsatia was coming awake.

'Allow me, sir.'

The driver tossed his whip aside and hopped down from his box, giving me an ingratiating smile. He had almost guided me back inside, when I looked up from the mire to see that a light had appeared in the window of the building nearest us: a tavern, from the look of it. Its signboard creaked faintly in the breeze. I squinted at its inscription. I could make out the head of some sort of animal and a wink of gold paint.

'Come along, sir.' The driver's hands pressed my shoulders. 'Sir? Is everything all right?'

'Yes . . .' I barely heard him. I was pressing a shilling into his palm, not looking at him. 'Here – your money. Take it.' I was already walking towards the tavern. 'Now go.'

I heard his incredulous voice behind me: 'Sir?'

'Go!'

The mud sucked at my boots and I had to wrench them free at each step. But a few seconds later I was on solid ground, a bricked footpath, and the tavern rose before me. The door opened, throwing a triangle of light across the bricks. I was moving forward, squinting at the signboard. And once again I saw the peeling portrait, clearer now: the head of a buck whose antlers had been painted gold. Above the antlers, three words: THE GOLDEN HORN.

Chapter Four

It was the smell that struck me first, stale pipe and coal smoke mingled with sawdust and vermiculated wood daubed with pitch: the smell of a chamber that had seen neither broom nor beeswax, neither light nor air. Then, as I stepped inside and my pupils adapted to the dim light, I caught what became the most pervasive scent of all: coffee. For the Golden Horn wasn't a tavern after all, but a coffee-house.

The door swung shut behind me and I took a few more steps through the hearth smoke, casting about for a chair. A coffee-house was the last thing I expected to find in the heart of Alsatia, though I shouldn't really have been surprised, because even then, as far back as 1660, it seemed that a coffee-house stood in every street. I had only ever been inside one of them, the Greek's Head, an airy place filled with would-be actors and poets, and its congenial atmosphere could not possibly have prepared me for the smoke and gloom of the Golden Horn.

I found a seat, a three-legged stool, and sat down well away from the fire, which was drawing poorly.

'Your pleasure, sir?'

A short and pot-bellied waiter had appeared beside me, wiping his hands on a grubby apron. Behind him, two unsavoury-looking men sat in grave discussion, while behind them a lone man, the one who had entered a moment earlier, sat with his back to us, paring the calluses on his palms with a knife. As I looked around me at the crude furniture, the tiny hearth, the curled handbills yellowing on the walls, I wondered what tangled thread could possibly connect the Golden Horn to Pontifex Hall. All at once I doubted whether the patterns I was seeing – the cipher, the keyword, the strange verse, Strabo, now the Golden Horn coffee-house – had any significance beyond my own imagination. Was there a meaning behind this series of clues, or only chance and coincidence?

There was only one way to find out. I reached into my pocket and withdrew a penny. 'A dish of coffee, please.'

But no clues or mysterious powers revealed themselves; at least, not yet. By the time I finished the drink – a bitter, sludgy brew – the room had filled with more customers. A dozen-odd men had arrived, singly or in twos, each of them shabbily dressed, with scuffed boots and patched coats. Conversation was sporadic and quiet, punctuated by guttural laughter. The waiter moved back and forth from the counter to the tables, dishes clattering on his tray. Everyone seemed to be waiting for something to happen, but nothing did. I had been wrong about the significance of the name; it must have been a coincidence, nothing more. There were probably half a dozen taverns or coffee-houses called The Golden Horn, none of which had any connection with Pontifex Hall, least of all this one.

It was only after a few more minutes that I noticed the cabinet. It stood in the corner of the room, a small cabinet of rarities of the sort used by proprietors to attract custom. But from my seat I could see how this particular case was a sorrier collection than most, a witch's cupboard unlikely to convince even the most gullible patron. But I was curious, if not gullible, so I rose from my chair and crossed the floor.

The corner was darker than elsewhere, and no one else was paying the least bit of attention to the half-hearted display. Misspelled cards inscribed in a shaky hand identified a half-dozen uninspiring objects that seemed to cringe behind the glass. I leaned forward, squinting through my spectacles. A worm-eaten piece of cloth was identified as part of Edward the Confessor's shroud, while, beside it, an unremarkable wooden branch, half rotted, was reported as coming from a tree against which glanced the arrow that killed King William Rufus. According to its label, another even more undistinguished fragment had been chipped from the tomb of Sebert, King of the Saxons.

I almost burst out laughing at the sight of these bogus fragments of history, but then another of the cards caught my eye. Yellowed and curling, propped at the back of the cabinet, it identified a few square inches of frayed canvas as part of the main topsail of the *Britomart*, one of the ships in Sir Walter Raleigh's Orinoco expedition of 1617. I frowned and leaned forward again. I doubted the scrap was any more authentic than the others, but it reminded me of the patent in the coffin at Pontifex Hall, the one for the construction of the *Philip Sidney*.

And then I saw the last exhibit in the cabinet, by far the most gruesome. It, too, was at the back of the cabinet and looked like the severed head of a man. I started, then leaned forward again, goggling at this gruesome curio from what must have been some barbaric and heathen cult. It made a horrific sight. Matted brown hair hung over a tallow-coloured brow, beneath which two eyeballs goggled back, one pointed at the ceiling, the other at the floor. The left eyelid drooped, suggesting a wink, while the lips – grotesquely thick and painted red like a harlot's – were twisted into a cynical and knowing grin. But no sooner did I realise that the head was a fake, made of wax and velvet, than I was startled again, this time by the placard propped beneath the protuberant chin and inscribed in the same childish hand as the others:

> *The Head of an Automaton from*
> *the Kingdom of Bohemia,*
> *once Belonging to*
> *His Imperial Majesty, Rudolf II*

By the time I crept back to my table, the windows had darkened and hearth smoke was wreathing about the joists. My hand shook as I held the dish to my lips. I wondered whether the grisly head was more authentic than the other objects. Had it somehow found its way here from Pontifex Hall? Via Cromwell's soldiers, perhaps, or some other band of looters?

I sat in the chair for another thirty minutes, feeling ever more exhausted and anxious, throwing the occasional glance at the waxwork skull that seemed to wink back at me, smug and knowing, from behind its pane of glass. The dish of coffee, far from soothing me, as I had hoped, seemed to have set my nerves on edge. When my waiter shuffled past, however, I managed to point at the cabinet and ask how the item had been acquired. But he claimed to know neither how nor when it might have arrived in the Golden Horn. Indeed, it almost seemed from his surprised and then puzzled expression that he had never so much as noticed the cabinet before, let alone its most horrific inhabitant.

I decided to return home, now regretting that I had dismissed my driver so quickly. The journey back to Fleet Street was bound to be dangerous. I would have to travel on foot, I knew, because it was unlikely that a hackney-coach would stray into this street, especially after dark. My mind filled with all sorts of unpleasant encounters, which I tried to thrust aside as I threaded my way to the door.

It was then that I made my last discovery of the evening. As I reached the door I noticed a handbill pasted on the wall beside the jamb. There was nothing unusual about it, because the walls of the coffee-house were papered with all sorts of these notices. From where I sat I had been able to read a score or two of flyblown playbills, tradesmen's cards, obscene ballads printed on fox-marked broadsheets, together with bits of graffiti, also obscene, either carved into the benches and tables or else daubed on to the beams. So I almost passed the handbill without a thought, but as I stood aside to allow others to enter through the doorway, the inscription, a murky copperplate engraving, attracted my eye:

NOTICE OF AN AUCTION
to be held at the GOLDEN HORN, Whitefriars,
on the 19th Day of July, at Nine o'clock in the Morning,
at which time many diverse and uncommon Books
shall be exposed to View and auctioned
in 300 Lots
by Doctor Samuel Pickvance

I stood staring at the handbill as several customers pushed inside and then several more pushed past me into the night. A book auction? It was as if I had stumbled across an edition of Homer or Virgil in the forests of Guiana. I thought I knew everyone in the London book trade, including all of the auctioneers, but I had never heard of anyone named Pickvance, if that was in fact his real name. I wondered what 'diverse and uncommon' books he would be selling and what sort of collectors might turn up to bid for them. But most of all I wondered why he had chosen to auction them in the Golden Horn. It would be easy enough to find out, though, because the nineteenth, the day of the auction, was only two days hence.

Alsatia seemed almost peaceful as I stepped on to the tessellated path, the evening air cool and pleasant compared with the hellish climate of the Golden Horn. The illusion did not last long. A moment later I smelled the Fleet and was bumped roughly aside as four or five men, all wearing falchions or daggers on their hips, swaggered towards the door of the coffee-house. Other figures were moving about in the shadows. Alsatia had come brutishly to life. I shuddered at the prospect of the journey that now awaited me.

But I would make a return trip in two days. I knew this already as I turned round for a last look at the gold antler and the inscription above, neither more than a shadow in the failed light, but each one now a glinting hieroglyph. For there must be a connection, I was suddenly certain, between the parchment I was seeking and the 'strange and uncommon' books of Dr Pickvance.

The journey back to Nonsuch House was, in the event, without incident. I followed the wheel tracks down towards the river and found a waterman dozing at his oars alongside one of the coal wharves. For two shillings he agreed to row me downstream on the tide, which was ebbing once more. When he had fitted the oars into the rowlocks and shoved off with a grunt, I lay back in the sculler and watched the thinning spray of lights ashore. Buildings and spires slipped slowly past; a boat overtook us. Our oars dipped and lifted, dipped and lifted, mud from the shallows catching on the blades and dolloping back into the water. The pitched roof of the Golden Horn shrank, dwindled, disappeared. A few minutes later I could see the moon rising above the chimney-pots on London Bridge. I closed my eyes and felt the sculler slip between the stone piers and plunge, weightless, into five feet of roaring darkness and a sudden rush of spray and air.

Emerging on the other side, legs trembling, I disembarked to find a light burning in my corner of Nonsuch House. Monk had retired to bed, but Margaret was in the kitchen, pickling oysters. She scolded me for missing my supper, boiled brawn, which I ate cold, sitting alone in my study, exhausted. Thirty minutes later I, too, had crawled into bed. I lay still for a long while, listening to the tide gurgling through the piers and trying to steady my breathing. I felt for a moment as if I was still falling between the giant legs of the bridge; as if everything beneath me had, like the sculler, given way to empty air and exhilarated suspension. Because as I drifted asleep I was thinking not only of the handbill pasted to the wall of the Golden Horn but also of the letter, imprinted with a familiar seal, that had been propped on my desk, awaiting my return.

Chapter Five

I f the journey to the Elbe was arduous, then over the next few days, as the coaches and wagons left Bohemia behind, it grew much worse. Snow began falling from the sullen skies, at first a few aimless and circumspect flakes, then more heavily. The winds gathered in the east and blew across the crescent of the Carpathians, along the Moravian Highlands and into the Giant Mountains, howling among the boulders and snowdrifts through which the caravan fought its way. The few towns it passed through dwindled to villages whose dozen-odd houses clung like swallows' nests to the sides of steep hills. Then the villages shrank to only a few houses and soon disappeared altogether. The road, too, threatened to disappear. In some places it had been made almost impassable by rockslides, in others by snow. To travel in this season, the servants muttered among themselves, was uncivilised. After all, even wars – even Ferdinand, whose Walloons and Irish had stopped in Prague to begin their looting – waited for the spring. Yet each morning, no matter how foul the weather, no matter how steep the roads, no matter how many passengers had fallen ill with fever or how many horses were lamed by wind-galls or split hoofs, the sad journey continued. Soon there were no signs of life in the snowscape except for the wolves that appeared as the roads ascended in dog-legs through the forest. The wolves arrived singly at first, later in packs of ten or twelve, half hidden among the scarps of granite, following the wagons at a distance. Then they grew bolder, creeping close enough for Emilia to see their yellow eyes and the sharp outlines of their muzzles. Skinny and ill-fed as beggars, they scattered at the muffled report of a harquebus. The sound of the weapon also startled the passengers, for rumours had begun spreading up and down the caravan that the Emperor's mercenaries were in swift pursuit, though it was impossible to imagine how anyone, even the Cossacks, could have sped along roads as treacherous as these.

The first leg of the journey finally reached its end at nightfall on the ninth day. The caravan toiled past a monastery and, after crawling downhill, stopped not at one of the usual inns but before a castle whose lighted arrowslits shone unevenly in the invading darkness. Emilia, huddled in the chariot, her toes frostbitten, fancied she could hear the grumble of a river. Leaning forward, she peered through a crack in the window-curtains and saw a group of men in long coats and wide-brimmed hats hurrying across a courtyard, whose perimeter was rimmed with dozens of coaches of all sizes. The portcullis ground and scraped, then a pair of heavy doors boomed shut behind them. Breslau, someone said. They had reached Silesia.

The exiled court stayed for less than a week in the ancient Piast castle. This was not to be their final destination, merely one more staging-post for the fugitive court. Emilia found herself housed with three other ladies-in-waiting in a chamber that, though it had no windows, was prey to mysterious draughts and dustings of snow. The Queen slept in a chamber somewhere nearby. She had been taken dangerously ill almost as soon as the caravan arrived in Breslau, and so Emilia saw nothing of her. Only the physicians attended her, shuffling in and out of the royal apartments with their faces long and grim. After a day or two, rumours were bruited about the castle that she had died. Then a day later it was her unborn babe who had died – for another rumour, a more reliable one, claimed she was with child. Finally, the pair of them, mother and child, were said to have expired together. Truth became as scarce as firewood and fodder. More snow fell. The Oder froze. Then, on Emilia's fourth day in the castle, Sir Ambrose Plessington paid her a visit.

She was in her chamber at the time, alone, reading a book. When the knock came at her door she didn't rise from the cramped bed because she, like the Queen, was now indisposed. She had felt unwell for the second day in a row. Her monthly pains had arrived a few days earlier, but no monthly flow. Her head ached, as did her teeth, and she was sleeping poorly. Even reading had become a chore. For want of her own books she was reduced to reading ones from the Queen's collection. For the past day she had been reading Sir Walter Raleigh's *Discoverie of the large, rich, and beautifull Empire of Guiana*, with its blissful descriptions of warm climes and sepulchres filled with treasure. She had been lulled to sleep — her first in more than a day — when the knock on the door startled her awake.

She was surprised to see Sir Ambrose, of course. He had not spoken a word to her for an entire fortnight; indeed, he had not appeared to notice her at all. She, on the other hand, had watched his every move. From the quarter-lights of her chariot or the windows of inns she would watch him supervising the loading or unloading of the crates or riding alongside the Queen's carriage with the scimitar bouncing at his hip. Other times he galloped out of sight, travelling far ahead of the convoy, finding passages through the mountains or scouting for Polish troops, a band of whom he was reputed to have killed and left to the wolves. Three of his mounts were lamed by these antics and had to be destroyed, yet Sir Ambrose himself looked none the worse for wear.

'I do not disturb you, I hope?'

He had stepped nimbly into her chamber, which he, in his swollen boots and beaver hat, almost seemed to fill. Forced to duck his head under the lintel, he looked like a man entering a tent on a battlefield. When he straightened to his full height his appearance was no less martial, for the scimitar hung from one hip, the pistol from the other. But he was also bearing a lantern and, under his arm, a book. After making a bow, he paused, his bustling motions for once arrested. His head was cocked to one side like that of a painter critically examining his subject.

'You were asleep?'

'No, no,' she blurted, finding her voice. She had pushed herself upright on the bed and was holding Raleigh's *Discoverie* to her breast like a shield. 'No, sir. I was reading, that is all.'

He took another step forward, straw rustling under his boots and his dark gaze giving her a careful appraisal. The plume in his hat grazed the hammer-beams. 'You are unwell, Mistress Molyneux?'

'No, no,' she stammered again. She had no wish to tell anyone of her illnesses, least of all Sir Ambrose. 'I am perfectly well, thank you, sir. My habit is to read in bed,' she explained, raising the book and then feeling herself flush.

'Ah,' he was nodding his enormous hat, 'quite so. I am told you are a dedicated reader. Yes, a veritable Donna Quixote.' He smiled briefly to himself, then scratched at his beard with a forefinger. 'And in fact this charming habit of yours, Miss Molyneux, is what brings me to you.' He bent forward with a creak of boot leather and placed the volume on the table beside the door. 'The Queen wishes you to have another book for your pleasure. Along with her good wishes.' He bowed and turned to go.

'Please . . .' She had swung her legs over the edge of the bed. 'What news is there? Is the Queen unwell, sir?'

'No, no, the Queen is quite well. You must not believe everything you hear.' Pausing on the threshold, he winked. 'Nor should you believe all that you read.'

'I beg your pardon?'

'Sir Walter Raleigh.' His windburnt features had broadened into another smile as he nodded the brim of his hat at her book. 'Guiana is not the paradise that Sir Walter describes. I bid you a good day, Miss Molyneux.'

Then he was gone, disappearing down the corridor before she could ask about Vilém or indeed about anything else. But all at once she felt hopeful. He must have learned of her reading habits from Vilém. Or was it from the Queen instead? No, most probably Vilém, she decided. How else would Sir Ambrose have known of her liking for tales of chivalry? She had been careful not to tell the Queen of this passion, for the Queen detested all things Spanish.

A minute later the other ladies-in-waiting had returned to

the room. There was to be a church service that night to give thanks for the Queen's recovery, followed by a banquet. For the next twenty minutes the ladies chattered happily together, dressing themselves as of old in their flowing conches, in scarlets and purples, in laces and ribbons, as if Prague or Heidelberg lay outside; as if the past few days had been no more than a night terror from which they had been mercifully roused. Only when they departed did Emilia finally open the book left by Sir Ambrose. It was another tale of chivalry – Francisco de Moraes's *Prince Palmerín of England*. And only when she opened the cover did she discover the note between the pages, one inscribed in a familiar hand.

She met Vilém that night in the cellars, to which the note had summoned her. By this time the rest of the court was in the midst of an ecstatic and deafening intercourse. The feast had begun. Musicians conscripted from a local tavern were blowing krummhorns, battering tabors and singing lustily in Polish as dancers whirled about the floor of the crumbling hall with reckless fury – a tumult of spinning farthingales and flying elbows. The castle gates must have been flung wide to admit the good people of Breslau, burghers and beggars alike, because Emilia, dodging between them, failed to recognise a single face. She had no idea, either, where the food could have come from. Platters of beef and venison, pheasants and chickens, a roasted boar, dozens of quail, even a peacock still wearing its feathers, together with bowls filled with oysters, cheeses, boiled eggs, sweetmeats, nuts, plums, persimmons, Seville oranges, ices melting under the heat of a dozen blazing torches and even more candles – all were being served up to a band of exiles who only a few days earlier had been freezing to death in the wilderness, eating weevilled bread and frozen chunks of salted goose. But Vilém was nowhere among them. After an hour she managed to slip away and descend the stairs to the vaults, where she found him in an old wine cellar, stooped over a crate of books.

She was shocked by the sight of him. He had arrived in Breslau more than a fortnight earlier, before the snows, but he appeared to be the worse for the journey. He looked thinner and more ragged than ever. His breeches and doublet hung in tattered folds about his shoulders and hips like those of a scarecrow. Perhaps he too had been ill? He had a weak constitution, she knew – several evenings in Golden Lane had been spent nursing him through one complaint or another. A booming cough suddenly bent him double.

'Vilém . . . ?'

Their reunion was not what she expected. So busy was he checking the crates for damage, opening them one at a time, inspecting the oilskin-wrapped volumes, fussing and clucking over them before replacing dunnage, that he failed to notice her arrival. She moved quickly through the cellar towards him, weaving her way between empty wine racks and the dozens of crates. Most of the lids had been raised and tiny gilded characters glimmered in the torchlight as she passed. Later it would occur to her that the books had been crated in alphabetical order. Abulafia; Agricola; Agrippa; Artephius; Augurello. Then Bacon; Biringuccio; Böhmen; Borbonius; Bruno. The names meant little to her, as did the titles. *De occulta philosophia. De arte cabalistica.* Impious pursuits suggested themselves. *The Mirror of Alchymy. Occulta occultum occulta.* What would the Queen, a sworn enemy of popery and superstition, make of such works? FICINUM, she read on the spine of one of the thickest volumes, PIMANDER MERCURII TRISMEGISTI.

'Vilém!'

He showed no more surprise or delight when finally he saw her than when he discovered certain cherished volumes at the bottoms of the crates through which he kept searching for another twenty minutes. Indeed, over the next few days he would appear more concerned for the welfare of the books than for her. Like Otakar, he had become obsessed with the idea of the collection falling into what he called the wrong hands – being looted, burned or disappearing into the archives of Ferdinand or the cardinals in the Holy Office. Later he would tell her that he had assisted with the transport of the 'first consignment', some fifty crates of books. The second consignment was shipped from Prague by Sir Ambrose himself, for which reason Vilém would not find it odd that the Englishman was alone inside the library. Only when she described that episode – they were sitting on a pair of wine casks at this point – did he show any interest in her plight. Or, rather, he was interested in the leather-bound volume she had seen on his desk. Two times he forced her to describe the events of that evening but then, puzzled, claimed not to recognise her accounts of either the book or the horsemen. But he was especially interested in the elaborate binding. He sprang from the cask, squatted on the floor and rummaged through one of the crates for a minute, muttering to himself and grunting.

'You say it was bound,' he called over his shoulder, 'like one of these.' He swung round, clasping a fat volume to his chest. 'Is that so?'

In the torchlight she could make out the intricate swirls stamped on to the book's leather cover – a series of whorls and curlicues that reminded her, suddenly, of the fanciful lines of Prague Castle's maze garden seen from the upper windows of the Královský Palace. From its coloured fore-edges the volume looked like one of the Golden Books he had shown her a month earlier. She nodded.

'Exactly like that, yes. The same pattern, I would say.'

'Odd . . . very odd.' He was twisting a lock of his unkempt beard in his fingers as he studied the tooled leather. 'But you say the pages had not been dyed?' She shook her head. 'Mm,' he said into his stained ruff, frowning, 'how very odd indeed.'

'Did it come from Constantinople, do you think?'

'Oh, it's possible.' His head was bobbing. The idea seemed to excite him. 'Yes, it might have done. One doesn't judge a book by its binding, of course. But what you describe is a Muhammadan decoration known as *rebesque* or arabesque, which was used by the bookbinders of Istamboul. There were a dozen such books in the library, but this one that you describe, hmmm . . .'

He had opened the book and was thumbing slowly through its purple leaves, through pages that she remembered him saying had been made from the skins of unborn calves, sometimes as many as fifty per volume. Vellum, it was called. The calves were stunned and carefully bled, then flayed of their delicate hides. A lost art, he had claimed.

'But what could it be?' She was watching his face, wondering if he was telling her everything he knew. 'Was it something of value, do you think?'

He shrugged his narrow shoulders and laid the volume carefully aside. 'Oh, it could be anything – anything at all. And, yes, I should think it was of value. Perhaps of considerable value. Especially if it came from Constantinople. Its libraries and monasteries, you understand, were the world's greatest repositories of ancient wisdom.'

He was at his most pontifical now, plucking at his beard and staring glassily into the middle distance. The thumpings of the dancers in the hall were making themselves known through the groined ceiling, but he seemed not to notice.

'In the past few centuries, more Greek and Roman authors have been discovered in Constantinople than anywhere else. Priceless discoveries, mind! The eleven plays of Aristophanes . . . the seven of Aeschylus . . . the poems of Nicander and Musaeus . . . Hesiod's *Works and Days* . . . the writings of Marcus Aurelius . . . why, even Euclid's *Elements*, for heaven's sake! Not one of these works would survive today had it not been for the scribes of Constantinople. Every last one of them would have sunk without trace. And how much poorer would the world be for their loss!'

She nodded soberly, faintly amused, however, at his eager recitation, which she had heard before. He felt a strong kinship, she knew, with those humble men whose task it had been to collect and preserve documents that came to them from the burning or besieged libraries of Alexandria or Athens or Rome. A task that he no doubt saw himself re-enacting.

'But the Turks—'

'Oh, yes, yes,' he interrupted, 'the Turks. Quite so. A great disaster! How many other priceless manuscripts were lost when the Sultan invaded in 1453? Or, rather,' he added, 'how many priceless manuscripts have not yet been rediscovered?'

She nodded again, feeling the first twinges of a cramp begin to take hold of her stomach. The vault seemed suddenly airless and confined; she could barely breathe. Caulked with tow and oakum, the crates smelled of pitch – an acrid stink that, like so much else these days, made her nauseous on top of everything else. She was reminded of the hold of a ship, of her voyage from Margate to Holland on the *Prince Royal* seven years ago. She had been seasick then. Now her head ached and swam in exactly the same way. It seemed to revolve in one direction, her stomach in the other, as if she were indeed aboard a stinking, storm-tossed ship.

But she took a deep breath and tried to concentrate on what he was saying. She knew the story well, of course – he must have told it a half-dozen times. When the Sultan Mehmet captured Constantinople in 1453 his men had plundered hundreds of precious manuscripts from the churches and monasteries, even from the Imperial Palace itself. Only a few of these works had ever been recovered, by intrepid agents such as Jacopo da Scarperia, Ghiselin de Busbecq and Sir Ambrose himself. Vilém was both tantalised and appalled by the story of their discoveries – of ancient manuscripts rescued scant days before the merchants who owned them planned to rub out the lettering and sell the parchment for reinscription. What other treasures of ancient learning might be so poised on the knife-edge between destruction and discovery, like the lone parchment of the works of Catullus that had been found – so Vilém had claimed – bunging up a wine barrel in a tavern in Verona?

'. . . the books of Chaeremon. His treatise on the Egyptian hieroglyphs was mentioned by both Michael Psellos and John Tzetzes, but it has not been seen since – not since the sack of Constantinople. And many other books and scrolls might be found too. We know that Aeschylus wrote more than ninety plays, yet only seven survive, while less than half of the *Historiae* and *Annales* of Tacitus still exist, only fifteen books out of an original thirty – and half of *those* are fragments! Or Callimachus – he wrote *eight hundred* volumes, of which barely a few scraps are known. Possibly there are even other works of Aristotle himself awaiting discovery in Istamboul. His fame among the ancients rested on certain dialogues – the so-called exoteric and hypomnematic writings – but not one of these texts has been seen or read for centuries.' He paused for a second as his gaze slowly returned to her face. 'And so it was books such as these, you understand, that Sir Ambrose hoped to find in Istamboul.'

She nodded slowly. Sir Ambrose's journeys to Istamboul were the stuff of legend, for Vilém at least. Many of the works that the Englishman brought back from the lands of the Sultan – works such as Aristotle's treatise on astronomical research, the αστρολογικη δ ιστοριαδ, a work mentioned by Diogenes Laertius but never before seen in Europe – were, he claimed, among the greatest treasures of the library.

'He acted as one of Rudolf's agents,' Vilém was saying, 'as early as 1606. That was the year when the long war against the Turks finally ended and travel into the Ottoman lands became safer. But Sir Ambrose had travelled to Istamboul even before that, most likely as a dragoman in one of the English embassies. He was said to be on terms with the Grand Vizier himself, and he first gained access to the Emperor through Mehmet Aga, the Sultan's ambassador in Prague. He presented Rudolf with a manuscript of Heliodorus's *Carmina de mystica philosophia*, a priceless piece of occult learning – it's here somewhere – that was once owned by Constantine VII. Rudolf then sent him forth on his other missions. He negotiated the purchase of certain parchments from the Sultan. Others he found hidden away in the city's bazaars and mosques. And it was in such places,' he said, raising his voice to be heard over the din from above, 'that he discovered the palimpsests.'

'I beg your pardon?'

'Palimpsests,' he repeated: 'ancient parchments whose original texts were rubbed out and replaced by newer ones. Parchment was often reused, you see. It was always in great demand. But sometimes the original texts were not completely erased, or else they would begin seeping back through the reinscription. Sir Ambrose managed to recover them through alchemical means, by reviving the carbon in the original ink. One of them was Aristotle's work on astronomy, the other a commentary on Homer by Aristophanes of Byzantium.' He gestured at the crates ranged before them. 'They, too, are here somewhere. But as for the volume that you saw . . .' His narrow shoulders twitched. 'As far as I know, Sir Ambrose has not set foot in the Ottoman lands for some ten years, so I have no idea where the text might have come from. Nor which one it might have been.'

At that he fell silent and, pushing himself from the cask, resumed his work, inspecting each volume to ensure that it was packed neither too tightly nor too loosely. The festivities in the hall had grown louder, insinuating themselves through the stone ceiling in a series of rumbles and thumps. Emilia felt dizzier and more exhausted than ever. She no longer cared about Sir Ambrose or the parchment in the library – or about any of the books over which Vilém was fussing like a mother with her infants. She no longer cared about the Queen either. She merely wanted the journey to end, for the court to cease these arduous wanderings. Brandenburg – that was all she cared about now. Her mind had seized upon it. She had even begun to imagine the pair of them making a life for themselves. She might work as a seamstress, he as a bookseller or perhaps as the tutor to the son of a wealthy Brandenburger. Together they could live in a tiny cottage beneath the walls of its castle.

'Will the court go to Brandenburg, do you think?' she asked at last.

'The Queen may go wherever she wishes,' he grunted, 'to Cüstrin or Spandau or Berlin, wherever they will have her.' He had bent over the crate again. 'But Brandenburg will not provide refuge for long. Nor will anywhere else in the Empire, come to that.'

'Oh?' The seamstress and the tutor fled; their tiny cottage slipped over a precipitous and bloody horizon. 'And why should that be?'

'Because the Brandenburgers are Calvinists, that is why.' He shrugged. 'They will be prey to attacks from the Lutherans next door in Saxony who have already captured Lusatia. To say nothing of the fact that George William has already received an Imperial mandate from Ferdinand.' He had begun unswaddling one of the volumes. 'Have you not heard this latest rumour? The Emperor advises Brandenburg not to suffer the presence of either the King or Queen of Bohemia within his dominions. No, no, no,' he was shaking his head, 'the Queen would not be safe anywhere in Brandenburg for more than a few weeks. And the books would not be safe in Brandenburg either. Or anywhere else in the Empire for that matter,' he added. 'And so I shall not follow her to Brandenburg.'

'Not go to Brandenburg?' She felt her stomach heave with fright. 'But where, then . . . ?'

He had explained a few minutes earlier, when she tried to tell him of the terrible battle, of the dead in the river, that he cared nothing for the fate of Bohemia, and even less for its King and Queen, a pair of fools and wastrels who had been so willing to squander their treasures in return for soldiers and cannons. It had been reported that Frederick was offering the Palatinate to the Hansa merchants – the books in the Bibliotheca Palatina included – in return for sanctuary in Lübeck. So what evil bargain might he strike with the priceless volumes of the Spanish Rooms as his security? So Vilém would keep the books safe from King Frederick – and from the marauding Habsburg armies as well.

Boot heels were rasping and echoing on the stairway now, but Emilia ignored the sound. She pushed herself from the cask. The groined ceiling seemed to revolve overhead. 'What are you saying? Where, then, will you go if not to Brandenburg?'

'Ah, yes . . .' He seemed not to have heard her. He was holding aloft the unswaddled volume like a priest raising an infant at the font. Steam rose in curls from his sweating brow. 'The great Copernicus, I see, has made the journey in excellent condition.'

'Herr Jirásek . . .'

The bootfalls had stopped. A grubby-looking pageboy, the worse for drink, was performing a clumsy bow. Vilém was bent over another of his crates, once more in a devotional posture. Emilia staggered backwards and fumbled for the cask. She had bitten her lip so hard she could taste blood. Yes: these books were all he cared for. Nothing else.

'*Fräulein* . . .' Another clumsy bow. The boy clutched at the rim of one of the casks for support. '*Mein Herr?* Your presences are most gratefully' – he captured a belch in his gloved hand – 'most gratefully requested upstairs in the banqueting-room. An entertainment,' he said, stumbling over his consonants, 'for our Queen Elizabeth.'

There was a loud crash from above as a game of skittles was improvised with hats and crocks, with Seville oranges that began thumping across the floor of the hall and colliding with the legs of courtiers dancing their frantic quadrilles and gavottes. A wine cask was rolled across the floor – a rumble of thunder – to a roar of cheers. The boy turned waveringly on the steps, almost toppled backwards, then began to climb. Emilia sat down on the cask and gripped its iron hoops for support.

'A deal has been struck,' Vilém said at last. He was speaking softly, though the boy had disappeared. 'A favourable bargain,' he whispered. He added something else, but the words were lost as more thunder rolled across the ceiling and another boisterous cheer drifted down the stairwell.

'A deal?' She was leaning forward, straining to hear him.

'To England,' he repeated. Stooped over the crate, he was speaking as if to himself. 'We shall go to England, that is where.'

Chapter Six

Alsatia in the early morning was calm and quiet, with an air of hushed expectancy. As my hackney-coach paused at the top of Whitefriars Street the rows of buildings looked insubstantial in the dusty light, like canvas flats waiting to be struck by stage-hands and carried back to the scenery store. It was almost possible to see through or beyond them to the first settlement here, centuries earlier – the shaded cloisters, the church tower with its dozen bells, the monks in hair shirts and white hoods padding back and forth from the library or whispering matins and lauds together in the chapel. In the previous century, of course, the priory had been knocked down, much like Pontifex Abbey. There was no library any more, no chapel, no monks in white hoods, only their silent remains – the broken column, the abbreviated wall, a few stubborn bricks overgrown by chickweed and quack-grass. The rest had become a clutch of taverns and alehouses, along with other establishments of more anonymous but no doubt sinister occupation.

'Not through *here*, sir?'

'Yes, yes – keep going straight.'

I had been giving instructions to the driver, who claimed never to have set foot in Alsatia, a record he seemed anxious to preserve, until I offered the incentive of an extra two shillings. Trying to remember the haphazard course I had taken two nights earlier, I crouched forward, my face outside the window and upturned to the sun. The buildings stood at drunken tilts on either side of us, their doors sagging on their hinges and their windows shuttered. This time I had not heard the bleat of the horn as we entered; perhaps, half asleep those two days before, I had imagined it. Or perhaps there were other, subtler signals, a silent language that pulsed from building to building. I remembered a rumour I had once heard about Alsatia, that all of its taverns were honeycombed with cubby-holes, false floors and hidden passages, scores of secret places where fugitives and smugglers concealed themselves or their booty. Another Alsatia existed depths beneath the soot-rimed surface of timber, stone and thatch, behind a hundred wainscots and boarded entranceways. I twisted round in my seat and, for the dozenth time this morning, peered down the street behind us. Nothing. A minute later I caught sight of the blistered signboard.

I had no idea what I should expect, if anything, from the auction. I had attended only four or five of them by the summer of 1660, not through negligence or indifference, but because book auctions were, like coffee-houses, a recent phenomenon. In fact, the two were related in some ways. Most auctions in those days were held in rooms rented in coffee-houses, in the Greek's Head, for example, where the auctioneer, usually a former bookseller, would preside over the sale of as many as a thousand volumes, the owner of which was either bankrupt or dead. They were usually clamorous, well-attended affairs. The auctioneer advertised the auction in the newssheets and handbills, and catalogues listing the titles were made available in advance. The same people – booksellers or other collectors – always turned up to bid against one another for this edition of Homer, that one of Aristotle.

That, in my brief experience, was how auctions worked. But the one at the Golden Horn promised to be different. For one thing, it had not been advertised in the papers. I had been unable to find any mention of it in the gazettes, despite searching through the issues for the previous two weeks. Nor had I seen any more handbills like the one posted in the Golden Horn, even though I scanned the dead walls, cornerposts, pillories and all the various other spots favoured by the city's fly-posters, including the insides of a couple of taverns and coffee-houses. Nor, finally, had those few customers that I dared to ask – my best-known and most discreet clients – admitted to having heard of either Dr Pickvance or the Golden Horn coffee-house, much less of the proposed auction. Their looks had grown more dubious when I explained that the Golden Horn was in Alsatia, beside the Fleet River. I might as well have told them I would be travelling among the Patagonians or the Ottawas.

I was anxious for anything I might learn – about the parchment, about the verse, even about the Golden Horn itself – because over the previous days I had not discovered very much at all. I had spent several hours searching through my shelves for information about the *Corpus hermeticum*. I had no idea where to begin but started by looking at the editions by Lefèvre and Turnebus, which led me backwards to a handful of Greek and Roman writers, who in turn led me forwards along unexpected paths that wove strange and mesmerising patterns. I began to discover how the Hermetic texts were a sort of underground current slithering half seen through almost two millennia of history. They would bubble up somewhere on the surface – in Alexandria or Constantinople – only to slip away again into invisible channels beneath deserts and mountain ranges and war-ravaged cities . . . and then suddenly debouch somewhere else, hundreds of years later and thousands of miles away.

It was believed by most early commentators that the books originated in Egypt, at Hermoupolis Magna, which the ancients regarded as the oldest place on earth. The books were said to be the revelations of a priest known to the Egyptians as 'Thoth' and to the Greeks, who followed them, as 'Hermes Trismegistus', or 'Hermes the Thrice-Greatest', whom Boccaccio calls the '*interpres secretorum*', or the 'interpreter of secrets'. Thoth was the Egyptian god of writing and wisdom, who, according to Socrates in the *Phaedrus*, gave the world arithmetic, geometry and letters, and who in his spare time invented games of amusement such as draughts and dice. The wisdom of Thoth was said to have been first carved on to stone tablets before being copied on to papyrus scrolls and, in the third century BC, during the reign of Ptolemy II, brought to the newly founded Library of Alexandria, in which the Ptolemies had hoped to hold a copy of every book-roll ever written. It was here in Alexandria, among the thousands of scrolls and scholars in the great Library, that the revelations of Thoth were translated from hieroglyphics into Greek by a priest named Manetho, the famous historian of Egypt.

And it is at this point, in Alexandria, that the stream widens to Nilotic dimensions. From the great Library the texts spread outward to every corner of the ancient world, and for the next seven hundred years no respectable treatise – no matter whether its subject was astrology, history, anatomy or medicine – would be complete without a few choice references to the Egyptian priest whose revelations everyone agreed were the well-springs of all learning. But then, after so much expansion, the river suddenly contracts. The stream slows, thins, divides and – after the rule of the Emperor Justinian, who closed the Academy in Athens and burned the Greek scrolls in Constantinople –

disappears. The Hermetic texts are not heard of again until several hundred years later. At this point, early in the ninth century, copies turn up in the new city of Baghdad, among the Sabians, a sect of non-Muslims who had migrated from northern Mesopotamia. They proclaimed the revelations of Hermes as their Holy Scripture, and their greatest writer and teacher, Thabit ibn Qurra, refers to the Sabian texts as a 'hidden wisdom'. But some of this wisdom must not have been hidden all that well, because it soon made its way into the hands of the Muhammadans. Mention of Hermes Trismegistus can be found shortly after Thabit's time in the *Kitab al-uluf* by the Muslim astrologer Abu Ma 'shar, and a Hermetic text, *The Emerald Table*, part of a larger work known as *The Book of the Secret of Creation*, is studied by the alchemist ar-Razi.

But soon after the time of these Arab writers the stream had thinned and disappeared from Baghdad, again for political and religious reasons. After the eleventh century a strict Muhammadan orthodoxy was imposed throughout the Empire and no more is heard of the Sabians of Baghdad. However, the Hermetic works reappear almost immediately in Constantinople – the city alluded to in the cipher – where in the year 1050 the scholar and monk Michael Psellos receives a damaged manuscript written in Syriac, the language of the Sabians. And it is one of these manuscripts, copied by a scribe on to parchment, then removed from Constantinople after its capture by the Turks, that is brought to Florence, to the library of Cosimo de' Medici, some four hundred years later.

But where did *The Labyrinth of the World* fit into this long and complex history? I could find mention of the book neither among the editions nor in the commentaries on them – and not even in the *Stromateis* of Clement of Alexandria, who lists the names of several dozen sacred works written by Hermes Trismegistus. It seemed that *The Labyrinth of the World* was even more mysterious and shrouded in secrecy than all of the other books.

Discouraged, I therefore chose a different tack, catching a sculler to Shadwell in order to visit the papermill of John

Thimbleby. I had done business with Thimbleby for many years, and he proved to be, as I suspected, the 'JT' of the watermark on the interfoliated leaf. But he was unable to tell me either when precisely the mysterious piece of paper was made or where it might have been purchased.

The specimen was, Thimbleby admitted, an inferior effort. Did I see how flimsy the paper was? How it was already yellowing and curling? How it was almost transparent when held against the light? This meant it might have come from a batch made in the 1640s, probably between 1641 and 1647. During those years Thimbleby was mainly but not exclusively supplying Royalist printing-presses, including the King's Printer, who had been trailing the thinning and beleaguered Royalist armies round the country and cranking out their propaganda as soon as it could be written. The paper was of poor quality in those days, he explained, because demand had drastically outstripped supply.

Thimbleby took me into his workroom, where two men were dipping frames into a giant vat of what looked like porridge. Paper was usually made in this way, he explained as he gestured at the porridge, which a third man was endeavouring to stir: from linen rags, scraps of old books and pamphlets, various other oddments collected by the rag-and-bone men. These were cut into strips, shredded, boiled in a vat, marinated in sour milk, fermented for a few days, then strained, like so, through a wire mould-mesh. But with the shortage of linen scraps came improvisation. Seaweed, straw, old fishing nets, banana skins, hanks of rope, even cow dung and rotted burial shrouds from the skeletons exhumed for burning in the charnel-houses – Thimbleby had been forced to make use of almost anything. The result was paper of a dubious quality, which he nevertheless sent to the Royalist armies. Checking his records, he was able to tell me that large consignments had been shipped to Shrewsbury in 1642, to Worcester and Bristol in 1645, and to Exeter in 1646. But he had manufactured hundreds of reams every year, from any one of which, he told me, the mysterious page might have been taken.

And so I had returned to Nonsuch House that evening with

only a vague clue as to when Sir Ambrose might have encrypted the verse. Still, Thimbleby's account was encouraging. If the verse had been encrypted in the 1640s, at the outbreak, or even during, the Civil War, my theory made sense. The cipher must make reference to a treasure, including perhaps the parchment, which had been hidden – at Pontifex Hall or elsewhere – and was meant to be recovered once the Parliamentarians were defeated and it was safe to return to Pontifex Hall. But the treasure had not been recovered. Why not? Because Sir Ambrose had been murdered, as Alethea claimed? But murdered when? I realised I didn't know when Sir Ambrose died. It must have been before the end of the Civil War in 1651, when Pontifex Hall had been expropriated, but I couldn't remember Alethea's having said.

Before slipping the page back beneath the floorboards I had studied it for a moment, holding it to the light of the candle, looking first at the watermark, then at the close-set lines, the slight impression of the mould-mesh criss-crossing the surface. I thought of Thimbleby's disquisition and wondered what exactly this particular page had been made from. Fishnet? The pages of a book or pamphlet whose ink had been effaced? The winding-sheet from some ancient skeleton? I thought how odd it was that each page, no matter how flawlessly white, no matter what its inscription or watermark, always harboured another text, another identity, beneath its surface, palimpsested and invisible, like a secret ink that can be seen only when rubbed with magic dust or exposed to flame. But what dust or flame, I wondered, might bring Sir Ambrose's message back to the surface, back to life?

I had tucked the cipher between the scantlings, beside another piece of paper, one also, it seemed, of inferior quality and inscribed with a worn goose quill. This was the letter from Alethea, dated five days ago, which Monk had retrieved from the General Letter Office. What secret message, I wondered, was occulted beneath *its* blotchy ink, behind the politely cryptic words that rose from the page in Lady Marchamont's old-fashioned scrawl?

I had read it through once again, feeling a turmoil in my belly

and something insistent and unfamiliar nudging and squirming
behind my breastbone.

My good Sir:
  Please forgive the intrusion of another letter. I wonder
if you might meet me in a week's time, on the 21st of
July, at six o'clock in the evening? You may call for me in
London, at Pulteney House, on the north side of Lincoln's
Inn Fields. Suffice it to say, for the moment, that matters
of some importance have arisen.
  I shall look forward to your company. I fear the usual
discretions must still apply.
                                    Your most obliging servant,
                                                    Alethea

The usual discretions, I thought mirthlessly as, lying in bed
an hour later, I remembered the shellac in which her seal –
or a counterfeit of it – had been impressed. Alethea was, it
seemed, still no more discreet as far as the Post Office was
concerned: a puzzling bout of laxity, I thought, in someone
otherwise obsessed with secrecy. At first I didn't take her
warning too seriously. I even convinced myself, after the first
couple of readings, that perhaps I was wrong and the letter
had not been opened after all. But as I travelled back and
forth from Shadwell the next day I had the impression – the
vaguest impression – that I was being followed. Or perhaps
only watched. There was nothing specific, only a series of
peculiar incidents that I might not have noticed were it not
for the letter, which, like so many things these days, had set
my nerves on edge. The sculler that pushed off from the
quay a bare moment after mine. The image of the figure
behind me reflected in the door-window as Thimbleby and
I pushed into the Old Ship to eat our dinner. The narrowed
pair of eyes watching me through the slim gap in a shelf as
I browsed the aisles of a bookshop later that afternoon on
the Southwark end of London Bridge. Even Nonsuch House
seemed somehow altered. People I failed to recognise entered
and, after a few cursory glances along the shelves, departed

without a purchase; others simply peered through the window before slipping back into the crowds. And as I stepped outside to raise my awning a man across the carriageway started almost guiltily to life, then sauntered away.

No, no, it was nothing. Nothing at all. Or so I had told myself, sternly, as I set out the next morning for Alsatia. But why, then, was I craning my neck every minute to peer behind us, fearing what I might see framed for a second in the tiny oval of the hack's quarter-light?

But nothing appeared in the window, and I had forgotten my mysterious pursuers – indeed, I had forgotten almost everything else, including Alethea and her 'matters of some importance' – as I pushed past the waiter and stepped through the door of the Golden Horn.

At nine o'clock precisely Dr Samuel Pickvance stepped forward to a table, rapped its surface sharply with a mallet and cleared his throat for silence. He was in perhaps the fortieth year of his age, a tall, emaciated man with a widow's peak, a conspicuous nose and thin, ascetic lips that seemed to be curled in a moue of contempt. He loomed before us on a raised platform, which he occupied like a magistrate on his bench, or perhaps more like a priest at the altar, wielding his mallet like a sanctus bell or aspergillum. He rapped it a second time, even more sharply, and the room at last fell silent. The ritual was about to begin.

I had slipped into one of the last available seats, in the back row, nearest the door. The Golden Horn was still dark except for its single rush-candle and a smoke-roiling beam of sunlight that fell obliquely across the room like a toppled girder. But Pickvance now produced a lantern, which he lit ceremoniously with a taper produced by his assistant, a young man with reddish hair. Now the row of heads in front of me sharpened into detail, including that of the automaton in the corner. It grinned back at me, smug and clever.

Entering the room a few minutes earlier I had discovered myself in the midst of one of those milling crowds so loved by pickpockets. Most of the assembly had been claiming the forty-odd chairs that were arranged in rows before the platform, on which stood the table and, a minute later, Pickvance and his altar-boy. I had been expecting to recognise someone – one of my clients, perhaps, or another bookseller or two. But I didn't recognise a soul, not even when the lantern was lit. And I was taken aback by what I saw. Pickvance's audience – for so we seemed – did not look especially different from the patrons I had seen here two nights before; indeed, it could have been the same group, for all I could tell. Most were dressed in leather breeches and rucked linen, with broken felt hats jammed low on their brows; a few others wore the black homespun and grim expressions of Quakers or Anabaptists. Curiously enough, a few Cavaliers were also present among them, looking prosperous and wicked, smirking to themselves or winking lewdly at one another, legs crossed, V-shaped beards neatly cultivated. What mysterious enterprise could possibly have banded together such an ill-assorted company?

But when the auction commenced and the first of the lots were cried, I realised why I failed to recognise anyone – why I hadn't seen any of them in my shop and why there were no booksellers among them, or at least none of the reputable booksellers I knew. Dr Pickvance wasn't so much a priest or a magistrate, I decided, as a mountebank perched at his stall in Bartholomew Fair, hoodwinking a gullible audience. He was either an ignoramus or a cheat, because even from the back of the room I could see that he was embellishing and inflating each of the volumes which his assistant, introduced as Mr Skipper, held up for viewing. It was an outrage. Books bound in ordinary buckram or even plain canvas were called 'the finest *doublure*' or 'most excellent crushed levant', while everything else on show was 'hand-tooled', 'repoussé', 'opulent' and 'exquisite', with 'Aldine' this and 'Plantinus' that, bound specially by 'the late King Charles's binder' or even 'the incomparable Nicholas Ferrar of Little Gidding'.

I was tempted to stand up and expose the grotesque canard, but everyone else seemed to have fallen under Pickvance's spell. He often started bids at a penny or two, but they quickly rose to a shilling, then to a pound, and within a minute or two the mallet would be resounding and our perverse auctioneer shouting in triumph: 'Sold! For thirty shillings! To the gentleman in the second row!'

So appalled was I by this hoax that two or three lots had been sold before I realised what type of volume was being offered. The first ones had been bound collections of political or religious tracts, including pamphlets by such persecuted sects as the Ranters, the Quakers and, most numerous of all, the Bunhill Brethren – works, in other words, that would have run foul of the Blasphemy Act passed by Parliament ten years earlier. No respectable dealer would touch them for this very reason, at least no dealer who wished to remain in business for long, because the Secretary of State regularly sent his searchers into the shops to root out and burn whatever blasphemous or seditious books and pamphlets they might lay their hands on.

So this was the reason, I supposed, why Dr Pickvance held his auction in the Golden Horn – to escape the eyes of the searchers. For obviously none of his wares had been licensed by the Secretary of State. Yet this lack of sanction failed to deter the bidding one bit. I watched in amazement as the black-garbed sectarians competed for the pamphlets against a couple of smirking, rosecake-scented Cavaliers who appeared to regard even the most lubricious of the Bunhill Brethren's exhortations as some sort of joke. But I supposed the searchers were no more likely to enter Alsatia than were the bailiffs and catchpoles, so we were safe – if that was the word – from the graspings of the law.

Soon the lots grew more shocking, the bidding even fiercer. After thirty minutes the lots began to include hastily executed woodcuts and engraved prints depicting in the most vivid detail unchaste performances by masters with their kitchen-maids, or between ladies and their coachmen and gardeners. Others consisted of slim volumes of decidedly amateur verse describing a series of similar partnerships, along with prose volumes of specious medical authority illustrating inventive but surely impossible sexual postures that guaranteed, to the acrobats who attempted them, delights of a barely credible measure.

As each lot was cried, Dr Pickvance or Mr Skipper would

wave the prints about for general observation, like frantic puppet-masters. Or else Pickvance would read aloud passages from the books in his high-pitched voice, eyes going glassy as he did so, beads of sweat standing out on his brow as Mr Skipper stood meekly aside, his own face turning a deep crimson.

I had seen and heard enough. There could be nothing of relevance to my quest in these crude pages. The next ten or twelve lots dealt with the sort of occult literature I had seen at Pontifex Hall, but these were in much poorer repair and bound in inferior leather, mostly calfskin, and the ex-libris of Sir Ambrose Plessington would not, I thought, be found among them. I prepared to leave. But no sooner had I scraped my chair and risen halfway to my feet than I heard Pickvance crying a new lot, one similar, it seemed, to the previous couple of dozen.

'Gentlemen! You see before you Lot 66,' he called in his hectoring cadence, 'from the famous collection of Anton Schwarz von Steiner!'

I started at the name, which I knew I had heard before. I watched the volume flourish in Pickvance's hand, whose fingers looked strangely clawed, as if the digits were malformed. Then I remembered. I had been ascending from the crypt at Pontifex Hall, with Alethea, two steps ahead of me, describing Sir Ambrose's exploits, how he once negotiated for the Holy Roman Emperor the purchase of the entire library of an Austrian nobleman, a renowned collector of occult literature named – I was certain – von Steiner.

Bids on Lot 66 had started at ten shillings. Two men in particular were bidding against each other: one of them in the front row, the other two or three seats to my left. Pickvance was soliciting higher and higher offers. Twenty shillings . . . thirty . . . thirty-five . . .

My spit had dried up and I felt a shiver creep up my backbone like a bead of mercury. I squinted hard at the volume, which Mr Skipper held aloft as he paraded up and down the platform. What were the chances, given Pickvance's appalling record so far, that it had actually been part of the Schwarz collection, much less in the Emperor's library? But a link, however tenuous, had been forged, something that might connect Sir Ambrose Plessington to the Golden Horn, or at least to Dr Samuel Pickvance.

I leaned forward in my chair and licked my lips. The room seemed to have gone impossibly silent. The man in my row had ceased bidding. Pickvance raised his mallet.

'Thirty-five shillings, going once . . . going twice . . .'

By the time the last of the three hundred lots were sold the bells of St Bride's had rung four o'clock. I stumbled outside, blinking and squinting in the brilliant sunlight, bumped and pushed on the tide of the departing auction-goers, with whom I now felt, after so many hours together, an unwelcome kinship. To escape them I walked down to the Fleet and stood for a few moments on the bank, watching the water flex and gurgle as the tide pooled slowly inwards. A slick of oil shivered and coalesced on the surface, a perfect spectrum of colour. Then, as the voices finally subsided behind me, I reached into my coat-tails.

Lot 66 was, by the standards of this particular auction, a rather distinguished volume: actual morocco with strong stitching, its rag-paper pages unscathed by either damp or book-lice. It proved to be an edition of Cornelius Agrippa von Nettesheim's *Magische Werke* published in Cologne in 1601 and edited by someone named Manfred Schloessinger. I knew little about the work other than that it was a translation into German of *De occulta philosophia*, a book of spells in which one finds, among other things, the first ever reference to the word 'abracadabra'. It had cost me almost five pounds, which was far too much, of course. I wouldn't be able to sell it for even two pounds, let alone five. But what interested me wasn't the title or the author but the ex-libris pasted to the inside cover. It incorporated a coat of arms, a motto – '*Spe Expecto*' – and a name engraved beneath in a heavy Gothic script: Anton Schwarz von Steiner.

Of course, the ex-libris may not have been authentic. A bookseller learned to distrust these little tokens of identity. One cannot judge a book either by its cover, as the saying goes, or by its ex-libris. This one, for example, might have been soaked off another book – one that had belonged to von Steiner – and then pasted on to the inside cover of an otherwise undistinguished copy of Agrippa's *Magische Werke*. Unscrupulous booksellers had been known to resort to such tactics in order to increase the value of a book – something I would not have put past Pickvance. Or else the bookplate might not have been von Steiner's, but a forgery instead. And if this was the case, I wouldn't recognise the fraud unless and until I saw a true example of von Steiner's ex-libris, which didn't seem likely in the near future.

On the other hand, I told myself, it was well known how the contents of the Imperial Library in Prague had been pillaged and dispersed during the Thirty Years War. What was missed by the soldiers looting Prague Castle at the start of the war had been scooped up by Queen Christina of Sweden as it ended three decades later. So it was possible that the ex-libris was authentic and that the volume had found its way to England. It could have been brought over by Sir Ambrose, who would have been acquainted with it through his dealings with the Holy Roman Emperor. Possibly the Englishman had been unscrupulous in his dealings with Rudolf and had kept certain volumes for his own private collection, which in time must almost have rivalled the Emperor's own. But if this was the case, why was the volume not at Pontifex Hall? Why did it not show his ex-libris on the front pastedown? And if it had been pillaged or lost like many of the others, why had Alethea made no mention of it?

As I closed the hide cover, I remembered from somewhere that Agrippa, the so-called 'Prince of Magicians', a friend of both Erasmus and Melancthon, a secretary to the Emperor Maximilian and a physician and astrologer at the court of François I, was said to be the foremost authority in Europe on the Hermetic writings. Even so, the link between his *Magische Werke* and the Hermetic parchment stolen from Pontifex Hall promised to be a long and tortuous one. Authentic Schwarziana or not, the volume might have no connection whatsoever with either Sir Ambrose or his missing parchment. Had I merely wasted five pounds and an entire day's work?

Perhaps not. I fished in my pocket for the card Pickvance had given me after I had threaded my way to the front of the room to collect my prize. Up close, the auctioneer had been shorter and looked much older. Deep creases criss-crossed his consumptive face, and the whites of his eyes – or, rather, their yellows – were filigreed with red. His long fingers were, as I had noticed, strangely crooked, as if arthritic or even, perhaps, broken by a pilliwinks. I wondered if he had been tortured by one of Cromwell's Secretaries of State, or if his hands had merely been caught in a falling sash-window. As I accepted the copy of Agrippa from these gruesome claws I found myself bold enough to ask who had put the volume up for auction.

'I might be interested in other texts of a similar provenance,' I told him in a low tone. 'Ones from von Steiner's collection.'

Pickvance had seemed startled by the question. It occurred to me, not for the first time, that the volume might have been stolen: yet another reason why he chose to auction his wares in the Golden Horn. Possibly his inventory – those lots that weren't forged – consisted entirely of booty from the libraries of Royalist estates that, like Pontifex Hall, had been pillaged or confiscated. His reply did nothing to alleviate my suspicions. He shrugged and told me that he was 'not at liberty to divulge' his sources. His emaciated face had stretched into an unwholesome grin.

'Trade secrets, after all.'

I caught him by the coat-sleeve as he was turning away to attend to someone else. I suspected the jangle of a few gold sovereigns could easily put paid to what few scruples or discretions he might possess, so I told him in the same hushed tone that my client would be willing to pay a great deal – much more than five pounds – for the right volume. He had paused at that, then turned slowly to face me. For a second I wondered whether I was doing the right thing . . . and whether Pickvance was anything more than a thief or a charlatan. Whatever, he seemed to set aside his own reservations at once and rise eagerly to the bait.

'Oh, I dare say. Oh, it's possible, yes, that I might have something in that line.' His tone was more respectful now.

He was probably inventing plans for more 'Schwarziana' as he spoke, more forged texts. 'Of course, I would have to check my catalogues. But, yes, yes, yes, I may well have—'

Now it had been my turn to leap to the bait. 'You keep catalogues? Records of your sales?'

He seemed insulted by the question. 'Why, yes. Of course I do.'

'Yes, of course.' I pressed on, polite and earnest as ever: 'Would it be possible, I wonder, for me to consult—'

But I was interrupted by a shout from behind us. The Cavaliers and Bunhill Brethren had begun pressing forward to claim their unsavoury acquisitions, and Mr Skipper, anxious to requite them, was attempting to draw Pickvance aside. The auctioneer muttered something into his cravat, then turned back to me, fishing inside his waistcoat with his dreadful, pilliwinksed fingers.

'Tomorrow,' he whispered to me before a wave of bodies carried him off.

Now, looking down at the card, I realised that when I went to Pulteney House the next evening I would at least have something to report to Alethea – something of importance, if my appointment with Pickvance proved fruitful. I had no idea what, if anything, might be found in one of his catalogues. Lists of buyers and sellers, perhaps, or the name of whoever had put the edition of Agrippa up for auction. Possibly even a reference, a trail of sorts, that would lead to the parchment, or at least back to Sir Ambrose's library and whoever had pillaged it. Because whoever pillaged it might have sold the books – stolen books, after all – through an unscrupulous dealer such as Pickvance.

I started back towards the Golden Horn, into which a few customers were filtering. It was still early, I guessed: not yet five o'clock. With a pang of guilt, not to mention surprise, I realised I didn't want to return to Nonsuch House; not just yet. Perhaps I would walk back to the bridge, a leisurely stroll. It had turned out to be a fine day, even here in Alsatia. The stench of the Fleet Ditch wasn't so bad, I decided, once one got used to it. The wind had strengthened, dispersing the shimmering miasma and the clouds of insects. It had also borne up a few clouds that dragged themselves slowly overhead, bound for points east. Perhaps I would stop in a tavern on the way, I thought; or a coffee-house.

I tucked the *Magische Werke* back inside my coat-tails and then looked again, as if for guidance, at the slip of paper in my hand. An ordinary tradesman's card incorporating a coat of arms – no doubt fraudulent – and four lines of text, neatly engraved:

Dr ſamuel Pickvance,
Bookseller & Auctioneer,
at the ſign of the ſaracen's Head,
Arrowsmith Court, Whitefriars

I would be making at least one more trip into Alsatia; but for the first time the prospect didn't fill me with dread. Nor, I realised, did the prospect of visiting Lincoln's Inn Fields. Alethea's face suddenly rose before me, alarmingly distinct, and I realised also that I was almost looking forward to the appointment. And so as I travelled home along Fleet Street, where I did indeed stop inside a tavern, I wondered what was happening to me. I was becoming bold and unpredictable, a stranger to myself: as if one of Agrippa von Nettesheim's alchemical reactions, some profound and alarming transmutation, had taken place deep inside me.

Chapter Seven

Pulteney House stood on the north side of Lincoln's Inn Fields, halfway along a terrace of six or seven houses, all perfect replicas of one another, that overlooked the field: brick façades, white pilasters, tall windows reflecting a score of suns. I approached it along one of the dozen public footpaths through the overgrowth of pimpernel and cudweed. It was late afternoon, and I was sweating heavily after a long walk. My legs were faltering and my shirt clung to my back. I shaded my eyes from the lowering sun and looked about me.

Lincoln's Inn Fields had once been London's most fashionable quarter, a place where our lords and ladies – members of Charles I's doomed court – had lived in their insolent and audacious luxury. But during the Commonwealth they made haste for Holland or France, and so for the past ten years most of the houses had stood deserted. Now there was no smoke and no light, and as I drew closer I could see their blistered paint, a broken window here or there, the layers of soot on their sills and ovolos. The wrought-iron railings and gates about their gardens – rank with couchgrass – had been uprooted. Turned into Cromwell's muskets and cannons, I supposed.

Pulteney House was, marginally, in the best repair, with a young mulberry standing guard at the door and the polished panes of a window showing oriflammes of sunlight. The heavy fold of a gold-tasselled curtain was barely visible behind them. I didn't recall Alethea saying that either Sir Ambrose or Lord Marchamont had owned a London house, so as I manipulated the ponderous lion's-paw knocker I came to the distressing conclusion that Pulteney House must belong to Sir Richard Overstreet, the man to whom, according to Phineas Greenleaf, Lady Marchamont was betrothed. The 'matters of some importance' no doubt had something to do with plans for the wedding.

I was startled, therefore, when who should open the door but Phineas Greenleaf himself. He betrayed no signs of recognition, which I found odd given that we had spent six days on the road together and shared a number of humiliatingly intimate bedrooms. He merely widened the aperture enough for me to slip through and then ushered me down a corridor to what seemed like a drawing-room, dark on account of the yew-green curtains.

'If you would wait here, sir.'

I listened as he ascended an invisible staircase and then creaked across the floor above me. Events seemed to be replicating themselves in some disturbing and anticlimactic pattern. That first night in the library at Pontifex Hall he had left me alone, just so, and shuffled up the staircase in search of his mistress. So I was not unduly surprised when I saw that I had not been led into a drawing-room after all. Once again Phineas had left me stranded in the middle of a library. Or in the middle of what in some happier incarnation had been a library. The rows of shelves had been denuded, picked clean of their books, and even a number of shelves were missing. Burned as firewood, I wondered, by a regiment of Cromwell's soldiers? But a few of the house's other furnishings had been spared the holocaust or pillage, for there was a moth-ravaged tapestry on one of the walls and a marble-and-slate fireplace with tongs and firedogs arranged before it. Four padded chairs had been quadrated round a small rosewood table.

Yet the library was not quite empty of books. In the dim light I spied a pile of fat volumes arranged on the table – books that I supposed Alethea must have brought with her in the hope of whiling away the hours on the coach. I creaked open the cover of the one on top, fully expecting to see Sir Ambrose's ex-libris stamped on the pastedown. But straight away I saw that the volume was much newer than any of those at Pontifex Hall, as were its three fellows. I could smell the tawed leather of their bindings.

New books? I was surprised by the discovery. What on earth could the mistress of Pontifex Hall want with yet more books? I was sitting in one of the chairs now, riffling the leaves of the first volume with a mixture of curiosity and guilty pleasure. What choice texts, I wondered, might she have brought with her? Learned tomes like Ficino's translations of Plato or Hermes Trismegistus? Or volumes on witchcraft, or perhaps even necromancy?

But each of them covered more mundane territories, ones hardly preferable, in my opinion, to the company of the dour and surly Phineas Greenleaf. I frowned at the title-pages as I plucked up the volumes and then replaced them. All were on matters pertaining to the business of wills and property law. The names were familiar enough, but never had I troubled myself to open one of them, let alone to read as much as a page. Yet here, with a bookmark fully three-quarters of the way through, was Hobhouse's *A Treatise of Testaments and Last Wills*, while beneath it sat Blackacre's notoriously dull *A Touchstone of Property and Conveyances*. Its pages had been cut all the way to the bitter end, as had those in the third volume, Phillimore's gargantuan *Equity Law and the Practice of the Court of Chancery*. Only the last book seemed in keeping with the Lady Marchamont I thought I knew: a volume entitled *The Law's Resolution of Women's Rights*. Its pages too had been cut from front to back, while the notes scratched in the margin were composed in a familiar hectic scrawl.

By now a light tread was squeaking across the ceiling overhead. I replaced the last volume and sat back in the chair, aching with exhaustion. I had still not recovered either from my exertions – I had spent most of the morning and a good part of the afternoon in Alsatia – or from the shock of my discovery. I scrubbed my palms across my cheeks and brow, then took a couple of deep gulps as if drinking the dense, mulled air of the room from a heavy gourd. I fished the copy of Agrippa's *Magische Werke* carefully from my pocket and placed it on the table next to the other books. Yes, I had come far today. I had learned much.

Closing my eyes, I heard the soft outcry of treads and risers as Alethea descended the staircase. I sat back to await her arrival. How much, I wondered, ought I to tell her?

I had left for Alsatia early that morning, this time travelling up river by sculler. Arrowsmith Court, when I finally found it, proved exactly the kind of place in which I would have expected Pickvance to conduct his unsavoury trade: a small patch of mud-slimed cobbles round three sides of which a number of sooty tenements pressed four and five storeys upwards. A clowder of scrawny cats was busy in a heap of fishbones, while a couple of others groomed themselves in doorways and on window-sills. Last night's rain had collected in turbid pools and already stank like bilgewater. As I picked my way round them a chamber-pot was emptied from one of the upper windows. I leapt sideways in the nick of time. Yes, I thought ruefully: I had come to the right place.

The Saracen's Head stood directly opposite the courtyard's narrow, arched entrance. A swarthy, moustachioed face, its expression fierce and implacable, peered back at me from a signboard above the door. The tavern itself appeared to be closed. A tobacconist's stood to one side of it, a shop of more ambiguous designation on the other; both were also shut tight, their bottle-glass windows bleared with dirt and soot. Beside the tobacconist's door stood another, smaller door, whose tarnished brass sign read: 'Dr ſamuel Pickvance – Bookseller and Auctioneer'.

After pulling a fraying bell-rope I was admitted with much furtiveness and then conducted up five flights of stairs by Mr Skipper, who explained that Dr Pickvance was otherwise engaged, but that he, Mr Skipper, would be honoured to assist. The 'offices', from what I was allowed to see of them, consisted of a single room furnished with two desks, a pair of chairs, and what looked to be the tools of a bookbinder's trade: a stack of sheepskins and a beating-stone in a far corner, together with an assortment of gimlets, sewing-presses and polishing irons littered across the rest of the room. There was also a printing-press, an enormous mechanical beast to which Mr Skipper repaired after sitting me at one of the desks. On the desk sat a pile of perhaps two dozen catalogues bound in greasy brown leather.

'Good luck to you,' he murmured with a morose smile, then turned his back, I suppose to begin cobbling together more 'masterpieces' for Pickvance's next auction. I picked up the first of the volumes and opened its cover.

As I read through the catalogues for the next eight hours, nourished only by an unappetising rabbit pie fetched by Mr Skipper from a cookshop, a few facts about the mysterious Dr Pickvance gradually began taking shape. I was able to determine that he conducted his auctions roughly twice a year, going back as far as 1651, the year when the Civil War ended and the Blasphemy Act passed through Parliament. All of the auctions must have been as clandestine as the one in the Golden

Horn, because all had been conducted in Alsatia, roughly half in the Golden Horn, the others scattered among a handful of nearby taverns and alehouses, including two or three in the Saracen's Head. The works auctioned had been of a piece, it seemed, with those sold in the Golden Horn, and some of the auctions had comprised as many as 500 lots. The catalogues listed each work's author, title, date of impression, style of binding, number of pages and illustrations, general condition, and, finally, provenance. I was encouraged by this last detail. I noticed how Pickvance or some amanuensis had recorded not only the name of whoever put the lot up for auction but also that of whoever had purchased it.

I suspected, however, that many of these names and provenances were as fraudulent as the books themselves, for 1651 was the year that Cromwell sequestrated many Royalist estates, and I guessed that the contents of their libraries – or else volumes featuring their forged ex-librises – had passed through Pickvance's office. I noticed that one of the catalogues for an auction in 1654 advertised 'books once belonging to Sir George VILLIERS, Duke of BUCKINGHAM, removed from his admirable collection at York House in the Strand'. I knew that part of this 'admirable collection' – truly, one of the choicest in Europe – had been looted after the Civil War when York House was confiscated; the other half had been sold at auction a few years later when Buckingham's son, the second Duke, a Royalist, ran short of funds during his exile in Holland. But whether or not Pickvance had been selling bona fide volumes stolen from Buckingham's collection it was impossible, on the evidence of the catalogues, to discern.

My heart lurched as I looked at the dozens of titles in the York House collection. Ours was an age of great discrimination and taste, of aesthetes and collectors such as Buckingham and the late King Charles, but it was also an age of great desecration. How many treasures like those of Buckingham must have been lost to England because of our wars? Because of the Puritans and their superstitious zealotry? For when Cromwell and his cohorts weren't destroying works of art – beheading statues or tossing paintings by Rubens into the

Thames – they were selling them two-a-penny to the agents of the King of Spain and Cardinal Mazarin, perhaps even to unscrupulous merchants like Dr Pickvance. I noticed that a number of lots in Pickvance's catalogues had come from the salerooms of Antwerp, which for the past few decades had been the clearing-house from which plunder from the numerous European wars was sold at starvation prices to the greedy princes of Europe. As I reached for another volume I quailed at the task now confronting me. How on earth was I to find *The Labyrinth of the World* in such a mountain of other stolen volumes?

I discovered the copy of Agrippa, along with my own name, listed in the most recent catalogue, one of the first I inspected. The *Magische Werke* was recorded as having come from the collection in Vienna of Anton Schwarz von Steiner. But by now its more recent owner, the man who had put it up for sale in Pickvance's auction, was of much more interest to me. It was a man I had never heard of: Henry Monboddo. There was no trace of the volume's journey from von Steiner to Monboddo, so there was no way of knowing how Monboddo had acquired the volume – whether or not it had come to England via Sir Ambrose Plessington and had therefore been stolen from Pontifex Hall. The only clue to Monboddo's identity was an address, a house in Huntingdonshire, that had been pencilled into the catalogue. But there was no indication whether Monboddo was alive or – as was more often the case with the owners of auctioned books – deceased. I copied the name and address on to a piece of paper, then riffled through the rest of the catalogue, searching in vain for anything else he or his heirs might have put up for auction.

But the edition of Agrippa and even the mysterious Henry Monboddo himself were soon secondary to my purpose. I returned to the first of the volumes, that for 1651, and began working my way forward, auction by auction, year by year, wary of missing a familiar name or title that might lead to Pontifex Hall. The hours passed slowly. It was almost four o'clock by the time I reached for the last catalogue but one, that for an auction held some four months earlier:

Catalogus Variorum et insignium Librorum
selectissimae Bibliothecae,
or,
A Catalogue containing a variety of ancient and modern
English and French Books in Divinity,
History and Philosophy

The auction had been held at the Golden Horn on the 21st of March, and the wares proved to be much the same as those at all of the others. I traced my finger down the next page, turned it, ran my finger down another. I was almost seeing double by now. So exhausted was I, so addled was my brain, that when I came to the entry – almost at the very back of the catalogue – I registered no shock or surprise, and I had to read it several times before I could absorb its implications:

Labyrinthus mundi, or *The Labyrinth of the World*. A fragment. A work of occult philosophy attributed to Hermes Trismegistus. Latin translation from Greek original. 14 manuscript pages of the finest vellum. Arabesque binding. Excellent condition. Date and provenance unknown.

Through some oversight, or perhaps because of a deliberate omission, the entry failed to record the name of the vendor. But the new owner's name – the name of the man who had purchased it four months earlier – was inscribed clearly in pencil. It was the repetition of Henry Monboddo's name as much as anything else that jolted my brain from its torpor. Studying the entry carefully, I saw that Monboddo had paid fifteen shillings for the fragment – a pittance, I thought, remembering Alethea's insistence about its value and her eagerness to pay any price to retrieve it. But it was the object of my quest, I had no doubt of that. There was no mention of an ex-libris, though the omission was hardly surprising: presumably it had been removed, either by Pickvance or the previous owner, who would not, after all, have wished to advertise the theft from Pontifex Hall.

Still, I was puzzled by the price of fifteen shillings. Had neither Pickvance nor the anonymous owner known its true value? I could not imagine Pickvance selling anything for a penny less than its worth. I therefore decided that Alethea must have been been drastically wrong about the fragment. Perhaps, at fifteen shillings, it was no more valuable than anything else that Pickvance put up for sale.

I had not the courage to ask Mr Skipper what he knew about Henry Monboddo – Alethea had insisted upon discretion, after all – and so after copying down the details of the entry I closed the volume and returned it to the stack. My step grew light as I left the building a few minutes later and began walking through Alsatia. The Gordian knot, I decided, was almost cut in two. I would find Henry Monboddo, make him a generous offer – using Alethea's money – and collect my reward. Then I would be done with the business once and for all, and I would be able to resume my peaceful and sedentary life. It had been a good day, I told myself. I believe I might actually have begun to whistle.

I was in this same mood, exhausted but sanguine, when I heard the footfalls in the corridor growing louder. I pushed myself arduously from the chair. Lady Marchamont had arrived.

Ten minutes later I was seated at an enormous dining-table, listening to Alethea apologise for the dire condition of Pulteney House. She had appeared in the library doorway looking like what Horace calls *mentis gratissimus error*, 'a most delightful hallucination'. She was dressed exactly as she had been at Pontifex Hall – the leather buskins, the dark calash – despite the warm weather. I had already decided she must have purchased Pulteney House only recently, hence the massive tomes on the table downstairs. After all, as a widow she was now a 'feme sole' according to our laws, no longer a 'feme covert'. She was therefore able to buy and sell property, even to conduct a suit in the Court of Chancery if she wished. But in fact my first suspicions proved correct, because as we climbed the stairs to the dining-room she explained how Pulteney House belonged to her 'neighbour' (as she called him) Sir Richard Overstreet, who had 'kindly' lent it to her. Pontifex Hall was no longer safe, so she had come to London for the time being: for how long she could not say. But she thought that, despite the risks, the two of us should meet to 'exchange information'.

Pontifex Hall no longer safe? I was puzzled by her claim. Why on earth not? Because of the torrents of water from the spring that were supposedly eroding its foundations? Or was there some more menacing reason?

'Of course, no one has inhabited Pulteney House for almost ten years,' she was now saying, 'so it's hardly comfortable. The pipes from the conduit have been plugged or broken, therefore we have no water. Even more inhospitable conditions, I fear, than Pontifex Hall.' She smiled briefly, then her eyes flickered for the dozenth time to the copy of Agrippa's *Magische Werke*, which was still clutched in my hand. 'Please, Mr Inchbold.' She was gesturing at the plates of food – venison from one of Sir Richard's deer parks – which Bridget had served a minute earlier. 'Shall we begin? I believe we have much to talk about.'

And so as the candle flame did its fairy-dance between us I told her everything I had learned in the past couple of days; or very nearly everything. I was wondering how much I should reveal. I decided to say nothing of the cipher or my suspicions about being followed. But I told her about the Golden Horn, about the bizarre auction, about Dr Pickvance, and finally about the enormous pile of catalogues that I had finished inspecting only two hours earlier. Yet she was not as baffled by the name Henry Monboddo, I discovered, as I had been. We were eating our pudding, a syllabub, by this point. I paused for a moment and then asked whether she knew the name.

'Indeed I do,' she replied simply, then fell silent for a spell, contemplating her reflection in the silver cheek of the soup tureen. I could see the reflections of the candle, two perfect flames, in her dilated pupils. At length she set aside her spoon and picked up her napkin to dab carefully at her lips. 'In fact,' she said at last, 'Henry Monboddo is my reason for inviting you to Pulteney House tonight.'

'Oh?'

'Yes.' She was rising from the table, and so I did the same

– a little too quickly. My head felt giddy because of the wine. 'Come with me, Mr Inchbold. There is something I must show you. You see, I too have made a discovery about Henry Monboddo.'

I was led along the corridor, then through a small rotunda and into a bedchamber. It appeared that Sir Richard had at least attempted to make this part of Pulteney House hospitable for his guest, because the walls were newly papered and the room had been furnished with a four-post bed, a chair and a looking-glass whose foxed surface gave back my freakishly foreshortened and hunchbacked reflection as I stumbled into the room. There was also a portmanteau on the floor beside the bed with several garments protruding untidily from its top. I stood inside the door as if frozen, like a tobacconist's wooden Indian.

'Please, Mr Inchbold.' She pointed to the chair before bending over the portmanteau. The window had been pushed open, and I caught the gentle susurrus of velvet curtains. 'Won't you take a seat?'

I moved to the chair and watched, anxious and alert, as she rummaged in the trunk, first through a layer of the clothing – I caught sight of a series of shifts and smocks writhing beneath her touch – and then in a deeper sediment. At last she found what she was looking for, a sheaf of papers, which she extracted and then handed to me.

'Another inventory,' she explained, seating herself on the edge of the bed.

'Like that at Pontifex Hall?' I remembered the document well: those six wondrous pages, each signed by the four bailies.

'No, not quite the same. This one was compiled almost thirty years later. It includes only books, as you can see. The contents of the library at Pontifex Hall in the year 1651.'

'Immediately before the estate was seized.'

'Yes. Lord Marchamont had the contents of the library valued before we went into exile. He was planning to sell the entire collection. We were . . . embarrassed for funds. But no buyer could be found. Not in those days. No one, that is, to whom Lord Marchamont had any wish to sell the collection. So he next considered removing the library to France. He had even arranged for its passage across the Channel from Portsmouth on the *Belphoebe*, one of the few men-o'-war that hadn't deserted to Cromwell in 1642. But the plan fell through, of course. The *Belphoebe* went down off the Isle of Wight less than a fortnight before the books were due to be sent from Pontifex Hall. A freak storm. But the shipwreck was fortunate for the collection, as it turns out. I need not tell you what would have happened otherwise.'

Indeed not. A number of libraries that had been transferred to France for safekeeping during the Civil War had become the property of the French Crown, by *Droit d'Aubain*, upon the deaths of their owners. A fate that Sir Ambrose's books would no doubt have shared when Lord Marchamont died.

'I discovered the inventory in the muniment room,' she was continuing, 'in the bottom of the coffin, one day after you left Pontifex Hall. Otherwise I would most certainly have given it to you then.' She was leaning forward from the bed. 'Quite detailed, as you will see.'

'It mentions the parchment?'

'Of course. But that detail is not the most interesting piece of intelligence. Please, the last page, if you will. There you will see how the collection was inventoried and valued by the person whom Lord Marchamont had engaged to sell it.'

The document was at least fifty pages long, an endless swarm of authors, titles, editions, prices. My head swam. I had already read too many catalogues that day. But the last page was blank, I saw, except for a few words inscribed at the bottom: *This entire Collection valued at the sum of 47,000 pounds sterling, on this day, the 15th of February 1651, by Henry Monboddo of Wembish Park, Huntingdonshire.*'

I felt a tightening in my belly and looked up to find Alethea studying me closely.

'Henry Monboddo,' she murmured thoughtfully. 'A man well known among the Royalist exiles in Holland and France.'

'You knew him, then?'

'I did indeed.' She reached for the inventory and carefully

returned it to the portmanteau. 'Or, rather, I met him on one or two occasions. He worked out of Antwerp in those days,' she continued, the bedposts gently creaking as she resumed her seat. 'He was a picturemonger, an art-broker. He sold the contents of many libraries and galleries, including those from York House. You know of the collection?'

I nodded, remembering Pickvance's catalogue for the year 1654, with its description of the items from the 'admirable collection' of the second Duke of Buckingham.

'Those were difficult times for all of us. Buckingham was also embarrassed for funds. York House had been confiscated and many of its treasures, those collected by his father, were pillaged by Cromwell's men. So in 1648, in order to relieve the Duke's finances, Monboddo sold some two hundred of the paintings. He got him a fair price, because the Peace of Westphalia had recently been signed and therefore the supply of plunder was threatening to dry up. Indeed, after Westphalia the stream might well have disappeared altogether had it not been for our commotions here in England.'

'So Monboddo disposed of collections of books and paintings for insolvent exiles? For anyone whose estate was being sequestrated?'

She nodded. 'He found the buyers for their art collections. Dukes and princes who wished to stock their libraries and cabinets. He had connections in courts throughout Christendom. My father dealt with him on a number of occasions when he made purchases for the Emperor Rudolf.'

'You mean to say that Monboddo was known to Sir Ambrose?'

'Yes. Many years earlier, of course. He conducted the negotiations with agents such as my father and took a handsome commission in return.' Her gaze dropped to the copy of Agrippa clutched in my hand. 'I believe he even negotiated with my father over the purchase of the von Steiner collection in Vienna. But there were also rumours about Monboddo's work,' she added. 'He was said to have clients other than Royalists unable to pay the taxes imposed on their estates.'

She paused to withdraw from the folds of her skirts an

object that in the poor light I took a moment to recognise as a tobacco-pipe, which she then proceeded to fill, expertly, with tobacco. I expected her to hand it to me but was surprised to see her fit it with equal expertise between her molars. Her face flashed orange as she lit a taper and coaxed the bowl to life.

'Forgive me,' she said, gusting smoke and waving the taper through the air to extinguish its flame. 'Virginia tobacco. The fire-cured leaf of the *Nicotiana trigonophylla*, a particularly delicious species. Sir Walter Raleigh claims harmful effects for it, but I have always found a postprandial bowl an excellent aid to digestion, especially if smoked in a clay pipe. My father once owned a calumet,' she continued as a cloud of smoke unfurled into the space between us. 'It had a clay bowl and a stem made from a reed plucked from the shore of Chesapeake Bay. It was made a present to him by a Nanticoke chieftain in Virginia.'

'Virginia?' Sir Ambrose Plessington, that Proteus, that decagon with all of his mysterious side-facets, assumed yet another guise. But I was here on other business. 'You were mentioning that Monboddo—'

'Yes, yes, we were speaking of Monboddo, not of my father. Nor of Raleigh.' She had leaned back and was reclining on the bed now, on its half-dozen scattered cushions, her great tangled mane against the headboard. 'Yes, there were stories, I should almost say legends, about Henry Monboddo.'

'Legends of what sort?'

'Well . . . where shall we begin?' She cupped the bowl in her palm and for a few seconds studied the canopy above her head as if for inspiration. 'For one thing,' she resumed, 'it was said that he negotiated the purchase of the Mantua Collection in the year 1627. In those days he was the artistic agent for King Charles. That much was common knowledge. He was also the agent for the Duke of Buckingham. The first Duke, I mean – Sir George Villiers, the Lord High Admiral. Monboddo scoured the courts and studios of Europe on behalf of the pair of them, bringing back to England all sorts of items. Books, paintings, statues . . . whatever might have struck the fancy of those two great connoisseurs.' The clay pipe wavered and glowed before me as she took another slow draught of smoke. 'You have heard of the Mantua Collection?'

I nodded. 'Of course.' Who had not? Dozens of paintings by Titian, Raphael, Correggio, Caravaggio, Rubens, Giulio Romano, all purchased by King Charles for the sum of £15,000 – a bargain even at that price. The canvases hung in the galleries of Whitehall Palace until Cromwell and his band of philistines sold them off to pay their debts. It was the greatest disgrace, in my opinion, of Cromwell's reign – a despoliation of our entire nation.

'The silk industry in Mantua had collapsed in the 1620s,' she continued, 'and so the Gonzagas were starved for funds. King Charles was also starved for funds, but a detail such as that hardly troubled him where paintings were concerned, especially ones as marvellous and valuable as those in the Mantua Collection. He could scarcely believe his ears when he first heard the report from Mantua. A special tax was levied and Monboddo raised the remainder of the funds along with Sir Philip Burlamaqui, the King's financier. At the same time, of course, Burlamaqui was raising funds to equip a fleet of a hundred ships for Buckingham's expedition to the Île de Ré, where the Protestants of La Rochelle were besieged by the armies of Cardinal Richelieu. An unfortunate coincidence of events,' she murmured. 'The King was forced to choose between his ships and his paintings.'

But he chose the paintings. I knew the story well. He chose the paintings over the lives of his mariners and the Huguenots, beggaring the fleet in order to pay the Mantuans. Five thousand English sailors in their rotting ships starved to death or were slaughtered by French troops, and who knows how many Huguenots died at La Rochelle. The expedition was a disaster, even worse than Buckingham's raid on Cádiz two years earlier. So the paintings from the Mantua Collection – all of those images of the Virgin Mary and the Holy Family – were steeped in Protestant blood, paid for by the lives of Englishmen and the Rochellois.

'This most wonderful collection became the shame of Protestant Europe,' she said, 'as did the treasures assembled by

Buckingham at York House. For Buckingham had not only led the failed expedition, he had also arranged King Charles's marriage to the sister of Louis XIII and then loaned to the French navy the ships with which Richelieu proceeded to batter La Rochelle and later the half-starved English fleet. And so is it any wonder that Cromwell should have wished to sell both collections, York House as well as Whitehall Palace?' She paused to draw thoughtfully on the pipe. 'And that, Mr Inchbold, is where the other rumours begin.'

I was frowning in the darkness, trying to catch the twisted thread, to assemble in my head the cast of characters: Buckingham, Monboddo, King Charles, Richelieu. 'Are you saying that Monboddo was involved in the sale of the Mantua Collection as well as the paintings from York House?'

'So I believe.'

'He was in league with Cromwell, then?'

'No, he was in league with someone else. The rumours claimed that Monboddo was secretly acting as the agent for Cardinal Mazarin, the Chief Minister of France, Richelieu's protégé. It was well known that Mazarin hoped to lay his hands on the treasures that Cromwell was selling. Monboddo covered his tracks very well, of course, as did Mazarin, but my husband came to believe the rumours. For that reason he dismissed Monboddo as his agent and refused to part with a single volume even though in those years we were as poor as tinkers.'

'But why should Lord Marchamont have been so opposed to the sale? The collection would have been lost to England, it's true. It would have been a great pity. But we were no longer at war with the French. In those days they were supposed to be our allies in Cromwell's war against Spain.'

'Yes, but there were principles involved. Other concerns.'

She hesitated as if uncertain whether to continue. But at length, as another cloud of smoke twisted between us, she explained how any such transaction would have violated the letter of her father's will, which stipulated that the collection should be neither broken up nor sold, either whole or in part, to anyone of the Roman faith. Rome with its *Index librorum prohibitorum* was the enemy of all true knowledge. Sir Ambrose believed that Rome stood not for the dissemination of thought but, rather, its suppression. The works of both Copernicus and Galileo had been proscribed, as had the Cabala and other magical Jewish writings studied by writers like Marsilio Ficino. In 1558 the penalty of death was decreed against anyone who printed or sold condemned books. Hundreds of booksellers fled Rome after the publication of the *Index* in 1564, followed by thousands of Jews expelled by Pius V, who suspected them of abetting Protestantism. The Hermeticists soon found themselves under the same cloud as the Jews. The editor and translator of the polyglot edition of the *Corpus hermeticum* was condemned by the Inquisition as a heretic, while the greatest Hermeticist of all, Giordano Bruno, was burned at the stake. His crime had been championing the doctrines of Copernicus.

'Oh, I know all of this must sound peculiar to you, Mr Inchbold, like the ravings of a zealot. But my father was most determined on these points. He believed in the Reformation and the spread of knowledge, in a worldwide community of scholars, a Utopia of learning like the one described by Francis Bacon in *The New Atlantis*. So it would have been a disaster, in his opinion, for a single book to fall into the hands of someone such as Cardinal Mazarin, a pupil of the Jesuits.' She paused again, then dropped her voice as if fearful of being overheard. 'You see, my father had rescued the books from the bonfires of the Jesuits once already.'

'What do you mean?' I was leaning forward in the chair. 'Rescued how?' I remembered her description of the books, that evening in Pontifex Hall, as 'refugees', along with her claim that some of them had survived a shipwreck. I wondered if she was about to say something about the 'interests' and 'enemies' of which she had spoken.

'From Cardinal Baronius.' The pipe stem clacked quietly between her teeth. 'The keeper of the Vatican Library. Perhaps you know his work? He wrote at length on the *Corpus hermeticum*. You may read about it in his history of the Roman Church, the *Annales ecclesiastici*, published in twelve volumes.

178

In his time Cardinal Baronius was one of the world's foremost authorities on the writings of Hermes Trismegistus. He took up his pen in order to refute the work of the Huguenot theologian Duplessis-Mornay. In 1581 Duplessis-Mornay had published a Hermetic treatise entitled *De la vérité de la religion chrétienne*. He dedicated it to the Protestant champion of Europe, Henry of Navarre, whose counsellor he later became. The work was translated into English by Sir Philip Sidney.'

'Another Protestant champion,' I murmured, remembering how Sidney – that great Elizabethan courtier who died fighting the Spaniards – had been the namesake of the ship built for Sir Ambrose, according to the patent, in 1616.

I closed my eyes and tried to think. The name Baronius was familiar, though not because of either Duplessis-Mornay or the *Corpus hermeticum*. No: a cardinal of that name was the man responsible for the transportation – the theft – of the Bibliotheca Palatina in 1623, after the Catholic armies invaded the Palatinate. It was one of the most outrageous scandals of the Thirty Years War. Some 196 crates of books from Germany's greatest library, the centre of Protestant learning in Europe, were carted across the Alps by mule-train, with each mule wearing round its neck, on a silver label, the same inscription: *fero bibliothecam Principis Palatini*. The books and manuscripts had disappeared, one and all, into the Bibliotheca Vaticana.

Or had they? I opened my eyes. The wine and the smoke between them were addling my brain, but now I also remembered Alethea's claim that Sir Ambrose had worked in Heidelberg as an agent for the Elector Palatine. An idea slowly swam towards the surface.

'The books at Pontifex Hall have come from the Bibliotheca Palatina. Is that what you're saying? Cardinal Baronius didn't steal all of them after all. Sir Ambrose rescued them from—'

'No, no, no . . .' She shied the pipe in an arc through the air. 'Not from the Palatina.'

I waited for her to continue, but the Virginia tobacco seemed to have induced in her a mood of voluptuous repose. She leaned over the edge of the bed and rapped the bowl of the pipe against the hearthstone. I cleared my throat and chose another tack.

'And was it Cardinal Mazarin,' I asked as gently as I could, 'or his agents, who . . . who . . .'

'. . . who murdered Lord Marchamont?' Her voice came thickly from among the nest of pillows. 'Yes. Perhaps. Or so I believed at one time. My husband was murdered in Paris. Have I told you that? We were crossing the Pont Neuf in our coach when we were set upon near the spot where Henry of Navarre was murdered by Ravaillac. He was stabbed in the neck with a poniard,' she continued calmly, 'also like King Henry. There were three assassins, all on horseback, all dressed in black. I shall never forget the sight of them. Black livery with gold trim. It was dark, but I was meant to see them, you understand. I was allowed to see their uniforms, their faces. It was intended as a warning.'

'A warning from whom? From Cardinal Mazarin?'

'I thought as much at one time. But events have changed my mind. I now believe the assassins were hired by Henry Monboddo.'

I licked my lips and drew a careful breath. 'But why should Monboddo have – ?'

'*The Labyrinth of the World*,' came her voice through the muggy darkness. 'That is why, Mr Inchbold. No other reason. He wanted the parchment. Not the rest of the collection, only the parchment. He was obsessed with it. He had found a buyer who desperately wished to acquire it. Someone who was willing to have my husband murdered. And now it would seem that my husband's worst fear has been realised,' she added after a short pause, her voice once more growing faint. 'If what you say is true, then Monboddo has laid his hands on it at last.'

The tiny flame beside the window leapt and dived. The fields beyond were dark and silent. I could feel my sideburns prickling, the gooseflesh raising itself along my forearms. From somewhere below the stairs came the slow shuffling of Phineas's feet and the arthritic creaking of floorboards. When I looked to the bed I saw that Alethea had raised herself so that she now sat upright beneath the canopy, her arms wrapped round her knees. I could feel her eyes upon me.

'Arrangements have been made,' she said at last.

'Arrangements, my lady?'

'Yes, Mr Inchbold.' The bed gave a groan as she pushed herself to her feet. Her shadow fell lengthwise across me. 'A visit to Wembish Park seems in order, does it not? The manuscript must be recovered. And we must make haste to reclaim it before Monboddo can sell it to his client. But you must be careful,' she whispered as she led me to the staircase, 'very careful indeed. Take my word for it, Mr Inchbold: Henry Monboddo is a dangerous man.'

An hour later I was back in Nonsuch House, back in my study, nodding off over a tobacco-pipe and Shelton's translation of *Don Quixote*. I had reached the bridge without incident, without being followed. Or so it seemed, but my senses were dulled and the night black as tar. I dozed off a couple of times, and the driver had to shake me awake when we reached our destination. Now I could neither keep my pipe alight nor concentrate on the pages of *Don Quixote*, through which I was blundering without managing to glean a scrap of sense.

A visit to Wembish Park seems in order . . .

Yes: the faint, meandering scent I had been following was stronger now and seemed to direct me, urgently and unambiguously, to Wembish Park and Henry Monboddo. But whatever optimism I had felt earlier in the day, in Alsatia, had now vanished completely. I thought of Lord Marchamont murdered on the Pont Neuf and then of the solitary figures who had shadowed me.

Henry Monboddo is a dangerous man . . .

I pushed myself upright and then walked to the window. The sky rose black and starless; below it, the city looked lightless except for the wavering lanterns on the poop-rails of a few merchantmen far downstream in the Limehouse Reach. Unfurling their sails, I supposed, and putting to sea on the first of the ebb, which I could hear fluxing with its familiar rush between the piers.

I yawned again, clouding the window-panes with my breath. Hearing a faint chime from the floor beside me, I peered down to see a glint on the boards. A key. I turned it over in my hand, speculatively, watching the polished brass shine in the candle-light. Alethea had given it to me as we parted in the darkened atrium of Pulteney House. It unlocked a small strong-box that would be concealed beneath the stone lozenge on top of a grave in the churchyard of St Olave's, Hart Street, not far from the north end of London Bridge. We would have to use the strong-box for any future communications, she explained, because her post was being opened – a realisation that had come, I thought, a little late in the day. Nor could we meet again at Pulteney House, which she said she might, in any case, soon be departing. She would therefore leave any further letters for me in the churchyard, cached in the grave of a man named Silas Cobb.

I slipped the key back inside my pocket and took up my book. Once more I would be leaving London, I realised, for an unknown destination, somewhere fraught, possibly, with numerous perils. I felt like an old knight in a tale of chivalry: an impoverished hidalgo with his broken lance and dented shield setting off, at the whim of his beloved, into a world of intrigues and enchantments, bent on some impossible task.

But then I reminded myself that Alethea wasn't my beloved, that no enchantments would be waiting for me at Wembish Park, and finally that my task now seemed – on the basis of my discoveries today – far from impossible.

Chapter Eight

Winter's first panes of ice were thickening in Hamburg's canals by the time the *Bellerophon*, a merchantman of three hundred tons, cast off her lines and started the final leg of her 2,000-mile voyage from Archangel. The ship's log recorded that it was December in the year 1620. Martinmas was past, the start of the most dangerous and unpredictable seas, though the voyage down the Elbe to Cuxhaven began well enough. The *Bellerophon* was carried swiftly on the ebb, passing the crowded stalls of the St Pauli Fischmarkt on her starboard side, then the scattering of ropewalks and gabled warehouses opposite. Downstream in deeper waters, creaking at anchor, sat the nimble-looking *fluyts* of the Hanseatic fleet, each with its hull worried by a half-dozen lighters and bumboats. The *Bellerophon* cut a fine figure as she swayed past them with her stays taut and whistling in the breeze, her cream-coloured sails snapping and swelling as quickly as they could be unfurled. Though her hold was full with furs from Muscovy her passage was smooth and buoyant. Her hull rode high in the water, and the shadows of her cutched sails swept fleetly over the workmen squatting on quays or thrumming up the planks to the storehouses, humping barrels of Icelandic cod or sacks of English wool. A few crewmen could be spotted on her waist, waving their caps, while high above their heads, tiny against the steel-grey and snow-spitting December sky, the topmen were clambering up and down her ratlines and along her yards, tugging at bull-ropes and lengthening the topsails that gathered the wind in their bunts and swept her ever more rapidly along the brackish tide to the sea.

Standing on the quarterdeck, letting snowflakes alight and melt on his cheeks as the spire of the Michaeliskirche dwindled and shrank astern, Captain Humphrey Quilter watched his men going about their tasks. The voyage from Archangel had been a difficult one. The Dvina had frozen almost two weeks early, and the *Bellerophon* and her crew escaped its clutches by no more than a couple of days. Quilter had been trapped in its ice once already, two years ago, when the entrance to the bay was frozen solid in the first week of October. No one who remembered that dreadful experience had wished to repeat it. Six frostbitten months in the frozen jaws of the Dvina, waiting for the spring thaw, which came three weeks late that year. But it was always a dangerous voyage. This time the ship had escaped the spreading ice only to be battered by fierce gales in the middle of the White Sea. After limping into harbour at Hammerfest for repairs to a cracked mizzenmast, she was lucky to cheat the ice once again, this time by a single tide.

But now, four weeks on, Captain Quilter was able to relax. This last leg of the voyage, from Hamburg to London, would be the easiest, even though December and its unpredictable weather had arrived – and even though this was, as rumour had it, an inauspicious season for voyages. For soon it would be difficult to sail any ship abroad, ice or no ice, fair weather or foul. The ports as well as the sea routes between them would be shut to all vessels except warships, because new battles were looming. The entire continent of Europe was a budge-barrel waiting for a quickmatch that would not be long in coming. And no one, Quilter supposed, would be spared the explosion.

He braced himself on the creaking deck, legs wide apart, and tasted the breeze turn cooler, saltier. The heathlands and salt marshes with their dykes and wicker fences slid along the port bows. He knew the estuary well, its every sandbar and shoal, and would barely need to glance at the rolled-up sea-cards in his cabin. The ship would reach Cuxhaven by early afternoon and then, with good wind and weather on the North Sea, the coast of England two days later. Still not quick enough, he knew, for his forty-six crewmen, who were eager to return home after five months at sea, though at least they would have money in their pockets, even if the promised load of Wismar beer had gone astray somewhere between Lübeck and Hamburg. Yes, a good haul, well worth their troubles. There would be wages and bonuses for all, not to mention a handsome return for the shareholders in the Royal Exchange. For below decks the *Bellerophon* was carrying almost five hundred bales of top-quality fur bought from the Lapps and Samoyeds at the English fort in Archangel. She was bringing back to England enough beaver pelts, Quilter reckoned, for several hundred hats, not to mention muskrats and foxes for scores of fine coats, sable and ermine for the gowns of a hundred judges, along with a few dozen bear and reindeer skins, the former complete with claws and mummified heads, the latter with antlers intact, all destined to hang from the walls or cover the floors of various lordly estates. Last winter had been a cold one even by Muscovite standards (or so the Samoyeds had assured him) and therefore the pelts were thicker – even more valuable – than usual.

Then there was as well the other cargo, the more secret one, the one on which Captain Quilter hadn't paid so much as a single thaler in port duties. He shifted his stance and threw a glance in the direction of the hatchway. True enough, the mystery cargo had made a common smuggler of him, but what choice did he have in the matter? The two hundred casks of beer from the merchant in Lübeck had failed to arrive, which meant the *Bellerophon* would have needed a few dozen lasts of cheap Lüneburg salt to use as ballast. But Lüneburg salt would have been difficult to sell in London, even if there was some to be had at such short notice, which as it happened there was not. There was no woad or pig-iron either, or ballast of any sort, and so Quilter had agreed – with less reluctance than was truly proper – to take on board these mysterious boxes that had not been registered in the tally clerk's port book and, once on English soil, would not be reported at the custom-house either. Or that at least was the plan. Two thousand Reichsthalers he was to earn for his troubles, or almost £400, half of which had been paid already and was safely stowed in his sea-chest. Oh yes, he told himself as the fortress at Glückstadt shifted into view over the starboard bow, a very good haul indeed.

Still, something troubled Quilter about the whole affair. How, for example, had the man in the Golden Grapes known his name? How had he known about the fugitive consignment of Wismar beer? And who were the passengers that, for a few extra thalers, he had been persuaded to take aboard and hide below decks? Perhaps they were spies of the sort with which every port in Europe was supposedly rife these days. But spies for whom? And the stranger from the tavern, John Crookes – had he been a spy as well?

It had been a strange and unnerving business. Quilter listened to the familiar sound of the sheets humming overhead as the sails filled in undulant white billows, drawing the river's strengthening wind. The proposition had come two nights earlier, at a tavern in the Altstadt, on the wharfside, where he was drinking a pot of ale and eating a fried hake in the company of his bo'sun, Pinchbeck, and a half-dozen other crewmen from the *Bellerophon* who were scattered round the tables with their noses thrust into pint-pots. The night had been about to blur into every other evening spent in Hamburg – drink, cards and perhaps a prostitute from the Königstraße before a stumbling journey back to the waiting gangplank. But then the bells in the tower of the Petrikirche began pealing madly and a man stepped deftly through the door and took a seat at the empty table next to Quilter. Catching Quilter's eye, he introduced himself as an Englishman, John Crookes, of the firm Crabtree & Crookes, importers from the Hansa towns into England. Over a glass of Dutch gin he explained that his firm made use of the Hansa fleet, whose ships would otherwise have sailed to England with empty holds. Only now there was, he whispered, a deal of unpleasantness, the source of which was that the Hamburgers were quarrelling with the Danes, whose King had just built a huge fortress a few miles downriver at Glückstadt. And because King James of England had married the sister of the King of Denmark – this belligerent foe who wished to rule both the Elbe and the Baltic – not a single ship in the whole Hansa fleet was willing to carry the cargo of English merchants. At that point Crookes had withdrawn a pouch from his inside pocket and, without removing his eyes from Quilter's face, slid it in a knight's move across the table.

'Not to mince the matter, Captain Quilter,' he said in a low tone, 'I need a ship. Or part of one. Now . . .' He tapped the leather pouch with a forefinger. 'I wonder if you, a fellow Englishman, might possibly see your way to providing some assistance?'

The pouch contained a hundred Reichsthalers. The cargo was taken on board one night later, well after dark, without the use of either torches or flares; even the four lanterns mounted on the ship's poop-rail had been extinguished. Ninety-nine crates in all. Bribes were paid to the dockers to ensure prompt loading, also to keep their mouths shut, because the last thing Quilter needed was for one of the riverside gangs that prowled the Legal Quays of London and Gravesend to hear about some valuable cargo stowed in the hold of the *Bellerophon*. She would be marked down for plunder even before she set sail from Hamburg.

He had watched the activities from above, on the catwalk, gnawing at his lip, then at his knuckles. The crates were grappled through the lading port by the dockers and the grumbling crewmen who were already trying to guess what might be inside them but were unable to foresee what grief the strange cargo would soon bring them. So heavy were the boxes, and so numerous, that for a time Quilter thought they might overload and imbalance the ship. But the fear had proved unfounded; the *Bellerophon* was now swaying swiftly down the Elbe, perfectly ballasted. By the time the sun teased apart the clouds and appeared over the foreyards, the first slivers of Cuxhaven's steeples hove into view, a familiar and welcoming sight.

Captain Quilter permitted himself a smile of satisfaction. High above his head the luffs were shivering as the topmen lengthened sail. Cloud shadow swept over the deck, pursued by sunlight. The weather would hold. In two more days the *Bellerophon* would reach the Thames, or rather the Nore, the anchorage where the mysterious boxes would be offloaded on to a pinnace, and then he, with another thousand Reichsthalers, could forget all about them.

A minute later he was inside his cabin, among its litter of charts and compasses. Soon afterwards, as the *Bellerophon* nudged into Heligoland Bay, the pealing of church bells, a sign of ill omen, could be heard far in the distance. Yet Captain Quilter thought nothing of it at the time; nor did he give a second thought to the sight through the scuttle of another merchantman, the *Star of Lübeck*, which appeared a short distance off their port beam. Instead, he bent his head over the dog-eared portolano showing the shoals and sunken ships marking the entrance to the Nore and, beyond it, the Port of London.

The journey to Hamburg from the castle at Breslau lasted

more than three weeks. Snow had fallen across Bohemia and the Palatinate as well as in Silesia. For days on end the ravening armies were snowbound, brought to a standstill outside farmhouses or in the midst of puzzled villagers. From Heidelberg in the west to Moravia in the east, the Emperor's soldiers huddled in their billets or stood crotch-deep in the snow, chopping what little fodder could be found for their starving horses. In the courtyards and gardens of the Prague Castle the snow lay three feet deep. Looting had not ended until five days after the gates were finally breached; Otakar's prophecies had fulfilled themselves in the most brutal fashion. The palaces and the Spanish Rooms were sacked one by one, as were the churches and even the sepulchres and churchyards, whose corpses it was rumoured had gold in their teeth. The houses in Golden Lane and the laboratories in the Mathematics Tower were also pillaged, because of further rumours that Frederick's band of Rosicrucian alchemists had discovered ways of turning coal into gold. Whether or not any gold was found, or even any coal, the treasures of the castle and then the Old Town were plentiful enough that not a few marauding soldiers found themselves obliged to hire drudges to carry their sacks of booty.

In Silesia the fugitive court had stayed in Breslau for six days after the long *via dolorosa* from Prague. On the morning of the seventh the caravan, or part of it, shunted north and then west along the curves of the Oder, looking in the dawn light like a mangy herd of migrating beasts. Delays were constant. After a day the crates were loaded on to seven barges, but first the Oder and then the Elbe froze, and the ice had to be broken by men wielding barge-poles. Even so, one of the barges splintered its hull and had to be towed ashore and abandoned, entailing yet another delay before the journey resumed, as slow as ever. Boundary columns reared and then fell away astern. Friedland. Saxony. Brandenburg. Mecklenburg. The toll stations, each with its guards and cannons, loomed and dwindled. A handsome bribe was paid at each, and not one of the barges was boarded, not one of the crates was prised open.

In the end the journey from Breslau was something over three hundred miles as the crow flies, though with the ox-bows in the Elbe, and with the ice and the cold, it seemed much longer, an agonising voyage through sandstone-gorges and towns whose buildings cringed behind fortress walls on wooded slopes above the river. Finally the barges reached snowbound and windswept heathlands in which a few sheep-pens and juniper bushes projected themselves from sculpted snowdrifts like ruins. Only after the Elbe widened and cleared of ice, filling with colliers and fishing boats, did the sun appear and the weather improve. A day later the river widened further, its current quickening, its traffic thickening into chaos. A clutch of towers and steeples appeared above the watery Geestlands.

Emilia, rubbing her chilblained fingers together, could not even have begun to guess where they were, or how many days had passed since Breslau. She said nothing as the barge slithered between two others, then bumped into a busy quay. Nor did she say anything as a half-dozen men, led by a tall wharfinger, stumbled down the planks towards them. Though it was past dusk, no lanterns had been lit, and the figures hopping aboard were no more than shadows.

Vilém took her hand and together they disembarked, climbing the slippery embankment to where, at the top, the scene below was cast faint and shadowed in the rushlights of a waterfront tavern. Behind them the wharfinger was barking instructions in German. The crates were being carried to one of the storehouses that jumbled the riverside. The grip on her wrist tightened.

They stayed for three days in Hamburg, in the Gänge-Viertel of the Altstadt. Emilia spent each night in a different *Gasthaus*, in rooms of her own, narrow little cells in which she would wake each morning expecting to hear the chime of the Queen's summoning-bell next door. But there was no summoning-bell next door, not since the night when she had been roused from her bed, given two minutes to pack her bags, then escorted down to the Oder on Sir Ambrose's arm. She thought from the panic of the departure, as well as the expression on Vilém's face – for he had been there, lashing one of the crates to the top of a wagon – that the Cossack mercenaries had caught up with them at last. But they were not fleeing the Cossacks, she would later discover; rather, the Queen and her court. For only after the night ended and the sun rose, a dim iceblink on the smudged horizon, did she realise that the Queen's carriage with its piles of books and hat boxes was nowhere in sight. There were only the three of them now, along with a half-dozen workmen, Silesians who spoke neither English nor German.

What deal had been struck? As she watched the crates being borne up from the dock she wondered whether they had merely been stolen, whether Sir Ambrose was nothing more than a thief or pirate. In their fleeting moments together Vilém had claimed to know little of the Englishman's plan other than that they were to be met in London by a man named Henry Monboddo. Monboddo was an art broker, he said, a picturemonger and book dealer who supplied the wealthy lords of England with valuable paintings and manuscripts, as well as whatever other fascinating bric-à-brac he was able to prise loose from the princes and potentates of France, Italy or the Empire. Sir Ambrose had dealt with him many times before, because Monboddo had also prised loose a few odd bits and pieces that found their way into the collections of the Emperor Rudolf. Now it seemed that Monboddo had found a new client. Vilém had no idea who. But on their second night in the Altstadt he confessed what she already suspected. They were being pursued.

The two of them had been sitting at the table in her room, whispering over a chessboard, a single candle burning in an eight-armed candelabrum. He had recited a familiar litany, claiming to know neither who was in pursuit nor whether they had anything to do with the men in black-and-gold livery. Nor did he know whether the men in black-and-gold livery might be in the service of Cardinal Baronius, or the Emperor, or else some other party entirely. But he admitted that among the hundreds of books he and Sir Ambrose had carted from Prague in the ninety-nine wooden crates were those from the library's secret archive – books outlawed as heretical by the Holy Office.

Was the parchment one of them? Vilém claimed not to know. But the cardinals of the Inquisition would not take kindly, he said, to the liberation of the books from Prague Castle – nor to their transport to a heretical kingdom such as England. For included among the crates were such controversial treatises as the work of Copernicus that Emilia had seen in the wine cellar at Breslau. That particular volume, *De revolutionibus orbium coelestium*, had been suspended by the Congregation of the Index, he explained, following Galileo's brush with the Inquisition in 1616. Galileo's writings – both published and unpublished – were likewise found in the archives. And Galileo was, in the eyes of Rome, a most dangerous writer.

But still other documents were to be found in the ninety-nine crates. The secret sanctum in the Spanish Rooms had been greatly enlarged in the past few years, and not only because of the zeal of the Congregation of the Index. There were also stacks of lambskin in the archives, Vilém said, that catalogued the multifarious doings of the greatest empire on earth. For, some years earlier, when he was Archduke of Styria, Ferdinand had signed an agreement with his cousin and brother-in-law, the King of Spain. The treaty brought together the two Houses of Habsburg – the one in Austria, the other in Spain – who would henceforth work together to crush the the Protestants in their midst. In those days there was much brotherly mixing of blood. Documents in the archives in Seville found their way into the Imperial Library in Vienna, and vice versa. Philip even sent to Vienna a copy of the *Padrón Real*, the map of his domains in the New World. But Vienna was no longer safe, for both the Turks and the Transylvanians threatened it. So it was that over the past few years many of the documents from the Imperial Library were sent for safekeeping to Prague Castle, to the secret archive in the Spanish Rooms. But then of course everything changed. Ferdinand was deposed from the throne of Bohemia and replaced by a Protestant.

Emilia closed her eyes and felt the room begin to revolve. The King of Spain? The wind outside was howling plaintively in the chimney-pots like the ululations of a wolfpack. The cardinals of the Inquisition? The candle guttered in the draught, drooling icicles of wax. What fatal Pandora's box had been prised open in Prague Castle? Not for the first time she was sensible of the danger – one worse than the biting cold or the ice floes on the Elbe – into which Sir Ambrose had plunged them. And was the Englishman a danger too, someone to be feared as much as their mysterious pursuers?

He entered her room a few minutes later, knocking on her door before entering with a brisk step. He seemed in a cheerful mood. He handed each of them a passport and certificate of health – both forged in false names – then turned to Vilém.

'I regret to say that, if my information is correct, you may also have need of these.' He extended a small calfskin pouch. 'In the event that we should be caught up, you understand. I am told they have several unpleasant methods of persuasion.'

'Persuasion?' Vilém accepted the small calfskin pouch and loosened the drawstring. Emilia, watching from the corner, saw Vilém sprinkle into his palm three or four small seeds.

'*Strychnos nux vomitica*,' Sir Ambrose explained. 'From a tree in India. Brought back, I believe, from a Jesuit mission. Painless, apparently, and very fast. I've seen one work on a blackbird.' He paused. 'I should think one would do the trick; two to be safe.'

Vilém frowned. 'But how am I to . . . ?'

'To what?'

'To persuade the men to swallow them?'

Sir Ambrose looked perplexed for a second, then burst out laughing. 'My dear fellow!' he exclaimed. He made a terrific show of wiping his cheeks with a handkerchief and suppressing further eruptions of mirth. 'No, no, my dear fellow. They're for you. *You* are the one who must swallow them, should you have the misfortune to let them catch you. Oh, dear me . . .'

One night later she was smuggled aboard the *Bellerophon*, escorted up the cleated gangplank in pitch-blackness, then led down a hatchway to the stale air of the orlop-deck, the lowest inhabited level of the ship. Her tiny cabin – another narrow cell into which she was thrust – smelled of gunpowder and pitch and the poisonous water in the bilges. As the *Bellerophon* made its way down the Elbe, she watched through a scuttle, alone in her cabin, as the sea turned the colour of a desert and ruffled its skirts along the shore. Then a few leagues out to sea, as the sandstone cliffs of Heligoland swayed into view, she was violently ill, and for what seemed like days on end she lay swaddled in her hammock, feeling the *Bellerophon* heave and pitch and creak across the immense sea. The ship's doctor visited her cabin and fed her preparations of ginger and German camomile. But even then, of course, she knew her illness was not to be cured by a few herbs; it was something graver and yet more wonderful than mere seasickness.

Chapter Nine

S t Olave's Church stands in Hart Street, near Crutched Friars, in the shadow of the Navy Office and Tower Hill. As I arrived, its front doors were yawning open, exposing a candle-lit nave and a flock of departing parishioners. Evensong was letting out. I dodged past the small crowd, rounded a corner, then crept down a flexuous path towards the churchyard, whose gates were surmounted by a pair of stone skulls. The eye-sockets regarded me grimly as I passed on to the edge of the old burial-ground, hoping to look solemn and respectful, as churchyards demand, not like a miscreant bent on some sinister bit of mischief – which, for all I knew, I was.

It was the evening following my trip to Pulteney House, and for the second night in a row I was leaving Tom Monk alone in Nonsuch House. He had begun to suspect me, I believe, of some romantic attachment, a ridiculous suspicion, but one encouraged by the bouquet of flowers I was clutching in my hand. Yet this ritual – the flowers and the churchyard – had been a familiar one. Each Sunday for the past five years I had tiptoed into the outer churchyard of St Magnus-the-Martyr, holding flowers to my chest and threading my way past the victims of plague and consumption and a score of other misfortunes to a familiar granite tablet surrounded by four tiny lozenges. But I realised with a soft pang of grief and guilt that I had not visited Arabella's grave for some time now, not since my first letter from Alethea and the visit to Pontifex Hall. I squeezed the stems more tightly and stepped uncertainly forward.

I had spent much of the day in Whitehall Palace, in the offices of the Exchequer, examining countless rate-books and poll-tax returns. I was hoping to learn more about Henry Monboddo before I was forced to confront him. Forewarned is forearmed, as my mother used to say. I had considered returning to Alsatia and making enquiries of Samuel Pickvance, but I was wary of raising the auctioneer's suspicions. He and Monboddo might be in league together, after all. So I had settled for the palace instead, to which a waterman conducted me, travelling up river through the heavy morning traffic.

Whitehall Palace in those days was a haphazard maze of some thirty thatched, timber-framed buildings whose corridors and enclosures were as crowded with people and as filled with coal smoke and rat droppings as everywhere else in London. It was hardly a fit place for a king, I decided, or even his mistresses. I picked my way through a series of sunless courtyards and cramped passages until I reached the nondescript block of tarred buildings devoted to the counting and storing of the royal treasure. From the poll-tax returns, which specified occupations, I hoped to learn something of Monboddo's business dealings, and from the rate-books what properties he might own, if any, apart from Wembish Park. I suppose I must have, if not quite distrusted Alethea, then at least possessed a robust scepticism concerning her claims. But such scepticism was healthy, I assured myself. Trust, after all, is the mother of deceit. I therefore wished to uncover a few objective and independent facts about Henry Monboddo.

The search proved to be a long and difficult one. I looked as far back as 1651 before finding any reference to Monboddo, I assumed because he, like Alethea, had spent the last nine years in exile. What I read in the records accorded with everything

Alethea had said. Henry Monboddo was listed as a dealer of fine books and paintings who had been Keeper of the Royal Library in St James's Palace for five years during the reign of Charles I. There were no clues, however, as to the identity of his client, of whoever was so desperate to get his hands on *The Labyrinth of the World*. The rate-book for 1651 listed his address as Wembish Park, along with a house in Covent Garden – a house that, when visited two hours later, proved derelict. The records also mentioned an office in Cheapside that had become, I would discover, the premises of a silversmith who claimed never to have heard of anyone named Henry Monboddo.

Before leaving Whitehall Palace I had also searched the records, on a whim, for information regarding Sir Richard Overstreet. He did not rise in my estimation when I discovered that he was listed as a lawyer. But not all lawyers were necessarily scoundrels, I told myself, and Sir Richard did appear to have enjoyed a brilliant and lucrative career before he was forced into exile in 1651. He had practised privately as a conveyancer and then been appointed Solicitor-General in 1644. Later he held posts in both the Navy Office and the Foreign Office, for the latter of which he served as an envoy-extraordinary in Madrid. He had even taken part in a Royalist embassy to Rome.

Hunched over the crinkled documents, I had wondered for a moment whether Sir Richard, like so many of our gentry, was a crypto-Catholic, possibly even a spy for the Pope or the Spaniards. This was wild thinking, but I knew that in 1645 a secret embassy had travelled to Rome with the purpose of securing military assistance against Cromwell in return for the conversion of King Charles and his advisers to Roman Catholicism. Still, I had no clue whether Sir Richard's trip to Rome had been part of the same mission. Nor did these few facts, like those about Henry Monboddo, tell anything of his character, motives, or even his religion. So I had thanked the clerk for his assistance and then made my way back through the decrepit maze to the landing-stairs.

Now, picking my path through the churchyard, I saw two black-garbed mourners among the stones, a man and a woman, one on either side of the ground. The woman was veiled, the man wearing a broad-brimmed hat. I picked my way past a stand of yews to the first row of monuments, feeling conspicuous and also faintly absurd as I scanned the ground. A hundred-odd markers were pressing upwards from their hummocks of earth in odd angles and uneven rows, gapped here and there like a failed crop, their late-afternoon shadows striping the new-mown hay.

I discovered Silas Cobb's grave in the middle of the churchyard, half overgrown by the branches of a yew tree that screened it, partially at least, from the rest of the churchyard: a granite slab topped by a deep-socketed death's-head. By the time I had located it, one of the mourners had disappeared, but the other, I felt, had been watching me, his face half turned to follow my awkward progress. I decided that after he departed I would take a look at the monument before which he was standing. Then I took a deep breath and fumbled in my pocket for the key. As I did so I reread the inscription:

Hic jacet
SILAS COBB
1585–1620
ʃoli Deo laus et gloria in saecula

A small bouquet of hyacinths and camomile had been propped against the tablet. I was surprised by the sight. Was someone still grieving for Mr Cobb even after the passage of forty years? His aged widow, perhaps? I was soberly reflecting that no one would be placing flowers on my grave forty years after my death – not even forty days afterwards, for that matter – when I became even more puzzled by the tablet itself. The other granite markers along the row also dated from the 1620s, but while their death's-heads were periwigged with moss and their inscriptions partly eroded, Silas Cobb's tablet looked new and out of place. Certainly the granite did not look forty years old.

I knelt beside the lozenge and, with the yew's soft needles plucking at my hair, placed my own flowers against the tablet.

The lozenge was partly overgrown with nettles, which I cleared away with the tip of my thorn-stick before slipping my fingers underneath. The loam beneath was dark and warm and smelled of decayed tubers. A few handfuls had been scooped aside and a strong-box cached inside the hollow. I felt like a schoolboy exhuming a spurious treasure buried the previous autumn. When I fitted the key into the lock the catch sprang open with a startlingly loud report. I held my breath and looked over my shoulder, through the wind-quivering branches of the yew. The second mourner had departed.

I found no message from Alethea inside the box, so left behind a slip of paper confirming my intention to travel to Wembish Park at her convenience, as agreed. Then I locked the strong-box, replaced it, slid the lozenge back into place, and began creeping through the ranks of weathered granite. I was surprised that Alethea with her obession with secrecy had not insisted upon a code or an invisible ink.

The windows of the church were dark by now, and Hart Street for the moment looked deserted of traffic. I was moving in the opposite direction, diagonally through the churchyard, southeast towards Seething Lane, which also looked deserted. Much as I detest venturing abroad in daylight, amid the crowds and the stink, at night London is even worse. I had an unpleasant sensation between my shoulder-blades, as if some great bird had perched there and was slowly champing its beak and unfolding a pair of sooty wings. There was something sinister and dangerous about the way the houses in Seething Lane, beyond the gate, seemed to crouch together in the darkness. Beside them reared the great dark hulk of the Navy Office.

I stopped beside a grave to peer at the enormous structure rising above the screen of yew trees. Remembering the patent for Sir Ambrose's Orinoco expedition as well as the scrap of canvas in the Golden Horn, the supposed main topsail of the *Britomart*, I wondered if I should return the following day to make some enquiries. Perhaps the log for the *Philip Sidney* still existed, or possibly there was someone in the Navy Office who could tell me about his involvement with Sir Walter Raleigh's voyage to Guiana. I wondered idly if it was possible that a connection existed, however tenuous, between Raleigh's voyage and *The Labyrinth of the World*. After all, Alethea claimed that Monboddo had been the artistic agent for the Duke of Buckingham, and I knew that Buckingham, the Lord High Admiral, had supported Raleigh's enterprise in Guiana. I also remembered that the other books missing from Pontifex Hall – one of which had been Raleigh's *Discoverie of the large, rich, and beautifull Empire of Guiana* – all dealt in one way or another with the exploration of Spanish America. Or was I clutching at straws?

Of course, I already knew about Raleigh's ill-starred expedition. As an apprentice in Mr Smallpace's shop I had gobbled up accounts of the voyages of Raleigh and Drake as if they were adventure stories. I still stocked a number of books about Raleigh's Orinoco expedition, including first-hand narratives written by men who had sailed in the *Destiny* or in the other ships in the fleet. I had sifted quickly through them in the days after my return from Pontifex Hall, though none mentioned either the *Philip Sidney* or Sir Ambrose Plessington.

But what a story Raleigh's voyage makes! A daring sea adventurer spends thirteen years in gaol for conspiring against a crafty old king, who then releases him on condition that he fills the ever-dwindling royal coffers by finding a mythical gold mine across the ocean, thousands of miles distant in the middle of an ill-explored land filled with enemy soldiers. It might have come from the tongue of Homer or the pen of Shakespeare – the flawed hero, the treacherous king, the slippery advisers, the impossible task, the tragic death, all mingled into a wintry world of treachery and greed. I used to think I could glimpse, in Raleigh, the after-image of Jason as he is sent by the usurper Pelias to recover the Golden Fleece, or Bellerophon when he journeys to Lycia to fight the Chimaera after angering the treacherous Proetus – Bellerophon who, like Raleigh with his fatal charter, bears a warrant demanding his death. Who says we no longer live in an age of heroes?

The main events of Raleigh's sad tale are known well enough. He sailed from London with his fleet in April 1617, leaving behind squabbling factions and powerful enemies. His scheme was supported by King James's new favourite, Sir George Villiers – later to become the Duke of Buckingham – as well as the anti-Spanish faction at court, the so-called War Party led by the Earl of Pembroke and the Archbishop of Canterbury. Pembroke and the Archbishop had thrust forward young Villiers to topple the reigning favourite, Somerset, and to counter the pro-Spanish faction supporting him. Yet not even Villiers's blandishments could tempt the King to forsake his pro-Spanish policy. So while Raleigh's instructions were to locate the gold mine, his charter also stipulated that he must not attack any Spanish ships or settlements. If he violated these conditions, the Spanish ambassador in London, Count Gondomar – the most powerful of his enemies – would claim his head, as provided for in the charter.

Of course, things immediately went wrong. Two days into the voyage, while Land's End was still in sight, one of the fourteen ships sank in a gale, taking with her a crew of sixty men. When the fleet reached the mouth of the Orinoco, eight miserable months later, after storms and scurvy, Raleigh was too ill to continue and remained with the *Destiny* in Trinidad. It was then the dry season, a time when the level of the Orinoco falls and navigation becomes more hazardous even than usual. But Raleigh could not wait, and five ships were chosen to ascend the river. It was thought that the mine would be found hundreds of miles inland, near the elusive El Dorado, 'the Golden One', a city that was said to stand in the middle of a lake. The legend of this city and its unfathomable riches had been repeated by all of the Spanish chroniclers, and for seventy years the conquistadores, those knight-errants of the jungle, had navigated the Orinoco and its tributaries in search of it. But neither El Dorado nor its mines of gold had ever been seen except, supposedly, by a man named Juan Martín de Albujar, a fugitive from Maraver de Silva's 1566 expedition, an expedition for which, unusually, no chronicle exists.

Nor was the mine discovered by Raleigh's men. Instead, the fleet blundered upon the humbler town of San Tomás, a Spanish garrison of a hundred bamboo huts, a mud-walled church and a couple of rusty cannons, all clinging to the bank of the Orinoco. Then, disaster struck. Shots were exchanged, men died, the quest was abandoned, the fleet sailed into the Boca de la Sierpe – the 'serpent's mouth' – and rapidly dispersed. Raleigh and his men sailed home in disgrace. Raleigh feigned illness, then madness, then attempted to escape to France. But he was captured and thrown back inside his old rooms in the Bloody Tower. An inquiry into the disastrous affair was undertaken by Sir Francis Bacon. In October 1618, at the behest of Gondomar, Raleigh was beheaded. The official reason was treason against King James.

But I was uncertain how Sir Ambrose Plessington fitted into this tragic fable. Had the *Philip Sidney* been one of the ships in Raleigh's doomed fleet? If so, what were the connections between *The Labyrinth of the World*, Henry Monboddo and a long-ago voyage into the Guianan jungle?

I squinted at the Navy Office for a while longer, doubtful, all of a sudden, that it would hold an answer. Then I turned round and made my way to the spot where the second mourner had stood. It was a grave with a tiny granite pillar under the sprawling marquee of a cypress whose branches overhung Seething Lane. I had been expecting a fresh mound of earth strewn with bouquets of flowers, but the stone was cracked, the grave untended and the inscription all but unreadable. A root of the cypress was erupting through the soil, looking eerily like a protrudent knee. I bent warily forward and strained my eyes. The stone seemed to commemorate an infant named Smethwick – the first name was illegible – who had died in the third quarter of the last century. It seemed unlikely that anyone could still be mourning the child, so I decided I was mistaken about the location of the grave – and, no doubt, about the mourner's attentions as well. Besides, had I not been behaving suspiciously, slipping into the churchyard at dusk and then lurching about like a ghoul? All sorts of dreadful things happened in churchyards in those days. He probably took me for a 'resurrection man', one of those grave-robbers who excavates fresh corpses to sell to London's apprentice barber-surgeons and medical students. At least, that was the reassurance I made to myself as I began walking back towards the balefully staring skulls, resisting the urge to run and feeling the pair of talons sinking ever deeper into the quivering flesh of my back.

I returned home on foot. Later I would wonder what might have happened if I had hired a hack and arrived back at Nonsuch House five minutes earlier. But there were no hacks to be found, and so I began stumping homeward, reaching the bridge some twenty minutes later. Everything seemed as usual as I approached Nonsuch House, but outside an apothecary's closed-up shop I spotted Monk in the middle of the carriageway, reeling towards me, his face dazed and white. Beyond, the green door to Nonsuch Books stood partly open and was hanging lopsidedly in its frame.

'Mr Inchbold – !'

A number of onlookers were grouped about the front of the shop like the audience for a raree-show, poised between walking and standing, murmuring in subdued speculation in the way they do when a cart-horse kicks a stranger's child or drops dead in the street. Monk had staggered towards me and now began clutching at my sleeve and stuttering something unintelligible.

I pushed past him and tugged sharply on the doorknob. The door teetered downwards, even more awry now, hinges screaming in pain. The top hinges, that is, for the bottom ones were bent and dangled lopsidedly in the splintered frame. The whole thing threatened to come loose in my hand. But I had widened the aperture a few more inches – enough to step inside, my throat choking with fear and anger.

My feet skidded over something, and when my eyes adjusted to the gloom I saw how my books – every last one of them, it seemed – had been stripped from the shelves and scattered across every inch of the floor. Hundreds of them lay clustered together in haphazard cairns as if awaiting a bonfire: bindings snapped, covers awkwardly tented or flung open like wings, exposed pages lop-eared and riffling in the light breeze from the destroyed door. There was the smell of dust, hide, fustiness – of old, outworn things whose familiar, agreeable fug had somehow been strengthened as if through decoction, a pervasive but invisible cloud that swirled like cannon smoke above the delicate ruins.

I righted myself and staggered ankle-deep towards the counter, stumbling about in a full circle, unable to comprehend the compass of this destruction, let alone its purpose. I sank to my knees in the centre of the shop, only vaguely aware of Monk behind me. My precious refuge, my haven from the turmoil of the world – all of it was gone, destroyed. My chest began to heave like a child's. I remember a pair of hands on my shoulders but not whose they were or what happened next.

Indeed, of the next few hours I remember little: only a kind of dazed underwater progress through the shop, with Monk and I forlornly surveying the damage, picking up books and sorting through them, commiserating over the destruction of a volume or, more rarely, soberly celebrating the unlikely preservation of another. My walnut shelves, I discovered, had also been destroyed – ripped from the walls and flung to the floor, where they lay criss-crossed at rakish angles to one another and splintered like rigging after a tempest. Later I would decide that it must have taken an army to perform such desecrations, but only three men had done it, Monk told me, and it had probably taken them just five minutes. They took to their heels when, after hearing the noise, he crept down the turnpike stair and peered into the shop. They appeared be looking for something, he said, because they had been snatching each book from the shelf, frantically riffling through it, then tossing it aside before moving on to the next one. But sometimes one of them would stick out an arm and sweep an entire shelf on to the floor, or else rip the shelf itself from its brackets, all without so much as looking at a single one of the books.

'Scared me good and proper,' he finished, eyes bright and nervous at the recollection, 'and I don't mind tellin' you.'

'Who do you suppose they were, Monk? The searchers?'

'The searchers, sir?'

It was close to midnight by this point. We were sitting at the counter, in our usual positions, master and apprentice, as if these familiar poses might bring back something of the shop's shattered equilibrium. Dozens of half-dismembered books still littered the floor, but we had managed to put up some of the shelves and replace the few of their books that would not require rebinding.

'The Secretary of State's henchmen,' I prompted him. 'You remember.'

He looked even more alarmed now. He knew a little about these myrmidons since two years earlier John Thurloe, the Secretary of State at the time, despatched them on their rounds of Little Britain and London Bridge. They paid us a visit only days after a pregnant woman had arrived in Nonsuch Books following what she said was an arduous journey by barge from Oxford. As Monk watched, frightened and incredulous, she gave birth on the counter to triplets – three copies of Sexby's *Killing No Murder*, a treatise calling for the death of Cromwell. The searchers had come pounding on the door two nights later. Poor Monk had been roused from his bed when a lantern was thrust in his face and a loud voice demanded that he identify himself. He had not forgotten the episode.

'No . . . not the searchers,' he replied. 'Foreigners.'

'Foreigners?'

'Yes. French. Maybe Turkish. Dark-skinned, they were, sir. The dead spit of pirates, all dressed in black. One of 'em had a gold earring. Another a knife,' he added soberly.

'Did they say anything?'

'Not a word.'

'Did they take anything with them? Any books?'

'No, sir.' He shook his head. 'Not so I saw.'

'No. Nothing seems to be missing, does it?' He shook his head again. So far all of the volumes seemed to be accounted for, though the next day I would double-check my catalogue. 'Which way did they go?'

'Into Southwark. I ran after them, but they was quicker 'n what I am.' He dropped his eyes to the counter. His hands were fidgeting in his lap.

'I understand. Thank you, Monk,' I told him. 'You did well.'

I leaned back in the chair, closing my eyes and trying to think. For a moment I almost allowed myself to believe the desecration had nothing to do with anything else that had happened these past few days. Or perhaps they had been searchers after all. Perhaps the new Secretary of State employed Frenchmen to do his dirty work. But what would they have been looking for? Possibly the new King was going to be as troublesome to booksellers as Cromwell. I decided that tomorrow I would put a few questions about in Little Britain and Paternoster Row. Someone else might have had visitors as well.

I opened my eyes to find Monk watching me closely. I tried to offer a reassuring smile. 'Yes, you did well,' I repeated. 'Very well. But I fear our work tonight is not yet finished.'

'Oh?'

I nodded at the door, which was slumped awkwardly on its hinges. The carriageway was visible beyond. Every few minutes a passerby would peer curiously inside before quickly retracting his head and hurrying away.

'Tomorrow I shall find us a joiner and a locksmith,' I said. 'But for tonight . . .'

I reached into the counter and withdrew a pistol. Monk's eyes widened at the sight. It was an evil-looking weapon, heavy and awkward, a huge firelock I had purchased many years earlier from a blind, one-legged Civil War veteran who had taken to begging outside my shop. I had no idea if the flint and frizzen worked, or even how much priming powder to sprinkle into the pan. The old veteran had given me a lesson, but I had never expected to use the thing and had purchased it purely to relieve his misery.

'Tonight we shall take shifts guarding the shop,' I told him. 'Just in case someone should be tempted to avail himself of our stock.' I placed the dreadful instrument on the counter between us. 'Or in case our friends should wish to return.'

Monk's eyes grew even wider at these unpleasant prospects, so I attempted another reassuring smile, which came out as a pained grimace.

'Go to bed,' I told him gently. 'I shall wake you in two hours.'

But in the end I sat up the entire night by myself. I started the task of rebinding a few of the books, though every ten minutes I would leave my sewing-frame and creep to the door to peer on to the carriageway for signs of life, ears cocked to catch the sound of stealthy footsteps hurrying away. But there was no one about now except the watchman, an arthritic old fellow who hardly inspired confidence. He was half blind, I noticed. One of his eyes was filmed over like that of a dead fish, while the other rolled at me like that of the severed head as he advised me to repair my door in case I should offer a temptation too powerful for some poor soul to withstand. Then he shambled away with his lantern swinging.

Only after dawn broke in the east did I abandon my sewing-frame and wake Monk. And only as I trudged upstairs to bed did I allow myself to think about the three black-clad assassins who had murdered Lord Marchamont in Paris. Had they been the same men? It seemed possible – yet it made no sense. If the killers were agents of Henry Monboddo, as Alethea suspected, and if Monboddo now possessed the parchment, as I had discovered, then what could they have been searching for among my shelves? Possibly they were in the employ of someone else, even Cardinal Mazarin himself. I clambered into bed and tried to sleep. There were many things, I told myself, that I had yet to learn.

I lay on my side for several hours, exhausted but sleepless, staring at the wall, listening to the knocking of the death-watch beetles inside it. Suddenly the familiar sound was menacing and portentous, as if the insects were consuming the beams and supports of the modest life I had built for myself. As if Nonsuch House were about to collapse and tumble me head over heels into the current rushing past sixty feet below.

Chapter Ten

From the freshes of the Elbe at Cuxhaven the *Bellerophon* shaped a course westward along the Frisian Islands, past chains of snow-clad saltings and dykes, past sand-spits and moles projecting like ribs into the grey waters of the sea. She sailed in soundings, ten fathoms of water, for almost a full day until, setting a course southwest by south, she left the Dutch coast at dawn on the second day and, putting on more sail, holding a close wind, turned her bows towards England. Captain Quilter, peering through his spyglass, sighted the coast from the catwalk two hours later. All was going to plan. He lowered the glass and returned it to the pocket of his tarpaulin. In eight more hours, if all went well, they would reach the Nore and, riding at anchor, the *Albatross*.

But from that point in the voyage nothing would go well. Later, taking stock of the disaster, Captain Quilter would blame not only his own avarice – his greed for the two thousand Reichsthalers – but, even more, the ignorance of his crewmen. Not ignorance of their jobs, because he recruited only the most experienced and capable hands, but the pristine ignorance that bred the worst superstitions in men exposed to the cruelty of the elements. Yes, sailors were a superstitious lot, there was no avoiding the fact. Quilter had seen them at their strange rituals in the Golden Grapes, purchasing gruesome good-luck charms – the cauls of newborn children – from the old crones plying the taverns beside the port. The men believed with some bizarrely misplaced faith that one of these shrivelled membranes (or what Quilter's suspicions told him were in fact the bladders of pigs) would save them from death by drowning. And one day when the *Bellerophon* was becalmed in Dvina Bay he had caught a furtive party muttering a chant and then tossing a broomstick over the poop-rail, as if an action as petty as this, and not (as every educated man knew) the movement of the stars in the heavens, or the rotation of the earth, or the conjunction of planets, or an eclipse, or the rising of Orion or Arcturus, or a half-dozen other celestial rituals that were beyond the feeble arc of human endeavour, might cause a change in a force as powerful and unpredictable as the wind!

Then, of course, there had been the church bells. Their ghostly peals were heard on the upper deck as the *Bellerophon* slid past Cuxhaven – a sure sign, supposedly, that the ship and her crew would come to grief, for there was no omen so terrifying to a sailor as the sound of church bells at sea. Within a day the ship's surgeon had clambered up from the cockpit to report that three of the crewmen had come down with a fever. Two turns of the sandglass later came the news that another handful of men had fallen ill, but by then Captain Quilter had more serious dangers to worry about.

What, he later wondered, had caused the wind to blow this time, to twitch the dog-vane at the end of its line on the gunwale as the sun climbed overhead at the end of the morning watch? No notice was paid to it, however, for the sky was bright and clear, the wind steady, and most of the crewmen – those who hadn't yet taken ill – squatted on coiled lanyards in the messes below, peering at one another over hands of cards. But slowly a storm front appeared on the eastern horizon, implacable and bruise-black, and began edging its way across the sky like the shadow of an approaching giant. The deck-beams creaked noisily and water poured through the scuttles. Then the first of the spume broke over the bows and across the fo'c'sle deck, followed by stinging pellets of rain. Seconds later the ladders and decks were resounding with the boots of crewmen rushing to their stations. The midshipmen were already on their hands and knees on the waist, prising open the scuppers, while others who stuck their heads through the hatches were sent scrambling up the flapping ratlines. As they hastily struggled to reef the canvas – Pinchbeck was shouting orders at them from below – the first antlers of lightning split the sky.

The luck that saved the crew from the Scylla of the Dvina and the Charybdis of the White Sea had, it seemed, now deserted them. Pinchbeck clung with both hands to the mainmast, bellowing himself hoarse, until a heavy wave broke amidships and sent him staggering sideways like a drunken brawler. He righted himself only to be knocked down a second later as the stern plunged sickeningly downward and frigid water cascaded across the poop deck. Bodies scattered aft from the waist, knocked down like skittles. Then the stem dipped, the bowsprit sliced the water, and the bodies tumbled backwards. The familiar rituals turned to panic as a dozen desperate cries followed them across the decks. 'Helm astarboard!' 'Belay there!' 'Left full rudder!' Three men had lashed themselves to the tiller, which was rearing and tossing them about like an unbroken horse, its rope burning their hands and breaking one of their wrists. 'Hard alee!' 'Steady so!' And then, as one of the topmen sped spreadeagled through the air, his scream lost in the gale: 'Man overboard!'

But there was nothing to be done except to strike the sails and pray. From the leeward side of the lurching quarterdeck, Captain Quilter watched in helpless anger as the sky rapidly unscrolled itself above the heads of the struggling topmen, above the tops of the masts that, as the sheets of rain thickened, were almost lost to view. He regarded the storm as a personal affront, as impertinent and enraging as the attack of a Spanish picaroon. There had been no warnings beforehand, not the treble ring round the moon at sunrise that morning, nor a halo round Venus at sunset the night before, nor even the flocks of petrels circling the ship a half-hour earlier – none of those things that, in Quilter's long experience, always presaged violent turns of weather. The elements were not playing fair.

Now, with the deck awash, he slipped on a board, fell heavily on to his backside, then was struck on the ankle by a rogue bucket. He pulled himself upright and, cursing again, hurled the bucket overboard. A sodden chart wrapped itself round his head before he could claw it away. It flapped over the gunwale like a mad seagull, and through the rain he suddenly glimpsed the coast looming to leeward – a hazard now more than a refuge. To survive the ice of Archangel and Hammerfest, he thought grimly, only to be dashed to pieces on your own shore!

And it appeared that the *Bellerophon* and her crew would not be the only ones dashed to bits. Two bowshots astern, on their starboard quarter, another ship was wallowing and plunging in the troughs, showing two distress lights in her main topgallant. A minute later she fired off a piece of ordnance, a brief spark and puff of smoke, barely audible above the rain and wind. Her bowsprit and foremast went soon afterwards, the latter struck, Quilter saw, by a bolt of lightning that knocked two of her hands into the sea. He had steadied himself long enough to raise his glass, and now he could see the *Star of Lübeck*, another merchantman sailing from Hamburg to London. Her ballast had shifted, or else she was hulled and making water – tons of it – for she was listing badly to port, with her masts bent at a low angle to the heaving water. He only hoped she would keep a decent offing and not drift any closer towards the *Bellerophon* and take both of them down . . .

For the next two hours the *Star of Lübeck* faded rather than loomed, however. Only after the worst of the storm had spent itself – at which point, perversely, the sun lowered pillars of light from between a parting in the clouds – did she reappear. By then the *Bellerophon* was scudding under bare poles and listing badly to starboard. The damage was much worse, Quilter knew, than in the White Sea. The sails were in rags and the tiller was cracked. The mizen topgallant lay slantwise across on the poop deck, where it had skewered two deckhands and fractured the skull of a third. Who knew how many men had been lost overboard. Worst of all, the keel had dragged across the edge of a sandbar and then struck a rock with a deafening crack. She was probably bilged and filling with water at this very minute, giving them only minutes to plug the leak with a sail or a hawsebag. Something had to be done, he knew, or the rest of them would be lost too, turned into firewood and fishbait along the shore, which was rearing ever closer.

He made his way through the nearest hatch, beneath which, in the main and then the middle deck, the boards were slippery with provisions spilled from their casks and cupboards. The floors tilted at 45-degree angles; it was like balancing on the slope of a pitched roof. Soon the air thickened with a foul stench, and he realised, too late, how the pisspots had evacuated on to the floor. Then on the gundeck the smell grew even worse.

'The bilges, Captain.'

He had been joined by Pinchbeck, who was holding a begrimed handkerchief over his nose. The two of them were picking their way carefully across the littered boards. Water had surged through the gunports, and the floor, a litter of quoins and soaked cartridges, was a half-inch deep. Quilter could hear the cries of the sick men in the cockpit.

'Stirred up like a soup, I should think,' the bo'sun added in a muffled voice.

'Never mind that,' Quilter snapped. 'Get a team of men down to the pumps. And fetch some canvas from the sail-locker. Also a hawsebag, if you can lay your hands on one. If there's a leak it'll have to be fothered fast or we're drowned.' The bo'sun shot him an alarmed look. Quilter waved an impatient arm. 'Go on – quickly now! And find every man you can spare,' he called after Pinchbeck's retreating figure, 'and send him to the hold. The cargo will have to be shifted!'

Quilter clambered down the next ladder alone. The steerage and the wardroom both were empty, their jungles of hammocks dangling limply from the beams. When he reached the orlop-deck he was surprised to see that it, too, was deserted. He had been expecting to find his three mysterious passengers here – frightened out of their wits, no doubt – but they were nowhere in sight. So far they had kept to themselves; not once had he seen them on the upper decks. Greengills, he had reckoned to himself with some amusement a few hours earlier. But now he saw that their cabins were empty.

Not until he reached the ladder into the hold did he hear any signs of life. The stink from the bilges was stronger now; bile rose in his gullet as he descended the ladder. Voices from below. There seemed to be some sort of dispute in progress. He snatched one of the oil-lamps swaying from a deck-beam and picked his way down the ladder one-handed.

The cargo deck had suffered the worst of all. The trembling light showed Quilter a promiscuous litter of pelts among the scattered dunnage and crates, several of which had been upturned against the bulkheads. Other crates had broken apart and were sliding back and forth with the motions of the ship. He took a few faltering steps, straining to hear the voices at the other end of the hold, not wishing to think about the damage done to his furs. The way was blocked by a couple of crates, out of which a half-dozen books were spilling.

Books? He gave them a kick to clear his path, then hoisted the lantern and picked his way forward, feeling water seep through his shoes. Why should the firm of Crabtree & Crookes have been sending *books* to England? And why such secrecy about them? He had carried contraband a few times before, but never had a book crossed through his lading-ports. He peered at the scattered volumes in the wavering light. A few had already been damaged by the water, he saw. Their pages, sodden and swollen, looked like the pleats of a lace ruff.

He raised his eyes. Perhaps a dozen shapes were visible at the far end of the hold, their shadows quaking and darting across the dubbed planks.

'You there! What's happening?'

No one turned. He picked his way through the obstacle course towards them. More books. As he searched for footholds on the deck he felt his gut tighten. Was this some mutinous congregation? If so, Quilter had snuffed out more than a few kindle-coals of mutiny in his time aboard the *Bellerophon*.

'Get to work,' he growled at the motionless shapes. 'We've been bilged. Do you not hear me? The load must be shifted. The pumps must be rigged. Quickly now! Before we sink!'

Still no one moved. Then he saw a sword glint in the lamplight and heard a voice.

'Stand back, I say!'

It was a moment before Quilter realised that the command was not directed at him. The wall of figures shifted a few steps backwards amid unintelligible murmurs of protest. Quilter was close enough to see their faces in the arc of light: the three strangers had been backed up against the wall by a good ten of his crewmen. One of the strangers, the larger of the two men, had raised his sword. What sort of strange business was this? He took another step forward, gripping the edge of a bulkhead, but then recoiled with a gasp. What in the name of – ?

His foot froze in mid-air. Beneath his shoe, spilling from its splintered crate, was what appeared to be an enormous jawbone, one the size of a crossbow, with a dozen teeth glowing wickedly in the lamplight. Quilter lowered the lantern, blinking in confused alarm. Where the devil had *that* come from? He stepped over it only to recoil again, for beside the jawbone lay an even more startling sight, the corpse of a two-headed goat, complete with four horns. The creature was emerging from the wreckage of a shattered jar whose liquid, puddled on the floor, gave off a worse stench than the bilges. What, in the holy name of God . . . ?

Soon other strange creatures appeared, hideous monsters that his disbelieving memory would construct only much later and then weave into his nightmares for years to come. They spilled from their crates as he lurched towards them, their coils and tentacles askew, their mouths toothsome and horribly leering. Still more were represented not in the flesh but by carvings – grotesque and menacing creatures with two heads and dozens of flailing limbs – or in an enormous book whose pages were riffling back and forth with each heave of the ship. As he passed the spreadeagled volume, Quilter caught sight of a demon with horns the size of a bull's raping a young maiden with its enormous black pizzle. Then, as the ship rolled, a hag with shrivelled breasts biting the neck of a naked figure, a man, prostrate beneath her. He stared at the page, aghast, feeling his nape prickle under his soaked tarpaulin. Another roll. The demon reappeared.

But worst of all these sights by far – the image that Captain Quilter would carry with him through his tormenting dreams and into his grave – was a corpse-like creature that lay supine in one of the boxes nearest the wall, a man with a mask for a face whose stiffened limbs were jerking and thrashing as if the brute were attempting to rise from its coffin. Even the doll-like eyes were rolling frantically and the head was twitching and cocking like that of a curious bird. Several of the midshipmen were staring back with expressions of stupefied wonder; one of them was crossing himself repeatedly as he muttered a prayer under his breath. Quilter stood rooted to the timbers as if spell-cast. Why, even the grinning lips were moving as if the creature were attempting to speak, to deliver some ghastly threat!

'Ah! Captain! You choose to join us at last.'

The voice startled Quilter to life. He raised his eyes from the creature's mad gesticulations to see the man with the sword bow and then, straightening, inscribe a few initials in the air with the point of his weapon. The ring of crewmen edged a skittish step backwards.

'Do please call off your men, won't you, Captain? Otherwise I shall be obliged to cut their throats.'

'Devil,' sneered one of the midshipmen, Rowley, a veteran dockside brawler. He had armed himself, Quilter saw, with a bodkin from the sail-locker. What was happening? Several of the others were also gripping improvised weapons – priming irons, a serpentine, even a couple of broomsticks – that they now raised in menace like a pitchfork army of angry villagers cornering the local vampire. Rowley took a step forward. 'Have you not killed enough men already?'

'I assure you I have done nothing of the sort.'

'Sorcerer!' someone piped up from the back of the pack. The powder-monkey. 'Murderer!'

'How very like a play,' retorted the stranger with a kindly smile, whetting his blade on the fetid air. 'But do you think we might perform it later? In another place? You heard the Captain. Our ship is—'

Rowley interrupted, lunging forward with a guttural cry, bodkin out-thrust. But the ship chose that second to lurch wildly to starboard as more water flooded into the bilges. The crewmen tottered sideways into the crates and the luckless midshipman, unbalanced by his leap, fell to one knee, his bodkin uselessly plying the empty air. When he tried to rise he discovered the tip of the blade at his collarbone.

'Bastard,' he breathed through gritted teeth, leaning backwards on his haunches. The point followed him, pressing deeper, breaking the skin. A bead of dark blood appeared and then scuttled into his collar. 'Devil. Murderer!'

'Rowley!' Quilter was now pushing his way through the throng. 'For God's sake, we've been bilged.' He was trying to push them away from the wall, away from the backed-up trio. What was the matter with everyone? Could they not hear the roar of the water in the bilges? The breach was only a few feet below them, the inrushing sea deafening as rolls of thunder. Any second now the water would surge into the hold and the *Bellerophon* would sink like a stone. 'Do you not hear me? The cargo must be shifted! *Now*! Before we sink!'

Still no one moved. Then the ship gave a laborious shudder and heave as the keel scraped over a sandbar and tipped violently to starboard. The crewmen slipped across the cluttered deck and tumbled like lovers into each other's arms. Quilter, too, lost his balance and, before he could right himself, felt someone fall and brush against his leg. He turned to help but saw a pair of sightless eyes goggling at him from inside a leering mask. The creature, dislodged from its coffin, had rolled to the floor. He kicked it in the belly, sending it into ever more frenzied throes. When he turned round he saw someone else – Rowley – also contorting on the deck.

It had all happened very fast. The midshipman had seized his chance a second earlier, lunging forward with a cry, the bodkin aimed at the stranger's belly. But his enemy was too quick for him. As his two companions dived backwards the man took a half step sideways and then with a few lazy flicks of his wrist inscribed another set of initials, this time in red across the midshipman's Adam's apple. Rowley coughed as if choking on a fishbone, spattering the front of his killer's coat with flecks of blood. Then he dropped the bodkin and toppled to the wet boards, where he lay twitching, pawing feebly at his throat and rolling his glazed eyes – the very twin of the hideous gargoyle thrashing and quivering only a few feet away.

Quilter was picking himself up from the floor, watching as the man stood over Rowley, cleaning the blade of his weapon and frowning at the blood on his coat as if wondering whence it had come. His companions still cowered in his shadow, while Rowley lay motionless, a vermilion puddle enlarging about his head.

'Well? Any other arguments?'

The small crowd had taken a step backwards. The man was fitting the sword carefully into his belt. The sound from below was growing louder, like the growl of a beast clambering up from the bilges, fangs flecked and eyes aglow.

'No? Then I propose that we assist the Captain.'

Quilter was standing shakily erect by now, his incredulous gaze travelling from the weltered corpse to the figure standing over it. For the first time he forgot the in-rushing water, the fact that in less than a quarter of an hour all of them would be crushed to death or drowned.

'*Assist* – ?' He was panting with exertion and rage. 'Who the devil do you—'

But no sooner had he opened his mouth than the deck teetered sideways a third time. Rowley rolled with the motion, flinging one limp arm through the air before flopping on to his back as if he too had been inspired by the malevolent sorcery of the man still straddling him. The bewildered sailors stumbled another pace backwards. Then the first of the water gurgled into the hold.

The precise nature of the dispute below decks Quilter learned only later, though he had guessed much of it already. It seemed that the men, seeing the books and specimens – these devil's relics, as Quilter was to think of them – had blamed Sir Ambrose Plessington (as the man later introduced himself) not only for the storm but also for the sudden attacks of fever. How else could these tragic fluctuations of fortune be explained except as the judgement of the Almighty on the devilish books and monsters in their midst? And how else could they be diverted, and the ship saved, except by tossing the offending crates overboard?

Sir Ambrose had taken exception to this particular line of reasoning. He claimed that the men were looting the crates, though Captain Quilter failed to understand why anyone – even someone who kept in his locker the caul of a newborn child – should wish to avail himself of those grisly treasures. But in the end he supported the claims of his passenger, ordering that the ninety-nine boxes stay in the hold. They would yet provide ballast for the ship if moved – but *quickly, quickly* – to the port side.

So for the next half an hour, as the noxious water crept steadily across the deck of the hold and collected foot-deep in the corners, a team of men laboured to shift the crates to higher ground. They were resealed after their gruesome contents had been replaced – a horrifying task, one before which even the boldest of sailors queasily shrank – and then carried to the port side, stacked on pallets, lashed tightly together and packed with shattered timbers and other bits of dunnage scavenged from the deck. Another team of men was assigned the task of cutting scuttles through the decks so that a third team with canvas buckets at the ready could begin the job of bailing. But all of these frantic efforts were for naught, Quilter realised soon after he and the other half of the crew had scrambled up the ladders to the fo'c'sle, for the *Bellerophon* was listing as badly as ever. It was only a matter of time, a few minutes at most, before she went down, cargo and all.

The rain had ceased at last, but the northeaster was blowing as hard as ever. Humpbacked waves were rushing at the ship with their white scythes of foam. Pinchbeck and a handful of men were gathered on the fo'c'sle deck, attempting to stanch a leak in the starboard bow. Two of the hands were plunging a canvas-wrapped basket into the water near the hole, using a long pole, hoping to get the basket close enough to the breach for the rope-yarns inside the basket to be shaken loose and drawn inside to plug the leak. Pinchbeck had already tried, without success, to pass a sail under the bows of the ship. Now the canvas was floating helplessly away from the port quarter, an enormous squid billowing its tentacles and returning to its subterranean lair. Three men had been sent to the sail-locker for another, but Quilter could see how hopeless all of it was. He could make out, a short distance away on the leeward side, an enormous sandbar, the Margate Hook, half exposed by the ebbing tide. There was no hope now, he realised. The ship would break apart on the reef by the time the men returned.

'Not nearly enough water, Captain,' the bo'sun screamed over the howls of the wind as the basket was thrust below the water for the tenth time. 'Low tide! Barely four fathoms! We've run aground! Couldn't get the sail to pass under her! Too much wind!' He paused to point to where the men, their hands red and stiff in the cold, were grappling with the basket. 'The basket neither!'

'Keep trying!'

Quilter held his breath as the basket disappeared from view with a muffled splash. The *Bellerophon* had tipped further sideways by now; her foremast, bent awry at the top, was almost touching the water. It was impossible to stand on the mountainous slope of the slick fo'c'sle deck without clutching something for support. Already the first waves had begun flooding over the starboard gunwale. The shore wavered and beckoned on the port side, dangerously close. Quilter could hear the call of gulls and thought he smelled the scent of pastureland. So was this where death would claim them, no more than a musket-shot from shore? Within sight of trees and in view of flocks of sheep calmly chewing their cuds? A few seconds later the basket bobbed uselessly to the surface to a chorus of curses.

'There's no hope, Captain!' Pinchbeck had straightened and was wiping at his brow with a bloodied handkerchief. 'I say we abandon ship.'

But Quilter had turned away and was watching with dazed detachment the clouds piling up in the east and beginning their fleet journeys inland. His fingers and cheeks were frozen, his feet now half submerged in water. The Margate Hook was even closer now, the beacon winking palely in its ancient timber lighthouse. In a minute at most they would be driven by the waves on to the reef.

'I say we abandon ship!' Pinchbeck repeated, turning to the men on the fo'c'sle when Quilter made no reply. 'Prepare the longboats!'

'There's no time,' muttered Quilter to himself as a couple of hands started aft towards the boats suspended in their hammocks. But before they could take a half-dozen steps they were interrupted by a cry from the waist.

'Captain!' One of the sailors, a topman, was gripping the foremast with one hand and pointing astern with the other. 'Look! A ship! There!'

Quilter squinted into the wind. The vessel had appeared on the starboard quarter, her bowsprit and foremasts missing, the rest of her poles bare or else wrapped in shreds of canvas. She was hopelessly adrift, with her hull riding low in the water and one of her yards pivoting like the sails of a windmill. When Quilter narrowed his eyes he was able to make out a few men on her quarterdeck, another group struggling to lower one of the longboats into the sea leaping about her waist. Even from this distance he could read the name inscribed on her bow. The *Star of Lübeck*. A second later he saw that the three men on the quarterdeck were dressed in black. Through the mist they looked no more than shadows.

But then the view was lost, for at that moment the hull of the *Bellerophon* struck the submerged edge of the Margate Hook and began breaking apart. She slid along the reef for half the length of her keel, timbers screaming and masts toppling before she reached a shuddering halt with her stem and bowsprit nosing downwards into the exposed shingle. Then she tipped agonisingly to starboard with the bowsprit snapping and the hull rupturing as its planks bowed and cracked and their treenails popped free like corks. Roiling water crashed across the splintering decks a few seconds later, and Captain Quilter and his crew were flung into the grey jaws of the sea.

Chapter Eleven

The Navy Office was casting an enormous shadow across St Olave's when I returned to Seething Lane. The building appeared even larger in daylight, a massive structure that with its jettied storeys and tarred timbers looked like a huge frigate that had run aground in the middle of London. This impression was strengthened when I slipped past the porter's lodge and stepped through the heavy oak doors that had been unbattened a moment earlier. Dozens of clerks and messenger boys scurried about the wooden floor like deckhands making ready for a storm, and through the open door of a large office I glimpsed two or three captains conferring over a map whose corners were pinned to a table by anchor-shaped paperweights. The sight of their handsome faces raddled by tropical suns reminded me that, while I stayed home in my shop, other men were sailing to the ends of the earth, exploring new continents and navigating mysterious rivers. I felt hopelessly out of place.

Two days had passed since my shop was sacked. By the middle of the previous afternoon Nonsuch Books had been restored to normal, or nearly so. There is no disaster so great, in my experience, that it cannot be mended with a folding-stick, a gimlet and a sewing-frame. For hours on end the shop had gonged and echoed with the reports of frantic and unremitting industry. A joiner repaired the green door and restored it to its hinges, while a locksmith replaced the lock with an even stronger one. The joiner also measured and hung five new walnut shelves, which I quickly lined with books. Monk and I had collected the remainder of them from the floor and then set about refurbishing the most damaged ones. I estimated that we would be ready for business in a day or two at most.

This morning I left the shop in Monk's care and returned to Seething Lane – not to creep into St Olave's churchyard but to make enquiries at the Navy Office, which seemed as likely a place as any to investigate Sir Ambrose's voyage to the Empire of Guiana. I had decided that I might learn more about my mysterious antagonists – perhaps even about Henry Monboddo – if I knew more about Sir Ambrose. I was hoping the log book for the *Philip Sidney* might still exist, or perhaps its collection of sea-cards or some other memorabilia. I also thought it might be possible to lay my hands on a copy of the Lord High Chancellor's report on Raleigh's disastrous expedition of 1617–18.

But after two hours at the Navy Office I found myself none the wiser. I was kept waiting on a bench as the bells of St Olave's struck nine o'clock, then ten. The captains came and went with the rolled-up maps tucked under their brocaded arms. The clerks squeaked across the floorboards or bent over their desks, quills waggling briskly. It was eleven o'clock by the time I was summoned forward, only to find myself traipsing from one cramped cubby-hole to another. Not one of the clerks claimed to have heard of a captain named Sir Ambrose Plessington; nor could they think where either his ship's log or the Chancellor's report might be found. One of these manikins suggested the office's old quarters in Mincing Lane, while another plumped for the Tower, which he claimed housed some of the Chancery records. A third explained that the Navy Office was in a state of upheaval because Cromwell's old commissioners had been sacked and the new ones appointed by the King were unlikely to locate forty-year-old records, since they had not yet learned how to find their desks without getting lost.

Noon had arrived by the time I left the Navy Office, resolved that it was time to search elsewhere for Sir Ambrose. I threaded my way through the crowds to Tower Wharf, where dozens of lighters and pinnaces were gathered beside the quays like herds of patient livestock. For ten minutes I tramped up and down the wharf, bumping into dockers with their booming casks and cursing under my breath, before I finally found an empty scull and clambered inside.

On the incoming tide it took almost thirty minutes to reach Wapping. The hamlet stood a mile downstream from Tower Wharf and consisted of little more than a row or two of stilted houses that overhung the banks of the Lower Pool. From my turret-room I could sometimes see its timber-yard and the steeple of the church, but never had I set foot there. This morning, however, I hoped to find an old man named Henry Biddulph, who had lived in Wapping for the best part of seventy years. He had been Clerk of the Acts for the Navy until 1642, at which point most of the ships in the fleet had defected to Cromwell, and Biddulph, faithful to King Charles, had lost his job. Since then he had occupied himself by composing a history of the Navy from the time of Henry VIII – a gargantuan work that after eighteen years and three volumes had failed to reach the Spanish Armada of 1588. It had also failed to sell many copies, though I dutifully stocked all three volumes, since over the years Biddulph had become one of my best customers. He visited Nonsuch House several times a month, and I tracked down dozens of books for him. He knew as much about ships, I suspected, as I knew about books, and I was now hoping that he might give me some information in return.

'Captain' Biddulph (as he was known to his neighbours) appeared to be a man of mark in Wapping, though the house to which I was directed from the hamlet's lone tavern was a humble affair, a tiny timber cottage with a prolapsed roof and an overgrown garden. Two windows at the front overlooked the river, two at the rear a timber-yard from which there arose a terrific clamour of hammers and saws. But the noise failed to disturb Biddulph, who was at work on volume number four when I tapped at his door with the tip of my thorn-stick. He recognised me at once and I was quickly invited inside.

I had always liked Biddulph. He was a spry old man with merry blue eyes and a monkish fringe of white hair that stood erect over his ears like the plumicorns of an owl. And as I surveyed the clutter of his study I was pleased to see that he was a man after my own heart. All of his money appeared to have been spent on either books or shelves to hold them. Indeed, most of the volumes in their morocco bindings looked better attired than their owner, who was wearing a pair of scuffed breeches and a tattered leather jerkin. Having seen him only in Nonsuch House, in my own environs, it was strange to meet him on different ground, here in his own little nest with its yellowed engravings of ships pinned to the wall. As I watched a ginger tomcat crawl through the window and on to his lap I reflected with a pinch of sorrow how poorly I knew even my most faithful customers.

After he served us a dinner of spitchcocked eels cooked on a gridiron, we retreated to his study, where he urged me to sample a new beverage called 'rumbullion', or 'rum' for short. It was a hellish fluid that seemed to scald the gullet and cloud the brain.

'Twice as strong as brandy,' he chuckled merrily, noting my grimace. 'Sailors in the West Indies call it "Kill-Devil". It's distilled from molasses. A captain I know smuggles the odd keg back from Jamaica for me. He drops it in Wapping before his ship docks at the Legal Quays.' He chuckled again, but then his blue gaze turned serious and enquiring. 'But you have not come all the way to Wapping to drink rum, Mr Inchbold.'

'No, indeed,' I murmured, trying to catch a breath that the drink had pummelled from my chest. 'No, Mr Biddulph, I've come to enquire about a ship.'

'A ship?' He seemed surprised. 'Well, well. And which one might that be?'

At first neither the *Philip Sidney* nor her captain meant anything to Biddulph. But as I explained why I believed that the ship had sailed on Raleigh's final voyage, he proceeded to squint at the plumtree timbers overhead and chant softly under his breath, 'Plessington, Plessington,' as if the name were some sort of charm. A moment later he clapped his hands together, startling the ginger tom.

'Yes, yes, yes – now I remember. Of course, of course. Captain Plessington! How could I forget?' He had lodged a quid of tobacco in his cheek and now paused to void a stream of juice into a pot between his feet. 'It's just that these days I live in another century,' he said, pointing at his tiny work-table, on which I glimpsed among the pile of volumes a copy of Fazeby's *True Report of the Destruction of the Invincible Armada*. So the decisive events of 1588, I realised, had at long last been reached. 'I spend so much of my time in the reign of Queen Bess that sometimes my tired old brain gets fuddled. But Captain Plessington – yes, yes, I remember his ship.' He was nodding his head vigorously. 'Indeed I do, Mr Inchbold. Very well.' But all at once he ceased his nodding, and his merry blue eyes narrowed once more. 'What is it you wish to know about her?'

'Anything you might tell me,' I said with a shrug. 'I believe Plessington was granted a charter to build her in 1616. I'm curious about her voyage, if in fact it ever took place.'

'Oh, it took place, Mr Inchbold.' Biddulph was nodding again as he stroked the cat, which had draped itself across his knees. 'And you're in luck, for I can tell you about the charter. That and much more, if you so wish. You see, I was in the Navy Office at the time, assistant to the Clerk of the Acts, so I saw all of the various contracts and bill-books for the *Philip Sidney*.' He cocked a white eyebrow at me. 'And a strange tale they told, Mr Inchbold.'

For a moment the woodpeckering in the timber-yard seemed to fade, and I heard the waves slopping at the supports of the house. I tried to sound casual as I fumbled with my cup. 'What strange tale might that be?'

'Well, the entire expedition was a strange one, Mr Inchbold. As I have no doubt you're aware. But bear with me, please . . .' He was squinting at the timber-beams again and slowly working the cud in his bulging cheek. 'Old men must take things one step at a time. It's so easy for an old brain to confuse one thing with another.'

'By all means, Mr Biddulph.' I could feel a pulse beating in my throat now, slowly and thickly. I reclined in the chair and tried another scorching sip of rumbullion.

But Biddulph's old brain was sharp as ever, and details were not long in coming. 'The charter was granted, so far as I remember, in the summer of 1616,' he explained after a short rumination, still studying the cracked beams. 'Just after Raleigh was released from the Tower. Construction on the ship began soon afterwards. She was built at the dockyard at Woolwich, where all of our finest warships have been built. The *Harry Grace à Dieu* was built there for Henry VIII, and the *Royal Sovereign* for the late King Charles. God rest his soul,' he added after a short pause.

'And the *Philip Sidney?*' I prompted when another reflective silence threatened to grow between us.

'Ah, yes. The *Philip Sidney*. She was built by the master-shipwright, Phineas Pett. Quite a task, even for a man of Pett's abilities. Six hundred tons burden with better than a hundred guns on her decks. She was even bigger than the *Destiny*, which was also built at Woolwich. It was a good eight months from the day the team of horses dragged her keel timbers into place until the night when she lurched down the greased slipways and on to a spring tide. I was at the dockyards that evening. Prince Charles himself performed the honours with a goblet of wine. Scarcely more than a boy at the time. *"God bless her and all who sail in her . . ."* Well, that's a wheeze, is it not,' he muttered darkly, 'considering all that happened. I remember thinking that it was a wonder she was ever ready to sail in the first place.'

'Because of her size?'

'Not only that. You see, none of us in the Navy Office expected she would ever be finished. The whole Raleigh expedition looked like folly from the start. Sir Walter was a braggart, everyone knew that. First there was the business of founding colonies in the swamps of Virginia. Then he spent a baker's dozen years in the Tower hatching his crack-brained schemes about discovering some mine in the middle of the Guianan jungle. Sheer folly, I say. After all, the white spar from the *Lion's Whelp* tested at Goldsmiths' Hall by the Comptroller of the Mint—'

'Excuse me,' I interrupted. 'The *Lion's Whelp* . . . ?' The name sounded familiar.

He nodded at one of the engraved ships pinned to the wall above his desk. 'Raleigh's ship on his first voyage to Guiana.'

'Ah . . . yes.' I remembered Raleigh's *Discoverie of the large*, *rich, and beautifull Empire of Guiana*, a slim volume that I stocked on my shelves, and one I had seen on Alethea's list of books missing from Pontifex Hall. One that had gone missing along with *The Labyrinth of the World*. 'Of course.'

'As I say, the white spar brought back from Guiana in 1595 showed as little as twenty ounces of gold per ton of ore. A risible amount, one hardly enough to make digging a mine in England worthwhile, let alone one thousands of miles away in the middle of the jungle. Then there was also the fact that the waters of the Orinoco had never been reliably mapped, not even by the Spaniards, even though the best engineers from the School of Navigation and Cartography in Seville had been tramping through the Guianan forests for decades. As far as the gold mines went, the Spaniards had only the word of a few tortured savages to rely upon, and everyone knows that a victim always tells his torturer whatever fantasies he wishes to hear.' He paused to take another recourse to the spittoon. 'Worst of all, though, was the Spanish Ambassador.'

'Gondomar,' I murmured.

'Precisely. Everyone knew how King James was under his influence. Gondomar ruled over him even more than did Buckingham – plain Sir George Villiers he was in those days, of course. And Gondomar was said to be most unhappy with Raleigh's charter. You see, he considered Raleigh nothing more than a privateer, like Drake. And soon there were rumours that Villiers was no longer so enthusiastic about the venture either. So it was that for eight months we expected to see Pett's carpenters throw down their tools, or else to wake up one morning to find that the *Sidney* had burnt to cinders on her keel blocks.'

A wind was stirring through the window, bringing with it a stink of brackish tide. I watched a herring-gull swoop past the raised sash, then a rocking mast from a pinnace tacking slowly upstream. Biddulph had fallen silent and the hammers in the timber-yard seemed louder than ever.

'But neither of those things happened,' I prompted him. 'The ship sailed.'

'Indeed she did.' Biddulph shifted the bulge of tobacco to the other cheek and shrugged. 'Greed prevailed over both fear and common sense, as it usually does. The money for fitting out the ship and paying her crew had already been raised through investors in the Royal Exchange, so fear and common sense would have made bankrupts of half of London. Ergo, in June of the year 1617 the *Sidney* sailed from London to join the rest of the fleet at Plymouth. I watched that too. I saw her cast off her anchors and ride down the Thames from Woolwich. I can still see the name painted in gilt on her escutcheon,' he said reflectively, then added: 'Peculiar name for a ship, is it not? That of a poet.'

'Yes,' I replied. 'Peculiar indeed.' It had already occurred to me that there might be a connection between the ship and one of the books of Hermetic philosophy I had dusted off a few days earlier, Giordano Bruno's *Spaccio della bestia trionfante*, an esoteric work that glorifies the religion of the ancient Egyptians. Bruno had dedicated his treatise to Sir Philip Sidney, who was not only a poet and courtier, but also a soldier who had died while fighting the Spaniards in the Low Countries.

'As I say, I watched her sail away on her maiden voyage,' Biddulph was continuing. 'But I knew it would be the last time I'd see her. I knew even then that the *Sidney* would never return to London.'

'Because of Gondomar?' I thought I knew this part of the story. As Raleigh left Plymouth a fleet of Spanish warships was rumoured to be setting sail from La Coruña. 'There were stories that the Spaniards aimed to intercept the fleet.'

'No, there was more than that.' He shifted about in his little chair, from which horsehair stuffing was burgeoning. 'At that time I was in a position to see the contract-books for the ship. I read everything to do not only with the fitting out and provisioning of the *Sidney*, but with the other ships as well. In those days I was responsible for preparing all contracts and letters to and from the Navy for signature and despatch. These documents had to do mainly with the purchase of stores and timber, with cordage and sails and so forth. A fleet of ships is like a herd of great ravening beasts, you understand. They have to be watered and provisioned, then scrubbed and groomed like prize racehorses and afterwards fitted out in canvas like fine ladies at their milliner's or dressmaker's. I also looked after all of the plans and models made by the shipwrights,' he finished, 'along with the contracts for their services.'

'And what was it that you learned from the contracts for the *Philip Sidney*?'

His face remained expressionless. 'I learned that her captain had no intention of voyaging up the waters of the Orinoco. You see, Mr Inchbold, Captain Plessington's ship was different from the others in the fleet.'

I felt myself swallow. The rumbullion and the noise of the hammers were giving me a terrible headache. 'Different in what way?'

'The *Sidney* was a first-rate,' he explained. 'That meant she could carry a hundred guns or more. The *Destiny* was fitted with only thirty-six. So with such heavy cannon the *Sidney* needed a deep keel, of course, like most of our first-rates. That's why our warships are superior to those of the Dutch,' he added in a lower tone, as if fearful that a Dutch spy might be loitering beneath his crumbling eaves. 'That's why Cromwell was able to defeat the Dutch so soundly in '54. Their warships need shallow draughts so they can navigate their own coastal waters, and because they need shallow draughts they can't carry the same heavy cannon that we can. Ergo, we have much more firepower. With a couple of 32-pounders one of our first-rates can scatter their fleets like chaff. The Spaniards and their frigates, however . . . well, that's another matter entirely,' he added ruefully.

'But the *Philip Sidney*,' I prompted him again: 'her keel was deep?'

'Oh, indeed it was. She was a wonderful ship for slaughtering Dutchmen but a poor one for exploring rivers in Guiana. With so deep a draught she could never have navigated the waters of the Orinoco. You see, Mr Inchbold, that was another strange thing about the voyage. I asked myself why Raleigh's fleet was due to arrive in Guiana in December or January, a time when navigation of the river is most difficult. To sail inland on the

Orinoco you need a boat that draws only five or six feet of water, and in places you find that only on a flowing tide, even near the estuary. Even in the wet season. So in the month of January . . .'

'Yes,' I nodded, 'the dry season.' I tried to make sense of this information. 'But what if the guns were merely for protection? And what if the *Philip Sidney* was never intended to ascend the river in the first place? What if she was only meant to anchor off the coast? Sir Ambrose could easily have navigated the Orinoco in a shallop or another smaller boat.'

' 'True enough.' He shrugged his shoulders and then paused to void another jet of tobacco juice with the velocity of a Greenland whale spouting water. 'And his ship did indeed have a shallop lashed to her stern. But there were other things she did not have. You see, besides their casks of water and brined pork, the other ships were laden with all manner of digging and essaying equipment. Pickaxes, spades, barrows and trench-carts, quicksilver. The bills and contracts piled up in my office. Added to them were contracts for the soldiers and other crewmen, most of whom, it must be said, were villains who stank of either gaol or the bawdy-house, because the best seamen of London and Plymouth spurned the mission as folly.'

'But the *Philip Sidney*?'

Well, that was the oddest thing. There was, Biddulph explained, no essaying equipment on board the *Philip Sidney*, no mining or digging implements – nothing of the sort. Not that had been recorded at the Navy Office anyway. No contracts that had been sealed and stamped by the Assistant Clerk of the Acts. Only soldiers and guns, all arranged in what had seemed to the young Biddulph like the utmost secrecy. Also other items, sheaves of paper with tables and designs – though he could not say what for precisely. He claimed to have no expertise in such matters. But all manner of complicated drawings and tables of mathematical calculations were involved in the construction and rigging of the *Philip Sidney*. A sign of those times, he claimed. Somewhere in the Navy Office was a book called *Secret Inventions, Profitable and Necessary in These*

Days for a Defence of this Island, and withstanding of Strangers, Enemies of God's Truth and Religion. Its author, he explained, was a Scotsman named John Napier.

'You're not likely to find that volume on your shelves or anywhere else, for that matter, Mr Inchbold. It's a confidential document. Very few copies were ever printed.'

'John Napier? I fear you've lost me. Was he not a mathematician?'

So he was, Biddulph admitted. A man of many parts, Napier was the first mathematician to make use of the decimal point, and in 1614 he made his greatest invention of all: logarithms. In those days, Biddulph explained, whole new worlds were opening up, not just in America and the South Seas, but in mathematics and astronomy as well. Men like Galileo and Kepler explored the heavens just as Magellan and Drake once explored the oceans. Through his telescope Galileo first saw the moons of Jupiter in 1610. By 1612 Kepler had counted 1,001 stars, over 200 more than Tycho Brahe. A few years earlier Kepler, a staunch Protestant, had interrupted his stargazing to calculate for Sir Walter Raleigh the most efficient method of stacking cannon-balls on a gundeck. This new science, Biddulph explained, went hand in glove with exploration and wars over both gold and religion. Mathematicians and astronomers were at the service of kings and emperors. In Scotland, fearful of another Spanish Armada, of a Catholic invasion of the island, Napier had composed complex plans for his 'secret inventions', one of which was a gigantic mirror that would use the heat of the sun to burn enemy ships in the Channel. His logarithms were soon employed as an aid to navigation by Edward Wright, a scholar at Cambridge, the author of *Certaine Errors in Navigation detected and corrected*.

'War had become a sophisticated art,' Biddulph explained, 'waged through mysterious numbers and complex geometries. As was navigation. Francis Bacon was designing plans for better and larger merchantmen – vessels of 1,100 tons, with keels 115 feet in length and mainsails 75 feet in width. He was also experimenting with new methods of ordering and disposing tiers of sails for quicker trips across the ocean. There were even stories that Bacon himself designed the *Sidney*, which might have been the case for all I know. Like most people in those days, he grovelled before Villiers. If Villiers wanted a ship, Bacon would certainly have designed one. And he sold Villiers his house in the Strand, York House, when Villiers took a fancy to it. It's where Villiers proposed to keep all of the books and paintings he had begun collecting.'

'So what are you saying?' I managed to interject. 'That the *Philip Sidney* was armed with . . . I don't know . . . with one of Napier's giant mirrors?'

I was beginning to wonder if Biddulph's mind was not perhaps slipping after all. But then I remembered that Edward Wright's *Certaine Errors in Navigation* had also been on the list of books missing from Pontifex Hall, one of the volumes taken from the library along with *The Labyrinth of the World*.

'Of course not,' he replied evenly. 'I am merely explaining how the *Philip Sidney* appeared to have been equipped for tasks other than prospecting for gold along the Orinoco.'

'Which meant . . . ?'

'Which meant nothing much in itself, perhaps. As you say, there were plenty of dangers to be found on the high seas. It would have been folly not to carry as many cannons as possible. But to understand the true purpose of the *Sidney*'s voyage, you must understand how things stood in those days. I mean how things stood in both the Navy Office and the country at large.'

'Her true purpose?'

Biddulph paused. His eyes had closed and for a moment I thought he might have fallen asleep. I could feel myself begin to sweat and wheeze in the close little room. I was about to ask again, but his eyes suddenly opened and with a laborious grunt he pushed himself to his feet. The sleepy cat in the crook of his arm was blinking in the jaundiced beam of sunlight that had drifted round to the window.

'Yes. Her true purpose. But shall we take a short walk, Mr Inchbold?' He was scratching the cat's ears and peering down at me, squinting in the pillar of light. 'I shall tell you all about it as we stroll. A perambulation, you see, sometimes refreshes a tired old brain.'

The tide had turned by the time we left the cottage, and most of the traffic in the Lower Pool was now bound for points downstream. Oars hissed and slapped in the water, canvas soughed in the breeze. We walked along the wharf in the direction of Shadwell, the sun warm on our shoulders. I had to struggle with my thorn-stick to keep up with Biddulph, who was spry as a goose. He slackened his pace only to pluck primroses from the water's edge, point out the odd landmark, or else to perform gallantries for the ladies of Wapping as they lumbered home from Smithfield Market with their suppers peeping from straw baskets. We walked as far as the Limehouse Stairs, almost a full mile. Only when we were returning to the cottage, squinting into the bright sun, did he resume his story.

The story, as Biddulph told it, seemed like one of the Revenge Plays so popular in the theatres of the time, something by John Webster or Thomas Kyd. There were court intrigues, shifting alliances, plots and counterplots, blood feuds, bribes both sexual and financial, even a poisoning – all performed with grisly relish by a cast of scheming bishops, sycophantic courtiers, Spanish spies and informers, corrupt officials, assassins, and a divorced countess with a spotted reputation.

Yes, I thought as we picked our way past the salt-glazed webs of fishermen's nets spread in the sun to dry: it would have made excellent theatre. On the one side was the War Party, led by the Archbishop of Canterbury, a staunch Calvinist spoiling for a war with the hated Spaniards. On the other was the Spanish Party, led by the aristocratic Howards, a family of wealthy crypto-Catholics who held sway over the King by means of their creature, a smooth-cheeked young Scotsman named Robert Carr, who had been created Earl of Somerset. Somerset was a spy for the Spaniards, turning over to Gondomar all correspondence between King James and his ambassadors. But in 1615 he had been disgraced when his new bride, a Howard, was accused of poisoning Sir Thomas Overbury, who opposed the marriage of the favourite to a woman whose infamy was remarkable even for those days. At a stroke both Gondomar and the Howards found themselves deprived of influence at court.

And it was at this point that a new character capered on to the stage, Sir George Villiers, another smooth-cheeked young man, who quickly replaced the imprisoned Somerset in the lecherous old King's affections. Villiers had been fostered and promoted by Archbishop Abbott, an inveterate enemy of the Howards. Among his numerous schemes the Archbishop planned to use Villiers to replace the Earl of Nottingham – yet another Howard – as Lord High Admiral. Once the hero of '88, Nottingham was by then a doddering octogenarian, the dupe of both his unscrupulous relatives and corrupt underlings in the Navy Office, to say nothing of the fact that he still received a handsome pension from the King of Spain.

'A new regime would begin with Villiers in the Navy Office,' Biddulph explained. 'No longer would our ships be the tools of the Howards and the Spanish Party. No longer would the Navy Office be a nest of thieves and informers, rotten with corruption from top to bottom. It would have a purpose once more. New and better ships would be built, and the Navy could begin to act as it had acted in the days of King Henry.'

But the situation was urgent, because at this point more characters began appearing on stage, couriers and messengers from all across Europe. All arrived at Lambeth Palace with enciphered papers and smuggled documents that brought dire news for the War Party. Not only had a Catholic League been formed in Germany to counteract the Protestant Union, but the Union itself was falling apart. It looked to the Abbott–Pembroke faction more and more as if the truce between the Dutch and Spaniards was about to be shattered by cannon-fire, as if new wars in the Low Countries were to be fought on the scarred old battlefields where Sidney gave his life thirty years earlier – wars for which England was neither ready nor, under James and the Spanish Party, willing. Worst of all, though, was a new report from Prague, delivered by a courier in red-and-gold De Quester livery, describing how a Habsburg, Ferdinand of Styria, was soon to be elected Holy Roman Emperor with the blessing of his cousin and brother-in-law, the King of Spain. Not only would Ferdinand use Spanish troops to restore Catholic magistracy anywhere in the Empire he might see fit, he would also revoke the Letter of Majesty granted by Rudolf II to the Protestants of Bohemia.

'So to men like Abbott and Pembroke, and also to Villiers, the purpose was clear. Protestantism was wavering as never before, Mr Inchbold, not only in Europe but in England as well. King James had lost the support of the Puritans, who no longer believed that his reign would bring about a true reformation of the Church. There was a real danger of a schism, of the Church of England breaking apart or collapsing from within – and of Rome seizing the moment of chaos to regain its lost ground. Looking back, I believe that the publication in 1611 of the Authorised Version of the Holy Bible was intended to impose conformity on English congregations, but of course it achieved the opposite effect, because suddenly every coney-cutter and wool-comber in England was convinced that he could preach the word of God. Protestantism began breaking apart, parish by parish, into numerous sects and separatist movements. So what was needed in 1617 was some masterstroke, a triumph, a daring strike at the heart of Spain's empire. Something that would unify the Protestants in their struggle against the twin powers of Rome and Madrid.'

I was stumbling along at his shoulder, attempting to follow these swirling currents and cross-currents as they flowed and receded, as they swept the *Philip Sidney* down the Thames to her secret destiny halfway round the world, among dense jungles and uncharted rivers, thousands of miles from competing factions and squabbling sectaries of England. I tripped on something, the fluke of a rusty anchor, and, righting myself, looked up to see London Bridge far in the distance, spread across the river behind the chimney stacks of Shadwell.

'The treasure fleet,' I whispered after a second, almost to myself.

'Exactly,' replied Biddulph. He had stopped walking and was gazing across the river towards Rotherhithe. 'Raleigh's ships were going in search of silver, not gold. That's why they were due to arrive in Tierra Firme in the dry season.

Not so they could sail up the treacherous Orinoco in search of a gold mine that probably never existed in the first place, but to attack the annual silver fleet that was due to sail from Guayaquil to Seville. The whole fleet was probably worth as much as ten or twelve million pesos. Quite a sum – one that would pay for an army of mercenaries for the Palatinate or the Netherlands, or wherever else they might be needed.'

We had begun walking again, more slowly now, our hat brims pulled low against the sun. I tried to comprehend everything he now began telling me: that Raleigh's fleet was funded by desperate German princes poised on the brink of war, by Prince Maurice of Nassau, by English merchants hoping to expand their trade in Spanish America, as well as by assorted Calvinists in both England and Holland, all dreaming of a war of religion with the Spaniards, of driving Catholics from England, the Low Countries and the Empire in the same way that King Philip had driven hundreds of thousands of Moriscos from Spain only two or three years earlier.

'The capture of the fleet – or even its sinking – would also have sent ripples to every part of the Empire, every corner of the Catholic world. No Spanish fleet had been touched since the capture of the *Madre de Dios* in 1592. Even Drake' – he had turned round and was gesturing into the distance, across the river, with his stick, to where the *Golden Hind* sat in her drydock at Deptford – 'even Drake had failed in his attempt to capture it in '96.'

Such was the bold plan, then. Led by the *Philip Sidney*, the fleet was to violate Raleigh's charter in the most spectacular fashion by attacking the annual convoy as it sailed from Nombre de Dios. The War Party believed that James would refuse to invoke the death clause in Raleigh's charter, not merely because Villiers and his faction would control the Navy Office as well as the court, nor even because Gondomar's influence would be waning as a result. The clause would not be invoked for the simple reason that – according to another clause in the charter – the greedy old King, the greatest spendthrift in Europe, was due to receive for his personal enjoyment one-fifth of whatever Raleigh might bring back in the holds of his ships: one-fifth of the treasures from the wealthiest convoy on earth.

But things went awry even before the fleet left Plymouth. Biddulph blamed the disaster not on the elements, not on ill fortune or poor planning, but on the Spanish spies and informers who infested Whitehall Palace and the Navy Office. It was known from documents smuggled out of Madrid that one of Gondomar's informers held an important post in the Navy Office, someone codenamed 'El Cid', or 'The Lord', which led Biddulph to believe that it was old Nottingham himself. So perhaps the silver fleet had been alerted to the danger well in advance. Perhaps it remained in Peru, in the harbour at Guayaquil. Or it could have sailed south, round Cape Horn, whose windy straits the Spaniards still controlled despite the recent depredations of the Dutch. Whatever the case, in the end Raleigh's fleet sailed towards the Orinoco instead of the promised riches of Nombre de Dios.

At this point in the voyage Biddulph was seeing Spanish agents and plotters everywhere. The so-called unprovoked attack on San Tomás by Raleigh's men was actually, he claimed, a clever plot aimed at discrediting the voyage in the eyes of King James, a well-planned conspiracy on the part of Gondomar's *agents provocateurs*, some of them on board Raleigh's ships, others stationed in San Tomás itself. Far from being fearful of an attack on a Spanish settlement in Guiana, Gondomar and the Spanish Party welcomed it, indeed provoked it. There was little for Raleigh to gain in Guiana and everything for him to lose, not least his head. Even more important, Villiers, Abbott and the whole War Party itself would be disgraced by the episode, while the Howards, Gondomar's *bien intencionados*, would once more be in the command of both the Navy Office and the King of England.

'But what became of the *Philip Sidney* after the fleet broke up?' I asked, wondering again how much of Biddulph's version – this tale of plots and counterplots – I should let myself believe. 'Captain Plessington wasn't in the party that raided San Tomás. Not that I've been able to discover.'

'And I doubt you will ever discover what Captain Plessington did,' Biddulph replied. 'Not even Bacon's inquiry could sort through all of the details. Nor, I believe, was it intended to,' he added with a sombre chuckle. 'The official story, of course, is that after the raid on San Tomás the fleet dispersed. It's known that Raleigh tried to talk his captains into attacking the Mexican treasure fleet, the one from New Spain that would be sailing from Veracruz. But in the end most of the ships followed the *Destiny* to Newfoundland, where they took on board cargoes of fish and then returned to England. Can you imagine the looks on the faces of the investors?' Biddulph was shaking his white plumicorns. 'Newfoundland cod instead of Peruvian silver! Imagine the indignation of the dukes and princes of Germany and Holland when they learned how their religion was to be preserved by nothing more than a few crates of salted fish!'

So tragedy mixed with farce as the princes of Europe slid towards the precipice. As the months passed, more and more couriers arrived at Lambeth Palace and the Navy Office. Vienna had been besieged by the Transylvanians; Transylvania had been invaded by the Poles; the Poles had been attacked by the Turks – a deadly cycle of blows and counterblows, a return of evil for evil. Europe had become a fanged beast catching hold of its own tail. Negotiations were repudiated, treaties went unratified. In Prague, two Catholic delegates to a convention of the Bohemian Estates were hurled from a window of the castle but survived because they landed in a dunghill. Their survival was taken by *dévots* across Europe as a sign from God. Other armies began buckling on their swords. Three comets appeared in the sky and astrologers took them as irrefutable proof that the world was about to end.

'Which was not entirely wrong, was it?' Biddulph gloomily observed. 'Because there then followed thirty years of the worst wars the world has ever known.'

For a moment we walked beside the river in silence. I was still trying to understand it all, to discover a coherent pattern among these bizarre activities, these strange, half-hidden events with their mysterious players – ones that, so far as I could see, bore little relation to what Alethea had told me about Henry Monboddo and *The Labyrinth of the World*.

Biddulph had now begun describing how, soon, another piece of news was delivered to the Navy Office by a panting courier. This had been in the late autumn of the year 1618, a short time after the comets appeared and Raleigh went to the scaffold specially built for him in Westminster Palace Yard. The report claimed that a Spanish galleon, the *Sacra Familia*, part of the Mexican fleet, had gone down with all hands near the Spanish port of Santiago de Cuba. That she sank was a fact, though the circumstances surrounding the affair were more mysterious. It was whispered in the Navy Office that the *Sacra Familia* had been boarded and then sunk by soldiers from the *Philip Sidney*. For the *Sidney* had not returned to London. It appeared that, like a few of the other ships in the fleet, she was prowling the Spanish Indies, as the defeated Drake had done in '96. But details were almost impossible to find, even in the Navy Office. Fact and fable were flung hopelessly together.

Soon another report arrived that the *Philip Sidney* had sunk in the Spanish Indies, followed swiftly by yet another claiming that the *Philip Sidney* had captured the *Sacra Familia*, then a third that the *Sacra Familia* had merely sunk in a violent storm. But one rumour in particular enjoyed a long career – long enough for it to pass from rumour into the more august realms of myth. It thrived for many years in the taverns of Tower Hill and Rotherhithe, or wherever mariners gathered. Like other of the rumours, it claimed that the *Philip Sidney* had chased the galleon and then, after firing her broadside guns, watched her sink with all hands. Yet this had been a galleon like no other.

'I know the rumour,' Biddulph said, 'because I must have heard it a dozen times. It concerns certain passengers on board the *Sacra Familia*. Stowaways, you might say. Ones that survived her wreck by clinging to the shards of her hull or else swimming ashore.'

'Who were they?' I was listening intently now. 'Spanish sailors?'

He shook his head. 'No, not Spanish sailors. Not sailors of

any sort.' He chuckled to himself for a second before spurting a stream of tobacco juice into the grass. We had almost reached Wapping, and ahead of us a number of watermen were sunning themselves on the New Crane Stairs. 'Rats. That's what the crewmen of the *Sidney* watched swim ashore while the *Sacra Familia* sank. Hundreds of rats. The waters churned with them, and some even made their way aboard the *Sidney*. Oh, I know, what ship is not infested with rats? But these were not just any kind of rat, you must understand. None of the mariners had ever seen their like. They were twice the size of the rats on board the *Philip Sidney*. Great burly creatures, greyish-red in colour, with short legs and tails.' He paused for a second, chops twitching with an excited smile. 'In sum, Mr Inchbold, these creatures were nothing other than bamboo rats.'

I had never heard of such things. 'I thought a rat was a rat.'

'Far from it. Jonston in his *Natural History of Quadrupeds* lists a good half-dozen types, including the rice rat and the cane rat. But this particular species, the bamboo rat, is unique in that it survives on a diet of bamboo shoots.'

'Bamboo? I wasn't aware that there was bamboo in Mexico.'

'Nor was I,' he replied. 'None has ever been sighted. Not anywhere in the Spanish Indies either.'

'So where did the rats come from if not Mexico or the Spanish Indies?'

He shrugged. 'Is it not obvious? They must have come aboard the *Sacra Familia* from somewhere that bamboo *is* found. And where is bamboo found but in the islands of the Pacific? In the Spice Islands, for instance. Jonston tells us that the bamboo rat is especially numerous in the Moluccas.'

'So the *Sacra Familia* had been to the Moluccas?'

'Or to an island elsewhere in the Pacific. Yes. What she was doing there is a conundrum, because Spanish voyages into the Pacific were rare in those years. Mendaña made his final voyage in search of the Solomon Islands in 1595, then Quirós and Torres followed in 1606. After that, though, there is almost nothing. The entire Pacific was fast becoming the domain of Spain's fiercest enemies, the Dutch, who had found a new passage into the South Seas through the Le Maire Strait. Many of the sea routes were now controlled by the ships of the Dutch East India Company.'

'So the *Sacra Familia* must have found another route,' I said eagerly, remembering the terms of Sir Ambrose's charter with its mission to discover a new passage to the South Seas. 'A route into the Pacific through the headwaters of the Orinoco.'

Biddulph shot me a surprised look. 'The idea has never occurred to me,' he replied, shaking his head. 'Nor was it mentioned in the rumours. Still, I must own that it's an interesting notion. But whatever she might have discovered, or however she might have reached it, the *Sacra Familia* had sailed in the Pacific, that much seems certain. Only now she was disguised as part of the Mexican treasure fleet. Her travels must have been a great secret, because when she was attacked by the *Sidney* her crew jettisoned all of her charts and portolanos, the ship's chronicle, the captain's log – everything that might have betrayed her mission. They got rid of everything, I should say, except her smell.'

That was the last and perhaps the most curious part of the story. For the *Sacra Familia* had possessed, even from the distance, a remarkable smell. It was not the usual smell of a ship at sea – the stink of rotting provisions, of bilgewater, of damp wood and gunpowder, of chamber-pots overturned by storms. On the contrary, it was a beautiful smell that seemed to float across the water towards the *Philip Sidney*, a delicious scent that reminded the mariners of incense or perfume. It seemed to hang over the water for hours after the burning wreck finally disappeared under the water. The bewitching scent was not, the rumours insisted, that of the cargo – some cargo that might have been loaded in the Moluccas – but of the ship herself, as if the aroma emanated in some mysterious way from her beams and masts.

'I never knew what to make of the stories, of either the rats or the beautiful smell. Only that, if the tales were true, the *Sacra Familia* was plainly not what she seemed.'

Yes, I thought, intrigued: her voyage was as mysterious as

that of the *Philip Sidney*, to whom her fate was somehow bonded.

'So sorry, Mr Inchbold,' he said with a gentle smile as he creaked open the door to his house. 'I fear I can tell you no more. Rumour and gossip, that is all I was ever to learn of the episode.'

We stepped back inside the little house, where I was treated to another cup of rumbullion. For the next hour I listened to other theories that Biddulph's leisure allowed him to concoct, including the 'dark matter' (as he called it) of Buckingham's murder in 1628, an act carried out not by a half-mad Puritan fanatic, as history recorded, but by an agent of Cardinal Richelieu cleverly disguised as a half-mad Puritan fanatic. But I was barely listening to Biddulph now. I was thinking instead of how it seemed that Sir Ambrose had once again sailed over the horizon and – for me at least – eluded configuration. I was also remembering the mysterious 1600 edition of Ortelius's *Theatrum orbis terrarum*, along with the patents in Alethea's muniment room, and thinking of how Sir Ambrose had been in Prague in the year 1620, two years and 6,000 miles from his mysterious adventures in the Spanish Indies. So I wondered if there was some deeper connection between these two doomed ventures, some invisible history that might involve the lost Hermetic text that Henry Monboddo and his mysterious client so desperately desired. Or was I merely becoming infected by Biddulph's curious line of logic in which no two events, however far apart in time or space, were ever unrelated?

And then I remembered what I had intended to ask him an hour or two earlier. I had actually stepped outside at the time and was in the midst of bidding him adieu. The sun had dropped behind the distant silhouette of Nonsuch House, and the waters of the river were grey as a gull's wing. I could feel the rumbullion going about its stealthy work inside me. I had missed my footing on the front step and there was a faint ringing in my ears that seemed to change pitch as we stepped outside. Our two shadows stretched all the way across the tiny garden.

'I was wondering,' I asked after we had clasped hands, 'did you ever meet Captain Plessington? Did he visit the Navy Office?'

'No.' Biddulph shook his head. 'I never met Plessington. Not once. He was far too important to deal with someone like me, you understand. I was only a humble assistant to the Clerk of the Acts in those days. No, I saw him only once, and that was on the night when the *Sidney* cast off her lines and sailed down the Thames. Plessington was standing on the quarterdeck, and I could see him faintly in the light of the stern-lamp.'

'But all of the preparations for her sailing . . . ?'

'Oh, Plessington had a delegate for details like that. Everything was arranged either through him or the *Sidney*'s purser.'

'A delegate?'

'Yes.' He was squinting at his eaves now, frowning deeply. The wind sighed at our backs and riffled the waves. 'Now . . . what the devil was his name? It's just that I spend so much time in the reign of Queen Bess that sometimes my old brain gets befuddled by names. No . . . wait!' Suddenly his little face brightened. 'No, no, I remember his name after all. A strange name it was, too. Monboddo,' he pronounced triumphantly. 'Yes, that was it. Henry Monboddo.'

Chapter Twelve

There is no sight so sublime, the philosopher Lucretius tells us, as a shipwreck at sea. And the wreck of the *Bellerophon* did indeed make a spectacular sight for the onlookers who left their crofts and cottages to gather on the windy shores of the Chislet Marshes. She broke apart on the Margate Hook at some time after five o'clock in the afternoon. She had already been bilged in the midships, and with her starboard bow forced by the waves against the reef –

the largest and most dangerous reef along the entire coast of Kent – it was only a matter of seconds before she shipped a dozen tons of water through her hull and then heeled clumsily on to her beam-ends. Her masts had toppled like ruined steeples and her yards and shrouds were hurled away. The waves foamed white about her hull before bursting in cascades over her fo'c'sle deck. Everyone on the upper decks was swept into the roiling sea, while those still below decks fared no better. The men frantically working the hand-pumps were either drowned as fountains of water thundered into the hold or else crushed to death as casks and puncheons tumbled like rogue oxen across the tilting deck. Others broke their necks or skulls against the stanchions, which themselves were splintering to bits, and still others had the misfortune to be trapped by falling beams and then drowned as the tide of water burst through the hatchways. And so it was that by the time the *Bellerophon* was smashed to a thousand pieces on the Margate Hook, there was not a single soul left alive inside her.

Her wreckage was swiftly scavenged. Almost a hundred onlookers had gathered along the muddy stretch of beach, and three enormous stacks of driftwood were lit. The bonfires' garish light lent an almost festive atmosphere to the scene. The Margate Hook and the havoc it wreaked with the occasional passing ship made one of the few consolations of living on this desolate edge of Kent. Folk were hoping for a repeat of the famous episode three years earlier when the *Scythia* was cracked open like an oyster on the very same spot, making humble fishermen and winkle-pickers drunk as lords on two hundred butts of Spanish malmsey. So as soon as the sea grew calm enough, a flotilla of a dozen-odd cutters and smacks was launched into the waves. By first light more than a score of crates had been dragged ashore, as had thirteen sopping and dishevelled crewmen.

Among them was Captain Quilter. For more than ten hours he had clung to one of the ninety-nine contraband boxes as it bobbed and wallowed in the heavy swell, sucked back and forth by outgoing and then incoming tides. But as full tide had come a second time the bonfires suddenly loomed before him and the crate washed up with a bump in the shallows. He was exhausted and frozen from his ordeal, but no sooner had his feet touched shingle than three men wading rapidly forward – his saviours, so he thought – shoved him back into the combers. The crate was scraped ashore and stacked with a score of others.

'You people have no right of salvage here.' He had righted himself and was splashing through the mud and sand towards a group of figures gathered round one of the bonfires. More boxes and chests were being dragged from the waters, while a small convoy of donkey-carts laden with others began winding its way into the marshes. 'These crates are flotsam, the legal property of the *Bellerophon*, and I as her captain—'

A crowbar flashed, and again Captain Quilter collapsed to his knees. His hand fumbled in his belt for the firelock with which he had armed himself as protection against Rowley's gang, but of course the pistol had disappeared. Now what little remained of his ship and her cargo – what little return he could make for his investors at the Royal Exchange – was vanishing at the hands of these shoreline pirates.

In the warmth of another bonfire he discovered a handful of his crewmen, blue-lipped and shivering. Three of their number, Pinchbeck included, had died since being dragged ashore in the last hour. Their bodies had been lined up next to the eight other sailors whose soaked carcasses had washed ashore. The pockets of their sodden cloaks and galligaskins were being rifled by those too small or infirm to loot the greater riches of the washed-up chests. Quilter's heart sank at the sight. The looters pushing and shoving over the corpses looked like nothing so much as flapping turkey buzzards, but he was far too numb and weak to chase them away.

A few of the other scavengers on the beach proved more hospitable, however. Blankets were distributed among the survivors, along with chunks of bread and cheese, and even the odd bottle of brandy, from which the crewmen were helping themselves to feeble swigs. Some fifteen minutes later, one more of the crewmen had expired but Quilter himself was feeling revitalised by the twin blessings of the brandy and the flames, when suddenly there came – no one was quite sure from where at first – the crackle of musket-fire. For a moment Quilter thought the shot was intended for him, but then he saw the looters delving in the crates and among the corpses squawk with surprise and leap for cover. Then a second shot echoed across the beach.

By this time he was belly-crawling across the mud and wrack to shelter behind a waterlogged cask. The first streaks of dawn had appeared above the wreckage of the *Bellerophon*, which by now had spread itself across much of the horizon. The rain had thinned to a gentle mist and the Margate Hook was vanishing beneath the flooding tidewaters. Perfect sailing weather, thought Quilter with a pang. He watched part of the keel wash ashore on the heaving waves. Then another shot broke the silence and he lowered his head behind the cask. The bonfire was snapping and crackling in front of him, sending shadows and smoke across the sand. When he raised his head a moment later he was expecting to see Sir Ambrose wading ashore with his sword or pistol flourishing, but what he saw instead, swaying on the horizon, looking like her own ghost, was the *Star of Lübeck*.

The Hansa merchantman was barely visible through the spindrift. She was still listing badly and scudding recklessly under bare poles, but, for all that, she was intact and afloat. The crewmen could be seen on her upper decks, hoisting what little canvas was left on to the splintered masts. But the bursts of musket-fire, Quilter realised, were coming from much closer to shore.

A fourth shot crackled along the strip of beach. The looters cursed among themselves and retreated deeper into the safety of the osiers. Quilter could see them fumbling at their belts for their daggers and old-fashioned matchlock pistols whose tapers were impossible to light because of the drizzle.

He shifted his gaze to the left, to where a cutter with its sail flapping and swelling had emerged an instant earlier from the smoke and wreckage. After a second he made out a figure in the prow, a man bent on one knee as if paying homage to a superior. Except the man wasn't paying homage to anyone, Quilter immediately realised, he was taking aim with his musket at the few figures left among the pyramids of crates. At a fifth crack one of the figures shrieked like a kite, arched its back, then dropped in the sand. The cutter splashed forward, its prow nodding in the waves.

Yes, it was Sir Ambrose Plessington after all, Quilter had decided. Trust a rascal like him to survive when good men like poor old Pinchbeck had perished. Two other figures – Sir Ambrose's companions, he supposed – were hunched in the stern, barely visible behind the swollen sail. So they, too, had survived the shipwreck. Now they had come to claim what was left of their precious cargo, the unholy relics that some would say had been responsible for the whole dreadful misadventure.

He rolled out from behind the barrel and struggled to his feet. The boat was in the shallows now, its sail furled, one of the figures in the thwarts working a pair of oars. Quilter limped into the foaming water, waving his arms like a man in a London street frantically summoning a hackney-carriage.

'Sir Ambrose!' He took another step forward into the waves. The boat had run aground and the figure from the prow was clambering over the gunwale. 'Sir—'

Even before the musket-ball whizzed past his shoulder and sent him plunging again for the safety of the barrel he had realised that the man in the prow was not Sir Ambrose, nor the cutter that of the *Bellerophon*.

From a quarter-mile up the beach Emilia was also watching as the three men came ashore. She had landed on the beach almost an hour earlier. As it happened, the Captain was right. She and Vilém had indeed escaped the wreck of the *Bellerophon* along with Sir Ambrose. They had cut one of the longboats free from its canvas sling and clambered inside barely ten minutes before the hull collapsed. The journey from ship to shore, a distance of no more than a mile, surpassed even the one from Breslau to Hamburg for danger and discomfort. The gunwales of the longboat had been splintered and its paddles had gone missing. After an hour it had shipped so much water through a leak in the hull that Vilém and Sir Ambrose were reduced to bailing water with their hats, Emilia with panels of her skirts. But somehow the vessel remained afloat. For the next ten hours the three of them had drifted back and forth on the current, the bonfires looming as they neared the shore, then fading as they slipped away. Then at last the wind died and the sail, a tattered piece of canvas, was raised. Fifteen minutes later they scraped the boat across the shingle and into the sand.

Now Vilém and Sir Ambrose were dragging the crates ashore, sliding them across the bladder-wracked shingle, through winkle shells that crackled underfoot. Five crates of books had been pulled aboard. Sir Ambrose had explained that the other crates would have to be raised from the bottom. Fortunately there was a team of salvors in Erith, men who used special diving-bells and even a 'submarine', an ingenious invention by the Dutch magus Cornelius Drebbel, whom Sir Ambrose had met in Prague. Their services were employed by merchants and investors in the Royal Exchange to recover the cargoes of the thirty-odd ships that each year were wrecked on the Goodwin Sands or the other shoals in the mouth of the Thames. The submarine, a marvellous piece of engineering, a vessel made from balsa-wood and Greenland sealskin, featuring fins and inflatable bladders, would do the trick nicely.

'You must go ahead to London,' Sir Ambrose was saying as he struggled with another crate. 'Immediately. Monboddo will be expecting you. As will Buckingham. I shall send word to the Navy Office as soon as possible.'

Vilém gripped the other end of the crate and hoisted it from the mud, then together they carried it to the high-water line and set it in the sand. The lid had come off, exposing and even spilling a few of its contents. As the two men staggered to the longboat to recover another crate, Emilia replaced the books, the last of which, tented open, badly water-damaged, was a thick volume that she recognised from the Spanish Rooms, one from which Vilém had read to her only a few months earlier, the *Anthologia Graeca*, a collection of epigrams compiled in Constantinople by a scholar named Cephalas. The original parchment had been discovered among the manuscripts in the Bibliotheca Palatina in Heidelberg, though this translation had been printed in London.

She turned the volume over, but before closing the sodden cover that smelled like wet shoe-leather she glimpsed a verse in the middle of the opened page, in the muted light of the bonfires:

Where is thine admired beauty, Dorian Corinth, where thy crown of towers? Where thy treasures of old, where the temples of the immortals, where the halls and where the wives of the Sisyphids, and the tens of thousands of thy people that were? For not even a trace, O most distressful one, is left of thee, and war has swept up together and clean devoured all ...

Vilém had read the verse to her on a gloomy evening in September when word reached Prague that General Spínola's army had invaded the Palatinate and soon would lay siege to Heidelberg and – in a cycle of violence reeling backwards and forwards across hemispheres and centuries from the ruins of Corinth and Constantinople – what remained of the Bibliotheca Palatina, including the manuscript of the *Anthologia Graeca*.

A ragged shout reached her from the other end of the beach. The looters were on their way, stumbling in haste, heels tossing clods of mud and sand. Without knowing why, she slipped the volume into her pocket, then struggled to replace the wooden lid.

'. . . in the Strand,' Sir Ambrose was saying. He and Vilém had arrived with another crate. 'York House. Beside the river. I've had dealings with him before.'

'Yes?'

'He's one of the best. Paintings, marbles, books. Perfectly respectable, of course. Also kept a good many baubles out of the Earl of Arundel's grasping hands, I can tell you that.'

Vilém was breathing hard. 'He knows the plan?'

'Of course he knows it. He's known it from the outset. Not to worry.' The seaweed-draped crate thudded into the sand. 'He's perfectly capable.'

'And trustworthy?'

'Trustworthy?' Sir Ambrose chuckled, then cocked an eye-brow at him. 'Oh, Monboddo is a true coin, we have no worries on that account. You'll be safe enough, the pair of you. Provided you make it to London,' he added, nodding at the looters slipping and stumbling towards them. Not far behind were the three men who had disembarked from the boat. 'I seem to have lost my pistol, worse luck,' he said in a casual tone. He had begun walking, unhurried, towards the longboat. 'Not to mention my sword. It would appear, my friends, that we find ourselves in yet another spot of trouble.'

No coach moved as swiftly over the roads of England in those days as the ones belonging to the De Quester Post Office for Foreign Parts. Each vehicle in the De Quester fleet had been specially designed to cover the seventy-mile journey from London to Margate, or from Margate to London, in less than five hours, even with a few passengers on board and a heavy load of ten mail-bags strapped to the leather roof or bundled inside. Their perches and sway-bars were made from poles of the lightest pine, while the axle-trees were greased with plumbago and the wheels mounted on springs and rimmed with iron. The whole contraption was pulled along the road by teams of Barbary horses bred for the task at a stable in Cambridgeshire. And so as dawn broke over the Chislet Marshes, one of these swift vehicles must have made an unusual sight as it lumbered and jolted through the mire at an even slower pace than the crate-laden donkey-carts creeping along in the opposite direction.

This was a stretch of road notorious even in these parts for its pot-holes and its tendency to flood at the first sign of rain. The driver of the coach, a man named Foxcroft, was squinting through the drizzle and mist as he huddled inside his tarpaulin and guided the team along the treacherous road. He had left Margate almost six hours earlier and his bags of mail from Hamburg and Amsterdam were already overdue in London. He might have made London on time, storm or no storm, had he taken the main road through Canterbury and Faversham instead of this miserable detour along the windswept coast.

But of course he dared not ride along the main road, just as he no longer dared wear the red-and-gold De Quester livery. A dispute was now commencing before the Lords of the Council as to whether the De Quester monopoly infringed the patent of Lord Stanhope, Master of the Posts and Messengers, who had recently begun using agents of his own – bands of ruffians, in Foxcroft's opinion – to carry his letters to Hamburg and Amsterdam. Not a month earlier Foxcroft had been ambushed by a gang of masked men outside the walls of Canterbury; then another driver was set upon two weeks later, in Gad's Hill. Both times the robbers had worn the garb of highwaymen, but everyone knew that Lord Stanhope's ruffians were behind the outrages. And so for the past few weeks Foxcroft had been condemned to this circuitous route – a route so desolate and forsaken that not even the most desperate highwayman would ever think of haunting it, especially not on a December morning as cold and miserable as this one.

And so it was that Foxcroft could scarcely believe his eyes when he rounded a corner and saw the oncoming convoy of donkeys and, beyond them, some sort of conflagration – fire, smoke, running figures – along the beach. Another of Lord Stanhope's ambushes? He cursed in fright and reined in the horses, but it was too late, the Barbs had whinnied and then reared in their traces at a loud burst of what sounded like musket-fire. Foxcroft teetered out of his balance before righting himself and gripping the reins in one hand, the edge of the seat with the other. In the second before his hat brim slipped over his eyes he made out, far in the distance, what looked like the wreckage of a ship.

The horses were plunging forward through the muck, muscling past the chain of mules and thundering pell-mell along the narrow road in the direction of the beach and its orange bonfires. The futchels creaked and squealed as the vehicle swung round another corner, tipping on to two wheels and hurling gobbets of mud into the osiers blurring past on both sides. Foxcroft thought he saw a clutch of figures huddled among them. But then one of the wheels struck a stone and he began bouncing in his seat like the village scold on her cucking-stool.

From the muddy road it took less than a minute for the coach to reach the verge of the even muddier beach. By this time the wheels had struck two more stones and Foxcroft, dislodged, found himself clinging with both hands to the seat as his boots hung a bare inch from the whirling spokes. Two bags of mail had been lost, along with his hat. Then, as the iron-rimmed wheels hit the sand, the coach slowed with a hard jerk and he heard another crack of musket-fire, much closer now. The horses reared again. He braced a foot on the transom and with a desperate lunge raised himself into the seat.

And it was then that he caught his first sight of them, a group of shadows, a clutch of five or six figures, all rushing towards him. Yes – an ambush of some sort. He twisted round and fumbled for his whip, but the whip had disappeared along with his hat and the bags of mail. The horses reared again as he clutched at the reins, and suddenly the coach lurched to a stop, its wheels stuck fast and sinking into the sand.

'Giddap! Giddap!'

He reached for the musket behind the seat, but it too had disappeared, as had the bag of shot. He spun round in the seat to face his attackers – more of them even than in Canterbury. The horses reared, then dug in, though with its perch and axle-trees ploughing through the sand the coach shifted no more than a couple of inches. Then the horses lunged again and it slid forward with a creak of leather as the wheels found purchase on the shingle.

But it was too late, Foxcroft realised. His lordship's bravos – a good half-dozen of them – were almost upon him.

'Holy mother of God,' he whispered, bracing himself to leap.

Captain Quilter was watching the stranded coach-and-six from his shelter behind a cask of alewife thrown overboard from the *Star of Lübeck*. By now the barrel had been punctured by a musket-ball and brine was spurting through the splintered staves and into the sand. He had heard a shout from among the osiers and, turning his head, glimpsed the coach careering towards the water as it strewed a couple of sacks in its muddy wake.

Gripping one of the barrel's hoops, he raised himself a few inches higher. The sand was as soft and deep as a hassock under his knees. Another shout, this time from the opposite end of the beach. He turned his head to see a group of figures rushing the coach. The vehicle had stopped by now, run aground in the muck and sand at the edge of the beach. The horses reared and kicked in their traces as the lone figure in the coach-box struggled to free the reins from where they were tangled in the futchels.

Quilter was on his feet now, staring through the screen of drizzle at the strange scene unfolding before him. Three of the figures had reached the coach by the time the reins were loosened and the coach jerked violently forward. The other three, one of them wielding the musket, were only a few paces behind and closing quickly.

'Giddap!'

'Get on board!' It was Sir Ambrose, raising one of his companions, the lady, into the box-seat. 'Yes! Go!'

One of the pursuers had dropped to his knee. His musket flashed and gave a cough followed by a puff of smoke. But the coach was rolling again, tipping from side to side like a bark in a heavy sea. A second person, a man, thin and hatless, had also leapt aboard. He was clinging to the wooden boot while Sir Ambrose ran alongside, raising something aloft, a chest of some sort. The man in livery was reloading the musket while the one in the boot strained his slender body, arm outstretched.

But at that second Quilter's attention was caught by something else. One of the lanterns or fireboxes from the messes of the *Bellerophon* must have ignited a spilled budge-barrel or spirit cask, for suddenly a deafening explosion shook the sky. As Quilter fell to his knees and looked into the offing he saw a fountain of orange fire, a spectacular display of pyrotechnics that dwarfed the bonfires and even the new sun shying behind the clouds. The streaks of fire were still raining into the sea by the time he thought to turn his head and look for the coach.

But neither the coach nor its passengers was anywhere in sight. Peering along the strand of beach he saw only their pursuers, the three men whose black-and-gold cloaks had been bathed in copper by the thousand cascading fragments of his ship.

Chapter Thirteen

I awoke the next morning feeling slightly unwell. There seemed to be a strange taste, faint and sweet, on the roof of my mouth, and my tongue was parched. When I rose from the bed, waveringly, clutching a bedpost, limbs strangely enervated, I realised how slick I was with sweat, how my bedlinen was soaked as if I were feverish, or as if my slumbers had been hard work. Panicked, for a few seconds I thought I was falling ill with an ague or worse (I have been something of a hypochondriac ever since Arabella's death), but then with a pang of relief I remembered Biddulph's rumbullion. The evening came back to me – Wapping, Orinoco, Villiers, Monboddo – in a steady accretion of detail. With a soft groan I sank into a chair and listened for a few minutes as the herring-gulls squawked heartlessly below the window, feeding and flapping in the mud. I seemed to remember a dream, something violent and frightening. Another alarming effect of last night's rumbullion, I supposed.

By the time I ate a breakfast of radishes and black bread, then drank a morning draught and spent a quarter-hour perched on the close-stool, I felt somewhat better. I descended to the shop and for another quarter-hour performed the old rituals of the awning and the shutters, the unbarring of the door and the tidying of the counter, all the while stumbling round in a pleasant daze as if surprised to find my shop still standing and myself safely inside it. This morning the resinous scent of walnut and pine – the sweet tang of the forest – spiced the familiar fug of rag-paper and buckram. The shop was better than new, I decided, inspecting the shelving and the hinges of the green door. I felt like a sea captain whose ship has been wrecked and then expertly repaired on a foreign shore from which it is time to sail for home.

Yes, I was feeling much better. After Monk departed for the General Letter Office I stepped outside the door and loitered for a time on the footpath, feeling the newly minted sun on my skin and gazing blearily up and down the carriageway as if taking my bearings from one of the signboards. And all at once the dream came back to me, stark and horrible.

Ordinarily I do not set much store by dreams. The few I remember are mundane, vague, illogical and unsatisfying. But the previous night was different. After my return from Wapping I retired to bed with my copy of *Don Quixote*, in which I reached Chapter 6, the point where the priest and the barber inspect and then burn the contents of poor mad Quixote's library, the source of his fantastic delusions. The episode recycled itself in my dreams, except that it was no longer Quixote's books but my own that burned. I had watched in cringing horror as they were ripped from the shelves and tossed by the armload into a bonfire by a band of taunting culprits who refused to resolve themselves as they darted in and out of the firelight. Soon these figures vanished into the night and I found myself at Pontifex Hall, alone, first inside the library, where the flames were devouring the shelves, then outside in the hedge-maze a few seconds later, watching as ashes and scraps of pages were carried skyward on great tentacles of black smoke, before returning to the ground like the cinders of an exploded volcano. At which point Pontifex Hall metamorphosed into a burning ship and the dream concluded with the thunderous crash of falling timbers. I awoke to discover that *Don Quixote* had toppled from my belly to the floor.

Now I wondered what on earth I should make of this disconcerting chain of images. Plato claims that all dreams are prophecies of things to come, visions of the future that the soul receives through the liver, while Hippocrates says that they are portents of disease or even madness. And so on neither account was I especially heartened. I decided I should take instead the advice of Heraclitus, who tells us that all dreams are nonsense and are therefore best ignored.

I was still standing on the footpath, under the awning, gawping like an imbecile, when Monk returned from Dowgate with the post. Two letters had arrived: one from a bookseller in Antwerp, the other from a superannuated clergyman in Saffron Walden. I followed Monk inside the green door. Another day awaited.

An hour later I caught a hack to Seething Lane. I had no intention of revisiting either Silas Cobb or the Navy Office, but rather I hoped to speak with the vestry clerk of St Olave's. Morning Prayer was in progress as I arrived, so I slipped into a pew at the rear, where I fumbled with a Prayer Book – one of those little volumes that Cromwell and his generals had done their best to burn – and felt self-conscious and oddly guilty. I have never been a church-goer, unlike Arabella, who sometimes attended two services a day. I have no objection to the practice, neither to the Puritans with their riotous conventicles nor the Established Church and its incense, railed-off altars and other quasi-popish rituals. But I am at heart, I suppose, like the Quakers who believe in their so-called inner light that needs no priests or sacraments to kindle it.

As I sat in a sunbeam spilling through the stained glass I was not, however, contemplating spiritual matters. I was thinking about Henry Monboddo and Sir Ambrose Plessington, about what imponderable connection might exist between *The Labyrinth of the World* and their adventures in Spanish America, between the *Corpus hermeticum* and a group of Protestant fanatics. These fruitless musings were interrupted as the service ended, at which point I picked my way up the aisle, past the departing congregation, wondering if my habitually dishevelled appearance along with the ill effects of the previous night's drink made me look to the vicar like a repentant sinner coming to beg forgiveness for a profligate life. In any event, he directed me with no apparent qualms to the vestry, where I discovered the clerk and explained to him that I wished to consult the parish records in order to learn something about one of the parishioners – an ancestor of mine, I told him – who was buried in the churchyard. He seemed pleased enough to oblige and, after much truffling in one of the cupboards, presented me with a fat volume, a register-book for the year 1620, bound in cowhide. He bade me sit at his little desk, then disappeared into the church, which now was empty except for an old woman slowly working her way along the flagstones with a mop.

The register-book was divided into those three staging-posts of life: christening, marriage and death. I riffled quickly to the section on deaths. It made depressing reading in the gloomy environs of the vestry. I knew that before the parish clerks compiled and published the Bills of Mortality, as they do nowadays, register-books often recorded causes of death. But I was quite unprepared for the little biographies of doom that ran next to each name and date, column after column, page after page: apoplexies, dropsies, pleurisies, spotted fevers, bloody fluxes, 'murthers', starvations, plagues, poisonings, suicides – and so forth, an endless catalogue of long-forgotten tragedies. One poor soul had even been 'mauled by a Bear escaped from the Bear-pit in Southwark', another 'eaten by a Crocodile in St James's Park'. Also recorded were a few deaths of a more imprecise nature, men or women who had been 'found dead in the street' or 'killed in a fall', while 'cause of death unknown' had been inked beside the names of others.

Silas Cobb's death proved one of these more mysterious varieties. After some thirty minutes I discovered his name near the back of the volume, in the pages dedicated to the month of December, which looked to have been an especially dangerous month for the parishioners of St Olave's. But the information proved disappointing. A smudged italic hand simply recorded that Silas Cobb had been 'found dead in the river below York House'. Nothing more. No occupation, no address, no next of kin. No clues of any kind to his identity.

A waste of time, I decided. I closed the register-book and thanked the clerk, and not until I reached the door of the church did I suddenly remember something that Biddulph mentioned a day earlier, that York House had once belonged to Francis Bacon, supposed architect of the *Philip Sidney*, who eventually sold it to the Duke of Buckingham, who in turn kept his books and paintings inside until his son was forced to sell them, using as his agent (according to Alethea) none other than Henry Monboddo.

For a few seconds my sideburns prickled with excitement . . . but soon I decided that I had merely conceived a strange and unstable fantasy. Any connection between Cobb and either Bacon or Buckingham, or between Cobb and Monboddo, must be a distant one at best. Even the connection between Cobb and York House with its hundreds of paintings was probably no more than an odd coincidence, for his corpse might have floated either upstream or downstream on the tide, as much as a mile or two, before being pulled from the waters below York House. He might have fallen into the Thames – or been tossed into it, dead or alive – at almost any point between the Chelsea Reach and London Bridge. The newssheets in those days were full of tales of these little voyages; of despairing men who leapt from the palings of the bridge only to fetch up, days later, three or four miles downstream.

Before leaving the church I thought to ask the clerk about Cobb's gravestone, which looked so much newer than its neighbours, much newer, I pointed out, than a 1620 vintage. But the clerk only shrugged his shoulders and explained that the practice of erecting a new stone over an old grave was common enough. Not only that, folk who came into fortunes often gave themselves more honourable pedigrees by improving the siting of their ancestors' graves – even to the point, he said, of exhuming bones from their obscure plots in the corners of the churchyard and reburying them in more prestigious environs, such as the church's aisles or crypt, where the new resting-place was marked by a marble plaque, even by a bust or statue. So it was, he claimed, that humble watermen and fishmongers sometimes discovered themselves, fifty years after death, in the distinguished company of dukes and admirals, with their effigies proudly displayed in marble or bronze. He informed me that the church kept no official records of such improvements.

'You may consult with the lapicide or stonemason who carved the stone,' he suggested. 'Ordinarily they inscribe their name or a coat of arms on the rear of the slab.'

But I was loath to creep back to Cobb's gravestone in broad daylight – almost as loath as I was to enter the noise and dust of a stonemason's yard in both the heat of the day and the aftermath of Biddulph's rumbullion. And so I returned to Nonsuch House, wondering what I should make of the things I had learned; if in fact I had learned anything at all.

For the remainder of that day I went about my usual ceremonies among my shelves and customers. Ah, the pleasant balm of routine, what Horace calls *laborum dulce lenimen*, the 'sweet solace of my toils'. Afterwards I ate a dinner cooked by Margaret, drank two cups of wine and smoked a pipe of tobacco, then retired to bed at ten o'clock, my usual hour, with Wolfram's *Parzival* – I had decided against *Don Quixote* that night – propped on my belly. I must have fallen asleep soon after the watchman announced eleven o'clock.

I have never been a good sleeper. As a child I was a notorious sleepwalker. My strange trances and midnight perambulations regularly alarmed my parents, our neighbours, and finally Mr Smallpace, who once led me back to Nonsuch House, barefoot and confused, after I wandered as far as the south gate of the bridge. As I grew older, this nocturnal restlessness translated itself into bouts of insomnia that plague me to this day. I will lie awake for hours on end, incessantly checking my watch, plumping and punching my pillow, thrashing and turning on my mattress as if wrestling a foe, before sleep at last whelms over me only to subside a minute later when I am disturbed by the slightest noise or provoked by the jagged shard of an unremembered dream. Over the years I have sought out various apothecaries who have prescribed all manner of remedies for the condition. I have drunk by the pint-pot foul-smelling syrups made from maidenhair and the seeds of poppies (a flower that Ovid tells us blooms beside the Cave of Sleep), or rubbed on to my temples an hour before retiring, as per instructions, other concoctions mixed from lettuce juice, oil of roses and who knows what else. But none of these expensive elixirs has ever managed to hasten my slumbers by so much as a single minute.

To make matters worse, Nonsuch House is an unfamiliar and even frightening place after dark, especially so, it seemed, after Arabella's death – a vast echo-chamber where floor timbers creaked and groaned, shutters rattled, the chimney keened, the eaves gargled, beetles tapped, rats squeaked and scurried, and the elm pipes shuddered and moaned behind the walls as the water inside them either froze or thawed. I think of myself as a rational man, but in the months after Arabella's death I used to jolt awake several times each night, stark with terror, then hunch beneath the counterpane like a horror-struck child, listening to a platoon of ghosts and demons whispering my name as they went about their stealthy work in my closets and corridors.

Tonight I was awakened with a start by one of these noises. Jerking upright in the darkness, I fumbled on the bedside table for the firelock. I had considered sleeping with it under my pillow, as I believe people are said to do for fear of housebreakers, but had visions of it discharging itself as I rolled over in my sleep, and anyway it had been far too big and uncomfortable to fit under my tiny goose-down pillow. So I had placed it on the table instead, charged with a ball and powder, though with the barrel pointing away from the head of the bed. The rest of the ammunition was in the drawer, in a bandolier that the one-legged veteran had sold me along with the firelock: thirty balls of lead that looked curiously harmless, like the petrified droppings of a small rodent.

I found the pistol only after a few seconds of frantic scrabbling, then closed my fingers over the stock and held my breath, listening for the intrusive noise. It had been, I thought, some sort of faint rattling or jingling, like a pair of spurs. But all was silent now. The noise had been a dream, I told myself. Or the watchman with his bell.

Ka-chink, ka-chink, ka-chink-a . . .

I had just fallen asleep when I caught it again, more clearly this time, an unfamiliar sound not in the building's usual repertoire: a faint but insistent jingling, like a small dinner-bell or a set of keys on a chatelaine. Or perhaps like a set of traces, except that it was hours past curfew, the gates would be closed, and no horse-and-carriage was likely to be passing along the carriageway.

I pushed myself upright again, left hand grappling for the pistol. I struck a taper and squinted at my watch, which I also had to fumble for on the bedside table. Past two o'clock. Abruptly the noise stopped, as if the perpetrator had caught himself and swiftly muffled it. I swung my legs over the edge of the bed, imagining the instigator hunched against a wall somewhere, breath held and ears trained.

Ka-chink-ka-chink-ka-CHINK!

The noise had grown louder and more insistent by the time I stole along the corridor and then, drawing a deep breath, down the first few steps. I had trouble with my footing in the dark but managed to avoid the third tread from the top, which squeaked, and the fifth from the top, whose riser – in order to trip unwary housebreakers – was four inches higher than the rest. I had no wish to rouse Monk, who would have been frightened to death by the sight of me slinking about the house, pistol in hand. Nor did I wish to alert the intruder who – I was sure of it now – was either inside the shop or else attempting to prise his way through the outer door: for the sound had been caused, I realised, by a ring of picklocks.

Ka-CHINK-a . . .

My nape prickled with fear. Drawing a shuddering breath I tightened my grip on the weapon and searched with a bare foot for the next tread. The jingling had ceased, but now I heard the catch click and then caught the slow creak of my new hinges as the green door was opened inchmeal. I froze, club foot suspended in mid-air. The floor timbers complained gently as the intruder stole across the shop. I licked my lips and felt blindly for another step.

What happened next was inevitable, I suppose. The steps of the turnpike staircase are steep, shallow and worn, their risers of irregular height; and of course I am a cripple and half blind without my spectacles, which I had left behind in my bedchamber. So when I reached for another step, my club foot skittered over the edge of the next tread and I pitched forward with a yelp to the landing. Worse, I lost my grip on the pistol as I flailed through the darkness. It clattered noisily down the steps ahead of me.

I caught my breath and held it. Dead silence followed. I lay on the landing for a few seconds before cautiously unfolding myself and rising to a crouch. So silent had everything fallen that for a second I almost thought I had been mistaken, that all had been a dream, or the sound of the wind, or the building lurching and creaking with the tide. But then I heard the unmistakable tread of feet and, seconds later, whispering voices.

I felt my body tense, bracing itself to lunge. I might still reach the pistol. But there were at least two intruders, while even if I reached the weapon first I had only one shot. So I remained in a crouch on the landing, too frightened even to breathe.

A few horrible seconds passed before I heard the sharp gasp of a taper. Then a light welled upwards and shadows pivoted across the wall. I sprang into motion, lurching crabwise along the narrow landing, fumbling for the steps above me. But it was too late. Already a pair of boots was squeaking on the treads, only a few feet below now. I heard the soft whoosh of the burning torch, then a loud scrape as the pistol was recovered. Another few seconds and they would reach me.

I spun round and groped blindly at the steps. But no sooner had I found purchase than a cold hand seized the back of my neck.

Nonsuch House was over eighty years old in those days. It had been built in Holland in the year 1577 and then shipped in sections to London, where its carved gables and onion-shaped cupolas were fitted together without the use of nails, piece by piece, like the segments of a giant jigsaw puzzle. It stood halfway along the carriageway, on the north side of a small drawbridge whose wooden-cogged wheels creaked and ground together six times a day. And so six times a day all traffic on the carriageway was forced to halt for twenty minutes while that beneath floated through on the tide: hoys and shallops headed upstream with loads of malt and dried haddock, bumboats and pinnaces going downstream with hogsheads of ale and sugar for the merchantmen at Tower Dock, sometimes even the yacht of the King himself on its way to the races at Greenwich, masts swaying and sails crackling. A hush would descend on the bridge at these moments as the pack-horses and pushing foot-passengers all paused in their tracks before the dream-like parade of twenty or thirty boats. As an apprentice, I, too, used to stop and watch in wonder as the carriageway rose steeply skyward and the sails sidled past the windows, their bunts filled with wind and bulging like the waistcoats of giants. But then Mr Smallpace would shout at me from across the shop and I would dutifully return my attentions to the piles of books.

The ritual was impressive and inspiring, but it also wreaked violence on Nonsuch House, especially my corner, which directly abutted the drawbridge and, six times a day, shuddered and groaned under the exertions. As the wheels spun and the girders lifted I could feel timbers quaking under my feet and hear the window-panes thrumming inside their fittings. Books had been known to topple from their shelves, cups and plates from their cupboards, copper pots and joints of meat from their hooks in the pantry. Even worse, soon after Mr Smallpace's death I discovered how one of the upright beams in the study had shifted so far from the ceiling that one wall now bowed ominously outwards.

Something had to be done. I hired a blacksmith's apprentice to arrest the drift of the rogue upright, but in the midst of the renovations a hole was knocked through the rotting wattle-and-daub, exposing a small cavity. The hole was soon enlarged to reveal a chamber, seven feet high by three feet wide, into which I could squeeze with a little room to spare. Experimental tapping with an iron poker revealed that entry to the chamber had been through a hatch concealed in its ceiling, the boards of which now formed the floor of a tiny boot-cupboard one storey above.

Who had built the secret little compartment I could only

guess. I found nothing inside except a wooden platter, a spoon, the tattered remains of what looked like a leather jerkin, and a battered silver candlestick. I had been expecting to find, if anything, a few ancient altar vessels or the scraps of priestly vestments, for I knew that priest-holes had been common features of houses built in the reign of Queen Elizabeth – little hiding-places under staircases or hearthstones to shelter priests of Rome and other victims of our religious persecutions.

That night I had sat inside the chamber with my knees drawn up under my chin and a candle burning in the old candlestick, trying to imagine whoever had hidden here: a Franciscan friar in a hair shirt, possibly even a Jesuit? For a moment I could see him very clearly, a little man kneeling on a rush mat, whispering a miserere, breathing carefully in the cramped darkness as, inches away, the magistrate's searchers called out passwords to one another and sounded the floors and wainscots with the hilts of their swords. I was no papist, but I hoped he had managed to escape, whoever he was, and preserve his secretive life – a hushed, ascetic and almost hermetically sealed existence of the sort for which I suppose I had always longed. So perhaps that was why when I hired a carpenter to fill in the chamber I changed my mind at the last minute, on a sudden impulse, and instructed him to leave the little cavity as it was, but to conceal it behind another wall. This wall was then whitewashed and panelled, and the panelling covered with bookshelves. Once again the chamber was invisible.

I had no expectations of ever using my secret chamber – God forbid! I wished to preserve it as a memorial, that was all. Over the following few years I thought very little about it, though after the searchers began paying their little visits I used it to hide a few tracts and pamphlets that would otherwise have been confiscated and burned. No one else knew of its existence but Monk, to whom it had become a place of endless wonder. Often I could hear him thumping about inside, playing what I thought were mysterious little games. But then one day I raised the hatch in the boot-cupboard and peered inside to discover that he had furnished it with odds and ends such as a three-legged stool, candles, a blanket, reading material, even an old chamber-pot scavenged from somewhere. I suspected him of harbouring plans to take up residence. It was, after all, roughly the size of his own little bedchamber and probably no more uncomfortable.

But one evening as I sat in my armchair I heard a fierce banging from behind the wall and rushed upstairs to catch him in the act of driving nails through the soles of three pairs of old boots and into the top of the wooden hatch. Under interrogation he explained he was devising things so that when he opened the trapdoor and slipped inside the chamber – like so – the pairs of boots would remain in place after the lid was closed. The entrance was thereby disguised. Clever, was it not? He had popped out of the hole and was panting heavily. I agreed that it certainly was. There was no need to ask what had prompted his inspiration. Only three nights earlier the searchers had burst through his door and thrust the burning lantern into his face.

'Well done,' I repeated. I had decided to forgive him the boots, which I hardly ever wore. 'Yes, quite ingenious.' But as I peered into the tiny chamber I was reminded of the priest crouching in the darkness, praying for the preservation of his clandestine life and quiet mission. 'But let us hope we never have occasion to test it.'

We closed the door and crawled out of the cupboard. Then for months on end – sometimes much longer – I would think no more about the little cell concealed behind my study wall.

'Mr Inchbold.' A whisper. The grip on my neck had tightened. 'This way, sir. Up. Follow me . . .'

We ascended quickly, our shadows vaulting up the steps before us. Past the study and the bedchamber, round another landing, then up another curling flight. From below came flashes of torchlight and a rapid thunder of feet. All stealth had now been abandoned. I heard a voice shouting after us, then a thud and a curse as our pursuers were tripped by the fifth stair from the landing. They picked themselves up, cursed again, renewed their pursuit. I heard a voice shouting my name.

By that time we had reached the top. Monk led the way,

scrambling nimbly down the corridor while I staggered a few steps behind, stupefied with fright, looking over my shoulder for the first head to crest the top of the stairs. I had no idea what he was doing, other than running away, until I stumbled into him. He had stopped in front of the boot-cupboard and now held the door open, elegantly, as if we were to board a coach.

'After you, sir.'

I fell to my knees and lowered myself downwards, into the darkness, fingertips clutching the edge of the hatch until my feet found purchase on a stool. A second later Monk dropped lightly beside me, like a cat, then eased shut the camouflaged hatch. We found ourselves in total blackness, without so much as a chink of light from above. I could see no trace of Monk, even though I sensed him only a few inches away, stifling gasps. I turned round, also gasping, but bumped into something. Panic bulged its flimsy membrane inside my gut. The air was so dark it almost seemed material, dense.

I turned again and bumped into another wall. The hole was little bigger than a coffin. I was about to climb out but then felt Monk's hand on my arm and heard boots – what sounded like an army of them – thundering overhead. The intruders had reached the top of the stairs. A voice shouted my name again. I fumbled for a stool, somewhere to sit. I couldn't breathe. More stomping. Doors banging shut. I was going to faint . . .

But I did not faint. Monk slid a stool towards me, I seated myself, then for the next few hours the two of us listened to the commotions above us, faces upturned to the invisible hatch, frozen in silence as the intruders – three men, possibly four – opened doors and tapped every inch of the house with their swords and sticks. Our guests were very thorough. The staircase, the stone jambs of the fireplace, its mantelpiece and hearthstone, the ceilings and floors, the cupboards, wainscots, beds, curtains, every crumbling brick or worm-holed timber – nothing in the house was left untouched. Three times we heard them directly above us, thumping about in the corridor outside the boot-cupboard, then opening its door and tapping at its walls. But three times the cupboard door slammed shut and the footsteps and tapping receded. A moment later I heard soft blows a few bare inches from my ears as the end of a stick carefully sounded the wall of my study. But the partition was thick, filled with hair-plaster and pug, and the hollow sound, if there was one, must have been deadened. After a moment the tapping stopped. I expelled a sigh of relief and felt Monk's hand squeeze my shoulder.

'All right, sir?'

'Yes,' I stammered, a little too loudly. 'All right.'

I was trembling badly and hoped he couldn't tell, but I supposed it no longer mattered. Throughout our ordeal it seemed as if the roles of master and apprentice had been exchanged. From the first moment of our hasty escape up the staircase he had been patient and courageous, while I, his master, was nothing but terror, confusion and, later, complaints. I chafed terribly under the confinement. After only a few minutes on the stool my back ached; then my legs grew stiff and, a short time later, I realised that my bladder desperately needed relief. Then I couldn't breathe the thickening air. My chest gurgled, my diaphragm twitched and heaved as I stifled my basset-hound coughs, any one of which would have betrayed us. I bit my lip and tried to draw strength and comfort from the thought of the priest who had preceded us inside the cell, perhaps in circumstances like these, a little man kissing his Agnus Dei, telling his beads, reciting the Litanies of the Saints under his breath. But it was all *I* could do to keep from whimpering.

Yet Monk was in his element in the cramped, pitch-dark cell. It was as if he had long been preparing for this moment, or as if his earlier experiences with intruders had been a sort of crucible, making him patient and wise, no longer my obedient subaltern but an efficient, decisive leader, capable of planning and assessing. He was the one who decided that we could not afford a candle, who found the blanket to cushion my back, who whispered reassurances about our supply of air and chances of escape . . . and who, after the outside door banged noisily shut and everything fell silent, was able to tell that one man was still inside the house, standing perfectly still, waiting for us to emerge, which I had been only too anxious to do. A few minutes later, of course, we heard a low cough from inside the study. So we waited another couple of hours until he too had departed. Then Monk made a step with his interlaced fingers and hoisted me upwards. I clambered into the boot-cupboard, gasping for air and then emerging into the dawn-lit corridors and chambers like a survivor crawling from the rubble of a disaster.

Only there were no signs of disaster either in the house or the shop below. Certainly nothing like what had happened a few days before. We tiptoed through the rooms in semi-darkness, keeping away from the windows – another of Monk's wise recommendations – and looking for any signs of what had happened. But it was as if no one else had been inside the house; as if the past few hours had been nothing but a shared nightmare. I even discovered the firelock on the bottom step, apparently untouched. The only evidence of our visitors was a faint whiff of torch smoke added to the fug of the house.

'Who d'you reckon they was, sir?' Up here, pacing the familiar corridors, Monk had reverted to being my deferential apprentice. 'Same coves as before, d'you think?'

'No, I think not.' We were inside the shop now, poking about with an eye on the green door. 'They weren't after our books, were they? Not like the men the other night.'

He nodded his head, and for a moment we gazed about in silence. No, none of the books had been touched. They still stood in the perfect ranks into which we had assembled them on their shelves only a few hours earlier. Nor had the men come for our money. The lock on the iron chest under my bed was untouched, as was the pouch of coins behind the shop's counter and, more importantly, the store of sovereigns and papers under the floorboards. Not so much as a tin farthing was missing from the house. I became aware that Monk's baffled, querying gaze had come to rest on my face.

'You reckon they came looking for you, then?'

I shrugged, unable to meet his prising glance. I turned round to inspect the lock on the door, which was intact, like everything else. The cracksmen, whoever they were, had known their business.

But just then something beside the door, a smudge of dirt, caught my eye, and I knelt to examine it. A clot of grey powder, a fairy-dust that was gritty to the touch and faintly iridescent in the morning light.

'What is it, sir?' Monk was leaning over my shoulder.

'Coquina,' I told him after a moment's inspection. 'Limestone.'

'Limestone?' He was scratching his head and breathing audibly. 'From a quarry?'

'No, not a quarry. The sea. See this?' I blew on the powder to expose a tiny fragment, what looked like a bone chip. 'It's made from crushed cockle-shells.'

He ran a finger over the dust. 'Blimey, sir. How'd cockle-shells get in here? You reckon they was brought inside by . . . ?'

'I do indeed.' I straightened, still examining the fine chips in my palm. 'Coquina is used in road-making,' I explained. 'Carriageways in front of mansions, that sort of thing. It must have been tracked inside on their boots.'

Monk nodded solemnly as if waiting for me to explain something further, which I didn't. After a minute I brushed the dust from my palms and stood before the shuttered window. It was almost eight o'clock by now. I watched through the louvres as the morning sunlight striped the floor behind me and etched long shadows on to the carriageway. The bands of light hurt my eyes and sent sharp pains radiating to the back of my skull. But I leaned forward and – just as I had done a half-dozen times in the past two days – peered up and down the lengths of carriageway. It was filling with morning traffic, with its familiar cacophony of shouting voices, ringing horseshoes, the iron clanking of bolts and bars as shops opened along the bridge. Apprentices with broomsticks materialised before them and swept at patches of sunlight.

I felt a painful throb beneath my breastbone as I watched the scene unfurl. This was my favourite moment of the day, the time when I would swing open the shutters, lower the awning, beeswax the counter and bookcases, cleanse the grate, light a fire, then bring a kettle of water to the boil for the first coffee of the morning and retire behind the counter and wait for my first customers to open the green door and step inside. But this morning I suspected the ritual would never be the same again. For who else, I wondered, might appear on the bridge this morning and then push inside the shop? Who else was out there, what evil eminence with his secret powers, hiding in the porches and doorways, watching the green door and waiting for the next time? Because what I hadn't told Monk was that the carriageways and footpaths of Whitehall Palace were covered with coquina – it had crunched under my feet as I wove my way to the offices of the Exchequer.

My glum thoughts were interrupted by a loud shriek; then the window-panes hummed and the timbers of the shop trembled in anticipation beneath my feet. I squinted through the slats and saw the drawbridge rising skywards like a piece of enormous clockwork, casting its arm of shadow across the front of the shop. A familiar hush descended over the carriageway. Carts and wagons grouped outside my shop, while a dozen buff-coloured sails gathered the wind and drifted, rippling, through the gap. A few more minutes and the last of them had sauntered past the window. Then the ropes slipped and strained in their pulleys, the wooden cogs ground together, the floor timbers trembled, and the bridge lowered into place with a few more geriatric groans. The traffic in front of Nonsuch Books came back to life and surged across the cobbles, as it did every day at this hour, with its din of creaks and curses.

Yes, all of the familiar rituals had begun. But I knew, suddenly, that I would not be a part of them this morning, that I would not be opening the shop, that for the first time in my professional life I would be turning my back on my duties. For my little ship was not sailing homeward, as I had thought, but careering wildly off course, into unknown waters, without maps or compasses. As I climbed the turnpike stairway a few moments later, clutching at the wall for support, I knew that Nonsuch House, my refuge for the past twenty years, was no longer safe.

III

The Labyrinth of
the World

Chapter One

So began my harassed and vagabond life, my tumultuous exile from Nonsuch House. I had no idea, at first, where I might flee. As I climbed the stairs to my bedchamber I contemplated leaving London altogether, but soon I thought better of it. I had set foot outside of the city on barely more than a half-dozen occasions: twice to the book fair in Ely, three times to the one in Oxford, and once as far as Stourbridge, also for a book fair. Then, too, there had been the longer and much more arduous journey to Pontifex Hall, where it seemed that all of my problems had begun.

I thought of taking refuge in Wapping instead, but quickly decided against giving poor Biddulph any more grist for his mill, which already ground out quite enough fear and conspiracy on its own. So as I filled a small leather book bag with a change of clothing I thought next of a few of my other customers. There were several of them – quiet, gentle scholars – who would, I believe, gladly have taken me for a night or two, or even longer if I wished. But what excuses might I have offered them? I buckled the bag and slung it over my shoulder. No: there was only one place in London left for me to go; only one place for fugitives like me.

When I returned downstairs Monk had opened the shop, and several customers – cheery, familiar faces – were browsing among the shelves. I nodded to them and then whispered to Monk that I must leave Nonsuch House for a number of days and that the shop was once again in his hands. He glanced at my book bag but showed very little surprise. I supposed that after the events of the past few nights he had come to expect these sudden caprices from his master. I felt a pang of guilt at deserting him – as if I, of all people, might have saved or protected him. Then I took a last look round the shop and slipped outside, where I quickly lost myself among the thick crowds pressing five-deep along the footpaths of the bridge.

Five minutes later I had crossed under Southwark Gate, where the traffic was slightly thinner. After glancing over my shoulder I stumbled with my thorn-stick down the footpath to the landing-stairs along the river, where I engaged a sculler. The waterman grinned and asked me where I wished to go.

'Up river,' I told him.

He watched me suspiciously as he unshipped his sculls and shoved off from the pier, no doubt because I had pulled the canvas tilt over the wooden hoops and now, despite the sunny weather, sat hunched under the canopy, which reeked of mildew. I peeped out from under this shroud to confirm that no one had followed me down to the landing-stairs. The river downstream was empty except for a couple of fishing smacks anchored in the shallows, busily shortening sail and awaiting the drawbridge's next ascent. Beyond their masts Nonsuch House rose above the piers, before dwindling into the soft haze as if disappearing into thin air.

'What's your pleasure, sir? Where shall I take you?'

'Alsatia,' I replied. Then I ducked back inside the canopy and didn't emerge until our bow had scraped against the landing-steps of the coal-wharves beneath the Golden Horn.

I took a room at the Half Moon Tavern, which stood in Abbey Court, more or less the centre (as far as I could ever tell) of the labyrinth of courts and by-streets that was Alsatia. My room was on the topmost floor and could be reached only by means of a narrow, twisting staircase, up which I was guided by the proprietress, Mrs Fawkes, a small, dark-haired woman whose quiet and gentle manner seemed more akin to a nunnery than a tavern in the middle of Alsatia. I had signed her guest-book as 'Silas Cobb', then paid a shilling for two nights in advance, which entitled me, she explained in her soft voice, to breakfast and supper as well as a bed. And should I require anything else for my pleasure – ale, tobacco, the services of a chambermaid – I must not hesitate to let her know immediately. Her sloe-coloured eyes had been modestly lowered as she made the allusion to the young ladies whose faces had peered at us from curtained doorways as I followed her upstairs. I assured her that I anticipated no such needs.

'In fact . . .' I was fishing in my pocket for another shilling, which I slipped into her palm. 'It is urgent that I not be disturbed during the course of my stay. Not by anyone, day or night. Do you understand?'

I suspected from Mrs Fawkes's reaction that such requests were not unusual among her guests.

'Of course, Mr Cobb,' she whispered, smiling at me before shyly dropping her eyes to the chatelaine at her waist, then to the black cat that had followed us up the stairs. 'Not a soul shall disturb you. Not as long as you reside under my roof. You have my word.'

Once she and the cat had departed I placed my bag on the bed and looked round the room. It was as small and spartan as a monk's cell, furnished with nothing more than a ladder-back chair, a table and a four-post bed with a fatigued mattress. But it was clean enough and would suit me perfectly well. Through its tiny window I could see the bell-tower of Bridewell Prison and, far beyond it, the north end of London Bridge, a sight that cheered me greatly and seemed to make my exile – as I already thought of it – slightly more bearable. I sat down on the bed, drew a shaky breath and congratulated myself on my choice.

I had been depressed and utterly baffled when I arrived in Alsatia an hour earlier. I was exhausted after the ordeal of the night and possessed no plan other than to seek refuge, like so many others, in its precincts. I first considered taking a room at the Golden Horn, then at the Saracen's Head, but each time I ruled it out. In either place I might have encountered Dr Pickvance, and I didn't yet know the nature of his relationship with Henry Monboddo. Besides, the Half Moon Tavern looked slightly more respectable – if that was the word – than either of the other establishments. It had just opened its doors when I arrived, and Mrs Fawkes was bidding farewell to several richly dressed gentlemen, attended by the black cat that followed her everywhere like a witch's familiar.

The premises otherwise seemed empty except for the young ladies who peered at us from their curtained-off rooms.

Yes, I told myself as I lay down on the bed: I would be safe here. All the same, I removed the firelock from my book bag and set it beside the bed.

I fell asleep almost immediately and didn't wake until early evening, by which time the first yellow lights were kindling on London Bridge. My fob-watch informed me I had slept for almost ten hours.

I rolled out of bed and, still befuddled by sleep, withdrew two small vials from my bag: two of the three purchases I had made before renting the room. Inside the first vial was a decoction of bramble leaves bought from an apothecary named Foskett, who informed me how the preparation, created in his own laboratory, was a superb remedy for sores in the mouth or else those on what he winked and called the 'secret parts'. I winked back at him, winced emphatically, and allowed him to believe what he wished.

After bringing a kettle of water to the boil I poured the decoction of bramble leaves inside, stirred it, then mixed in those of the second vial, three grams of lye purchased in the same shop. I was fully awake now, hands trembling as I replaced the caps. When the mixture had cooled I poured it into the washbasin and used it to drench my hair, my beard and even my eyebrows. Whether he knew it or not, Foskett's preparation did more than heal venereal complaints. The shaving-glass confirmed that both my hair and my beard had turned from a greying brown to jet black. For good measure I trimmed my beard into a sharp point, in the fashion favoured by Cavaliers.

I then turned to my last purchase of the morning, a suit of clothes from a haberdasher in Whitefriars Street. I folded and tucked away my sober bookseller costume – my threadbare doublet, my breeches with their seat worn almost through, my laddered stockings – and donned the new suit, piece by piece. First a gold-buttoned purple surcoat; then a pair of beribboned breeches with matching silk stockings; finally a black velvet hat with a dangling purple ribbon and a cocked brim. I would be conspicuous enough, to be sure, but not recognisable by anyone – scarcely even by myself – as Isaac Inchbold. No, I thought as I inspected the image given back by the darkened window: no one would know me as I went about my business tonight.

Satisfied with these effects, I sent for my supper. A short time later it was delivered to the room by one of the so-called chambermaids, a big-hipped, damask-cheeked girl with a country accent. She placed it on the table, accepted a tuppence and my thanks in return, then made her discreet exit without so much as a glance in my direction. The meal, fried haddock and parsnips, was quite tasty, and I ate with a great appetite. I also consumed with relish a cup of double ale. A few minutes later I was descending the staircase with the pistol tucked into the waistband of my new breeches.

At this hour the Half Moon was filling with patrons whose harsh laughter, interspersed with the shrieks of a fiddle, drifted up the stairs. The creaking treads attracted the attention of a couple of the residents in the curtained rooms whose disembodied faces, also plump and damask-cheeked, emerged from the folds of the curtains, or whose curtains had been drawn back to reveal candle-lit rooms with looking-glasses and vases of bright flowers. Smells of perfume and tobacco smoke wafted towards me, followed by a few muffled chuckles. I ducked my behatted head, but not before catching another snatch of my reflection in one of the looking-glasses: a black-haired bravo with his buttons glinting and his hat tipped at a rakish angle. Only my trusty thorn-stick – which I had been loath to abandon – proclaimed my former identity. Later I would wonder at the concatenation of strange events that had fetched me up here, but for the moment I didn't stop to ponder how it had come to pass that I, a law-abiding citizen, a humble bookseller, should now be descending the steps of a brothel in the middle of Alsatia, at nightfall, in disguise.

The sky had darkened by the time I emerged into Abbey Court. I looked round for a moment, taking my bearings from a sun-faded signpost on the corner, before walking north towards Fleet Street. On the way I passed Arrowsmith Court and through its narrow opening caught a glimpse of the Turk's grisly visage leering back at me. The windows of the Saracen's Head glowed orange, but those in Dr Pickvance's rooms were shuttered and dark. I kept walking north, the firelock chafing at my thigh and poking my hip. Across the ditch, in Blackfriars, lines of washing hung between the newly built tenements, pale swallowtails of smocks and shifts, like the bunting from some vanished procession. In Whitefriars Street a fox darted across my path, snout lowered, brush raised. It seemed an omen of some sort, as did the snatch of boldly chalked graffiti I saw, seconds later, on a collapsing hoarding: the same symbol – the horned man – that I had seen twice, also in Alsatia. Except that it wasn't a horned man or the devil, I suddenly realised, but a man in a winged hat. For the mark was not only the alchemical symbol for quicksilver, I knew, but also the astrological symbol for the planet Mercury.

I almost dismissed the sign and resumed walking. After all, our city was full of charlatans casting horoscopes and scribbling prophecies. Indeed, the newssheets were full of accounts of King Charles consulting our most famous astrologer, the great Elias Ashmole, to cast a horoscope to determine the most auspicious date for the sitting of Parliament. But then I recalled that Mercury, the messenger of the gods, the patron of merchants and traders such as myself, was the name given by the Romans to Hermes Trismegistus. And Hermes Trismegistus was the author of the *Corpus hermeticum*, in which was found, of course, *The Labyrinth of the World*.

I stood before the hoarding, staring as if spell-stopped at the brief scrawl. Was this some kind of grotesque hoax? A coincidence? A clue? Like all else I had discovered, it seemed impossible to interpret.

I turned round and began walking rapidly northwards, the balls of lead clattering in the pocket of my breeches. The breeze had strengthened, and coal-ash dashed in a quick gust across the cobbles, stinging my cheeks. I quickened my pace. A minute later Fleet Street opened before me, and I raised an arm to hail an empty hackney-coach.

Once again my destination was St Olave's, through whose

gate I stepped, some thirty minutes later, to find the churchyard empty except for a single mourner at the far end, nearest Seething Lane, and a sexton digging a fresh grave by lamplight. The mourner, his back turned, seemed not to notice me; nor did the sexton, the top of whose head was barely visible above the lip of the grave. His spade was rasping in the wet London clay and chiming whenever the metal struck a stone.

I had no message to leave for Alethea. Earlier, as I ate my supper in the Half Moon, I debated whether or not I should tell her how my shop had twice been invaded by persons unknown and that I had therefore left Nonsuch House in fear of my safety. But in the end I decided not to. Alethea, like Biddulph, entertained quite enough wild fancies without needing further ones added to them. I also decided not to tell her of my residence at the Half Moon.

Although I had been instructed to check the strong-box each evening, I had yet to receive a letter from Alethea via this means, and so I was surprised and even a little gratified to find a piece of paper inside it. I sprang open its lock, as quietly as possible so as not to alert the mourner, who seemed to be studying Seething Lane, as if waiting for someone to come through its gate and into the churchyard. I angled the paper into the light of the grave-digger's flickering lantern and began reading what proved to be the information that I had been waiting for these past few days. Preparations for my journey, she wrote, were now complete. A coach-and-four would be waiting for me at the Three Pigeons in High Holborn the next morning at seven o'clock. Her name was signed with a flourish at the bottom.

I locked the strong-box, but instead of destroying the piece of paper I creased it along the folds and slipped it inside my pocket. But I had already decided I would obey its request and make certain I was aboard the coach the next morning. I didn't relish the thought of showing myself abroad during the daytime, but perhaps Huntingdonshire would be safer for me than London.

Five minutes later I was back in the street, pressing forward through the darkness, pausing briefly at each fork or intersection to peer down narrow, tenement-lined streets in search of an empty hack. None appeared. No one did. So I picked my way through the darkness, through streets as empty as if abandoned after the onset of plague or war.

Only after another twenty minutes did I reach an opening and enter the broad sweep of the Strand. From there it was just a short walk to Alsatia, which, outcast that I was, I had already begun to think of as home.

Chapter Two

The coach's progress through the Chislet Marshes was a slow one. Foxcroft guided the horses through the mud of the coastal road until they reached one of the De Quester posting-inns. There the exhausted Barbs were exchanged and the arduous journey recommenced. White fogs hovered all day in the ditches and over the flooded hopfields, but Foxcroft dared not light a lantern for fear of Lord Stanhope's ruffians. Nor did he light one as dusk arrived. The coach made its way blindly along overgrown cattle droves and paths that slunk through decrepit orchards.

By this time his unexpected passengers had been reduced to two. The only member of the strange trio who had spoken a word, the larger of the men, had disembarked in Herne Bay. Foxcroft's remaining companions were now huddled under a blanket, crouched low among the sacks of mail. A half-dozen times he had tried unsuccessfully to draw them into conversation. He fed them all the same, cheese and black bread from the inns, along with cups of cider. He even offered them swigs from his own wineskin, which were declined with brief shakes of the head. The woman would sometimes turn her head to peer at the road behind, but the man, a thin little fellow, sat perfectly still. Some sort of bejewelled cabinet the size of a large sugar-loaf was clutched to his breast.

'What's that, hmm? A treasure chest?'

Silence from the back. Foxcroft shook the reins and the horses stepped up their pace, tossing their heads and blowing white plumes into the air. In a few minutes they would reach the high road to London, where the dangers increased of Stanhope's ruffians. But if the coach was ambushed the attackers might be appeased, he reckoned, by a prize like the chest. It was for that reason alone that Foxcroft was suffering their presence in his coach. The pair of them might spare him another dented crown.

'Yours, is it?' He had twisted round in his seat. 'I say, very nice.'

Still no reply. In the darkness he could barely make out their two heads, only inches apart. The thin little man stared fixedly at his feet. Perhaps they spoke no English? Foxcroft knew as well as anyone that these days London was full of foreigners, Spaniards for the most part, all of them either spies or priests, often both. The infestation was a sign of the times. The Spanish King and his ambassador lorded over old James. First that modern-day Drake, Sir Walter Raleigh, had been sent to the chopping-block for daring to fight the Spaniards on their own ground. Next King James had begun turning priests loose from the gaols and even daring to talk about marrying his son to, of all people, a Spanish princess! And now, worst of all, the old dolt was too niggardly to send an army to help his very own daughter even though her husband's lands in Germany were being invaded by hordes of Spaniards.

Still, he reassured himself, neither of his passengers looked at all Spanish. The woman, from the little he could glimpse of her, looked uncommonly attractive despite her bedraggled appearance. She was also young, scarcely more than a girl. What on earth was she doing with such a milksop, unless it had something to do with the box the fellow was clutching to his scrawny breast?

After another hour the smells of the country gave way to those of the city, silence to intermittent noise. The coach-and-six crossed the high road to London in darkness, then swiftly bore riverwards in the direction of Gravesend. Foxcroft intended to cross the river from Gravesend to Tilbury on a horse ferry, then ride into London along the north shore, where Stanhope's bruisers would scarcely expect to find him. If all went well he would reach the Ald Gate by the time it was creaking open, and from there it would be a short jaunt through the streets to the De Quester offices in Cornhill. What he might do with his other cargo, however, his two mysterious passengers, he had no idea.

He need not have worried himself. When the coach finally reached Gravesend it was obliged to wait almost two hours for the next ferry to Tilbury. He arranged for a new team and then tramped the streets until he found an alehouse that was open, in whose tap room he emptied three pintpots and demolished a pigeon pie, before returning to the posting-inn in time to watch the ferry disgorge its handful of passengers. His own passengers were quite forgotten at this point, and not until he had paid his two shillings and reached the middle of the black waters did he suddenly remember them. When he turned round in the box-seat he was surprised to discover that they had vanished into thin air, along with their glittering cargo.

As it happened, Vilém and Emilia were in a boat of their own at that moment, travelling upstream towards London, which lay some twenty miles to the west. The small barge had pushed off from the dock at Gravesend almost an hour earlier and, after threading its way among the pinks and merchantmen riding at anchor before the custom-house, reached the middle of the swirling current. From there it would be at least three hours to the dock at Billingsgate, the barge-master had informed them, even on a flowing tide. And from Billingsgate it might then take them as much as another hour to reach their final destination.

Emilia shivered and huddled deeper inside the canvas tilt as the water slapped and gurgled against the hull. Four more hours of cold and fear. But at long last she knew where they were going. They were bound, Vilém told her, for York House, a mansion in the Strand, near Charing Cross, where they would be met by Henry Monboddo. Vilém had been instructed to hand over the casket containing the parchment to Monboddo and no one else. Monboddo was experienced in such dealings, Vilém insisted, as the boat wallowed in the current. He was a friend of Prince Charles, and at present he was furnishing the galleries of York House to the extravagant but discriminating tastes of its new owner, George Villiers, the Earl of Buckingham.

Emilia watched the lights of Gravesend dim and disappear as the river turned north. The name was a familiar one. Rumours in Prague had set him to work fitting a fleet of men-o'-war to sail into the Mediterranean to attack Spain. But whether the ships had been fitted, whether or not they ever sailed, the attack never took place.

'So that is who the books are intended for, then? The Earl of Buckingham?'

Vilém shook his head, then raised his eyes from the casket wedged between his boots and glanced in the direction of the barge-master, who was grunting rhythmically as he leaned on his pole. Bewhiskered, wearing a leather jerkin, he had greeted them suspiciously in the barge-room a short time earlier, squinting at the pair of them – and then even more insistently at the casket – in the weak candle-light. Sir Ambrose had warned Vilém that the boatmen on the Thames were in the pay of the Secretary of State or Count Gondomar, the Spanish Ambassador, so to ensure discretion he paid the fellow an extra two shillings. This act only made the grizzled old rogue even more suspicious; as did the request to travel upriver without a lantern.

'No, not Buckingham,' he whispered, leaning closer. 'He, like Monboddo, is only an intermediary, an agent for another party, someone even more powerful.'

'Yes?' She too had leaned forward. Someone more powerful than the Lord High Admiral? The canvas awning stretched over their heads smelled of mildew and a glazing of salt. Outside, the cold wind was flapping its stiffened sides. 'Who, then?'

For the wealthiest and most discriminating collector in all of England, that was who. Because Monboddo and Sir Ambrose had furnished not only the libraries of Frederick and Rudolf but also, Vilém explained, that of their own countryman, England's finest connoisseur, the Prince of Wales himself. Young Prince Charles was not an iconoclast like his sister Elizabeth with her Puritan pastors poised at the ready to sniff out any sign of popery or turpitude. No, Charles loved images and other relics as much as his sister despised them. It was well known that he hoped to purchase the great Mantua Collection from the impoverished Gonzagas, but less well known, according to Vilém, was the fact that he was equally determined to lay his hands on the treasures of both the Bibliotheca Palatina and the Spanish Rooms. For these thousands of books, manuscripts and assorted curiosities were not only valuable in themselves, prize additions to the Royal Library in St James's Palace, but they were also the only means left of keeping the rampaging Spaniards at bay and thereby preserving religious toleration and freedom across half of Europe.

'Oh?' Emilia saw rearing before her eyes the desiccated serpents, the mummified heads with their grotesque grins. 'How might that be?'

Vilém had begun rubbing his palms slowly together. She could sense his excitement. The absence of Sir Ambrose seemed to have done him good: he had not spoken this much in weeks.

'I need not tell you,' he whispered, 'that both collections are in danger of falling into the hands of either the Spaniards or Cardinal Baronius, if the soldiers don't destroy them first, I should say, or the looters in the marshes. But the Prince proposes to purchase the whole lot from his brother-in-law – the complete contents of both libraries, along with the treasures from the Spanish Rooms. At what price I have no idea, but his financier, Burlamaqui, has been raising funds for the past three months. Frederick will then use the money to equip armies and repel the invaders from both Bohemia and the Palatinate.'

She was surprised by this plan, remembering Vilém's alarmed reaction to rumours about secret inventories, about deals struck with bishops and princes – 'turkey buzzards', he called them – who had sent their agents and emissaries scuttling to Prague ahead of their armies so they might pick at the carcass of Bohemia while there was still something left of it.

'So the rumours in Prague were true, then? Frederick was seeking to sell the collections after all?'

'Yes, yes – but the strategy is more involved than that,' he replied quickly, 'more complicated than an exchange of books for musket-balls. The collection will remain intact, and the crates of books and manuscripts will themselves become the means by which the Catholics will be forced from both Bohemia and the Palatinate. Or that is the plan, one that Sir Ambrose worked out with Buckingham and the Prince of Wales. But the business must be carried out in the utmost secrecy,' he added solemnly.

She drew the blanket, stolen from the De Quester coach, more tightly round their shoulders. 'Because of the Spaniards.'

He nodded. 'Neither King Philip nor Gondomar must know of the plan, that much is obvious. Burlamaqui is raising the funds in secret because many of them come through his connections with bankers in Italy and Spain. Nor must the plans for the Prince's betrothal to the Infanta go astray. Such double-dealing is distasteful, true enough, but cheap at the price, I think, because the Infanta's hand is worth all of £600,000. Such a sum will buy many books and paintings, will it not? To say nothing of how it will keep a good many soldiers – the best mercenaries in Europe – in powder and shot for years to come. Ingenious, is it not, using the King of Spain's own money to snatch back Bohemia and the Palatinate? To secure the Bibliotheca Palatina as well as the treasures of the Spanish Rooms?'

She followed his gaze as he squinted through the opening in the tilt. Were they alone on the water, or was that another barge in the distance, barely visible in the light of one of the guard-boats? So far the river had been empty except for the odd collier or a convoy of smacks heaped with their catches of mackerel. Each time one of them approached Emilia and Vilém leant back inside the tilt and averted their faces. But for the past ten minutes they had seen no one.

'But there's more to the plan than that,' he resumed after a moment. 'The situation is complicated. Other interests must be considered.'

The arrival in England of the books and other treasures also had to be kept secret from King James himself. The sale could not be completed through what Vilém called the 'normal channels' – a continent-wide network of brokers and financiers – because then it would have been discovered by the numerous agents of the Earl of Arundel, one of England's wealthiest collectors of statues and other artefacts, including books. Arundel was a Howard, a Roman Catholic, a member of the powerful family whose hatred for Buckingham was as well known, he said, as its close ties with the Spanish Ambassador. Neither was it a secret that for the past few years King James had been little more than Gondomar's creature, the plaything of the Spaniards. Did she need reminding that he received an annual pension of 5,000 *felipes* from the King of Spain? That he sided with Philip over the rebellion in Bohemia? That he lent no support to his daughter and her husband, his own flesh and blood? That he betrayed them to the Catholics just as he had betrayed Raleigh two years earlier? And so the King and most of his courtiers and ministers, including Arundel, were not made privy to the plot. Arundel would have reported it at once to Gondomar, Gondomar would have reported it to King James, and King James – 'an old fool in his dotage' – would have regarded it as nothing more than an act of robbery.

'Yes, yes,' he finished, 'and no doubt he would regard a man like Sir Ambrose as nothing more than a common pirate. No doubt Sir Ambrose would meet the same fate as Sir Walter Raleigh . . .'

The barge nosed round the bend and into the waters of the Long Reach. At Greenhithe a few fishing smacks had left the dock and were heading downstream into the estuary. Emilia watched them riding against the tide with their fore-and-aft sails luminous as ghosts. Vilém had fallen silent. She shifted her weight on the hard thwart, wondering how much of what he said was true and how much an elaborate fiction.

The boat was poled forward on the tide, a length at a time, round another bend and into the Erith Reach with its roadsteads on one side, the bell-foundries and anchorsmiths on the other. Daylight was still more than an hour away, but so too was London even though the wind had swung round to the west. She scented the first traces of its musk and smoke, what smelled like the foul hide of an ancient beast. Spires and the rhombic shapes of warehouses, dark and silent, loomed and fell away, as did the merchantmen against whose monstrous hulls the splashes of the pole were echoing. She turned her head and peered past the barge-master's dark form. Was someone behind them in the river, pulling a pair of oars?

She turned to Vilém, but he seemed to have noticed nothing. He was bent almost double, eyes fixed on the casket.

The casket contained a Hermetic text, fourteen pages of an ancient manuscript bound in arabesque – a text more valuable, he said, than all of the other crates of books put together. It was a copy made two hundred years earlier from an even more ancient document brought to Constantinople by a refugee, a Harranian scribe fleeing the persecutions of the caliph of Baghdad. When Constantinople was invaded by one of the caliph's descendants, Mehmet II, the Ottoman Sultan, it was saved by another scribe who smuggled it from the Monastery of Magnana before the library and scriptorium could be pillaged by the Turks. And now almost two centuries later the parchment was being smuggled to safety yet again, escaping another conflagration, another war of religion, this time in the Kingdom of Bohemia.

Emilia knew nothing about the *Corpus hermeticum*. The name reminded her, though, of some of the books she stumbled across in the castle in Breslau on the night of the feast, those whose titles suggested impious pursuits. But Vilém swore there was nothing impious about the Hermetic texts. Indeed, parts of them were even thought to foretell the coming of Christ. Together they consisted, he explained, of some two dozen books, along with who knew how many others that had disappeared over the centuries following other invasions, other wars. Some of the books dealt with philosophical subjects, others with theology, still others – the ones that attracted the most readers and commentators – with the arts of alchemy and astrology.

None of this made the least bit of sense to Emilia. How could a manuscript of fourteen pages – a few scraps of goatskin scribbled with a mixture of lampblack and vegetable gum – possibly be valuable enough for someone to kill for?

Vilém was still talking as the boat wound its way along the edge of the Hornchurch Marshes, twisting and then righting itself in the currents that eddied dangerously at each bend. His words tumbled out of him so quickly she could barely follow them. The *Corpus hermeticum* described a whole universe, he said, a magical place whose every part, from the moons of Jupiter to the smallest mote of dust, formed the threads of an ever-radiating web in which each atom was connected to every other atom. The parts also attracted and otherwise influenced one another so that a subtle but intimate connection existed between, say, the flow of the blood in the body and the flight of the stars through the heavens. These amazing influences could be detected by means of secret signs inscribed across the surface or in the core of every living thing and, once detected, could be manipulated and exploited so that wounds would be healed, diseases cured, events foretold or forestalled – the destinies of entire kingdoms interpreted or even changed. The man able to read these bristling hieroglyphics, these secret scriptures, was therefore a magician possessed of stupendous powers, capable of turning the influences of the heavens to his own ends. And any book purporting to describe these secret marks, to catalogue and explain them . . . well, the value of any such volume would be past measure.

'So the parchment is a magical book of some sort?' she managed to interrupt at last. 'And that is why Prince Charles wants it?'

'So it would seem, yes. No doubt he wants it to ornament his library in St James's Palace. But perhaps there is another reason as well.' Vilém raised his eyes from the casket. 'For the manuscript now possesses political as well as magical powers.'

The place of the *Corpus hermeticum* in the pantheon of literature was now more complex, he explained. Rome had grown suspicious of the Hermetic texts. Some of the books may well have predicted the coming of Christ, if interpreted in a charitable light by the Vatican's consultors. But other Hermetic teachings were a threat to orthodoxy. Of special concern were those passages on the structure of the universe and the divinity of the sun. After all, Copernicus himself had quoted from the *Asclepius* at the outset of *De revolutionibus orbium coelestium*, the heretical volume that dethroned the earth in favour of the sun. But even worse were the political dangers now coming from those who fingered the pages of the Hermetic texts, which were currently appearing in dozens of new editions and translations. Philosophers like Bruno and Duplessis-Mornay had dreamed of ending the wars of religion between Catholics and Protestants by promoting the philosophy of Hermeticism as a substitute for Christianity. But to the authorities in Rome the Hermeticists were, like the Jews, supporters of the Protestant cause who wished to erode the powers of the Pope. The suspicion was not without foundation. By the year 1600, when Bruno was martyred, the books had become the lodestone for all manner of heretics and reformers. Dozens of sects and secret societies began burgeoning all over Europe, like mushrooms in nightsoil: occultists and revolutionaries, Navarrists and Rosicrucians, Cabalists and magicians, liberals, mystics, fanatics and false Messiahs of every hue, all demanding spiritual reform and prophesying the downfall of Rome, all quoting the ancient writings of Hermes Trismegistus as their authority for a universal reformation.

'The Counter-Reformation is losing its footing,' Vilém explained, 'despite the armies of Maximilian and the bonfires of the Inquisition. A Pandora's box has been opened which Rome is trying to slam shut by whatever means. Sorcery and magic now rank with dogmatic heresy. Cabalist literature has been put on the *Index* and in 1592 Francesco Patrizzi, one of the translators of the *Corpus hermeticum*, was condemned by the Inquisition. The Jesuits at the Collegio Romano have begun an *Index* of their own, a list on which the works of Paracelsus and Cornelius Agrippa have been placed alongside those of Galileo. Johann Valentin Andreae, founder of the

Rosicrucians, has been pronounced a heretic by the Cardinals of the Inquisition. Traiano Boccalini, Andreae's mentor, a supporter of Henry of Navarre, was murdered in Venice, while Navarre himself, the polestar of all of these hopes, was assassinated in Paris. But the movement is Hydra-headed and unstoppable. With Navarre's death came a new hope, a new axle round which everything else could gather and spin.'

'The Elector Palatine,' murmured Emilia. 'King Frederick.'

'Yes.' He gave another shrug. 'Another hope that proved a sad delusion.'

A few lights along the shoreline wavered slowly past. The barge had shunted into Gallion's Reach, avoiding the landing-piers that projected into the ink-black water. The boat's wake as it passed stirred to life the strings of moored lighters whose hulls bobbed in the swell. Beyond the jetties and mud banks lay nameless hamlets and tumbledown cottages. They had been in the barge for over two hours now, but the river had narrowed only slightly. At times the shore seemed to vanish.

'So the parchment is a danger to orthodoxy.' She was beginning to understand the stakes involved, or thought she did. 'Rome hopes to suppress it, to stamp out its heresies before they can take hold.'

'Very possibly. At the moment Rome is terrified of any threat to its dogma, of a split that would undermine its fight against Protestantism. Galileo with his moons was one such threat, but four years ago he was silenced by the Holy Office, warned by Cardinal Bellarmine not to write another word in defence of the heretic Copernicus. The appearance of another document in support of Copernicanism or any other heresy would, however, be a drastic blow, especially at this time.'

'And especially if it came from an authority as great as Hermes Trismegistus.'

'Yes. So the manuscript will be locked away in the secret archives of the Bibliotheca Vaticana if the cardinals and bishops lay their hands on it. Perhaps it will even be destroyed.' Once more he lowered his gaze to the cabinet between his feet. 'Except there is something else,' he said slowly, 'something I fail to understand. For in the past few years the authority of Hermes

Trismegistus has been challenged, even destroyed. Not by the theologians of Rome, but by a Protestant, a Huguenot.'

There had been a recent dispute, he said, between a Protestant scholar, Isaac Casaubon, and a Roman Catholic, Cardinal Baronius, Keeper of the Vatican Library – the man who, Vilém claimed, now wished to cart off to Rome both the Bibliotheca Palatina and the manuscripts in the Spanish Rooms. Years ago the Cardinal had published a massive study about the history of the Church, the *Annales ecclesiastici*, in which Hermes Trismegistus was described as one of the Gentile prophets along with Hydaspes and the Sibylline oracles. This treatise was much admired by Vilém's teachers, the Jesuits in the Clementinum, but since then it had been soundly refuted by Casaubon, a Switzer, a Huguenot who had come to England at the invitation of King James. And Casaubon's magnum opus, *De rebus sacris et ecclesiasticis exercitationes XVI*, published six years earlier in 1614, was said to prove beyond doubt that the whole of the *Corpus hermeticum* was a forgery composed not by some ancient Egyptian priest at Hermoupolis Magna but instead by a band of Greeks living in Alexandria in the century after Christ. These men had cobbled together a mishmash of Plato, the Gospels, the Jewish Cabala, together with a few scraps of Egyptian philosophy, and had managed to hoodwink scholars, priests and kings for more than a thousand years.

Vilém was shaking his head morosely as they swayed from side to side with the motions of the barge. It made no sense. Why should Sir Ambrose have been so intent on smuggling *The Labyrinth of the World* out of Prague? Sir Ambrose, a good Protestant, certainly knew the work of Casaubon. And why, too, if it was a fake, should the Cardinal wish to suppress it? Because that was who had pursued them from Prague, Vilém now told her: the agents of Cardinal Baronius.

'Can it not be opened?' Emilia, too, had returned her gaze to the cabinet. 'Is there a key for the lock?'

He shook his head again. 'Only the one kept by Sir Ambrose. I know of no other.'

The barge had now reached the deep waters and rushing

currents of Woolwich. The skeletal frames of the Navy's half-finished men-o'-war could be seen in the drydocks slipping past on the larboard side. Emilia had shifted to the opposite side of the barge, from where she could watch the waters behind them. Figures with flares and lanterns were moving back and forth in the yard entrances and among the wooden cranes whose profiles reared against the sky. As they shunted astern she thought she caught sight of another barge in the brief funnels of light, or rather a glimpse of a canvas tilt beneath which other figures could be seen. About a hundred yards of water separated them. She thrust her head out from under the awning.

'How much further before Billingsgate?'

The barge-master plunged his pole into the water, leaned on it, then raised it hand over hand. 'Eight miles or so,' he grunted before plunging it again. The boat yawed to starboard and he very nearly lost his balance. 'Two more hours,' he added after a moment. 'And that's if the tide doesn't turn.'

Emilia retreated under the awning and peered at the waters ahead. The ox-bow of the next reach with its dangerous currents lay before them. The Greenwich Marshes looked desolate, but moored along the other bank were a half-dozen Indiamen, the lanterns on their taffrails lighting thickets of masts swaying overhead. Behind them lay the East India Company's storehouses. As the barge approached the wharves, moving south now, Emilia turned her head to see the boat behind them lit by a ship's lantern. It had gained several lengths, perhaps more, since Woolwich. Two watermen were perched in the stern, while their passengers – a trio of shadowy figures – were huddled under the tilt. When she turned to Vilém she saw that he was holding something in his palm.

'Take one.'

'What?'

'It's them,' he whispered. 'The Cardinal's men.' He extended his hand a few inches. 'Eight miles. We won't make it . . .'

One of the East India warehouses loomed to starboard, its smell of molasses carried to them by the stiffening breeze. In its brief light she could see what he was holding: the leather pouch given to him by Sir Ambrose. *Strychnos nux vomitica.* Instinctively she shrank against the canvas.

'And as for the casket ...' The light slid away and they were in darkness. A gull screeched overhead as he stooped, still clutching the pouch, and then raised the casket to his lap with a soft grunt. 'It will have to go overboard, I fear. Those are the instructions.'

'Whose instructions?'

No answer. He was staring fixedly at the chest. She glanced up. More wharves crowded the banks and mazes of buildings pressed up behind them. The boat slewed sideways and a wave broke over the bows, showering her cheeks and soaking her petticoats. They had gained speed but lost control in the treacherous current. The barge-master cursed and struggled to keep the vessel on a steady course, using the pole as a rudder. Their own wake overcame them as they slowed, and the barge weltered even more. After a moment the current slackened and the waterman wearily began poling again. But their pursuers had gained another few lengths.

The next hour passed with Emilia perched on the edge of the thwart, swivelling to look astern first and then at the waters ahead. Another sharp ox-bow untwisted before them at Greenwich, along with more fierce currents that set the barge moving from side to side and the barge-master cursing all over again. The sky flushed with a few hints of pink and orange and the tide slowed. Soon the river began to fill with traffic, with dozens of lighters fighting their way to the Legal Quays below the Tower, and with eel-ships and oyster-boats on their way to Billingsgate. Armadas of shallops and pinnaces dodged and feinted among them, sweeping downstream with their sails puffed. Their pursuers closed the gap but then receded after Shadwell as they were slowed in the Lower Pool by the traffic swirling about like flocks of angry birds.

A few minutes later, straining her eyes, Emilia saw the arches of London Bridge girdling the river. When she turned round she saw the tilt-boat breaking into view again. The barge-master pushed hard, dripping with sweat, but it was no use. When they finally drew even with the crowded quays in front of the custom-house, the boat was only two lengths behind. The Cardinal's men had crawled from under the tilt, and in the awakening sunlight she could see their tanned brows, their jet-black livery with its stripes of gold. All three wore lace ruffs, and one of them – the man crouched over the prow – was clutching a dagger. When she turned to Vilém he was kneeling on the floor of the barge with the casket in his hands.

'Too late . . .' He was crawling out from under the tilt and into the bows, where he struggled to raise the casket to the gunwales. 'We won't reach York House,' he grunted. 'We won't even reach Billingsgate!'

'No!'

Emilia clambered over the thwarts, barking her shins, then caught him in a clumsy embrace and laid a hand on the casket, before he pushed her backwards. He hoisted the cargo and once more leant over the gunwales with the treasure outstretched in his hands.

Emilia picked herself up from the boards, but at that moment the barge was bumped in the stern by the tilt-boat. She heard the master curse as the barge slewed sideways and then an instant later broadsided an oncoming skiff. The collision was violent. The last thing she saw as she was thrown to the deck was a pair of boots disappearing over the gunwales.

'Vilém!'

The barge was rocking wildly from side to side by the time she raised herself. They had been boarded. She heard, rather than saw, two of the Cardinal's men scuffling with the barge-master. The poor old devil defended himself valiantly with his pole before the dagger slit his leather jerkin, then his belly. He sank to his knees with a last oath and then tumbled over the stern as the barge was struck again, this time on the starboard quarter by a fishing smack knocked off course by the careering skiff. The Cardinal's men tumbled into one another's arms before sprawling full-length in the stern. The knife clattered to the boards.

'Emilia!'

The smack was floating past, drifting upstream with its sail flapping, while the mast crazily pendulated and the master fought hard to keep his balance in the stern. Emilia caught a glimpse of Vilém prone on the teetering deck, tangled in nets and half-buried in an avalanche of silvery fish.

'Emilia! Jump!'

The smack was moving more quickly now, skimming past the floundering barge as the wind caught in her half-furled bunts. She stepped hurriedly on to one of the rocking thwarts and was bracing herself to leap, when a hand on her skirts tugged her backwards. But at that point the barge was rammed by the fourth and last boat, a wherry filled with a dozen passengers. Then the hand disappeared and she found herself plunging towards the smack through five feet of spray and air.

Chapter Three

The countryside in flood. Rain had fallen steadily throughout the night and was still pouring down as the sky above Epping Forest changed shade from charcoal to cinder-grey: so heavily that the fishponds and flint-pits were overflowing their banks. Overnight the mossy woodlands had become a morass. The worst of the storm had passed, but a strong gale was still blowing from the southwest, and still the rain came down. Oak and beech trees stood in the middle of rivers as if stranded; the splintered trunks of others, felled by winds or lightning, lay across the most windswept stretches of the road from London.

In the middle of the forest, near the cottages of its game-keepers and vermin-killers, four horses could be seen splashing along the Epping Road, drawing behind them through the mud and water a leather-topped coach. It was a little past seven o'clock in the morning. The horses were bound northward through Essex, staggering and straining, their wet manes flapping like pennants and the wheels of the coach flinging great divots of mud into the air. But at the lowest point in the road, where the water from the flint-pits stood the deepest, the coach halted with a violent lurch. The driver, who had already cleared the trunks of three trees from his path that morning, bawled a curse at the horses and cracked his whip over their rumps. They struggled for a moment, but the coach failed to move.

'What's happening?' I had lifted the leather flap to peer through the window. The droplets spattering my face felt like spindrift on the high seas.

'Stuck in the mud,' complained the driver as he hopped into the road with a splash. His boots squelched and sucked as he nearly lost his balance. He was already soaked to the skin. 'Not to worry, sir,' he growled into his collar as he pulled his hat low on his brow. 'I'll have us out in a tick.'

I sat back and removed an oatcake and a wedge of black cheese from my pocket. We had been on the road for more than an hour, since before first light. I had found the coach-and-four waiting for me as promised in the underground stable-yard of the Three Pigeons, its horses already harnessed. I was expecting to see Phineas again but had not been disappointed to discover that a different driver would transport me to Wembish Park, a burly man who introduced himself as Nat Crump. He was proving a more garrulous companion than Phineas, though one equally ill-tempered. As I sat in the back of the vehicle – different from the one that had carried me to Pontifex Hall – I chewed my breakfast and listened to his curses, cries of encouragement and rueful observations about the inclement weather.

'Should have taken a different road,' he was saying as he thrust a thick branch beneath one of the rear wheels and tried to jemmy it free. He urged the horses forward, their traces taut and creaking. The coach gave a small lunge and the iron-shod wheels groaned mulishly, but we moved only a few inches before settling back into the mud. I was alarmed to see that water had risen as high as our rear axle. Crump and the horses stood knee-deep. 'Should have gone through

Puckeridge,' he explained, bracing himself for better leverage. 'Higher ground over that way.'

'Puckeridge?' I was rocking with the motion of the coach. Overhead, elm branches were thrashing wildly. 'Well, why on earth did you not, then?'

'Orders,' he said with an angry grunt of exertion. 'I was ordered not to, wasn't I?' He paused and glanced in my direction. He appeared to regard the whole business as some fault of mine. 'I was told to ride through the forest.'

'Oh? And why was that?'

He had gripped a spoke and the wheel rim and now began forcing the branch with a dripping boot. The foremost horses reared a pace forward at his command but then splashed down four-square in the mire. This time the wheels hadn't budged so much as an inch. He cursed again as he waded arduously forward.

'Why?' He had begun scraping mud from before the wheels with the end of his stick. 'For the same reason that we're not taking Lord Marchamont's coach, that's why. Because it's safer.'

He laughed mirthlessly but then paused in his labours long enough to swing a thick arm proprietorially at the surrounding woodlands. His hat had fallen into the water and I saw how his thatch of blond hair was flattened to his skull by the rain. Earlier, in the poor light of the stable-yard, I almost thought I recognised him but decided that, as with so many things these days, I could no longer trust my instincts. I also thought he seemed to be surprised by my appearance – by my darkened hair and clipped beard – but supposed it was because I didn't answer my description. Whatever the case, he had taken me aboard without any fuss.

'Through the forest,' he was explaining between gasps and grunts. He had found another branch to use as a fulcrum and then waded to the rear of the coach, where he was working again on the wheel. The coach was rocking back and forth like a boat on the tide. 'Won't be followed if we go this way.'

I raised the leather flap on the rear quarter-light and peered into the bough-canopied lane that twisted away behind us. The morning was still half dark. Through the grey air I could see a couple of fallow deer watching us from the copsewood, a buck and a doe, both poised to bolt. But there was no human life to be seen, not even the poachers for which Epping Forest was notorious. The dreadful weather was keeping the roads empty. We had met only the occasional London-bound wagon or pony-cart since reaching the Epping Road.

'Giddap! Go on!'

One of the branches splintered and snapped with a loud crack, and suddenly the vehicle pitched jerkily forward, almost sprawling me on to the floor. The window-flap had flown open and through it I could see our wheels tossing breakers on to the muddy bank. Crump fought for a handhold on the side of the coach and pulled himself aboard. Then we were on our way again, ploughing north into a dense screen of trees and rain. I settled back for what promised to be a long ride. We did not expect to arrive at Wembish Park until the next afternoon.

Onward we rolled for the rest of the morning, the miles swaying slowly past. I dozed in and out of wakefulness, exhausted because I hadn't arrived back in Alsatia until after midnight and then, because the Half Moon after dark was as noisy as a witch's sabbath, had slept only in snatches. Feet trod the stairs at all hours, fiddles squealed in the tap room, dancers disported themselves up and down the corridors amid shrieks of laughter. There was peace at last an hour or two before dawn, but all too soon I was roused by a knock on my door and the voice of one of Mrs Fawkes's chambermaids informing me through the woodwork that my hackney-coach was waiting.

My journey to Wembish Park began under a familiar omen. As the coach approached Chancery Lane I had seen another chalk figure scrawled on a wall – one of the hieroglyphs I now remembered from my Hermetic studies that Marsilio Ficino had called a 'crux Hermetica'. Beneath, also crudely in chalk, faded by the rain, was a single sentence, like a caption: *We the Invisible Brethren of the Rose Cross.*

I had leaned back in my seat, puzzled, wondering if I had read the legend right. Was it a hoax of some sort? For it seemed far too strange, too cryptic, to be genuine. I had heard of the secret society known as the Brothers of the Rose Cross, of course. I stumbled across their strange story the other day as I was flipping through a few of my treatises on Hermetic philosophy. I was only surprised that Biddulph's narrative with its secretive Protestant conspirators had not included them. From what little I could make of them, the Rosicrucians were a secretive band of Protestant alchemists and mystics who had opposed the Catholic Counter-Reformation earlier in the century. They supported Henry of Navarre as the champion of their faith and then, after Henry's assassination in 1610, Frederick V of the Palatinate. Their graffiti and placards mushroomed on the walls of Heidelberg and Prague in 1616 or 1617, about the time, that is, when Ferdinand of Styria was named king-designate of Bohemia. The Rosicrucians must have regarded Ferdinand, a pupil of the Jesuits, with terror and loathing, but their placards and manifestos were strangely optimistic, prophesying a reformation in politics and religion throughout the Empire. These reforms were to be brought about through magical arts such as those taught by Marsilio Ficino, the first translator into Latin of the *Corpus hermeticum*. By means of the 'scientific magic' in the Hermetic texts and in Ficino's *Libri de Vita*, the Rosicrucian Brethren hoped to turn the debased and blackened debris of modern life – the world of religious strife, of wars and persecutions – into a kind of Golden Age or Utopia, in much the same way as they hoped to manufacture gold in their laboratories out of lumps of coal and clay.

Their desire for reformation was understandable enough, I supposed. What did the Rosicrucians see as they gazed back over the last hundred years of European history but slaughter-benches drenched in Protestant blood? There was the massacre of Huguenots in Paris on the Feast of St Bartholomew and the bonfires at Smithfield and Oxford during the reign of Queen Mary. There were the horrors of the Spanish Inquisition and the Holy Office, along with the wars of the Spaniards in the Low Countries, where Sir Philip Sidney lost his life. There were the Lutheran clergymen expelled from Styria and the bonfire of 10,000 Protestant books in the city of Graz, from which Kepler was banished. There was Copernicus, bullied and silenced, and Galileo, summoned to Rome in 1616 for examination before Robert Bellarmine, one of the cardinals of the Inquisition who had burned the Hermetic philosopher Giordano Bruno in the Campo de' Fiore. There was Tommaso Campanella tortured and imprisoned in Naples. There was William the Silent murdered by Spanish agents and Henry IV stabbed by Ravaillac on the Pont Neuf.

In the end, though, the Rosicrucians themselves became a part of this tragic litany. They discovered neither the philosopher's stone nor their cherished Golden Age, because in 1620 King Frederick and the Bohemian Protestants were crushed by the armies of the Catholic League. Undoubtedly most Brothers of the Rose Cross were superstitious charlatans and foolish idealists, but I had felt a sorrow for these men who had wished to ward off with their books and chemicals and feeble magic spells what they saw as the evils of the Counter-Reformation, of Spain and the Habsburgs, only to be swallowed up themselves in the horrors of the Thirty Years War.

But this morning as the coach jolted past Chancery Lane something else about the Rosicrucian Brethren had struck me. I realised that their manifestos had appeared in Prague at roughly the same time that Raleigh's fleet – financed by another band of zealous Protestants – was setting sail for Guiana. Indeed, the most famous of the Rosicrucian tracts, *The Chemical Wedding of Christian Rosencreutz*, a copy of which I discovered on my shelves, was published in Strasbourg in 1616, the same year that Raleigh was released from his cell in the Bloody Tower. So I wondered again if Sir Ambrose with his Hermetic text was some sort of link between these two doomed ventures, the first with Raleigh in Guiana, the second with Frederick in Bohemia. I had no idea; but the other day as I glanced through my copy of *The Chemical Wedding* I noticed something else about the text, something even more dramatic than its date, for engraved both in its margins and on the title page were tiny Mercury symbols, exact duplicates of these figures scribbled on the walls of London.

Then the coach had reached Bishopsgate, where the gates were scraped open to admit a flock of geese being driven to market for slaughter. I had pulled the window-curtain and closed my eyes, but as the coach creaked about me I found myself thinking of the dozens of alchemical works at Pontifex Hall, along with its well-stocked laboratory, and I wondered if Alethea's father, a devout Protestant, had been a Rosicrucian too. But at that point my thoughts had been interrupted as the cackling of the jubilant geese fell about my ears – the riotous clamour of creatures oblivious to the fate that lay only a few minutes away.

'Hungry, sir?'

'Mmmn . . . ?' The voice had startled me awake, and for a few seconds I was too disoriented to move or speak.

'Shall we stop for a meal, sir?'

I pushed myself upright and peered through the window-flap, confused and blinking, feeling the dislocation I always experience when I abandon the city for the country. A flat landscape was slowly reeling past, its fields and wood-lined droves half underwater. Rain was still falling in curtains, drumming across the leather rooftop.

'How long before Cambridge?'

'An hour,' replied Crump.

'No.' I fell back into the seat. 'Carry on.'

In fact it took two more hours to reach Cambridge, but by that time the rain had stopped and the sky at last blew clear. An impressive sunset one hour earlier had turned to soft pink a herd of sheep straggling across the flat chalklands. When I thrust my head through the window I had felt a damp wind pluck at my hair and noticed a mud-speckled coach-and-four trailing us at a distance; then a horseman on a blue roan trailing the coach. But I thought little of them at the time. The road as we neared Cambridge was thick with all sorts of coaches, riders on horseback, stage-wagons bound for London or Colchester. I leaned back in the seat and closed my eyes.

The plan had been to stay the night in Cambridge and set out at first light for Wembish Park. To that end, Crump proposed a posting-inn called the Bookbinder's Arms, which he claimed stood by Magdalene College, overlooking the river. I readily consented. So far Crump had proved himself a remarkably capable guide.

But it was at this point that our journey suffered a bewildering setback. It might have been the growing darkness, or Crump's exhaustion, or the crowded streets with their rows of overhanging buildings. Or it might have been the reluctance of the post-horses, who were refusing each gate or unlighted by-street and worrying at their snaffles. Whatever the reason, however, the aplomb with which Crump had found our way through Epping Forest and the fifty-odd storm-racked miles now seemed to desert him. For the next three-quarters of an hour we wound through narrow streets barely an arm's span wide, passing college after college, post-inn after post-inn, circling back upon ourselves, squinting and craning our necks, blundering across causeways and bridges only to be brought up short by ditches or cul-de-sacs, all without coming upon either Magdalene College or the Bookbinder's Arms. So at last Crump invited me to share the coach-box with him: I would watch for the inn, he said, while he concentrated on the business of driving.

There was barely room enough for two in the seat, but for a long while we rode in this fashion, our feet side by side on the footboard, our shoulders rubbing together. He had fallen silent and kept his eyes trained on the street ahead, while I twisted back and forth, looking out for signboards and, at the same time, studying him more closely. He was an ox of a man with pale eyes, blond hair and a drinker's nose that was pitted like a Seville orange. I had met him before – I was certain of that by now – but could not remember where. He might have been one of the labourers at Pontifex Hall, I thought, or one of the patrons blowing on his coffee in the Golden Horn.

For an instant a memory seemed to shimmer and rise on the edge of the horizon, but then we struck a bump in the road and I had to grasp the edge of the seat to stay aboard. As I did so, I felt a sudden pressure on my hip and, looking down, saw the butt of a pistol in Crump's waistband. I raised my eyes to his face and was alarmed to see something new – a look of worry, maybe even fear – inscribed across its weathered furrows.

'Shall we stop here?' I asked, pointing to an approaching inn whose unscrubbed stable-yard could be smelled even from this distance. We had passed its signboard twice already. 'This one looks adequate. What does it matter? They're all the same, these inns.'

'Keep your mouth shut and your eyes open,' he growled, working his mandibles fiercely and giving the reins a hard shake. 'You might miss something.'

The St George & Dragon slipped past, as did the Shepherd's Crook, the Shoulder of Mutton, the Faggot of Rushes, the Merrie Lion, the Leathern Bottle, the Sow & Pigs, plus at least a half-dozen other inns and taverns, all of which Crump refused to consider. I decided I would jump down on to the street and make my own way – with or without Crump – to one of the other inns. But just as I rose from the seat and balanced myself on the footboard, steadying myself to leap over the wheel and on to the bridge, I suddenly caught sight of the Bookbinder's Arms, a pale hulk with flickering windows and a steep roof that rose against the sky like a ziggurat. It stood directly across the river from us, on the opposite side of a narrow bridge on to which Crump was guiding the horses.

'There,' I told him. I could now hear the familiar gurgling roar of water, the River Cam funnelling between the pylons of the bridge. 'See it? The Bookbinder's Arms.'

But Crump made no reply. Jaw tightly set, he glanced over one of his enormous shoulders again, shook the reins, and the horses moved forward at a swift trot. Perhaps he hadn't heard me over the roar of the water. I pointed at the building and then made to tap him on the forearm – we were nearing the end of the bridge and would pass the inn at this pace – but my fingers touched something cold and hard instead. Looking down, I saw the pistol gripped in his right hand.

'Giddap! Go on! Giddap!'

The horses plunged forward across the bridge so quickly that I was almost thrown from my seat. When I righted myself I heard Crump's oath and, turning my head, saw that we were no longer alone. The mud-spattered coach-and-four was approaching from the opposite side, blocking our path, and ahead of it a blue roan with a horseman astride was charging towards us.

I turned in confusion to Crump. He grimaced, cursed again, then raised his pistol in the air and pointed it at the figure rearing in the stirrups. The roan veered sideways into the stone balusters as the weapon discharged itself with a bright shower of sparks, stinging my left cheek. Our own horses bolted forward, panicked by the report, the coach swaying wildly behind them. I clung to the edge of the seat as Crump fumbled with the reins and another cartridge for his pistol. In a few more seconds we would draw level with the other coach.

'For God's sake help me!' Crump was thrusting the pistol and its cartridge towards me. The hub of one of our wheels ground against the balustrade, and our heads came together as the coach lurched violently sideways. 'They'll kill us!'

But I didn't take the pistol, which clattered on to the bridge behind us. Instead I recoiled from him as the coach righted itself, then I twisted round in the seat and hoisted myself with a clumsy bound on to the rocking coach-top, where I crouched for a second on my haunches, gripping the edge. Then, without heeding Crump's shouts or looking downwards, I leapt over the balustrade and into the swirling din of the rain-swollen Cam. But as I hit the waters with a splash and was sucked below the surface, then through the middle arch, then downriver past the Bookbinder's Arms, it wasn't the thunder of the flooded river I was hearing but the echo of Crump's wooden teeth clicking together like rattlebones.

For I had remembered, at long last, where I'd seen him before. But then for a long time, as the current carried me downstream, I remembered nothing at all, because suddenly the whole world had gone black and silent.

From Magdalene Bridge the River Cam flows northeast towards the Isle of Ely, several miles below which, on the edge of the peat fens, crosscut by ancient Roman drainage canals, its waters run into the Great Ouse and then seaward to the Wash, thirty miles to the north, where they flow towards a desolate horizon. With the day's downpour the fens were even more flooded than usual, and that evening the river's current was turbulent and swift. How many miles it might have swept me downstream I had no idea. I only know that I awoke sodden and chilled on the floor of a lighter that was being poled against the current by a fenman on his way to market, an ancient turf-cutter named Noah Bright. Stars were reeling overhead and muddy embankments wavering past. I coughed up a lungful of water and fetched my breath in ragged gasps. It might have been hours or even days later.

Of the journey back to Cambridge I have only the vaguest memories: the old fenman leaning on his pole; the motion of the lighter in the water as a dark riverscape slid over the gunwale of the boat; the sweet odour of the sun-dried peat against which my cheek was pressed. Bright kept up a spirited monologue as he poled us along, though what he might have been talking about I have no idea, for I barely listened or responded. I was thinking all the while about Nat Crump, about what I had seen when our heads clashed together on the bridge: the set of wooden teeth bared like a cur's with fear and anger.

An accident in Fleet Street. Cart-horse dropped down dead, sir . . .

The discovery had been a shock. Even now I had no idea what to make of it. But Crump had been the driver of the hackney-coach in Alsatia, that much I knew at once. Crump was the one who took me on that apparently fortuitous detour to the Golden Horn. I was as certain of that, at this moment, as I was of anything.

An accident in Fleet Street . . .

For I could no longer know anything, I realised, except that a few days ago someone named Nat Crump had followed me to Westminster, to the Postman's Horn, where he picked me up from the street, to all appearances at random, and then delivered me to within sight of the Golden Horn, also apparently at random. But the journey must have been carefully planned and executed so that the elaborate design would appear as an accident, a coincidence, a rare piece of good luck. Which meant that everything that had happened since the first trip to Alsatia, as well as everything that had followed so smoothly from it – the auction, the copy of Agrippa, the catalogue – had also been staged. As, of course, had the journey to Wembish Park. I was being led astray, coaxed into ever deeper and more dangerous waters. Even if the house actually existed I had no doubt that it, like all else, would be nothing more than a blind. But a blind for what? For whom?

We seem to have reached a dead end . . .

And the loquacious turf-cutter, Noah Bright, who was rearing above me in the stern? What of him? He seemed to be watching me closely as he spoke, bending upon me a pair of eyes as bright and alert as an old pointer dog's. I had managed to explain that I was a bookseller from London, Silas Cobb by name, who had come to browse among the shops and stalls of Cambridge's Market Hall, but who had toppled into the river after enjoying the hospitality of one of the town's numerous taverns. I had no idea if he believed my hasty fibs – or if I could trust him. Suddenly I was suspicious of everyone. I wondered if the old fenman wasn't yet another Crump or Pickvance, an actor brought on stage to play a part, a marionette whose strings were twitched from behind canvas flats by someone else. Had he found me in the river only at random, by pure chance? Or was even my leap overboard under some sort of precise control, determined by a set of indices whose author and purpose remained a mystery? I wondered where the limits of this control might lie. I wondered if Biddulph with his tales about the Navy Office and the *Philip Sidney* had been arranged for me like everything else. If the graffiti had been scrawled on the walls of London and the curiosities placed in their dusty cabinet for my eyes alone . . .

'What the devil . . . ?'

The lighter had skidded sideways in the current, yawing frantically to starboard. Water splashed over the gunwales and the load of peat wobbled unsteadily beside me. I raised my head to see that Bright had ceased poling and was squatted in the stern, peering anxiously across the flooded river. Turning my head I saw the faint lights of Cambridge in the waters ahead of us. We must have been a good mile or more north of Magdalene Bridge. The lantern teetered on the thwart and threatened to tumble into the waves. I turned my attention back to Bright, a wave of goose-flesh creeping across my nape and shoulders.

'What is it?'

'Over there,' he whispered, nodding to the embankment. 'There's something on the riverbank.'

I turned my head again and saw a dark shape half hidden among the waterlogged sedge: what looked like some sort of amphibious creature that had crawled halfway out of the water. Light from the lantern played towards it as Bright sank the pole in the mud and pushed off, carefully drifting the nose of the lighter across the treacherous current. He almost lost his balance but managed to hold the course, ruddering with his pole as we wallowed in the onrushing water. A few seconds later the keel slid with a soft rasp into the mud. I could see an arm outstretched in the sedge. Bright raised his pole from the water with a grunt.

It was a man, spreadeagled face-down on the bank, his legs submerged in the swollen river. Bright swung the pole boom-like across the edge of the bank, but even before it prodded his shoulder and rolled him on to his back it was obvious he was dead. In the ghastly light of the lantern I could see that his throat had been cut from ear to ear, almost enough to sever the head, which flopped horrifically sideways. I felt my gorge rise in my throat and looked away, but Bright was disembarking, splashing knee-deep through the water and holding the lantern aloft. No sooner had he reached the body than the current struck both of them, but before the lantern was extinguished and the body rolled into the sedge I caught a swift glimpse of the face – of the bulbous nose and, beneath it, the pair of wooden teeth tightly clenched as if in some inarticulate rage.

Chapter Four

One of my earliest memories is of watching my father write. He was a scrivener, so writing was his profession, an affair governed by all sorts of precise and complex rituals. I can still picture him hunched as if in supplication over his battered escritoire, his hair hanging over his face, a turkey quill pivoting back and forth in his slender hand. In appearance he was, as I am, unimposing, a small man with dark garb and the morose, worried eyes of a puffin. But to watch him at work was to marvel at the genius of the scribe's hand. I used to stand beside his desk, holding aloft a candle as he mixed his ink or trimmed his quills with a penknife as carefully as if performing the most delicate surgery. Then he would dip the tapered point into the ink-horn and, magically, begin inscribing the chalked and pumiced parchment spread on the desk before him.

What was my father writing? I had no idea. Those were the innocent days before my hornbook taught me how to decipher the bowing heads and flourishing limbs of his curious ink-figures, and so at the time they were as irresistible and beguiling as the hieroglyphics of the Pharaohs. In fact my poor father must have been writing passages of the dullest possible sort. Letters patent, court rolls, parish registers: that type of thing. The scrivener led a life of rare drudgery. Only when I was older did I realise that my father's back was permanently bowed from hunching over his desk and his eyes dim because he was too poor, much of the time, to afford a candle. His labours in the tiny garret room that served as his study were relieved once a week when he visited the shops of ink-makers and parchment-sellers, or when he delivered the fruits of his efforts to the Inns of Chancery in whose pay he was so precariously kept. As I grew older I sometimes accompanied him on these forays through the streets of London. With the rolled-up parchments tucked under his arm or inside a weather-worn scrip strapped round his neck he would present himself at Clement's Inn, or one of two dozen others, and I would sit in quiet anterooms, watching through the doorway as my hunchbacked father in his dirty ruff shyly and with trembling hands unscrolled his wares on the desk of thin-chopped unsmiling law clerks.

How well I remember those voyages, even now. Hand in hand through the streets the pair of us would roam, into strange and forbidding buildings, worlds of power and privilege far removed from our tiny house and my father's ink-stained escritoire. Twice we were even ushered by silk-clad pages into the Signet Office in Whitehall Palace itself. Most often of all, though, on these weekly odysseys we visited Chancery Lane, because it was here, on the east side of the street, near the gaming-house in Bell Yard – another favourite haunt of my poor father, alas – that the Rolls Chapel stood.

My father, a man with atheistical leanings, often joked that the Rolls Chapel was the only church he ever attended. And from the outside the building did indeed look exactly like a church. It had a stone bell-tower, hexagonal in shape, together with stained-glass windows that overlooked the barristers and magistrates bustling up and down Chancery Lane. Inside a nail-studded oak door was a chancel and a long nave filled with row upon row of pews. Yet the pews were filled not with pious parishioners and their prayer-books but with heavy morocco-bound books and stacks of paper and parchment three feet high. And those who came inside – little groups that huddled in the northwest corner – prayed not to God but the Lord Chancellor, or rather to the Master of the Rolls, his adjutant, who heard suits from where he perched priest-like on his bench in the chancel. For the Rolls Chapel may have been a church at one time – built, my father told me, for the converted Jews of England – but it had long since been converted itself, and now it housed in its bell-tower and in the crypt under its grey flagstones the voluminous records of the Court of Chancery.

I crossed my childhood ghost – the tiny Isaac Inchbold dressed in his russet frock and moth-holed hose – as I took my place on a pew beside the door on the morning after my return from Cambridge. The sun in the stained glass was casting across the flagged aisles the brilliant blossoms of light I remembered so well from those distant mornings when I sat kicking my feet against a prie-dieu and awaiting my father's descent from the tower or ascent from the crypt. Now, as then, the Rolls Chapel was silent and smelled mustily of old parchment and ancient stone.

But it was far from empty. From where I sat I could see dozens of clerks and scriveners threading carefully amongst the kneeling-stools and choir stalls, while my pew was shared by a congregation of a dozen gentlemen, most of whom looked like Cavaliers. And behind the worm-eaten chancel screen, before a small audience of lawyers in horsehair wigs, the Master of the Rolls, a fat man in scarlet robes, was holding court. I removed my fob-watch for inspection, then returned my anxious gaze to the tiny door to the bell-tower through which a clerk had vanished a few minutes earlier. Above the door was a sign: 'Rotuli Litterarum Clausarum.' I sighed and replaced the watch. I was in a desperate hurry, for I was in grave danger – and so, too, was Alethea.

It was now two days since my departure for Cambridge. I had arrived back in Alsatia the previous night after spending another entire day on the road. I had made haste for London because a terrible thought had occurred to me, one that set my nape and sideburns prickling. I realised that all of the strange concatenations – everything that some unknown person or persons had staged for me – led straight back to the cipher in the copy of Ortelius, a text I was obviously meant to discover and solve. Which meant that whoever was laying the trap had access to Pontifex Hall and its laboratory. Which meant that he was most probably one of only two people, either Phineas Greenleaf or Sir Richard Overstreet, or perhaps the two of them in league together. Whatever the case, the culprit had access not only to Alethea, but also to her trust. And one of them, most likely Sir Richard, had murdered Nat Crump.

Yet the events of the past few days had still perplexed me. I could not begin to guess why Crump should have been killed, nor how the various other strands – the break-ins at Nonsuch House, Henry Monboddo and his mysterious client, the Orinoco expedition – were connected to the errant parchment itself, the alpha and omega of the mystery, the Holy Grail that seemed to be receding ever farther beyond my grasp.

But then suddenly I had realised how I might cut through the Gordian knot after all – how I might get to the bottom of the mystery of Henry Monboddo and Wembish Park . . . and then, through them, to the identity of whoever lay at the heart of the whole affair. For the villain had not quite covered his tracks. The answer lay not at Wembish Park, I knew, but here in London, in Chancery Lane – in a few lines of text inscribed on a roll of parchment.

I arrived in the Rolls Chapel that morning, still in disguise, after a fruitless trip to Pulteney House, which had looked dark and deserted. I explained my mission to a clerk seated at a desk by the baptismal font, who informed me with a sneer that what I wanted was impossible, for all of the clerks superintending the Close Rolls were, I must understand, very busy at the minute. No one could requite my desire, he explained, for another few days at least.

'The Act of Indemnity and Oblivion,' he explained with a shrug of his narrow shoulders.

'I beg your pardon?'

'The land settlements,' he said in a tone of derisive hauteur. 'The clerks are researching land entitlements so the estates confiscated by Parliament can be restored to their rightful owners.'

'But that's why I'm here!'

'Is it, indeed?' He peered over the edge of his desk, giving me a frank scrutiny from head to toe, quite rightly sceptical, I suppose, that a person of such a humble and even shabby aspect could have any possible connection with an aristocratic estate, confiscated or not. 'Well, you will just have to wait your turn like everyone else.' He nodded at the slumping gallery of

Cavaliers. Then slowly his eyes returned to me. 'Unless, that is, of course . . .'

The fellow had coughed delicately into his tiny lace-beruffed hand and tossed a furtive glance in the direction of the chancel. With a mental sigh I reached for a shilling. I knew, of course, that greed was essential to a lawyer's craft, but I had not realised that the vice had filtered down to their clerks as well. When the coin was granted only a dubious glance I was forced to add another. Both coins were conjured into thin air. He returned his gaze to the papers on his desk.

'Be seated over there, please.'

Then, for a whole hour, nothing. Two suits were heard in the chancel and their plaintiffs dismissed. Clerks and lawyers shuffled to and fro, rootling among the volumes on the pews or in the vestry to my right. The brilliant garden of light crept slowly across the flagstones until it almost reached the toes of my boots, which, as of old, were tapping impatiently at the padded prie-dieu on the floor in front of me. At last I heard my name called and, looking up, saw a clerk, a thin young fellow, standing in the tiny door to the bell-tower.

'You may see the enrolments now, if you please,' the clerk at the desk informed me. 'Mr Spicer will show you the way.'

The climb was a difficult one. There was no hand-rail other than a frayed rope, and so narrow was the stairwell that my shoulder rubbed against the sandstone newel at every step. I twisted round it and ascended in pursuit of the nimble Mr Spicer, but after a dozen steps I imagined the tons of stone pressing in upon me and felt the same freezing tremors of panic as in my priest-hole a few days earlier. I have always detested enclosed spaces, which remind me, I suppose, of that eternal confinement shortly to claim me. To make matters worse, young Mr Spicer saw no need for a candle, and so I was forced to wriggle upwards through a musty darkness relieved only by the occasional arrow-slit window.

Panting heavily, I reached the top at last to find Spicer waiting in a small hexagonal room. I realised at once why he had not lit a candle on the way up, for the room was stacked with sheaves of parchment, some of which had been sewn head to foot and rolled into fat spools several feet in diameter. Scattered about, and so numerous that they took up most of the floor space, were dozens of wooden boxes from which protruded even more parchments, some of them sallowed, others new.

My eyes flitted over the rolls and boxes, over the parchment tags with their bright seals of wax hanging down like tassels. It was the world of my father the scrivener. But I was intrigued by the sight for a quite different reason, for I knew that the answer to my persecutor's identity would be here among these documents. How many documents had I studied thus far in search of answers? Rate-books, patents, parish registers, auction catalogues, editions of the *Corpus hermeticum* and tales of Raleigh's voyage – all of which had led me further and further astray. But now at long last I was about to discover the truth. It would be inscribed here, I knew, somewhere among these parchments.

'Every last will, patent, writ and charter in the country is enrolled here,' Spicer was explaining with some pride as he caught my transfixed gaze. 'These documents are the overflow from the crypt and vestry. In the crypt there are already more than 75,000 parchments of them on something like a thousand rolls.'

He picked his way to his desk and stooped to scrape open a deep drawer, from which he removed, with an exaggerated grunt, an enormous folio bound in leather. It must have been a good foot thick.

'I am a busy man,' he sighed, taking his seat, 'as I hope you will appreciate. So if you wouldn't mind . . .'

'Yes, yes. Of course. I shall come straight to the business.' I stepped forward, leaning on my stick. 'I'm in search of a title deed.'

'You and everyone else,' he muttered under his breath. Then with a creak of leather he opened the cover of the cartulary and took up his magnifying lens. 'Very well. A title deed.' He licked his thumb and riffled through the heavy pages. 'What year was it enrolled? The season would be helpful too, if you can. Summer? Autumn?'

'Ah, well . . . now there, I fear, is the rub.' I attempted an ingratiating smile. 'I'm not quite certain when the transaction took place.'

'Is that so. Well, what is the name of the purchaser, might I ask?'

'Another rub, I fear.' I hoisted my smile a little higher. 'That is precisely what I'm hoping to find, you see – the name of whoever owns the property.'

'But you have no date of purchase? Not even a rough guess? No? Well then,' he said through pursed, renunciatory lips as I shook my head, 'you have rather put the cart before the ass, if you don't mind me saying so. You must know one or the other, the name or the date. Surely you can understand that.' The enormous cover, held ajar, creaked again and then fell shut with a gentle thud. 'As I say, Mr Inchbold, I am a busy man.' He was stooped over again, replacing the cartulary in its drawer. 'I trust you can find your own way down the stairs.'

'No – wait.' I was not going to be dismissed that easily. 'I have a name for you,' I said. 'Two names, if you please.'

Yet Spicer was unable to find mention in his book of any property in Huntingdonshire belonging to either Sir Richard Overstreet – the first name I had him search for among the tidy columns that ran up and down the rag-paper pages – or Henry Monboddo. However, he eventually discovered in his cartulary a record for a property in the name of some-one named not Henry, but Isabella, Monboddo. Almost an hour had passed by this time. I was leaning forward, trying to read upside-down the print that someone, one of Mr Spicer's predecessors, had inscribed in a neat chancery hand. The house was a jointure, he explained in a bored mono-tone, settled on Isabella by her husband who was named – yes, yes – Henry Monboddo. He bent forward with his nose pressed to the reading-glass. A freehold estate named Wembish Park.

'That's it,' I stammered. 'Yes, that's—'

'The jointure was granted,' he continued as if oblivious, 'in a will made by Henry Monboddo in the year 1630. Since then it has been compounded by Parliament, later confiscated, then restored to its owner under the terms of the Act of Indemnity and Oblivion.'

'Restored to Isabella Monboddo?'

'That is correct. She is described as the relict of Henry Monboddo.'

'The relict? But when did Monboddo die?'

'These are not parish records, Mr Inchbold. The cartulary does not tell us such things.'

'Of course,' I murmured placatingly. I was trying to make sense of the information. Monboddo dead? Did Alethea not know? I leaned forward even further. 'So ... Isabella Monboddo is the owner of the estate?'

'*Was* the owner. Wembish Park appears to have changed hands since the recent land settlement.'

He was hunched low over the page now, like a jeweller examining stones of rare quality through his lens. From where I sat I could see the columns shrink and swim beneath it. Then he turned the page with a sharp crackle and, laying the glass aside, looked up for the first time in twenty minutes.

'Yes,' he said, 'it's been sold. Quite recently, from the looks of it. The deed was enrolled only a few weeks ago. Though of course it may have been registered in the county with the Clerk of the Peace up to a month before that. We're a little behind in our work—'

'Yes, of course, all of the land settlements . . .' I was hardly daring to breathe. 'To whom was it sold?'

'Ah. Well.' He indulged himself with a smile. 'That the cartulary does not tell us.'

'But the deed?' I could barely contain my urge to wrench the register from his hands and read the entry for myself. 'You say it's been enrolled?'

'Of course it's been enrolled. It's the law, you understand.'

'Well, in that case, where is it found?'

Spicer seemed to ignore the question. He took up his reading-glass and once again hunched his back, applying himself like a laborious schoolboy to the page. After a few seconds he plucked up one of his quills and with elaborate care trimmed its nib and then copied on to a scrap of paper rummaged from one of the drawers a bristling thicket of numerals that, still leaning forward, I was barely able to decipher: CXXXIIIW. DCCLXXVIII. LVIII.

'There you are,' he said, sliding the cryptic message across the top of the desk towards me with the tip of an index finger. 'This, I believe, is what you wished to learn.'

I took up the paper and held it by the edges, careful not to smear the ink. I frowned and raised my eyes to Spicer. He was watching me with a complacent smile.

'What do you mean? What is this?'

'The crypt, Mr Inchbold.' The cartulary gave a valedictory flump as its cover was slammed shut. Spicer's smile had disappeared. He replaced the quill in the ink-horn and then slipped the reading-glass into a drawer. 'That is where you'll find what you're seeking. In the crypt.'

The sun had shifted to the west windows by the time I picked my way down the narrow staircase and into the nave. The chapel was even emptier now; I could see only a pair of clerks in hushed conference in the chancel. I sculled along the aisle on my thorn-stick, faint from hunger because I had not eaten since the previous day. But there was no time for food. Bracing myself against a pew I swung my club foot over a stool, holding tightly to the slip of paper. Yes, there was too much to do before I could think about my belly.

The door to the crypt stood at the front of the church, near the chancel beneath which I supposed it extended. It bore the same legend as the one leading to the bell-tower, 'Rotuli Litterarum Clausarum', and creaked open on to a set of steps equally shallow and narrow. There was no light, so far as I could see, except a muted glow at the bottom. I ducked my head beneath the scarred wooden mullion and, taking a deep breath like a diver, began a slow descent.

I was to be met in the crypt by a clerk named Appleyard who would decipher the paper and locate the deed. But I had already guessed that the numerals referred to the shelf mark of the roll in question. As I descended I could see that the shelves and cases in the catacomb below were all numbered, as were the boxes and the scores of rolls bound with ribbons and crammed on to the shelves. Still, it would have been impossible to locate the roll on my own. As my eyes adjusted to the poor light I saw that the crypt was a vast labyrinth extending far beyond the chancel to encompass the area beneath the nave and then, for all I could tell, Chancery Lane and perhaps even a good part of London as well. Narrow corridors barely two feet in width and overhung by the rolls of parchment – some as big around as saucers, others thin as pipe stems – slithered away into darkness on either side, then divided into other, equally cramped tributaries. It was only because I was short and my belly of modest dimensions that I was able to pick my way along the widest of these passageways towards the thin glow of lamplight and, squatted within it, the tiny desk occupied by Mr Appleyard. The lamp had been trimmed low and Mr Appleyard was fast asleep.

It took a minute or two to rouse him. He was a frail-looking old man with a coronal of white hair over his ears and a bald dome that had yellowed to the colour of the parchments surrounding him. Twice I shook him gently by the shoulder. On the second occasion, he snorted and coughed, then jerked erect with pale eyes ablink.

'Yes?' His hands were fumbling on the desk. 'What is it? Who's there?'

I slipped the paper on to the desk and explained that I had been sent from the tower by Mr Spicer. 'I'm searching for a deed,' I explained. 'My name is Inchbold.'

'Inchbold . . .' His hands froze in mid-air above the blotter. Then he paused for a moment, frowning deeply and tapping the tip of his nose with a forefinger as though lost in some private reverie. 'Of the Inchbolds of Pudney Court? In Somersetshire?'

I was surprised by the question. 'The attachment is a distant one.'

'Of course. But your attachment to Henry Inchbold, I think, is not so distant. Correct? Your voice no less than your name is very like his.'

Now I was quite taken aback. 'You remember my father?'

'Very well indeed. A fine selection of scripts. The ascenders in his court hand were, I recall, most emphatic in their execution.' He shrugged and offered a toothless smile. 'You see, in those days I still enjoyed the pleasures of sight.'

Only then did I realise that Appleyard with his fumbling hands and blinking gaze was as blind as Homer. I felt my heart slip. Was this some joke on the part of Spicer? How would a blind man – even a man with a memory evidently as prodigious as Appleyard's – lead me through the wanderings of the crypt?

'But I take it, Mr Inchbold, that you have not come to discuss your father.'

'No.'

'Nor Pudney Court either. Or is that perhaps the deed you seek? I remember it as well, you know. A fine example of the floreate charter hand before the so-called reform of penmanship in the thirteenth century. Reform,' he repeated disdainfully. 'An emasculation, I call it.'

'No,' I replied, 'not Pudney Court either. A property in Huntingdonshire.'

'Ah.' His sallowed head was bobbing.

'A house called Wembish Park. I believe it was recently sold.' I retrieved the slip of paper from the desk. 'Mr Spicer has given me the shelf mark. Shall I read it to you?'

The paper was decoded much as I suspected. The parchment would be found on shelf number CXXXIII, which stood in the west wing of the crypt. Hence the 'W' in the code, Appleyard explained. Roll number DCCLXXVIII was one of those on which deeds for the present year had been enrolled. The deed itself would be the fifty-eighth parchment, which meant that it would have been enrolled roughly halfway along, 'so far as I remember, mind'. He was feeling his way through the corridor in front of me as he spoke, ticking off the shelves as he passed them, moving so swiftly that I had some difficulty keeping pace. I was carrying my stick in one hand, and in the other the lantern, which he had advised me not to drop unless I wished to see its flames engulf four hundred years of legal history.

'Here we are,' he said at last, after burrowing like a mole

along a branching series of ever-narrowing aisles. 'Shelf number one-thirty-three. Correct?'

I held the lantern aloft. Its glow lit the legend inscribed on a yellowed and curling paper fixed to the end of the shelf: CXXXIIIW.

'Correct,' I replied.

'Well, then, the rest is up to you, Mr Inchbold. You are conversant in Latin, I trust?'

'Of course.'

'And the law hands? Chancery? Secretary?'

'Most of them.'

'Of course. Your father . . .' He was struggling with the roll, which I helped him lower from where it had been shelved. It was an awkward bundle, surprisingly heavy, and had been fastened with a red ribbon. 'You must read it here. I regret there is no better place. But this corridor and the next should be long enough.'

'Long enough?'

'You will have to unroll it, of course. Mind the lantern, though. That is all I ask of you.'

With that he shuffled away down the corridor, humming to himself and leaving me to squat on the floor, bones cracking, with the curious prize clutched in my arms. As I untied the ribbon – slowly, like someone unwrapping a precious gift – I could hear the subdued thunder of traffic trundling overhead. So the crypt extended under Chancery Lane. Was that how the old clerk found his way through the corridors? By sound? Or had he been gifted, like the blinded Tiresias, with preternatural powers?

The ribbon came undone, and I slipped it into my pocket for safekeeping. Then, having fixed the tail of the roll against the wall and weighed it down with my thorn-stick, I began carefully to unroll the enormous spool. After a minute I reached the entrance to the corridor, moving on hands and knees, feeling like Theseus crawling through the labyrinth with Ariadne's golden thread unravelling behind him. Then I entered the next corridor, which after a few paces made a dog's-leg at a 120-degree angle. Then the next, dog-legging in the other direction. Shelves crowded to either side of me. The roll grew thinner, its tail longer. What would I discover at its end? A Minotaur? Or a passage out of the labyrinth and into the light of day? The floor declined slightly as I crept forward. 66 . . . 65 . . . 64 . . . 63 . . .

At last I reached it, midway through the roll and midway along the corridor. I caught my breath as it unfurled, even though the fifty-eighth deed on Chancery Roll DCCLXXVIII was utterly indistinguishable, at first glance, from the others: a piece of parchment, perhaps eighteen inches in length, with a seal suspended on a tag at the foot, which had been slit and then stitched to the head of the previous document. Well? What had I been expecting to see? I propped the lantern on the floor and seated myself cross-legged beside it with the parchment spread across my lap.

I had thought as I unrolled the documents that within seconds of reaching the deed I would know the culprit's name. But as I studied it front and back, it must have been a full minute before the import of the document finally struck me. The first thing I noticed were the signatures on the dorse, both illegible. Those of the witnesses, I supposed: law clerks, very likely. I turned the roll over, holding my breath. Still there was no revelation, though immediately I noticed the jagged line at the top of the page. As I ran my forefinger over the crude serration – the parchment was obviously an indenture, cut in two – a memory shot briefly to life, then abruptly faded. I had seen a similar document, an indenture very like this one. But I could not, in that brief second, remember where or when.

Sciant presentes et futuri quod ego Isabella Monboddo . . .

The first line, inscribed in black ink, leapt from the page. The lettering had been executed by a scrivener whose talents, I decided, fell short of my father's, though it was done in the elegant curves and dagger-sharp strokes of chancery script. So mesmerised was I by the script that it was another few seconds before I realised what exactly I was reading.

Sciant presentes et futuri quod ego Isabella Monboddo quondam uxor Henry Monboddo in mea viduitate dedi concessi et hac presenti carta mea confirmavi Alethea Greatorex . . .

But then, as the words unravelled from the page, I understood. Yet I couldn't believe what I was seeing. Squinting in the poor light of the cramped corridor I held the document so close to the lantern that its edge touched the casing. My eyes swept across the dense thicket of figures, returning to the top of the page to read it through again:

> *Let men present and future know that I, Isabella Monboddo, sometime wife of Henry Monboddo, have in my widowhood given, granted, and by this my present charter confirmed, to Alethea Greatorex, Lady Marchamont of Pontifex Hall, Dorsetshire, relict of Henry Greatorex, Baron Marchamont, all lands and tenements, meadows, grazing lands and pasture, with their hedges, banks and ditches, and with all their profits and appurtenances, which I have in Wembish Park, Huntingdonshire . . .*

But I could read no more. The document dropped from my fingers and I slumped against a shelf, numb with shock, still not quite daring to comprehend what I had read. My foot must have struck the roll, for the last thing I remembered was the sight of it tumbling a few feet along the slight decline of the corridor before beginning its long unravelling, gathering its own momentum as one by one the documents unfurled and snaked into the darkness of the next corridor.

Chapter Five

Y ork House stood less than a mile up river from Billingsgate, where the storehouses and manufactories overhanging the embankment gave way to mansions that pushed themselves like palisades from the Thames. One after another they drifted past, each with an arched gateway framing a riverfront garden and a barge moored below. York House was found at the westernmost edge of the row, near the New Exchange, at the point where the river bent south towards the dingy clutter of Whitehall Palace. The eddies of current heaved and flexed about its stone steps that led to an arched watergate, on either side of which a stone wall encrusted with limpets held back the high tides. Tarred wooden bollards beside the steps made fast a multi-oared barge whose lacquered hull, in the morning sunshine, gave back a warped riverscape. Beyond the gate sprawled the garden: drooping willows, pollarded aspens, a forlorn pomegranate, all throwing spindly shadows across a knot garden filled with the shrivelled husks of last summer's flowers. Sparrows hopped about the box hedge, pecking for seeds and leaving hieroglyphics in frost that the low sun had not yet melted.

As she breasted the stairs, Emilia was surprised to see how the mansion – one of the largest on the river, late home of the Lord High Chancellor – appeared to be in ruins. Empty window sockets and a gap-toothed balustrade looked down on piles of stone blocks littered before the west wing. Baskets of bricks and roof slates stood against the wall of the east wing, halfway up whose crumbling surface a wooden scaffold jutted. Pulleyed ropes hung downward from the platforms like nooses, wagging in the breeze. From inside the house came the sound of hammers.

It was now eight o'clock. The post horn of one of Lord Stanhope's departing mail-coaches was sounding in Charing Cross as Emilia followed Vilém across the garden to the tradesmen's entrance. Her left knee and ribs were aching from her brush with the gunwales of the fishing smack an hour earlier. At the last second Vilém had grasped her arm and pulled her aboard the smack as it knifed past on the current. When it docked at Billingsgate the two of them had disembarked and, limping and dripping, made their way through the fish market to the other side of London Bridge. A scull was waiting. The Cardinal's men seemed to have disappeared into the thicket of masts and sails.

Progress to York House had been a slow one on account of

the tide, which had turned by the time the watermen pushed off from the stairs beside the Old Swan Tavern. Vilém had chosen the two burliest specimens and a sleek-looking pair-of-oars, but the journey upriver still took almost an hour. To make matters worse, the watermen had trouble finding the house. Essex Stairs ... the Strand Bridge ... Somerset Stairs – all had looked exactly the same as the boat slipped past. One of Emilia's hands gripped the wet fustian of Vilém's coat. He had been oblivious, perched in the bows with his head raised as if sniffing the breeze. But at one point, halfway along the row, he nodded at one of the mansions.

'So that is Arundel House.'

Turning to look at the palace sliding past on their starboard side she saw a wintry-looking garden filled not with people, as she first thought, but dozens of statues. A cluster of robed figures was standing erect beneath the trees, frozen as if at a stroke, gesturing arms immobile, sightless marble eyes gazing across the river to Lambeth Marsh. Others wrestled together, while still others lay supine in the grass like corpses on a battlefield, staring at the clouds, their arms and torsos fractured in the middle of heroic postures. She could see yet more ruins under the wings of the house, a promiscuous heap of rubble, what looked from this distance like the fragmentary remains of urns and pediments whose shards had been bleached bone-white by ancient suns. Above them, on the keystone of the arch, the inscription: 'ARVNDELIVS'.

The name was familiar. She craned her neck as the garden slowly receded in their unfurling wake, trying to remember what Vilém had said a few hours earlier about Arundel and the Howards, about their rivalry with Buckingham.

'From Constantinople,' Vilém was now saying, almost in a whisper. 'The finest collection in all of England, if not the whole world. Arundel has an agent at the Sublime Porte who ships them to London by the crate-load. He suborns the imams. He convinces them that the statues are idolatrous so they can be removed from the palaces and triumphal arches. Most of the other statues are from Rome, where Arundel has good connections with the papal authorities.'

'And good connections with Cardinal Baronius?'

Vilém nodded grimly. 'Arundel and his agents have been working for Baronius, spreading their sticky web, trying to catch whatever they can of the treasures from the Spanish Rooms and the Bibliotheca Palatina. Reports from Rome say a deal has been struck. In return for Arundel delivering the Hermetic manuscript, the Pope will sanction the export of a number of statues on which the Earl has set his heart. Included among them is an obelisk from Egypt that now lies on the site of the Circus of Maxentius. Also a few ornaments from the Palazzo Pighini. Arundel plans to erect them in his garden, I fancy. A fine sight they would make. Monuments to Rome in the heart of London.'

Now, pushing aside draping willow branches, ducking among the aspens, Emilia hurried to catch Vilém, who was three steps ahead, the cabinet clutched awkwardly in his arms as he crept round the knot garden of York House. There was a side entrance beside a basket of bricks, under the scaffold, cast in shadow. When Vilém knocked hesitantly on the door, a cacophony of yelps and snarls arose from within. Both of them shrank backwards, Vilém fumbling with the cabinet. Claws scrabbled angrily against the inside of the door.

'Quiet, quiet! No, no! Achille! No!'

But the muffled voice from behind the door did little to silence the beasts. A few seconds later came the rasp of a judas, and Emilia caught the wink of an imperious eye.

'Who knocks?'

Vilém, apparently thinking better of announcing himself, made no reply, only hoisted the cabinet high enough for the eye to see. Then came more howling and the sound of crossbars sliding in their wooden grooves. Seconds later the door squealed open a crack to reveal four snouts, clamorous and slobbering. A pack of buckhounds. Emilia stumbled backwards, her heels slipping in the frost.

'Achille! Anton! No!'

The hounds spilled outside, leaping over one another's lithe backs like a troupe of acrobats. Emilia recoiled another step but tripped over the basket, then one of the tumultuous hounds. Its tail struck the hollow of her knee and she collapsed with a cry to the grass. Seconds later she felt on her throat and hands the hot breath of the pack, then their noses and tongues.

'Salt,' explained a calm voice from somewhere high above. 'They adore the taste of salt. Obviously, my dear, you've been perspiring.' Hands clapped loudly. She looked up through a chaos of ears and tails to see a liveried figure tickling the jowls of one of the capering hounds. 'Here, lads. Here, my boys! Auguste! Achille! Anton! Good boys!'

'We have come on important business,' Vilém was saying from where he cowered beside the door, holding aloft the cabinet as two more of the hounds, lean and spotted, stood on their hind legs and pawed at his belly and chest like children patting his pockets for sweets. 'We would speak to Mr Monboddo!'

'Do come in, please,' said the footman, sniggering. 'Mind the carpet, though, won't you? That's it. The Earl is most particular where his carpets are concerned. Oriental, as you can see. Very fine, this one. Hand-knotted. All the way from Turkey.' He was ushering the hounds inside. 'A gift from the Grand Vizier!'

The walls of the corridor were lined with busts and marble figures like the ones in the garden of Arundel House, their ancient noses and lips obliterated like those of syphilitics. Some were still inside wooden crates packed with straw, where they looked like poets and emperors reposing in their coffins. Marbles snatched from Arundel, Emilia supposed. Further on, portraits in their heavy frames leaned towards them from hooks on the wall; others still in paper wrapping bound by twine sat upright on the floor.

Emilia barely registered any of them as she passed. The baying of the canine pack, its numbers now enlarged, was deafening in the close quarters. Excited tails thumped the walls and thwacked the canvases. Pink tongues drooled glittering necklaces across the Vizier's carpet, which seemed to stretch endlessly in front of them.

'Good boys,' the servant in his mallard-green tunic was shouting above the din. 'Stout lads! Hearty fellows!'

They were led through a succession of rooms, each one in poorer repair than the last. The interior of the house, like the exterior, seemed to be in a state of either destruction or reconstruction, it was difficult to tell which. They followed the footman up a flight of stairs, along another corridor, and finally into a large room bursting with more busts and fragmentary urns, more wooden crates, more portraits propped against a half-finished oak wainscot.

'If you will wait here, please.'

The servant disappeared with the hounds flinging themselves about him in frantic orbits, their claws clicking like dice on a gameboard. The sash had been raised and the room was freezing cold. Emilia's heart sank. She turned round to reach for Vilém's hand, but he had already crossed the room and was squatting beside a half-finished line of shelves. The shelves were lined with books, some of which had been packed into three crates, also stuffed with straw, that stood in the corner furthest from the window. Vilém was lifting a volume from the shelf when a warped floorboard creaked. Emilia turned round to catch sight of a white ruff, a black cloak and a wink of gold earring.

'From Hungary,' boomed the voice. 'The Bibliotheca Corvina.' The tone was deep and golden, like that of an orator or politician, though the speaker, from what Emilia could see of him in the poor light, was short, almost squat. 'Or I should say from Constantinople, where it was taken by the Vizier Ibrahim after the Turks invaded Ofen and pillaged the Corvina in 1541.'

Vilém, startled, had almost dropped the book on the floor. Now he was rising to his feet, awkwardly. From down the stairs came the echoic yelp of a dog, then the bang of a door.

'Corvinus's ex-libris is found on the inside,' the basso profundo was continuing. 'The purchase was negotiated by your friend Sir Ambrose. I believe he discovered it among the incunabula in the Seraglio.' The dark head turned to appraise the room: Emilia only very briefly, the jewelled chest in the middle of the floor more keenly. 'Is Sir Ambrose not with you this morning?'

Vilém shook his head, still clutching the book. 'No. There's been some difficulty. He—'

'Neither is the Earl, I regret to say. Pressing business at the Navy Office. A pity, Herr Jirásek. I believe Steenie very much wished to show you round the library himself. Though perhaps I might be of service instead?' The warped board gave another angry squawk as he stepped forward and made a polished bow. 'Henry Monboddo is my name.'

Only when Monboddo straightened and stepped another pace forward on the warped board and into the glow of the sash-window – an actor striding centre stage, Emilia thought – did the ruff, cloak and earring finally resolve into a complete person. He was scarcely taller than Vilém but still gave off an air of unmistakable imperium, one enhanced not only by his voice – a heavy millstone grinding bolts of velvet – but also an aquiline nose, a neatly cropped beard and a head of black hair as thick and glossily oiled as the highly prized pelt of some aquatic animal. There was also, Emilia thought, a raffish gleam in his dark eyes, as if he had glimpsed in some corner of the room, over Vilém's shoulder perhaps, some ridiculous but titillating object or scene that only he could appreciate.

'I must apologise on behalf of the Earl,' he was continuing, 'for the condition of the house. But improvements must be made if it is ever to do justice to his collections of marbles, paintings and, of course, his books.'

'It's a . . . a most impressive collection,' stammered Vilém.

'Yes, well . . . dare I say, *mein Herr*, that you have brought your hogs to a fair market?' He chuckled softly at that, a phlegmatic rumble that seemed to rise from the bottom of his blacked boots. But a moment later he looked altogether more serious. 'Not quite so impressive a collection, I fear, as Arundel's. But of course everything will be more favourably disposed once the shelves and cabinets' – he gestured with a broad sweep at the rickety shelving – 'have been completed. You see, this entire house will be devoted to them, every last closet and chamber. Steenie purchased the lease from Sir Francis Bacon. At present he is in the process of negotiating the purchase of another property, Wallingford House, also very convenient for Whitehall Palace. Viscount Wallingford is selling it at a most favourable price.' Laughter welled up again, thick and rich as molasses. 'A deal has been struck, you understand. Wallingford is selling it for just £3,000 in exchange for the life of his sister-in-law, Lady Frances Howard.'

At this point the raffish eyes seemed to glimpse in the gloomy peripheries of the chamber a scene more preposterously endearing than ever. His broad features flirted with a mocking grin that gave him the look, Emilia suddenly thought, of a schoolboy contemplating some glorious prank. She looked quickly away, unnerved, and saw through the window Buckingham's lacquered barge casting off from the landing-stairs, then slipping into the middle of the current, bows pointed downstream. Two figures sat inside, clad in green livery.

'Perhaps you have heard of Lady Frances? No? The Earl of Arundel's cousin,' he explained, clasping his hands over his velvet, fob-chained belly as if stifling another rich chortle. 'Now she sits in the Tower, all forlorn, waiting for the axeman to come tapping at her door. Possibly news of this dreadful little scandal has reached Prague? The poisoning of poor old Sir Thomas Overbury? The disgrace of Somerset? No, no, no,' he was waving a ruffed hand through the air, looking more serious now, 'of course it has not. And why should it? You Bohemians have more important matters to consider than our petty squabblings here in London. But come . . .' He gestured with a flourish. 'May I have the honour of showing you something of Steenie's treasures?'

For the next thirty minutes Monboddo swaggered through chamber after chamber with the pair of them in tow, listening to his burly voice booming off crumbling plasterwork and warped wainscot. The treasures made an impressive sight even if York House itself did not. Monboddo would unswaddle each, then lift it to the light, his swart face beaming with pride. He seemed to know, intimately, the provenance of each, whether it had come from a library in Naples after Charles VIII's Italian campaign of 1495, or from a church in Rome following its sack by von Frundsberg in 1527, when the *Landsknechts* invaded the

Sancta Sanctorum and pillaged the tomb of St Peter itself – or from any one of a dozen other battles, lootings and assorted atrocities. He recounted all of these stories of bloodshed, theft, betrayal and destruction with hearty relish. To Emilia, lagging behind, gazing at canvases sliced from their frames and marbles prised from their plinths, it seemed that beauty and horror had been fused together in Buckingham's precious *objets*, as if behind every glint of gilt or gemstone lay a story of violence and suffering. She was unnerved by the sight of Monboddo's hands as he fondled each item; of each thick knuckle with its floccus of black hair. They seemed not so much the hands of a collector or a connoisseur – hands trained to touch vases or violins – as the brutal paws of a lecher or a strangler.

The horrid perorations rolled over her. Carthage. Constantinople. Venice. Florence. Cities of beauty and death. Heidelberg. Prague. She had turned to the window and between the glazing-bars caught a glimpse of the river's tawny back with a couple of sails teetering along. The barge and its occupants had disappeared downstream.

'... And now it has made its journey from Bohemia to London,' Monboddo's Jovian voice was finishing its latest dreadful litany, 'just as the pair of you have done.' His full lips in their fringe of jet beard twisted into an indulgent smile as he set a goblet back inside its straw-filled crate. 'It was a gift to Steenie from King Frederick, an acknowledgement of his support for the Protestant cause in Bohemia. Arrived only a few months ago, one step ahead of yet another battle. But no need to tell you two about that little commotion, is there?'

His glossy black stare had come to roost on Vilém, who slowly shook his head. All at once Monboddo's features became solemn and formal.

'Speaking of which ...' His eyes now dropped to the cabinet that Vilém was still clutching in his arms. 'I believe we have some business, Herr Jirásek. A matter of some other errant treasures? But let us discuss details over breakfast, shall we? You look worn out, my dears!'

Chairs were brought, then a table was laid with plates of food – roasted pig's pluck, a peasant's dish for which Monboddo apologised, explaining with a wink how Steenie was fond of such humble fare since his mother had been a maidservant. Neither Vilém nor Emilia managed to eat more than a few bites, but Monboddo's appetite, undaunted by the meanness of the dish, stopped his mouth long enough to allow Vilém to tell his story. Patiently and without faltering he told of the *Bellerophon*'s wreck, of the *Star of Lübeck* and the liveried pursuers, of the looters on the beach, of Sir Ambrose's plans to hire salvors with diving-bells to raise the crates, and his arrangements for another ship to transport the salvage.

When Vilém finished, not so much reaching a conclusion as blundering suddenly into a bewildered and anxious silence, the house seemed to have fallen completely still. Through the window there came the distant gong of a church bell and a cool, scentless breeze. As the arras curtains gave a lazy shrug Emilia heard the sound of oars in the water and, seconds later, caught sight of a long barge nosing its way beneath the watergate, a frieze of figures aboard. Carefully she returned her gaze to Monboddo.

He was leaning back in his silk-upholstered chair, nodding a black boot in the air. It almost seemed that he was flirting with another smirk, even trying hard not to laugh, as if Vilém were telling some involved but amusing story, some ribald anecdote whose comic outcome he already knew. He belched softly and wiped his beard with the back of his hand. His dark eyes rose from the nodding boot and came to roost on Vilém. A scull lisped in the water and the boot ceased its restless motions.

'Well, well,' he said in a philosophical tone, expelling a sigh from his deep chest, 'a blow to the cause, that much is certain. A tragedy indeed. To escape Ferdinand's armies only to be shipwrecked on the shore of England! Oh, dear me, Steenie will be most upset, I can assure you of that. As of course will the Prince of Wales. Most upset. And I understand from what Steenie tells me of his little plot that Burlamaqui has already come up with most of the money. The Lord only knows where from, or what fantastic tale he might have told to his Italian bankers. But all is not lost, is it? By no means. Diving-bells, you say? A submarine?' He seemed to find the thought richly amusing. 'Well, Sir Ambrose is nothing if not resourceful. And the parchment . . . well . . . that at least has survived, has it not?'

His gaze had dropped to the cabinet that seemed to crouch between Vilém's feet. Vilém was perched on the edge of his chair, straight-backed and anxious.

'Yes,' he said slowly, 'the parchment. We made certain of it.'

'Yes, yes. The parchment,' Monboddo repeated. '*The Labyrinth of the World*. There is that at least to be thankful for.'

His voice trailed dreamily away. He was studying the new plasterwork of the ceiling, a pattern of swirls and lobes incorporating Buckingham's coat of arms. Through the window behind his head Emilia could see a pair of green-liveried figures warping the sleek barge along the bottom of the landing-stairs. There were others in the boat now, also in livery. The hull struck one of the bollards with a hollow thud. Then the arras shrugged and the sight abruptly disappeared.

'Do you have the key, I wonder?' The bass voice was casual.

Vilém seemed to start. He raised his head, looking as if he were sniffing the air for some elusive scent, like a buck in a forest clearing who hears the soft snap of a twig.

'The key, sir?'

'Yes. The key to the chest. Has Sir Ambrose entrusted you with it by any chance? A pity,' he said in the same casual tone when Vilém, eyes wide, shook his head with nervous vigour. 'A great pity. It would have saved us a deal of effort.'

Then with a lazy motion and a creak of his silk-upholstered chair he leaned backwards and grasped in his hairy paw a tool – an iron crowbar – propped on the window-sill.

'Well, then, what do you think, my dears?' He waggled the tool in the air. 'Dare we open it?'

'No,' Vilém stammered. 'We must wait for . . .'

But Monboddo had already leaned forward and seized the casket in his thick paws. Vilém rose shakily from his chair. There came, from outside and below, the sound of feet crunching through the frost in the garden.

* * *

The cabinet took several minutes to prise open. It was a sturdy piece, having been fashioned from the wood of a mahogany tree felled on the shores of the Orinoco. It was also very valuable – one of the most valuable of Rudolf's many cabinets in the Spanish Rooms. The jewels encrusting its surface included diamonds from Arabia, lapis lazuli from Afghanistan and emeralds from Egypt, along with 24-carat gold that had been mined in the mountains of Mexico and shipped across the ocean on the Spanish treasure fleet. Yet Monboddo the great connoisseur showed scant respect for either its beauty or its value. He had struck three violent blows across its lid and hinges before Vilém could intervene.

'Stop this, I say.' He had taken hold of Monboddo's burly arm as it drew back for yet another blow. 'Stop this before—' But he was sent sprawling across the floorboards as the larger man twisted round and gave him a violent push.

'A man must kill a few hogs,' Monboddo growled into his ruff as he struck the lid another blow, 'if he wishes to make a blood pudding.'

He was on his haunches beside the cabinet, grunting and red-faced like someone at his close-stool. Beads of sweat had formed in the deep furrows of his brow. He inserted the end of the crowbar under the hasp, then the staple, then the hook of the padlock, trying to force one of them free.

'Damn!'

The crowbar slipped and the lock rattled. The lid screeched as if in protest and then gave a dense ring as Monboddo reared back and struck it another furious blow with the iron bar. One of the jewels shattered and its fragments, bright and blue as damselflies, skittered across the floor and into the corner. Vilém, picking himself up from the boards, murmured another protest. Emilia stepped backwards a pace. She could hear, from below, the bang of a door and the sudden, fierce commotion of the hounds.

'Achille! Anton! No, no, no, no, no!'

Monboddo was kneeling on the cabinet now, cursing under his breath as he fitted the flat beak of the bar under the hasp and then forced the other end downwards with both hands, using his weight for leverage. His head trembled with the strain. Then the hasp's golden hinges gave another squeak as the metal warped and one of the pins popped free.

'Ha! We shall have it yet, my dears!'

The buckhounds were on their way upstairs, thumping and yelping. Emilia thought she could hear behind them, beneath their excited clamour, the sound of spurred boots treading the first of the steps. She looked to Vilém, but he was staring at the cabinet. A second pin had popped free. Monboddo was noisily freeing the bar from the warped hasp, head lowered like a bull, puffing heavily as he readied himself for another try. The cabinet gave a soft rattle as if its contents were shifting.

'Auguste! Aimé! No! No!'

The first of the hounds bounded into the chamber, followed by three companions, one of which knocked over a suit of rusted armour suspended on a wooden rack. A buckler and a visored helmet gonged to the floor, then skidded and spun towards Monboddo. He didn't so much as bat an eye. Four more hounds burst into the chamber, lunging at the scraps of food on the table. A plate was knocked to the floor and shattered. The spurred boots reached the corridor.

'By God – !'

With a loud groan the hasp broke free from its hinges. Monboddo gave another crow of triumph. He was still on his thick hams, bent over the cabinet, sweat dripping from his nose; Vilém knelt beside him, his face curiously pale. Emilia squinted in the poor light. She felt frozen, trapped in the eye of this whirlwind of rumbling boots, leaping hounds, clattering plates and armour. The cabinet gave another rattle as Monboddo grasped it between his hairy, looter's paws. Then, slowly, he raised the lid.

'Achille!'

Inside was another cabinet, exactly the same in every detail as the first, from its polished mahogany and gold hinges to its brilliant jewels. Monboddo raised it in his hands, holding it to the light and inspecting the ornate sides, brow knit. A nuzzling hound was thrust aside. Vilém was still beside him, head cocked, also looking puzzled. Monboddo lifted the lid of the second box to expose a third, even smaller, then a fourth, smaller still – a series of wooden shells that he tossed aside one by one.

'What? What's this?' He had reached a fifth casket, which was barely larger than a snuff-box. He swung his bullish head to face Vilém, who had turned even paler. 'What is the meaning of this? A joke? What have you done?' He hurled the tiny casket against the wall, where it shattered to expose a sixth. 'Do you toy with me? The parchment! Where is it, damn you!'

The spurs had ceased their jingling and now the hounds fell silent. Arduously Monboddo pushed himself upright, his boots crunching broken glass. Emilia, staring at the litter of boxes, felt Vilém recoil beside her.

'Gentlemen!' Monboddo had turned to face the door. 'Bad news, my good sirs. It would appear that Sir Ambrose and his friends have enjoyed a small joke at our expense.'

He gestured with his crowbar at the mahogany cabinets. Emilia, raising her head, saw three men in the doorway, the gold on their dark livery lit by the sash-window. Then a board creaked piteously and the first of them stepped into the chamber.

Chapter Six

Was there ever a summer when the rains fell so heavily? Whenever I look back on those days it seems that rain is streaming from a leaden sky. The sun disappeared for weeks on end behind sullen scuds of cloud; it might have been October or November instead of July. In London the gutters filled and flowed, feeding the swollen Thames. The window-sills and clothes-lines no longer bore their swags of laundry, for there was never enough sunshine to dry anyone's linen. In the countryside the rivers overflowed their banks, running in torrents across stunted fields, sweeping away roads and bridges. Fasts were observed and days of humiliation observed, because in time it was decided that the incessant rains must be the Lord's angry judgement on the people of England for failing to punish the regicides. Before the year was out the traitors would be hunted down in Holland and hanged at Charing Cross, Standfast Osborne among them. Huge crowds thronged Whitehall and the Strand to watch the spectacle, and a thousand voices cheered as the bodies were cut down and the butchers stepped forward to begin their work. One by one the bellies of the regicides were expertly slit and the dripping lengths of viscera thrown on to bonfires that sizzled and snapped under the bleak October rain. Nothing like it had been seen since the days when Queen Mary martyred Protestants in Smithfield, or Queen Elizabeth Jesuits at Tyburn. Even death was considered a punishment too soft for Cromwell, so his carcass was excavated from its tomb in Westminster Abbey and hauled in a cart to Tyburn, where it was hanged and then beheaded. The rotted corpse was buried under the scaffold while the skull was slathered with pitch and stuck on a pike on Westminster Hall, from where it glowered at the crowds hurrying past the bookstalls and printsellers below. Small boys threw stones at it; others laughed and cheered as the ravens fought over the eye sockets. Revenge, revenge – everyone in those days was bent on revenge.

And was I, too, bent on revenge? Was it that which made me embark, feverish and ill, on that final, fateful journey? Was it retribution that I hoped to find as I set out from Alsatia, in the midst of the deluge, in the back of a mail-coach jostling along the Strand and into Charing Cross, heading slowly westward?

I remember the sodden morning of my departure, in contrast to those preceding it, in vivid detail. It was still only July, but already the scaffolds were being built for our little auto-da-fé. Or perhaps it was the beginning of August. I had lost all track of time. How many delirous days had passed since I had returned to Alsatia from the Rolls Chapel? Four or five? As much as a week? I recalled very little of those intervening days, and nothing at all of my journey back to the Half Moon Tavern from that dark labyrinth under Chancery Lane. How did I return, by hack or by foot? What must the hour have been when at last I found myself, dazed and alarmed, inside my tiny room?

The next few days – or the next week – had passed horribly. I fell into a nightmarish sleep, from which I awoke now and again, sweating and sore, unable to move, tangled in clammy bedlinen like a panicked beast trapped in a net. At one moment the chamber seemed unbearably hot; the next, it was freezing cold. I was hungry and thirsty but too weak, when I tried, to rise from the bed. I have vague memories of footfalls along the corridor. At some point after dusk I was aware of a jingling of keys, the sighing of hinges and, in the doorway, the alarmed face of a chambermaid. Mrs Fawkes must have arrived shortly thereafter. I seem to remember someone else, a man, shuffling about on the squeaking floorboards. He inspected my tongue, whoever he was, and pressed his ear to my chest and the back of his hand to my brow. It seems I was agued; the result, doubtless, of my little excursion in the Cam, along with my exertions, my travels, my lack of food. I have always possessed a weak constitution. My body as much as my mind craves regularity and custom. To cap it all, my asthma had worsened. My chest was making a braying noise that seemed to alarm all concerned. In one of my few lucid moments it occurred to me how my clients would wonder and exclaim at the news that Isaac Inchbold, the respectable bookseller, had died in a brothel.

Yet Mrs Fawkes had no wish to let me die; perhaps she was mindful of the reckoning. And so it was that over the next few days I suffered all manner of attentions from a succession of her chambermaids. Every few hours I was spoonfed broths and gruels, and my aching limbs were rubbed with chamois-leather gloves. I was bled by a barber-surgeon, in whose cup my drained blood looked as bright and volatile as quicksilver. In time I was made to totter down the stairs and into a sweating-house – a hitherto unknown facility – where I bathed in a cistern whose ordinary function (judging from the cavorting pink nymphs painted on the tiles above) was something less salubrious. But the bath seemed to help, as did everything else, and in time I felt better.

One morning when the rainclouds were prowling the horizon I rose from my sickbed, dressed my shrunken limbs in the Cavalier clothing that someone had thoughtfully laundered and folded, then took hold of my thorn-stick and hobbled down the stairs to pay Mrs Fawkes for her hospitality. Through the windows of each landing I could see, sinking into the rooftops, steadily shrinking as I descended, the turrets and pennants of Nonsuch House, all looking exact and familiar, but also unreal, as if the building were an apparition or a model of itself, or something glimpsed in a dream. The drawbridge was lifting itself skyward in a languid pantomime. At the last turn, the scene vanished from sight, and all at once, wobbling on my stick, I felt choked with grief, hopelessly cut off from my past.

'But, Mr Cobb . . .' Mrs Fawkes had seemed startled by the sight of the gold sovereigns I pressed into her palm. 'But . . . where will you go, sir?'

'My name is Inchbold,' I told her. I had had enough of lies. 'Isaac Inchbold.' I had turned and was already halfway to the door. Rain was falling heavily now. I watched a stream of water pulsing along the middle of the street. 'I shall go to Dorsetshire,' I told her, realising for the first time what dark skein my fevered brain had been slowly spooling as I lay sweating and trembling in my bed. 'I have urgent business in Dorsetshire.'

Six post roads left London in those days: six roads that radiated like the cords of a great web, at whose centre crouched the Postmaster-General and his superior, Sir Valentine Musgrave, the new Secretary of State. Between the radiations of the new royal monopoly, woven into its meshes, was a finer, almost invisible grid of by-posts and 'common carriers': independently run couriers who served the small market towns and remote areas of the kingdom that the coaches of the Postmaster-General had yet to penetrate. These were woefully primitive and disorganised, but spying and smuggling – and the shipping or receiving of unlicensed books – would have been tricky to accomplish without them. In 1657 Cromwell had tried without success to suppress them, and now I supposed they would become the *modus operandi* of the new King's numerous enemies, the secret channels for new forms of dissent. I caught the first of what would be a half-dozen of them somewhere to the west of Salisbury: a small, slow vehicle, barely more than a covered wagon, that ran a whimsically irregular route through the countryside, through ten miles of detours, flooded hamlets and forced stops, until it was time to wait three hours for the connecting coach to trundle into town, an even smaller vehicle heaped high with demijohns of Tewkesbury mustard and Hampshire honey. But the last coach I caught – the one that finally delivered me to Crampton Magna – was considerably larger and swifter than the others. It also had a familiar symbol, a crux Hermetica, painted on the door in sun-faded gold, just visible between streaks of mud the colour of mature rust.

It was late in the afternoon by this point, and I had been four days on the road. The other passengers had disembarked long before. I stood under the dripping awning of a tobacconist-cum-post-office, staring in disbelief at the image, wondering if I was hallucinating, if the fevers had not yet left my body. Was there no escaping the radius of signs and vectors, not even here, in this anonymous hamlet, miles from anywhere?

'Mercury,' explained the driver, a huckle-backed old fellow named Jessop, when he caught me staring at the door. He was hitching the horses to the harness and the harness to the poles. 'Letter-carrier to the gods. The coach was part of the old De Quester fleet,' he added with some pride, thumping the spattered door with a finger-shy hand. 'More than forty years old but still going strong. The Mercury symbol was part of De Quester's coat of arms.'

'De Quester?' Where had I heard the name before? From Biddulph?

'Matthew De Quester,' he replied. 'I purchased the coach from the company when it lost its charter. This was a good many years ago. Well before your time, I shouldn't wonder, sir.'

With an effort he clambered into the coach-box and signalled for me to follow. I climbed aboard, filled with dread and dismay. For the next few hours, as the exhausted horses stumbled hock-deep through the mire, I wondered if I was ever to get to the bottom of these strange matters, if whatever mysterious truth that Alethea harboured was destined always to escape me. All of my investigations seemed to have added up to so much dross. I felt like the alchemist who, after hours of labours, after endless alembications, decoctions and distillations, is left not with the dazzling lump of gold of which he dreams, but rather the *caput mortuum*, a worthless crust, the residue of burnt chemicals. In the past few days I had begun to doubt my powers of reason. I who considered myself so rational and wise suddenly found that I knew nothing and doubted everything. All comforting certainties seemed to have disintegrated.

'Here at last, sir.'

Jessop's voice startled me from my gloomy reverie. I glanced up to see a church tower looming over a huddle of bleak cottages. Lanterns and voices were approaching.

'Crampton Magna.' He had twisted to the ground with a splash. 'The end of the line.'

It was to be another twelve hours before I reached my destination. At the village inn, the Ploughman's Arms, none of the five taciturn patrons could be persuaded to undertake the journey to Pontifex Hall. I had just resigned myself to a long walk in the rain when I was approached by a newcomer, a young man with a freckled face who pledged to take me in the morning, if I pleased to wait. His father, he explained, was the gardener at Pontifex Hall.

The bartender seemed taken aback by the request for a room, but at closing-time I was ushered up a creaking flight of stairs and into a tiny chamber whose walls were festooned with cobwebs and whose linen had yellowed with age. It looked as if no one had opened the door, let alone slept in the bed, for a good many years. But I toppled gratefully on to the lumpy bolster all the same, then into a series of restless and interconnected dreams from which I awoke hours later, heartburned and unrefreshed. Through a lone window that showed an expanse of dirty thatch and a corner of the church I could see that it was raining still, as hard as ever. I doubted my young driver would appear in such weather. But after I trudged downstairs to eat a substantial breakfast, then took my easement in a foul-smelling jakes, a small two-wheeled chariot forded the flooded stream and approached the inn at a brisk trot. The final leg of my long journey could at last begin.

What would I say to Alethea when I saw her again? For the past few days I had rehearsed in my head any number of accusing speeches, but now as Pontifex Hall drew steadily closer I realised that I had no idea what to say or do. Indeed, I had no idea what I hoped to achieve other than perhaps to cause some dramatic scene that would bring the whole affair to its conclusion. I also realised with a flutter of panic that, in grasping the nettle in so bold a manner, I could well bring myself into danger. I thought of the corpse of Nat Crump in the river and of the men who ransacked my shop and then pursued me to Cambridge. Once again the doubts took hold. Were these really the same men who had murdered Lord Marchamont? Or were they instead, like all else, the inventions of Alethea? Perhaps she, and not Cardinal Mazarin, was their mysterious paymaster, the one who set them on my trail. After all, she had traduced the entire situation, had she not? And she had betrayed me.

After a time the horses slowed and I looked up to see the archway opening its wide piers and the house behind it swivelling slowly to face us. Above the piers loomed the familiar inscription. The ivy had been cut back and the words chiselled afresh on the keystone. I could see that a number of improvements had already been made. The dead lime trees had been hewn down and replaced with saplings, the ivy was cut back, the road freshly gravelled. The hedge-maze also looked more defined: a great swirl of green hedges, seven feet tall, that stretched away in a hieratic geometry. I had the sense of a gradual peeling away or exfoliation, of old things renewed. Pontifex Hall seemed to have changed as much as I had. On the north side of the house a small garden had been planted with eyebright and mouse-ear, along with dozens of other herbs and flowers. All had burst into bloom, their leaves and petals shivering in the wind. I recalled none of them from my previous visit.

'The physic garden, sir,' explained the boy, catching my gaze. 'It hasn't bloomed, say the villagers, in more than a hundred years, not since the monks left. The seeds were buried too deep; at least, that's what my father reckons. Nothing grew until he ploughed the soil in the spring.' For a second he regarded me shyly from under the brim of his hat. 'It's like a miracle, isn't it, sir? As if the monks had returned.'

No, I thought, strangely moved by the sight: it was as if the monks had never truly vanished, as if through the years of exile something of them had persisted and endured, lost but redeemable, like the words of a book that awaits the reader who, by blowing at the dust and opening the cover, will revive the author.

'Shall I wait for you here, sir?'

The chariot had reached the house, whose broken dripstones were slobbering torrents of water. I could hear the eaves gulping overhead. The house, despite the improvements, looked as morose and forbidding as ever. What would become of the underground watercourse, I wondered, with so much rain? I hoped that the engineer from London had arrived to perform his crucial task.

'One moment, please.'

I twisted down from the chariot and looked more carefully about the grounds. There were no signs of occupation or industry. The windows with their broken panes – those, at least, had not been replaced – looked dark. Perhaps the house was deserted? Perhaps I was too late?

But then I smelled it: a wraith of scent on the damp morning air, sweet and pungent, as slight and swift as a hallucination. I looked up again and saw in one of the opened windows – that of the strange little laboratory – the silhouette of a telescope. My stomach gave a languid heave of fear.

'No,' I told the boy, feeling a pulse begin to beat in my throat. 'I shall have no need of you. Not yet.'

I stepped under the pediment. The smell of the pipe smoke – of fire-cured *Nicotiana trigonophylla* – had already vanished. I raised my stick to strike the door.

Chapter Seven

'Inchbold!'

The voice was accusing. The door, which had opened to expose the dour mask of Phineas Greenleaf, now began to shut as the dull eyes flickered after the departing chariot. I stepped hastily forward and fumbled for the brass knob.

'Wait . . .'

'What is it?' he demanded in the same stern tone. 'What brings you here?'

This was not the reception I expected, even from Phineas. I thrust my club foot into the shrinking aperture. 'Urgent business,' I replied. 'Allow me inside, if you please. I come to pay my respects to your mistress.'

'In that case, Mr Inchbold, you come too late,' he hissed through his gapped teeth. 'I regret to say that Lady Marchamont is not at home.'

'Oh? And is her ladyship at Wembish Park, then, may I ask?' I gave the knob an impatient twiddle. 'Shall I find her there, perhaps?'

'Wembish Park?'

His expression had turned innocent, even confused. Was it that he played his part so well, or did Alethea not make him privy to her secrets?

'Allow me inside,' I repeated as my thorn-stick insinuated

its way against the stone jamb. 'Or shall I knock down the door?'

This was an idle threat for someone of my stature, but one I found myself obliged to make good when the door suddenly swung shut in my face. I applied a shoulder to the solid oak, bellowing curses, before trying a boot to no better effect. I would probably have broken my toe or collarbone had I not thought to try the brass doorknob. As the catch clicked I heard a muffled curse from within, then the door flew wide and again I found myself confronted by Phineas. This time he was even less cordial. He came at me with his teeth bared, threatening to cast me out of the door like the insolent cur I was. I advanced across the threshold and struck him on the haunch with my stick, then after several more physical discourtesies the two of us found ourselves grappling together on the tiled floor.

And so began my final visit to Pontifex Hall. What a scene it must have made, shameful and comic, two grotesques feebly wrestling in the deep chasm of the atrium, elbows and curses flying. I am by no means a brawler. I abhor violence and have always taken pains to avoid it. But put a coward to his mettle (as the saying goes) and he will fight like the devil. So as I engaged my geriatric opponent I found that the bites and punches – the whole brutal dockside repertoire – came all too readily. The toe of my club foot found its mark in the middle of his belly and my teeth in his thumb when he tried to throttle me. The ignominious proceedings concluded when I put him 'in chancery', choking him in a headlock and pummelling his nose with my fist. Not until I saw the bright spurt of blood did I allow him to slither away, moaning like a bull calf and dabbing at his horror-struck face with the back of his hand. Yes, yes, it was a shameful scene, but I regretted it not a whit. Or not, at least, until I heard a voice call my name from somewhere high above. I rolled over with a groan – Phineas had landed a few solid blows of his own – and peered upwards up to see Alethea leaning over a banister at the top of the staircase.

'Mr Inchbold! Phineas! Stop this at once!' Her voice came echoing down the stairwell. 'Please – *gentlemen!*'

I staggered to my feet, panting and scuffling, flinging

droplets of rain like an ill-mannered hound clambering from a duck pond. A gust of wind through the yawning doorway swung the glass chandelier, which belatedly announced my arrival with a series of dissonant chimes. My stockings made a squishing noise as I awkwardly shifted my stance, and so fogged were my spectacles that I could barely see through them. I was aware of having lost a certain advantage. Wiping at my beard, I felt a righteous fury at my predicament. I must have looked both a ruffian and a fool.

But Alethea seemed not at all surprised either by my appearance or my conduct, or even by the fact of my sudden arrival. Nor did she seem angry as she descended, merely puzzled or distracted, as if awaiting something further, the true climax that had yet to happen. For a second I wondered if she had somehow been expecting my arrival on her doorstep. Was even this wild gambit, my flight into Dorsetshire, part of her mysterious design?

'Please,' she said as her eyes returned to me, 'can we not be civil?'

I gaped at her, a spasm of laughter rising in my gut, bitter as wormwood. I could hardly believe my ears. *Civil*? All at once my anger, along with my well-rehearsed speeches, returned in a flash. I lunged a step forward and, waving the stick like a pike, demanded to know what she called 'civil'. All of the lies and games, were *they* civil? Or having my every step dogged? Or my shop ransacked? Or Nat Crump murdered? Was all of that, I demanded with furious hauteur, was all of that what she dared call *civil*?

I believe I continued for some time in this vein, venting spleen like a wronged lover, accusing Alethea of everything I could think of, my voice rising to a shriek as I punctuated each misdeed with another rap of my stick. How I bellowed and roared! My bravura delivery impressed me; I had not thought myself capable of mustering so fiery and commanding a tone. Through the corner of my eye I could glimpse Phineas crawling across the tiles, leaving asterisks of blood in his wake. Halfway down the stairs Alethea had frozen in mid-step, clutching the banister, her eyes wide with alarm.

Slowly my tirade petered out. *Ira furor brevis est*, as Horace writes. I was panting with exhaustion, fighting back sobs and tears. I had caught my reflection in an oval looking-glass propped against the wall: a tottering Cavalier, starved and tattered, his chops hollow and his eyes feverish. I had quite forgotten the transformation, the work of the ague in tandem with Foskett's concoctions. I looked like the frantic spectre of someone returned from the dead to wreak unholy vengeance – a likeness that was not, perhaps, so far from the truth.

Alethea allowed a moment to pass, as if gathering her thoughts. Then to my surprise she denied none of the charges – none except for the murder of Nat Crump. She even seemed disturbed by the news of the coachman's death. It was true, she said, that she engaged him to pick me up outside the Postman's Horn and drive me past the Golden Horn. But of his murder in Cambridge she knew nothing.

'You must believe me.' Her features worked themselves into an agitated smile of reassurance. 'No one was to be killed. Quite the contrary.'

'I don't believe you,' I murmured peevishly, as my fury lapsed into a sulk. 'I no longer believe a word you say. Not about Nat Crump or anything else.'

She was silent for a moment, twisting a strand of hair and thinking. 'He must have been murdered,' she said at last, more to herself than anyone else, 'by the same men who killed Lord Marchamont. By the men who followed you to Cambridge.'

'The agents of Henry Monboddo,' I snorted.

'No.' She was shaking her head. 'Nor were they the agents of Cardinal Mazarin. Those were also lies, I regret to say. You are right – so much of what I told you was a lie. But not everything. The men who killed Lord Marchamont are real enough. But they are agents of someone else.'

'Oh?' I was hoping to sound scornful. 'And who might that be?'

She had reached the bottom of the stairs by now, and I caught another whiff of Virginia tobacco. And of something else as well. At first I took the pungent scent wafting from her clothes for bonemeal and thought she had been tending the knot garden. But a second later I knew it for what it was: chemicals. Not the garden, then, but the laboratory.

'Mr Inchbold,' she said at last, as though delivering a prepared speech, 'you have learned much. I am most impressed. You have done your job well, as I knew you would. Almost too well. But there is much left to learn.' As she extended a hand, I blinked in alarm at the fingertips, which looked strangely discoloured. 'Please – won't you come upstairs?'

I refused to budge. 'Upstairs?'

'Yes. To the laboratory. You see, Mr Inchbold, that is where you will find it. In the laboratory.'

'Find what?'

'Lock the doors, Phineas.' She had turned round and begun climbing, lifting her skirts and swaying up the steps. 'Allow no one inside. Mr Inchbold and I have matters to discuss.'

'Find *what*?' I was bellowing again, feeling the anger rise inside me. Somehow I had been wrong-footed. Yet again I had lost my advantage. 'What are you talking about?'

'The object of your search, Mr Inchbold. The parchment.' She was climbing still, ascending the great marble helix. Once more her voice echoed in the vast well. 'Come,' she repeated, turning to beckon me. 'After so many troubles do you not wish to see *The Labyrinth of the World*?'

Borax, sulphur, green vitriol, potash . . . My eyes roved over the legends inscribed on the vials and bottles littered among the bubble-shaped still-heads with their coiled glass tubes. Yellowish chemicals, green ones, white, rust, sky blue. The stink was even stronger and more tart than I remembered. My membranes prickled and my eyes began to water. Oil of vitriol, aqua fortis, plumbago, sal ammoniac . . .

Reaching for my handkerchief I paused in mid-gesture. Sal ammoniac? I glanced again at the vial, at the colourless crystals, remembering the recipes for sympathetic ink, for inks that, like those made with sal ammoniac, could only be read if the page was heated by a flame. I felt a soft thrill of excitement briefly rouse itself; I also felt dizzy, as if my fever were returning.

'Ammonium chloride,' explained Alethea, catching my gaze.

She was standing beside me, breathing audibly on account of our climb. 'Essential to alchemical transformations. The Arabs made it from a mixture of urine, sea salt and chimney soot. The first mention of it is found in the *Book of the Secret of Creation*, a work that the Muhammadans in Baghdad attributed to Hermes Trismegistus.'

I nodded dumbly, remembering my researches of a week or two earlier. But by now I had spotted something else in the room, the vial marked 'potassium cyanide', which was sitting three-quarters empty on the table before the open casement. Beside it stood the telescope, still on its tripod, pointed at the heavens. The copies of Galileo and Ortelius had been removed and replaced by another volume, a slimmer one half buried in the detritus of the laboratory, a score of pages bound in a cover of tooled leather.

'The laboratory belonged to my father,' Alethea explained as she crossed to the table. 'He built it in the undercroft, where he conducted many of his experiments. But I've moved what little equipment remains into this room.' She paused briefly to lean across the table and pick up the vial of potassium cyanide. 'I required better ventilation for my purposes.'

I watched nervously as she unstoppered the poison. I was still trembling from my outburst in the atrium. I was also embarrassed. It had all been so unlike me. I wondered briefly if I ought to apologise – and then had to bank down yet another wave of anger and self-pity.

She had set the vial back on the table and begun rummaging among the other objects. She seemed to be shifting into and out of focus, so I lifted my spectacles from the bridge of my nose and wiped at my eyes with the handkerchief, which came away smudged with blood. When I replaced the spectacles she was turning round, the leather-bound volume – a volume bound in the style known as *arabesco* or arabesque – in her hands.

'Here, Mr Inchbold.' She extended the book. 'You find it at last. *The Labyrinth of the World.*'

I made no move to accept the volume. By now I was wary of her talent for drawing the wool over my eyes; for making me feel like an awkward schoolboy. I would not be made a fool of again, I told myself. Besides, at this point I was more interested in that tiny bottle of poison, which I seemed to remember had been fuller before. Once again I considered the stories about the fine ladies of Paris and Rome poisoning their husbands. But then I felt her eyes searching mine and so asked, grudgingly, where she found it.

'I didn't find it anywhere,' she replied, 'because it was never lost in the first place. Not in the way that you understand. It's been at Pontifex Hall all the while. It's been here in the house, carefully hidden, for forty years.'

'It's been in your possession all this time? You mean to say that you hired me to locate a book that—'

'Yes and no,' she interrupted, opening the front cover. 'The parchment has been in my possession, that much is true. But matters are not quite so simple as that. Please . . .' She motioned me forward. The bitter scent of almonds had added itself to the *mélange* of smells. In the poor light I could see the ex-libris embossed on the volume's inside cover: *Littera Scripta Manet*. 'Stand over here, if you please. You're just in time to see the last wash.'

'The last wash?' Once again I didn't budge, only watched as she took up the vial again and sprinkled a measure of crystals into a solution of what appeared to be water.

'Yes.' She was unstoppering another bottle. 'It's in palimpsest. Do you know what that means? The parchment has been reinscribed, so the writing must be recovered by chemical means. The process is a most delicate one. Also highly dangerous. But I believe I've finally discovered the proper reagents. I made potassium cyanide by adding sal ammoniac to a mixture of plumbago and potash. The process is described in the work of a Chinese alchemist.'

I crept forward, made curious almost despite myself. I had heard stories of palimpsests, those ancient documents that had been discovered in monastic libraries and suchlike: old texts effaced from parchments on to which new ones had been inscribed. Greek and Latin scribes were known to recycle parchment whenever they ran short, erasing one text by soaking the leaves in milk and then scrubbing at the ink with a pumice-stone before reinscribing the surface, now blank, with a new one, so that one text lay dormant and hidden between the lines of another. But nothing disappears for ever. Over the centuries, because of atmospheric conditions or various chemical reactions, the effaced text sometimes returns, barely legible, to deliver its forgotten message between the interstices of the new script. So it was that a number of ancient books had been occulted and then discovered, centuries later: the frolics of Petronius interrupting the earnest Stoicism of Epictetus, or *priapeia* insinuating their bawdy verses between the Pauline Epistles. *Littera scripta manet*, I thought: the written word abides, even under erasure.

I was leaning forward, squinting at the cockled page. Alethea had opened the window even wider and was now prising the lid from another vial, this one marked 'green vitriol'. So was that, I wondered, how Sir Ambrose had come upon *The Labyrinth of the World*? Between the lines of another text? I was intrigued. What bookseller has not dreamed of finding a palimpsest, some text that for a millennium has been lost to the world?

'I tried an Aleppo gall at first.' She was carefully mixing the solution. I coughed gently into my handkerchief. The bitter smell had grown even stronger. 'The tannin should have bitten deeply into the parchment even after the gum arabic was dissolved. I thought a tincture of crushed gall might bring it back to the surface but . . .'

'Tannin?' I was trying to recall what I knew about ink, which was hardly anything at all. 'But the ink will be made from carbon, will it not? From a mixture of lampblack or charcoal? That was how the Greeks and Romans made their ink, after all. So an oak gall will be of little use if you wish to—'

'That's true,' she murmured absently. 'But this text was not inscribed by the Greeks or Romans.' She was bent over the volume, adding a tincture to the surface of the parchment, across which I could see lettering, which appeared to be Latin, or perhaps Italian, inscribed in black. Her hair was whipped by the breeze and the door slammed shut. 'It was written much later than that.'

'At Constantinople?'

'Not at Constantinople either. Would you open the door, please? Cyanide becomes toxic when it vaporises. Next I tried a deliquescent sal ammoniac,' she continued, adding another drop. 'I made a solution by heating ammonium chloride and trapping the gas in oil of vitriol. I thought that the iron could be recovered if the tannin could not. The iron in the ink would have corroded over time, but I hoped to restore its colour if possible. But that method also failed. The erasure seems to have been made almost too well. You can understand that the process has been most time-consuming. It's taken several weeks altogether. Quite a number of successive washes.'

'Which is why I was hired,' I muttered. I was feeling ill now; I could barely stand. 'As a decoy. A pawn.'

'You created a diversion.' Another drop was added. I stumbled towards the window, bumping into her chair. Alethea, bent over the volume, seemed not to notice. 'You bought me several weeks of precious time,' she said. 'You see, not everything that I told you in Pulteney House was a lie. There is indeed a buyer for the parchment, someone willing to pay a handsome sum. But there are also those – our new Secretary of State is one – who wish to take it without paying. I believe his men paid you a visit the other night.'

I knocked the telescope from its tripod as I swung the casement wide. A pawn. A diversion. That's what I had been – nothing more. My head reeled as it had done in the crypt of the Rolls Chapel. She began describing in the same absent tone the whole grotesque ruse – the cipher, the graffiti, the curios in the coffee-house, the volume of Agrippa, the auction catalogue. All planted for me to find. All intended to lead me further and further away from Pontifex Hall and *The Labyrinth of the World*. And to lead others astray as well. For why should she have sent her letters through the General Letter Office unless she wished them to be opened by the agents of Sir Valentine Musgrave?

'But there are others involved,' she was saying in a distracted voice. 'Agents of powers even more treacherous than those of the Secretary of State. They too had to be led astray. Secret knowledge can be a dangerous thing. In the end even my father wanted to destroy the parchment. It was a curse, he said. Too many people already had died for it.'

I was barely listening now. Overcome by nausea I thrust my head between the mullions and sucked at the cool air. The rain was sibilant against the brickwork, and above my head the gutters roared. I could see beneath me the pointed roof of the pediment sluicing yet more rain. Then my spectacles blurred, and when I wiped them with my handkerchief I thought I glimpsed a coach beyond the stone arch, far in the distance – something barely visible as it moved through the dense foliage and rising mist. But then I was startled by an exclamation from behind me. I turned round to see Alethea holding the book aloft. Between two rows of black lettering another line, smudged and indistinct, had appeared in bright blue.

'At last,' she said. 'The reagents are beginning to take effect.'

'What is it?' The blue characters, a series of figures and letters, dipped and swam before my eyes. Again my anger began to dissipate and I found myself intrigued. 'The Hermetic text?'

'No,' she replied. 'A different one. One copied by Sir Ambrose.'

'Sir Ambrose made the palimpsest?' I could feel my hairline dampening with sweat. I sank into the chair, trembling, bewildered by the turn of events.

She nodded and once more the dropper hovered above the page. 'He was the one who copied the text and then effaced it. You see, he had already discovered two palimpsests in Constantinople. One was an Aristotelian text, the other a commentary on Homer by Aristophanes of Byzantium. Both were concealed behind parchments of the Gospels, but the old lettering had begun seeping back. It's called "ghosting", as if the former text had returned to haunt its successor. He realised soon enough how it would be the perfect disguise.'

'Disguise?'

'Yes. To hide one text within another.' More blue characters had appeared on the page, bleeding into it like ink across blotting paper, though from where I sat I could read none of them. 'It was the perfect way to smuggle a text. Especially if the reinscription was considered valueless.'

'What do you mean? Smuggle a text from where?'

From among the contents of the Imperial Library in Prague, she gradually explained as she continued her work, bent over the table as if performing delicate surgery. This had been in the year 1620, at the outset of the warring between the Protestants and Catholics. Frederick had been elected King of Bohemia one year earlier, a Protestant on a Catholic throne, and so his followers across Europe had suddenly gained access to the contents of the magnificent library assembled by the Emperor Rudolf. The nuncios and ambassadors scuttling back to Rome and her allies among the princes of the Catholic League were alarmed at this turn of events, because a library is always, like an arsenal, a locus of power. After all, had not Alexander the Great planned a library at Nineveh that he claimed would be as much an instrument of his rule as his Macedonian armies? Or when one of Aristotle's other students, Demetrius Philareus, became counsellor to Ptolemy I, monarch of Egypt, what did he advise the King to do but collect together all of the books that he could on kingship and the exercise of power? So the idea of Rudolf's great collection in the hands of Rosicrucians, Cabalists, Hussites, Giordanisti – heretics who for years had been undermining the power not only of the Habsburgs but of the Pope as well – set the tocsins ringing all over Europe. Thus as the armies of the Catholic League marched on Prague in the summer and autumn of 1620, one of their foremost aims, Alethea claimed, was the recovery – and the suppression – of the library.

'Dozens of heretical books were held in the collection,' she continued, 'copies of them had been burned in Rome and placed on the *Index*. Now the floodgates were about to burst. No sooner had Frederick arrived from Heidelberg than scholars from all over the Empire began their pilgrimages to Prague. The cardinals in the Sant'Uffizio realised they would soon lose control over who was allowed to read what book or manuscript. Knowledge would have been disseminated from Prague in a great explosion, fostering sectaries and revolutionaries both within Rome and without, creating still more heresies, still more books for the bonfires and the *Index*. The library in Prague had become a Pandora's box out of which, in the eyes of Rome, a swarm of evils was about to fly.'

I was sitting beside the window, letting the breeze cool my brow. The rain was falling harder than ever. The ceiling in the corridor had begun to leak and the vials and cuvettes were chiming together on the table. Heretical books? I scratched at my beard, trying to think.

'What manner of evil?' I asked when she fell silent, bent over the parchment. 'A new Hermetic text that the Holy Office wished to suppress?'

She shook her head. 'The Church no longer had anything to fear from the writings of Hermes Trismegistus. You of all people must know that. In 1614 the antiquity of the texts had been challenged by Isaac Casaubon, who proved beyond a doubt that they were forgeries of a later date. In the end, of course, Casaubon, for all his brilliance, turned his magnificent guns upon himself. With his book he hoped to refute the papists, Cardinal Baronius in particular. But instead he merely succeeded in destroying one of their greatest enemies.'

'Because the *Corpus hermeticum* was used by heretics like Bruno and Campanella to justify their attacks on Rome.'

'And dozens more besides them. Yes. But with one stroke Professor Casaubon did away with a thousand years of magic, superstition and, in the eyes of Rome, heresy. After the texts had been dated, a new one was valueless, hardly of interest to anyone except a few half-mad astrologers and alchemists. It therefore made the perfect disguise.'

'Disguise?' I shifted uneasily on my chair, still struggling to understand. 'What do you mean?'

'Have you not guessed, Mr Inchbold?

She laid the thin volume aside, and before the wind riffled the pages I saw that the top half of the front one was now covered in the blue script, the ghost of a former text summoned back to life by her poisonous concoction. She dabbed carefully at the ink with a piece of blotting paper and then closed the cover. The wind had begun whistling in the necks of the flasks, raising an eerie chorus. A piece of dislodged slate clattered against the gutter and fell to the ground. The casement slammed shut. Alethea pushed back her chair and rose from the work-table.

'*The Labyrinth of the World* was only the reinscription,' she said at last, 'only the surface text. It was a forgery like the others, an invention used by Sir Ambrose to occult another text, one that was much more valuable. One in which the cardinals in the Holy Office would have interested themselves.' Carefully she stoppered the vial of cyanide. 'Many others as well.'

'Which text? Another heresy?'

'Yes. A new one. For if one world died in 1614, another was being born. In the same year that Casaubon published his attack on the *Corpus hermeticum*, Galileo printed three letters in defence of his *Istoria e dimostrazioni*, which had been published a year earlier in Rome.'

'His work on sunspots,' I nodded, perplexed. 'The work in which for the first time he defends Copernicus's model of the universe. Though I fail to see what—'

'By 1614,' she continued, oblivious, 'Ptolemy had been vanquished along with Hermes Trismegistus, his fellow Egyptian. Together the two of them were responsible for more than a thousand years of error and delusion. But the cardinals and consultors in Rome were less willing to accept the downfall of the astronomer than the shaman, and so the letters that Galileo published in 1614 are a plea for them to read the Bible for moral instead of astronomical lessons, to continue their practice of reading the Holy Scripture allegorically wherever it conflicts with scientific discoveries. All in vain, of course, since in the next year one of the letters was laid before the Inquisition.'

'So the text is one published by Galileo?' I was remembering Salusbury's translation of the *Dialogo*, the volume responsible for the astronomer's persecution by the Pope, the one whose contents Galileo had been forced to recant. 'One suppressed by Rome after the Holy Office banned Copernicanism in 1616?'

She shook her head. She was standing before the window with her hand resting lightly on the telescope, which she had carefully replaced on its tripod. Through the fogged panes I could see that the coach toiling through the mud had drawn a little closer. Nearer to the house I could make out through the curtains of rain the whorled outlines of the hedge-maze; even from this height, it looked hopelessly confused, an endless warren of curlicues and cul-de-sacs.

'No,' she replied, taking a small bucket from the work-table and picking her way into the corridor. 'This particular document was never published.'

'Oh? What is it, then?'

Water was not so much dripping as streaming through the ceiling. I watched as she stooped and placed the bucket beneath, in the middle of the puddle, then straightened.

'The parchment will keep for now,' she said. 'Let us continue our talk elsewhere.'

I took a last look through the window – the coach had disappeared behind a stand of trees – and followed her to the top of the staircase. Who was inside the vehicle? Sir Richard Overstreet? All at once I felt even more uneasy.

I gripped the banister and began to descend. I was about to say something, but after only two steps she stopped and turned round so quickly that I almost bumped into her.

'I wonder,' she said, looking at me with a kind of avid amusement, 'how much you know about the legend of El Dorado.'

Chapter Eight

The smell of the library was in sharp contrast to that of the laboratory. Everything about the cavernous chamber was precisely as I remembered, only now the pleasantly musty air was spiced with the familiar aromas of cedarwood oil and lanolin, as well as a resinous tang of new wood, for a few of the shelves had been repaired and the railing in the gallery replaced. The scents reminded me of my own shop, for smells always return us to the past more keenly and swiftly than any other stimulation. All at once I felt the same gust of heartsickness as on that last morning in the Half Moon Tavern. It might have been years rather than days since I last saw my home.

Alethea was motioning for me to take one of the leather-upholstered chairs beside the window. These too were new, as was the walnut table separating them and the hand-knotted rug, complete with monkeys and peacocks, on which they sat. I shuffled across the floor and obediently creaked into one of the chairs. Phineas was nowhere to be seen. Even his trail of blood had disappeared. For a second I entertained the notion that the disgraceful altercation had been only a product of my feverish imagination.

I crossed and uncrossed my legs, waiting for Alethea to speak. In those days I knew a little about the myth of El Dorado, or 'the Golden One', that will-o'-the-wisp that for the best part of a century had lured countless adventurers into the dangerous labyrinth of the Orinoco river. It is mentioned by chroniclers of the Spanish conquests such as Fernándo de Oviedo, Cieza de León and Juan de Castellanos, all of whose works I had briefly consulted in those first few days after my return from Pontifex Hall, and all of whom tell conflicting versions of the story. Rumours of El Dorado had reached the ears of the conquistadores soon after Francisco Pizarro's conquest of Peru in 1530: a city of gold governed by a valiant one-eyed chieftain, *el indio dorado*, whose practice it was to paint his body each morning in the dust of gold fished from the Orinoco, or perhaps from the Amazon . . . or perhaps from one of their hundreds of tributaries snaking through the jungles. The Spaniards were intrigued by the rumours, and in 1531 a captain named Diego de Ordás received a *capitulación* from the Emperor Charles V to ascend the Orinoco in search of this new Montezuma and his city of gold. Although he found no sign of it, other would-be discoverers were undaunted, and for the next few decades one conquistador after another set off into the jungle like knight-errants in the romances of chivalry so popular at the time. One of them, a man named Jiménez de Quesada, tortured any Indians he found by burning the soles of their feet and dropping bacon fat on their bellies. Under these encouragements his victims told stories of a hidden city of gold – now sometimes called either 'Omagua' or 'Manoa' – in the middle of the Guianan jungle, or perhaps even, like Tenochtitlán, in the middle of a lake.

But Quesada found nothing; nor did his niece's husband, Antonio de Berrío, a veteran explorer of the Orinoco and its tributaries whom Sir Walter Raleigh captured after the sack of Trinidad in 1595. That same year the Englishman, fired by the legends, ascended the Orinoco with a hundred men and provisions for a month. Only when the supplies were exhausted did he return to England, taking with him the son of an Indian chieftain and leaving behind to explore the river two of his most trusted crewmen. One of them was captured by Spanish soldiers, though not before he sent back to England a crude map showing the supposed site of a gold mine at the confluence of the Orinoco and Caroní rivers. But it would be another twenty years before Raleigh returned to Guiana for his disastrous final voyage, this time in the company of Sir Ambrose Plessington.

The serving-girl, Bridget, had entered the room with a pot of tea whose fragrant steam was curling through the air. I was gnawing at my lower lip as I perched in the chair, studying the rows of atlases overhead. I could see Martin Waldseemüller's *Universalis Cosmographia* and several editions of Ptolemy's *Geography*, including the one by Gerardus Mercator. Alethea, catching my gaze, set down her cup and pushed back her chair.

'A number of these maps and atlases are extremely rare,' she said, rising to her feet. 'Some are among the rarest and most valuable items in the entire collection. This one, for example.' She was standing on tiptoe, reaching for one of the volumes, which she then proceeded to flump on to the table between us, rattling our teacups. I was startled to see the water-damaged copy of Ortelius, the *Theatrum orbis terrarum*, the same volume I had inspected in the laboratory: the one from which I had cut the cipher. 'Do you know it?'

'I sell copies of it, yes,' I replied as she opened the buckram cover. I cocked my head and tried to read the colophon. 'This is the Prague edition?'

'Yes, published in the year 1600.' She began riffling through the crimped pages. 'It's extremely rare. Only a few copies were ever printed. Ortelius had travelled to Bohemia at the invitation of the Emperor Rudolf. Unfortunately he died in 1598, soon after his arrival in Prague. Some of the physicians claimed that he died of an ulcer of the kidneys, which Hippocrates tells us is nearly always fatal in old men.' Slowly she turned over one of the pages. 'Others believed that the great Ortelius was poisoned.'

'Is that so?' I glanced at the atlas, recalling the rumours mentioned by Mr Barnacle. The volume was now open at a sheet displaying the legend 'MARE PACIFICUM' – the very point at which I had discovered the cipher. 'Why should that have been?' I was trying to remember what Mr Barnacle had said about voyages through the islands in the high latitudes. 'Because of the new method of map projection?'

She shook her head. 'No such method of projection has yet been perfected. How those rumours started I have no idea, unless they were the invention of whoever murdered Ortelius.'

'So Ortelius *was* murdered?'

She nodded. 'After his death the plates from which the maps were engraved disappeared from the printshop. Or I should say one plate disappeared, that from which this particular map was engraved.' She tapped the rippled sheet with her forefinger. 'You see, the map of the New World in the Prague edition of the *Theatrum orbis terrarum* is different from those in any of the others.'

I was still scanning the page, wondering if I ought to believe her account any more than Mr Barnacle's. There was an elaborate cartouche – 'AMERICAE SIVE NOVI ORBIS, NOVA DESCRIPTIO' – and a representation of the Pacific Ocean, complete illustrations of islands and fully rigged galleons. Everything on the sheet looked precisely the same as on those dreamy afternoons at Molitor & Barnacle, including the scales of latitude and longitude.

'Map making is a speculative art,' she said as she turned the atlas 180 degrees on the table to face me. Again she tapped it with her finger, this time just above the cartouche. 'Look here. What do you see?'

Beneath her index finger I could make out a cluster of a half-dozen islands and the legend 'Insulæ Salomonis'. I shrugged and looked up. 'The Solomon Islands,' I replied cautiously.

'Precisely. But no one knows if the Solomon Islands are actually found at the spot where Ortelius places them. Indeed, no one even knows if they truly exist or if they were only the fantasy of Alvaro de Mendaña, who claimed to have sighted them in the year 1568. He named them the Islas de Solomón because he believed them to be the islands on which King Solomon mined the gold for his Temple in Jerusalem. But King Solomon must have been a better navigator than Mendaña, because the Spaniard never again found the islands. He made a second voyage in search of them in 1595, but with no luck. His pilot, Quirós, made a third in 1606, and many have searched since then. But they appear to have sunk into the ocean one and all, like Atlantis. They remain as elusive as *Terra australis incognita*, which Mendaña and Quirós had also hoped to discover.' Her finger had drifted down the page before stopping to the left of the cartouche, where I could read the inscription 'TERRA AUSTRALIS'. The rest of the space, a large continent whose coast ran down the map's two-hundredth meridian, was blank and featureless. 'Another mythical land portrayed by Ortelius.'

'The continent described in Ptolemy's *Geography*,' I said, wondering what such legendary islands had to do with Galileo or the libraries of Prague.

'And in Arab and Chinese documents as well. Rumours of its existence have circulated for centuries. The Spaniards sent numerous expeditions to discover it, all in vain, though in 1606 Quirós discovered a landmass, in fact only islands, that he named Australia del Espírito Santo. Afterwards it was sought by the Dutch, likewise in vain until a number of their ships bound for Java were blown off course and made landfalls along the coast of an enormous island guarded by coral reefs. Twenty years later some of their ships explored a coastline that stretches from the tenth parallel of latitude below the equator to the thirty-fourth. So it now appears that *Terra australis incognita* is something more than a myth. And if *Terra australis incognita* exists, then who is to say that the Islas de Solomón do not also exist?' She leaned forward and with her forefinger traced a path across the Pacific to the right-hand side of the sheet. 'Look here. You'll see that the Prague edition includes an interesting variant.'

I peered closely at the page. The light from the rain-streaked window was so dim I had to strain my eyes to see its image. But there, some thirty or forty degrees of longitude west of Peru, a dozen parallels south of the equator, in the middle of Ortelius's vast Mare Pacificum, was a tiny rectangular island marked 'Manoa'. This particular detail was not included on any of Mr Smallpace's editions, of that I was certain.

'But I thought Manoa was in Guiana or Venezuela.'

'As did everyone else. But to Ortelius it was an island in the Pacific Ocean, that great cavity left in the earth when the moon broke free. It would be found to the west of Peru and to the east of the fabled Islas de Solomón, on the 280th meridian east of the Canary Islands, which is what Ortelius, following Ptolemy, uses as his prime meridian. Or that, at least, is where Manoa is placed in the Prague edition of 1600.' She rose to her feet and carefully slid the volume back on to its shelf. 'You see, none of the other editions of Ortelius portrays Manoa,' she explained as she returned to her chair, 'either in the Pacific or anywhere else. That is what makes the Prague edition unique. And that, of course, is what Sir Ambrose found so intriguing.'

'But there were other maps of Manoa,' I protested, remembering Raleigh's map, engraved in Amsterdam by Hondius, that I used to explore with my fingers as I crouched between the shelves in Mr Molitor's shop.

'Yes, but most were crude affairs. Manoa was located all over the continent. But after Mercator it became possible for navigators to make use of latitude and longitude when plotting their courses. They could steer a straight course over a long distance without continually adjusting their compass readings. All that was needed was a ruler, a divider and a compass. Mere child's play.'

'Yes,' I nodded. 'Except for the minor detail that no one knows how to find the longitude at sea.'

'Yes, there is the rub,' she replied, returning to the shelf. 'Finding latitude is easy enough, even below the equator where the Pole Star cannot be sighted. One merely finds the sun's altitude at noon by means of a sundial or suchlike. But longitude is as difficult a proposition as squaring the circle.'

It was the ancient problem, I knew, that bedevilled all mariners. Longitude is merely another name for the time difference between two places. In principle its calculation, as I understood it, was a simple enough exercise. Whether over London or the Solomon Islands, or anywhere else on earth, the sun always reaches its maximum altitude at twelve o'clock, the local noon. Thus if a navigator in the Solomon Islands could know, at the moment of *his* local noon, the precise time in London, he could calculate the longitude of his position by the difference between the two times, since each hour equals fifteen degrees of longitude. That was all well and good, but how could someone possibly know the time in London when he finds himself stranded halfway round the world, on the shores of the Solomon Islands?

'Not even the ancients with all of their wisdom could solve the problem,' Alethea was saying. 'Ptolemy in his *Geography* discusses the method of Hipparchos of Nicaea, who advocates using observations of lunar eclipses as a way of measuring the differences in local time east or west of a fixed point. Then Johann Werner of Nuremberg' – she pointed to a volume on the wall – 'proposes in his edition of Ptolemy the so-called lunar-distance method by which the moon and the zodiac form a celestial clock that determines local time at every point round the globe. But neither of these methods succeeds either at sea or in distant lands to which reliable timekeepers cannot be transported.'

'Which is why Mendaña and Quirós were unable to find the Solomon Islands when they returned to the Pacific.'

'Precisely. Because in 1568 Mendaña recorded them at the 212th meridian east of the Canary Islands, only to find when he returned to search for them in 1595 that the 212th meridian was as troublesome to locate as the islands themselves.'

'So Ortelius's map is valueless,' I said. 'It's no more accurate than any of the others.'

She resumed her seat and poured two more cups of tea, which was a rare drink in those days, one I had sampled only two or three times before. It seemed to set my nerves on edge. My hand was trembling as I reached for the cup.

'No doubt the scale of longitude is nothing more than informed guesswork,' she replied at length. 'But the island? Is that also a fiction? And, if so, why should the map have been suppressed?'

'Who suppressed it, then? The Spaniards?'

'So Sir Ambrose believed. And they would have had good reason to do so. Prague would have been the last place on earth where the King of Spain and his ministers would have wished such a secret document to appear. Its colleges were rife with Protestants, Hermeticists and Jews, along with every sort of mystic and fanatic. Exactly the sort who, twenty years later, so terrified the cardinals in the Holy Office. And so the great Ortelius was poisoned and his map suppressed.'

She closed the book and regarded me carefully. I could hear someone crossing the atrium and rain splashing from the downspouts. A large pool of water was enlarging about the sundial, and more was spilling over the cracked rim of the fountain. In the distance, beyond the stunted orchard, I saw the dip-well and cress-pond, also overflowing, their swollen surfaces pocked and bubbling. I shuffled my feet nervously on the carpet, remembering the approaching coach.

'That might have been the end of the story,' she said at last, 'except for one small detail. It concerns a ship, Mr Inchbold. A Spanish galleon. One discovered quite by accident in the waters of the Caribbean.' Thunder crackled louder now and rain dashed against the window. 'Perhaps in your investigations you have learned something about it? It was called the *Sacra Familia*.'

Streaks of lightning were followed by mortar-bursts of thunder. In the midst of one of the loudest crashes Bridget appeared in the library doorway with a fish-oil lamp. She set it on the table and removed the tray of tea, her shoes scuffing along the tiles. Alethea too had crossed the floor. For several minutes she worked busily at the shelves, standing on a step-ladder and plucking down books like someone picking apples in an orchard. But then she returned to the table clutching an armful of volumes, which she began scattering in an avalanche across its surface. I caught one of the tumbling books before it slipped over the edge and was surprised to see Duplessis-Mornay's *De la vérité de la religion chrétienne*, the work of Hermetic philosophy translated into English by Sir Philip Sidney.

'. . . republished in new editions and translations,' she was saying over the din of the rain as the books tumbled over each other and on to the table. 'The *Apologia* of William of Orange, *The Spanish Colony* by Bartolomé de Las Casas, the *Relaciones* of the English informer Antonio Pérez . . .'

As she sorted through the pile, I caught a glimpse in the lamplight of the treatise by Las Casas, the Spanish priest who had catalogued atrocities committed by the conquistadores among the Indians.

'Even the printers and booksellers had joined the fight against Spain. These books and dozens of others, all were smuggled by their thousands into every corner of the Spanish Empire to rouse bands of defeated rebels and other malcontents in Catalonia, Aragon and Calabria. They were even translated into Arabic and smuggled into Africa to be read by the Moriscos whom Philip III banished from Spain. Now thousands of Moriscos, like the rebels in Calabria and Catalonia, were poised to pluck up their arms and once more fight the Castilians. Only this time all of Protestant Europe would be fighting at their side.'

So it was that I found myself listening for a second time to the story of Raleigh's expedition, to the tale of scheming bishops and princes from all across Europe making secret plans for a *coup de main* against their common enemy, the King of

Spain. But on this telling King Philip had lost something of his omnipotence. The English and Dutch spies along the waterfront of La Coruña and in the limestone alleyways of Cádiz were reporting that his navy had not yet recovered from the destruction of the so-called Invincible Armada, whose loss in '88 was but the first straw in the wind foretelling the end of his vast empire. The galleons were not being replaced or repaired because timber stocks on the Iberian peninsula had been badly depleted, and because there was no money to build them anyway – for spies in the House of Trade had reported that bullion imports from America had dropped from nine thousand tons per annum to a little more than three thousand. Philip was heavily in debt to the *hombres de negocio* as a result, as were dozens of merchants and shipowners in Seville who could only watch helplessly as silver collapsed and the galleon trade shrank. A major European war – a war the Spaniards could not possibly win – would put an end once and for all to the Spanish convoys which twice each year swept the treasures of the New World five thousand miles across the Atlantic to Andalucía. All that was wanting was the quickmatch to light the powder-train – a match that was due to be struck by Sir Ambrose and the soldiers on board the *Philip Sidney*.

But the planned mission ended in débâcle. I listened again to the story of how the daring enterprise was scuppered by informers in the Navy Office and on board the *Destiny* herself. At least, the enterprise failed until the *Philip Sidney*, sailing homeward through the Windward Passage, came upon the remnants of the Mexican fleet, which had been scattered along the coast of Cuba by one of the fierce storms that Spanish navigators call a *huracán*. What followed was an accident, a rare stroke of good fortune in the midst of disaster. Indeed, Sir Ambrose might never have stumbled across the convoy, Alethea said, had it not been for a peculiar smell reported by the deckhands while the ship was in soundings some ten leagues west of the Spanish harbour at Santiago de Cuba.

'A smell?' I remembered Biddulph's description of the aromatic galleon. 'What manner of smell?'

'Perfume,' she replied. 'The entire sea smelled of perfume,

or perhaps incense. Can you imagine anything so strange? At first the men on board the *Philip Sidney* thought it nothing more than a hallucination, for hallucinations are common enough at sea. Most have to do with colours, such as when the waves look green so that the ship appears to be moving across fields of grass. Yet no one on board the *Philip Sidney* had ever known the like of this particular hallucination, not even Sir Ambrose. Then, as the smell grew stronger, a sailor in one of the fighting-tops spotted something on the horizon.'

'A galleon,' I murmured.

'A fleet of galleons,' she replied.

It was the convoy from New Spain, three weeks out of Veracruz: fourteen galleons shaping their course northeast-by-north through rough seas towards the Tropic of Cancer and then the higher latitudes, the 40s and 50s, to escape the northeasterly Trades. Fourteen ships alone on the shimmering water that funnelled and whirlpooled between Hispaniola and the Cabo Maisí, most of them so heavily laden that their lower gunports were all but under water. They should have been met already by the *armada de la guardia de la carrera* which would escort them as far as the Canaries, but the squadron had failed to arrive, probably on account of the same winds that for the previous two days had battered the convoy along the coast of Cuba. Now thirteen of the ships were huddled together in formation like a pod of whales as they rounded the windswept cape, but the fourteenth was listing badly. Already it had fallen several bow-shots off the pace.

'The *Sacra Familia*,' I prompted when she paused.

She nodded slowly. 'At first the galleon seemed no more than an apparition. As the *Sidney* drew closer the strange scent grew stronger and the mariners could see that she looked golden in colour, as if her mast-heads and yard-arms were glowing in the sun or lit by St Elmo's Fire. Only the threat of keel-hauling could convince the most superstitious of the sailors to stay at their posts. But Sir Ambrose knew the smell almost at once. It was not perfume, he realised, but sandalwood, a tree whose oil is used to make soaps and incense. A tree whose golden heartwood

King Solomon is said to have used to build his Temple in Jerusalem.'

'The *Sacra Familia* was carrying a load of sandalwood?' I was puzzled but also disappointed by the revelation, by the reduction of this magical vessel, the subject of so many myths, to a cargo ship, a mere transatlantic mule.

'Not a load, though at first Sir Ambrose thought as much. But then he saw that, despite her list, the galleon was riding high in the water. He realised that the *Sacra Familia* carried no sandalwood and no silver or gold from the mines of New Spain; no load of any kind, even though she was sailing with the Mexican fleet. You see, the smell was coming from the galleon herself,' she explained, 'from her planks and masts. She had been built from stem to stern of sandalwood, exactly like Solomon's Temple. And so at once Sir Ambrose forgot about the other thirteen ships in the fleet and gave the order to pursue the galleon instead.'

Thirteen ships gorged with silver from the Mexican mines, or perhaps gold bullion, or bales of Chinese silk from Manila. I tried to imagine the scene. The wealthiest convoy on earth bound unescorted across five thousand miles of treacherous ocean for the Gulf of Cádiz. Yet Sir Ambrose forsakes them – and forsakes his holy mission – to pursue another ship, one with an empty hold. A galleon made from sandalwood.

'Such wood may have been fine for Solomon's Temple,' Alethea had resumed, 'but it's hardly suitable for ships. The heartwood is so heavy it barely floats. This must explain why she was lagging so far behind the other ships. It also explains why the *Philip Sidney* caught her so easily. It was like an Arabian stallion overtaking a mule.'

'But why sandalwood? Why not oak or teak?'

'That is precisely what Sir Ambrose had asked himself. And then he realised. He realised that the *Sacra Familia* had not sailed from Veracruz with the rest of the fleet. He knew at once that she had travelled from much farther afield.'

'The Pacific,' I murmured, thinking of Biddulph's bamboo rats, his belief that the ship had come through the Strait of

Magellan, that narrow passage of shoals and islands at the bottom of the globe.

'He knew that the galleon must have been built from oak once upon a time,' she was continuing, 'because the shipwrights in La Coruña would never have built a ship from sandalwood, no matter how badly their timber stocks were depleted. But at some point a shipwright must have found himself with no choice in the matter. Sir Ambrose understood that the *Sacra Familia* had been wrecked and then rebuilt by her carpenters in a land where no oak trees grew, a land where sandalwood was the only timber to hand. This must have been on one of the islands of the Pacific, which is the only place where one finds sandalwood forests.'

Yet not even Sir Ambrose realised the significance of this fact until the galleon was overtaken in the hour before dusk. This had been a league off the desolate eastern shore of the Cabo Maisí. The *Sacra Familia* stood no chance at all, even without a cargo, for the *Philip Sidney* was the most formidable man-o'-war ever to sail the seas, and her crew was well prepared for battle. At Sir Ambrose's command the soldiers began tallowing the ends of their pikes and the marksmen scrambled into the fighting-tops with their muskets and serpentines. Below decks the gunners filled the wooden cartridges with powder and primed the cannons before roasting fireballs on the brazier like so many enormous chestnuts. But the battle was over almost before it started, because the *Sacra Familia* was unable either to fight or to flee. Her powder was still wet from the storm and her bottom was barnacled and so fouled with the weed the Portuguese call *sargaço* that her rudder budged only with the greatest effort. The English ship had come within cannon-range barely an hour after sighting her, at which point a 32-pounder was sent careering across the galleon's beak-head. There was no reply, so two rounds of grapeshot shredded her sails, to say nothing of what they did to the yardmen putting on more canvas in a vain attempt to hoist sail and escape.

The remainder of the battle lasted less than an hour. The marksmen opened fire from above, while fire-pikes were thrown from the decks and flaming arrows shot from slurbows. One of the arrows sailed through a scuttle and started a fire in the forward deckhouse, from which sailors could be seen leaping into the sea. Then more men jumped as the fire spread rapidly through the hull. By this time the galleon was being driven towards the cape, towards a coral reef on which sat, like a gibbeted corpse, the battered shell of an ancient galleon whose name, *Emperador*, was still legible on her rotting escutcheon. The *Sacra Familia* joined her soon afterwards and then broke apart in several fathoms of water just as the longboats of the *Philip Sidney* were being despatched with a boarding party of fifty soldiers carrying rope-ladders and grappling-hooks. The few Spaniards who didn't drown were eaten by the sharks, though not before they were seen throwing overboard or into the flames the galleon's log, her collection of portolan charts, the wooden traverse board, a *derroterro* – everything that might have betrayed the secret of her voyage. In the end, only the rats survived the wreck, enormous bamboo rats that deserted the ship and swam for the banana plantations along the shoreline.

'Dusk had fallen at this point, and a bright sunset foretold the end of the storms. Sir Ambrose took soundings and ordered his men to drop anchor a mile off the cape, where the *Sidney* rode out the last of the storm. The galleon burned all night on the reef, and in the morning a party was sent to survey the wreckage and scavenge what was left of her. They were forced to work quickly. The flames would have been seen from the shore and word of the wreck would soon reach Santiago if the smell had not warned the Spaniards already, for by sunrise the wind had turned to the southeast and now the smoke was flowing inland with the smell of sandalwood.'

'And was anything found?'

'For several hours, almost nothing. Nothing that might have rewarded the men for their dangerous work in the shark-infested waters. There was no sign of the log and portolan charts, documents for which the Navy Office would have paid a handsome sum. By noon there was little left of the galleon but her keel, and what the fire had spared the wind and waves dispersed. Sir Ambrose was about to order his men to return – a Spanish frigate had been spotted along the coast – but then a party of them raised something from the shallows. It was scorched and waterlogged but still intact.'

'Yes?' I was holding my breath. 'What was it?'

'A sea-chest,' she replied. 'But not just any sea-chest, for it was made of the same wood as the ship. Carved on one of the sides was the coat of arms of a man named Pinzón.'

'The captain,' I said eagerly.

She shook her head. 'Francisco Pinzón was the navigator, and a famous one at that, a graduate of the School of Navigation and Cartography in Seville. He had been the pilot of the Quirós expedition in search of the Solomon Islands in 1606. He must have thrown the chest overboard with all else, but it survived both the fire and the wreck, because sandalwood is as durable as it is beautiful. Once opened, it was found to be filled with books, for the distinguished Señor Pinzón was apparently an avid reader. Most were stories of knightly endeavour, but there was another book inside the chest besides these tales of chivalry, one that told its own tale of a dangerous and impossible quest.'

'The copy of Ortelius.'

'Yes. The Prague edition of the *Theatrum orbis terrarum*, a book so rare that in those days not even Sir Ambrose had seen a copy. He had just opened the cover when suddenly one of the salvors rushed into the cabin. Something else had been found in the water.'

It was another clue: dozens of scraps of paper from a log or journal that someone had attempted to shred before throwing overboard. The pieces were painstakingly collected from the water, then Sir Ambrose dried the scraps and carefully reassembled them on the desk in his cabin. The task took the better part of the afternoon and was made difficult because many of the scraps were missing or else illegible. At first he could take his bearings from only a few words: TOLEDO, LONGITUDO, IUPITER. By this time the Spanish frigate was scarcely a league away, and a larger fleet had been sighted off the coast of Hispaniola. But the *Philip Sidney* would not be caught. She weighed anchor and soon after nightfall had reached the islands of the Bahamas. And so it was there among the palmed cays, in dark waters infested with both sharks and pirates, that Sir Ambrose finished assembling what remained of the scraps and, with them, the secret of the *Sacra Familia*.

'Was it another map?' I asked.

'No,' she replied. 'Something much more intricate than a map. Perhaps you wish to see it?' She had risen to her feet. 'What remains is still quite legible.'

I too found my feet, but the motion seemed to unsettle me and I felt dizzy once again. I wavered on my feet as I followed her across the tiles into the atrium, which was filled with an eerie storm light. The rain on the windows seemed louder now, and the chandelier was chiming noisily overhead. Water had begun trickling down the marble staircase, dripping from the banisters and puddling on the floor, but Alethea was either oblivious or apathetic, for she guided me past the little waterfall, tugging gently at my arm and saying something about an almanac. Her voice was half muffled by the rain. The floor seemed to tremble underfoot as we picked our way along the corridor, passing the Great Room and the breakfast parlour. Suddenly the crypt plunged abysmally beneath us.

'. . . transits, eclipses, occultations,' her voice was echoing against the copper-sheathed walls as we descended into the entombed air. As we reached the bottom of the stairs I felt water beneath my feet. It seemed to be flowing down the walls, for when I brushed against one of them my shoulder came away wet to the touch. Oily-looking waves streamed past us. Alethea was walking more swiftly now, splashing along in her buskins, still apparently oblivious to the conditions.

'Everything in the tables has been calculated with the utmost precision.' Her voice seemed distant as she strode into the darkness ahead of me, hoisting aloft the creaking lantern. From all round came the sounds of invisible water lisping and hissing as it coursed swiftly along the rocky striations. 'The almanac was compiled, you see, by Galileo himself.'

So it was that I found myself back inside the muniment

room, the place where I first encountered, through his many fragments, the mysterious Sir Ambrose Plessington. I lingered on the threshold. The floor, like that in the corridor, was running with water. The sodden rushes squelched as Alethea picked her away across to the coffin, which still sat on the trestle-table, safe for the time being. As she hooked the lamp to the wall sconce I was surprised to see how the water was almost crimson in colour. A droplet of what looked like blood fell from the ceiling and spattered my knuckles.

'Venetian red,' she explained. 'I've been using it in my search for the underground waterways. I pour dye into the cress-pond in order to determine what course it takes. I suppose I might have used a colour that was less gruesome, but as it happens the dye has done its work and I've managed to track down a number of the hidden channels. An engineer is laying pipes and building drains so that the springs can be tamed and the water diverted for use in fountains.'

I wiped my hand on my doublet and stood in silence as she creaked open the lid of the coffin and began to rummage among the papers. I could hear the dull roar of the water as it carved its mysterious channel behind the stone. *Tame* such waters? I had to admire her optimism, the unfailing buoyancy of her dreams. Even in the midst of such wreckage she could still cling to her grandiose visions of the house. But I had to admire her, I supposed, in other ways as well. For I had come to Pontifex Hall in anger and hatred but now found, almost to my chagrin, that it was impossible to dislike her. Perhaps I was as deluded as she was; perhaps I too was dreaming and desiring even as I trod the rising waters.

'Here it is.'

Her voice startled me from my reverie. She had turned round and was extending in her hand a piece of paper, or some other backing, on to which dozens of scraps had been pasted. Yet another text, another scrap to tell the story of her father's life. As she angled it into the light of the lamp I could see three or four columns of figures, each broken by an occasional gap.

'The puzzle of the *Sacra Familia*,' she was saying, 'fitted together by Sir Ambrose. Can you read it? The tables predict the eclipses of each one of the Jovian satellites.'

I blinked hard at this piece of handiwork, still perplexed. 'The Jovian satellites? But I fail to understand what they have to do with—'

And then suddenly I did. The print jumped into focus and seemed to detach itself from the page. The paper was spattered with Venetian red, but I had just made out the words IUPITER and LONGITUDO, when a stone burst from the wall like the stopper from the bung-hole of a cask, followed by a reddish tide.

I stumbled backwards a step, feeling the ice-cold water seep through my boots. Another stone broke free and even more water spilled inside, unfurling like tumbling bolts of russet to curl round our feet. The cataclysm had begun. For a paralysing moment I imagined the entire wall buckling and the pair of us crushed to death beneath tons of water and shattered masonry. Then I splashed forward and snatched Alethea's hand.

'Come,' I said. 'Quickly – or we'll drown!'

But she broke my grasp and scooped an armful of papers at random from the coffin, which now balanced precariously on its stand. 'The papers,' she said. 'Help me!'

But I was not going to drown for the sake of Sir Ambrose Plessington. I stepped forward and, seizing her arm, pulled her towards the threshold. The papers clutched to her chest spilled into the water, then the ink blurred and ran on the parchment, effacing itself in the eddying current. I could see among those sodden scraps the paper recovered from the galleon – the secret of the *Sacra Familia* once more cast upon the waters.

It would not be retrieved a second time. I reached down the lantern and, still clutching Alethea's arm, forced the door a few inches wider. The water must have broken through elsewhere in the crypt, for in the corridor it was two feet deep and flowing in a torrent from the direction of the staircase. Thrusting the lantern aloft I tried to make out the distant stairs. Already my feet were numb. I could hear the water whorling in the corners and slapping against the copper-sheathed walls. I swung round to face her.

'Is there another way out?'

'No.' She was still struggling to salvage what remained of her father's papers, which now flowed past like trout in a brook, trailing seals and ribbons. 'Only the way we came!'

I dragged her away and waded knee-deep into the current. The water was black now instead of red. After a few steps I heard the coffin fall from the trestle-table and overturn. I pressed forward. When I raised the lantern I saw that the other doors in the tunnel had burst open under the tremendous force of the waters. Their tributaries deepened and quickened the flow. Soon the fragments of wooden barrels and hanks of old rope were washed into our path, followed by the bone-urns from some ancient ossuary. Then came the bones themselves, bobbing skulls and femurs, the jumbled remains of a hundred monks shifting and sliding towards us.

I picked my way round the grotesque flotsam with Alethea still in tow. We had no more than a minute, I reckoned, to make our escape, before the crypt filled with water. When the water reached the middle of my thighs I heard another noise, a frantic squeaking which I mistook for the hinges of the lantern until I saw dozens of rats – fat, matted creatures – swimming against the tide and using the floating casks and skulls as stepping-stones. I lost my footing, then my grip on the lantern, which toppled into the water and extinguished with a hiss. I could see nothing in the darkness but, far in the distance, a weak light from the hatchway glowing overhead. I began struggling towards it, but so weakened was I when we reached the stairs that I could barely stand. The water had risen to my chest; it took three attempts before I finally found purchase on a submerged tread. Then I gripped the banister and climbed hand over hand until, exhausted and frozen, followed by Alethea, I breasted the hatch.

The corridor was running with water, adding to the torrent in the crypt below. We staggered towards the atrium, passing on the way the breakfast parlour and the Great Room. In the latter the cornices and their brackets were streaming, as were the stalactites of lime-washed plasterwork. A segment had fallen from the centre of the ceiling exposing the laths and joists beneath. Cracks like lightning-strokes had begun appearing on the walls, spilling yet more plaster in the water. Then, over the rush of water, we heard a desperate voice – that of Phineas – summoning Lady Marchamont.

'The books!' Alethea was saying over the roar of the water behind us. 'We must rescue the books!'

But we were not to reach the library, or not just yet. For on stumbling into the atrium we discovered Phineas with his back turned towards us, endeavouring to block the entrance door as he had done against me. It was shaking in its frame under some furious assault from the outside. He had no better luck the second time, for after another blow the door burst wide with a shriek of tortured wood and a gust of wind. I heard the crystal pendants of the chandelier chiming high overhead and felt Alethea's frigid hand in mine. Our visitors had arrived at last.

It was their coach, framed in the doorway, that I noticed first: a fleet-looking vehicle with a domed roof and four horses stamping and foaming in their traces. Then I heard a crunch of gravel and a broad figure stepped through the splintered frame, followed swiftly by three men in black-and-gold livery.

'Sir Richard?' Alethea was standing stock-still and open-mouthed beside me. Was she remembering the murder on the Pont Neuf? Quickly she dropped my hand. 'What are you doing here? What is – ?'

Phineas was the first to respond, scuttling forward to grapple with one of the men. But the contest was unequal, for his opponent produced from his belt a short dagger with which he artfully parried two feeble blows before driving the blade home with a swift and practised gesture. The footman crumpled without a word while his conqueror, a fat man with hooded eyes, wiped the stiletto on his breeches and advanced towards us.

'Sir Richard?' Alethea took a faltering step across the tiles. Her face had gone white. But Sir Richard directed his gaze not at his shocked affianced but at me.

'Mr Inchbold,' he said in a level tone as he removed his hat with a sweep of his arm. 'Well, well, I find I am not misinformed after all. How resourceful you must be. I saw you drown in the river with my own two eyes, though my sources insisted otherwise. I can but hope you were as resourceful in your search.' He unfastened a brass button to expose the pistol tucked in his belt. Water eddied between his boots. 'So where is it, then?' He stepped a few paces towards us. The black-clad trio at his heels eagerly followed suit. '*The Labyrinth of the World*,' he said in the same even tone. 'Where is it?'

But as he took another step, reaching for his weapon, the floor of the atrium shifted like the deck of a foundering ship and the four of them lost their balance. No sooner had they righted themselves than the chandelier broke free from its mooring with a shriek and plunged to the floor, shattering into a thousand pieces between us. Sir Richard staggered backwards, still fumbling for his pistol. I felt glass skittering against my boots and then a pair of hands in the middle of my back.

'Go!' It was Alethea. 'Run!'

Chapter Nine

All four of Jupiter's moons, even Callisto, the largest, are far too dim to be sighted with the naked eye. Galileo first saw them on a winter night in January in the year 1610, using a telescope with a magnitude of 32: four moons that orbit Jupiter in periods of one and a half to sixteen and a half days. Four new worlds that no one, ancient or modern, had ever seen before. He published his discovery in *Sidereus nuncius*, the 'Messenger of the Stars', and within a year the sightings were confirmed by Jesuit astronomers in Rome as well as by Kepler in Prague. They were also confirmed by a German astronomer, Simon Marius, who gave the moons their names: Io, Europa, Ganymede and Callisto.

Even from the beginning the discovery provoked as much

controversy as amazement. Not only were the four new satellites incompatible with the Scriptures but they also challenged Aristotle's claim in *De caelo* that the stars are fixed in the heavens. Worst of all, they opposed the description of the universe given in another hallowed book, Ptolemy's *Almagest*. Enemies of Copernicus attacked his system by arguing that if the earth is not, as Ptolemy claims, at the centre of the universe, then why should the earth, and the earth alone, possess an orbiting moon? But the revolutions of Jupiter's moons now led Galileo to recognise that the stars could orbit a planet at the same time as the planet itself orbits the sun. Jupiter and its four satellites became, for Galileo, a model for the earth and its own moon. So it was that in 1613 he wrote in the appendix to his letters on sunspots – a work opposing the Jesuit astronomer Christopher Scheiner – that the moons proved beyond all doubt the truth of Copernicanism.

But for Galileo the moons also had a practical significance that he kept a closer secret even than his Copernicanism. Galileo was a most practical man, of course. He dropped cannon-balls from the Leaning Tower of Pisa to refute Aristotle's theory of motion, and at the Auditorium Maximum in Padua he lectured students on the best methods of fortifying cities and constructing cannons. Now he realised that Jupiter's moons – and, more specifically, the eclipses occurring when they pass into the planet's shadow – could be used to solve the ancient problem of finding the longitude at sea; a problem for whose solution the King of Spain had offered a prize of 6,000 ducats and the States-General of Holland, not to be outdone, 30,000 florins. The truce between the two nations, signed in 1609, was soon to expire – that is, if it was not shattered by cannon-fire first. A new war would see the Spaniards and the Dutch fighting among the islands of the Pacific as well as on the old battlefields of Europe. Indeed, a few Dutch raids on the *presidios* of Tierra Firme had already been reported. So it was that Galileo, a devout Catholic, calculated a table of eclipses and approached Philip III through the offices of the Tuscan ambassador in Madrid. These tables – the index of Spanish fortunes in the Pacific – predicted the times and durations of the eclipses of each of the moons: eclipses that, like those of the moon, happen at the same instant anywhere on earth. Unlike lunar eclipses, however, these occur with great frequency, almost daily in the case of Io. Jupiter and its satellites therefore became, for whoever could predict their eclipses, a celestial clock telling the difference in time between any two places on earth.

'By the middle of 1615 the spies for both the War Party and the States-General were sending back from Madrid reports that Spanish ships in the Pacific had begun making trials using Galileo's tables. These tables were highly secret, of course.' Alethea was two steps ahead of me, leading the way through a darkened corridor whose carpet was an inch deep in water. 'Galileo never published a word of them.'

'And the *Sacra Familia* was one of the ships?'

She nodded her head. 'Sir Ambrose had read all of the reports that came to Lambeth Palace, and so he recognised the name of the ship as soon as he read it on her escutcheon.'

Pursued by Sir Richard, we had run from the atrium, splashing and sliding, into the library, where so much water had collected on the floor that the books on the bottom shelves were already half submerged, while dozens of those shelved higher had toppled to the floor. Already the pasteboard covers were wrinkling and the rag-paper pages degrading into the cast-off scraps of linen and hemp from which they were fashioned. I was stooping to salvage one of them – a futile gesture – when Alethea ordered me to keep running. We climbed the ladder to the library's gallery, then raised it beyond the reach of our pursuers. Now I could hear their boots on the stairs as we picked our way past the obstacles – collapsed plaster and fallen timbers – that littered the maze of dark corridors on the first floor.

'So the *Sacra Familia* had found a method of calculating the longitude at sea?'

'No,' she said, hurrying forward. 'Galileo's method fails to work at sea. On dry land or in an observatory, yes, it is the best method so far conceived. But at sea it is impossible. It is difficult enough to use a backstaff, let alone a telescope, on a moving ship, especially on a rough swell such as one finds in the Pacific. Jupiter might be spotted for a few seconds, but the slightest motion of the deck makes it impossible to train the lens on the satellites, even with the special binocular lenses that Galileo invented.'

How much longer before we were captured? From beyond the plaster walls came the sounds of thunder, or perhaps the boots of our pursuers. Or was it the water rupturing its way through the heart of the building? The floor seemed to tremble underfoot. Limping from pain, I stumbled after her. I was wet and exhausted but still curious. I demanded to know what secret it was that, in all likelihood, I was about to die for. 'What did the *Sacra Familia* discover?'

'An island of bamboo, sandalwood and gold,' she explained as we rounded a corner. She had taken my hand. 'The *Sacra Familia* was driven aground on an island somewhere in the southeast Trades that blow to the north of the Tropic of Capricorn. Or rather the island was covered not in gold but white spar, the yellow crystals that the Muhammadan alchemists call *markasita*, a substance never found anywhere that gold is not. It was the same island, Pinzón knew, as the one portrayed in the Prague edition of the *Theatrum orbis terrarum*. You see, Pinzón had been past the island once before, in 1595, on Mendaña's last voyage in search of the Islas de Solomón.'

'Mendaña missed the Solomon Islands and discovered Manoa instead?'

'Or possibly it was one of the fabled Islas de Solomón themselves. Who can say? Mendaña and Pinzón may have regarded the new island, with all of its sandalwood and white spar, as the site of King Solomon's mines. But of course, like the original Islas de Solomón, no one was able to find it again, though it was plotted in the Prague edition of the *Theatrum*.'

We rounded another corner and passed chambers whose doors yawned wide to show scriptors, writing boxes and a knee-hole desk. Their floors, too, were under water; the wainscots were warped and streams of water were running down the walls. Then the corridor swung left. Where were we fleeing to?

'But now the island's longitude could be determined,' Alethea was telling me. 'Galileo's tables revealed the precise time at which each of the eclipses would be seen in Toledo, which is where the Spaniards situate their prime meridian. Pinzón then recorded the exact times of the same eclipses on the island. Then, once the ship was rebuilt with sandalwood, she sailed for Spain, from which a new expedition would be despatched to locate the island, using the proper co-ordinates. But of course the *Sacra Familia* never reached Cádiz.' I could feel her grip tighten, then as we rounded another corner she added: 'And even had she reached Spain, her information would not have been worth the paper it was written on. In the space of a year it had gone from being one of the most valuable documents in Christendom to a dangerous heresy whose followers were burned at the stake.'

For if the moons of Jupiter were controversial, then their eclipses were even more so. Galileo did not discover them until 1612, two years after his first sighting of the moons themselves. He had begun calculating their motions by 1611, but he used the Ptolemaic instead of the Copernican tables – accepting the earth, that is, and not the sun as the centre of Jupiter's motions. Only when he refined his calculations by employing the Copernican tables did he discover how the moons were being eclipsed by Jupiter, whose shadow blotted out the light reflected from the sun. Predicting these eclipses was henceforth a simple enough task, but such predictions could not be made using the Ptolemaic tables, which caused errors both in the prediction of the time at which an eclipse begins and the position of the satellite against the stars as it enters and then emerges from the eclipse. Predicting the eclipses – these keys to the secret of the longitude – therefore entailed the acceptance of Copernicanism, a heresy for which Giordano Bruno was burned in Rome only a dozen years earlier.

What followed was a story that I knew well enough: one of ignorance triumphing over reason, of orthodoxy and prejudice over invention. In 1614 Galileo wrote to Christina of Lorraine a letter attempting to render Copernicanism consistent with the Holy Scripture. The effort was in vain, however, because the letter was laid before the Inquisition, whose dark machinery was set in motion by Pope Paul V. The cardinals in the Palace of the

Sant'Uffizio summoned Galileo to Rome and, after examining him, affirmed Copernicanism as a heretical doctrine. This had been in the winter of 1616, shortly after the *Sacra Familia* set sail on her long voyage into the South Seas. Galileo's method was therefore not only impractical by the time the battered convoy returned to Cádiz: it was also heretical.

'In another time such a heresy might not have been so catastrophic. Come, Mr Inchbold.'

We were moving almost blindly now. I could hear more rats, a whole pack of them, scampering and squealing underfoot.

'But in 1616 a war between the Catholics and Protestants was looming. Rome could ill afford new threats to its orthodoxies, especially ones propagated by someone as eminent as Galileo. Isaac Casaubon may have demolished the myth of Hermes Trismegistus, but now Hermetic philosophers all across Europe were catching at this new and, in the eyes of the Roman Curia, equally dangerous wisdom. Astronomy had replaced the learning of the *Corpus hermeticum* as the greatest danger to Church authority. Galileo was censured and his writings placed by the Jesuits on their *Index* along with the works of occultists such as Agrippa and Paracelsus. His project was dropped by the Spaniards, and the search for the longitude at sea – and for the mysterious island in the Pacific – came to an end.'

And so that might have been the last of the story, she claimed, had word not reached London that all was not lost when the *Sacra Familia* was wrecked on the reef. Other copies of her sea-chart existed. At first the reports were as spurious and untrustworthy as those regarding the island itself, though in time they were confirmed by spies in Madrid and Seville. These reports claimed that the *Sacra Familia*, after sailing from Veracruz, docked with the rest of the Mexican fleet in Havana, where, fearing the dire weather, her captain deposited duplicates of her charts, written in cipher, at the Jesuit mission of San Cristóbal – documents later shipped to Seville for safekeeping in the archives of the House of Trade.

'But that was not the only place the documents were housed. In March of 1617, just as Raleigh's fleet was preparing to sail for Guiana, Archduke Ferdinand of Styria concluded with the

King of Spain a treaty under whose terms Philip recognised Ferdinand as the successor to the Emperor Matthias in return for the German territory of Alsace and two Imperial enclaves in Italy. The treaty brought together the two most powerful families in Europe, the two Houses of Habsburg, one in Spain, the other in Austria. The two great empires would now work together, uniting to share their armies and their knowledge, and in so doing to crush the Protestants of Europe once and for all. Among their most powerful arsenals, of course, were their libraries.'

A roof slate thundered overhead as it fell. Part of the ceiling had fallen to expose the beams of the garret overhead. Water was cascading through, spilling into our path. I heard a shout from somewhere behind us, then Alethea gripped my hand and pulled me through the cataract.

'But the arsenal in Vienna was in danger,' I gasped as we emerged on the other side.

'Yes. In 1617 the Protestant armies of Count Thurn were at the gates of Vienna.'

'And so the chart was taken to Bohemia?'

'Along with dozens of other treasures from the Imperial Library in Vienna. It was placed in the archives of the Spanish Rooms, which already held reams of Tycho Brahe's astronomical data as well as forbidden books by Galileo, Copernicus and other heretics.'

And so it was that the new plot unfolded in London: one that sent Sir Ambrose to Prague Castle in the entourage of the Elector Palatine. He was given the task of recovering as many of the volumes from the library of the Spanish Rooms as possible, but in particular he was charged with finding the sea-chart and bringing it to England. The decisive *coup de main* would be struck after all – albeit belatedly – against the King of Spain.

'But the plan miscarried,' I said. 'The palimpsest was never delivered to Lambeth Palace.'

'No,' Alethea replied. 'At the last moment Sir Ambrose betrayed the War Party.'

'Betrayed them?' We had stopped before a closed door,

which Alethea was attempting to force with her shoulder. 'But why? Are you saying Sir Ambrose was a Spanish agent?'

'No, not Sir Ambrose. But both the Navy Office and Lambeth Palace had been infiltrated. Word of the palimpsest had already reached both Rome and Madrid.'

She was pressing with her shoulder at the door, which refused to budge. I heard a long-case clock chime from somewhere behind us, and then the sound of distant voices.

'*Ven acqui!*'

'*Vayamos por otro lado!*'

The door groaned and gave an inch. It was the same door, I realised, that had impeded my progress that long-ago morning. I lunged forward to help push. It creaked open another inch, then I felt a breeze and heard more frantic chiming: not spurs, as I thought at first, but the vials and cuvettes on their shelves in the laboratory.

'The fact that the palimpsest survived at all is a miracle,' Alethea said as we burst through a second later, then righted ourselves in another darkened corridor. 'In the end Sir Ambrose wanted it destroyed. Although he had risked his life to save it, his final wish was that it should burn.'

A chunk of plaster fell with a violent splash ahead of us, and the timbers above our head were creaking under an immense strain. We picked our way more cautiously through the corridor. Some more plaster collapsed, less than ten feet ahead of us.

'The Puritans wanted the chart,' I said. 'Standfast Osborne—'

'Yes,' she replied. 'As do the Spaniards. And now it appears that the new Secretary of State has also learned of its existence. Sir Ambrose claimed it was cursed, and he was right, because ten years ago he was poisoned by Spanish agents. They feared he would sell it to Cromwell, for in those years we were short of money and the Puritans were preparing for their holy war against the King of Spain. By then, of course, I knew that Sir Ambrose was not my true father,' she added in an undertone. 'That's who these men are, of course: Spanish agents. The same men who murdered Lord Marchamont.'

For a second I wondered if I had heard her aright. 'Sir Ambrose was not your father? But—'

'Yes,' she replied. 'That is my last deception. My real father was also murdered by Spanish agents – by Henry Monboddo, as a matter of fact. This was many years earlier. You see, Henry Monboddo was not only an art broker but also a Spanish agent. He learned of the palimpsest through the spies in Prague. But Sir Ambrose already knew of his treachery because of the failure of the Orinoco expedition, and he therefore used my father as a decoy. My mother, who had travelled from Prague with my father, died in childbirth shortly afterwards—'

'Your mother?'

' – and I was raised by Sir Ambrose as his daughter. I believe he regarded it as his duty, perhaps even as a form of penance, for betraying my father along with the greedy dukes and bishops in the War Party. My father was a Bohemian, a gentle man devoted to books and learning. But Sir Ambrose felt he could not trust him because he was a Roman Catholic.'

Voices echoed in the maze of corridors behind us. Alethea was moving more quickly now. We stepped over a fallen tapestry and passed a chamber whose window flashed with lightning. Through it I could see the lime trees stretching into the distance.

'*Caray!*'

'*Por Dios! Las aquas han subido!*'

The corridor turned to the left and we found ourselves splashing through a wide but empty saloon. I thought I heard a pistol shot from behind, followed by the shriek of splintering timber. Halfway through, my club foot slipped on the tiles and I sprawled headlong into the water. Within seconds I was back on my feet, hurrying, I was certain, to a horrible death.

'I was raised in Pontifex Hall,' Alethea was continuing as though oblivious to the dangers, 'and it was from Sir Ambrose that I learned all that I know. We were like Miranda and Prospero on their island, awaiting the tempest that would bring the usurpers to their shore. In time he even told me of the palimpsest and its history. He wanted it destroyed, as I have said, and I would happily have complied. But my husband

and then Sir Richard each dissuaded me. The document was to be sold, you see. I would be paid £10,000. Sir Richard was acting as the agent. I had no idea who the buyer was, nor did I care. I wished to be rid of the palimpsest, that was all. I trusted Sir Richard implicitly. We were to be married. The money would have been used to restore the house. We would have lived here together.' She paused for a second. I could hear shouts coming from behind us. 'But now the usurpers have arrived,' she intoned sadly. 'And now I know what I—'

Her last words were lost to me as the wall beside us buckled and more plaster toppled from the ceiling, striking me a glancing blow on the shoulder. I reeled sideways and fell flat for a second time. When I picked myself up, sodden and gasping, I groped for Alethea's hand; but by then she had already disappeared down the corridor. Somewhere at the end of it, in the laboratory, the dozens of glass vials were ringing their alarum.

And now I know what I must do . . .

Fear gives us wings, they say. But it is also, as Xenophon claims, stronger than love. I must confess that my thoughts were no longer for the books, or even Alethea, but only for myself as I rushed along the corridor a few seconds later. My frantic claudications echoed against the sodden plasterwork until, skidding wildly, I reached not the laboratory but the top of the staircase, which I realised had been my true destination. I hesitated at the sight of it, surprised to have negotiated my way so easily through the maze of corridors. But the marble steps were treacherously slick, and as I began the descent my dizziness returned. From the top step I could see almost the whole of the atrium, the whole dreadful tableau of death and ruin spread before me. The oval looking-glass in the atrium had been knocked over; its cracked face now reflected the gap in the ceiling where the chandelier had broken free. The chandelier itself lay nearby, in the middle of the floor, a mangled bronze bird. Beyond its wreckage I could see Phineas lying on his belly beside the door, his arms flung wide.

There were no more sounds from the laboratory – no ringing

vials and no cries for help. For a moment I wondered if I should return for Alethea, but then, gripping the banister, I continued my cautious descent. I was not prepared to die, I told myself, for the sins of Sir Ambrose Plessington. Through the open door I could see that the rain had finally stopped. The wind had steadied and the sun was threatening to appear. Such is the mockery of fate. As I crossed the atrium, my boots crunched the shattered crystal. I felt palsied and unstable until I realised that the floor was trembling underfoot. The blood had spread outwards from Phineas's prostrate body like the tendrils of a bright, submarine plant. I had just stepped past the gaudy slick when I heard a shout and then saw a lone figure in the library doorway, dressed in black. I caught a last view of the felled shelves and the chaos of the sodden masses on the floor before rushing through the doorway and into the dun-coloured light.

The horses, spooked by the commotions, tossed their heads in alarm and shied backwards as I flung myself towards them. The park, half waterlogged, wavered before me, reflecting a lurid sky. I thought of boarding the coach and so making my escape, but there was no time. I could hear my pursuer shouting in Spanish, while another figure had appeared from round the side of the house, near the physic garden. So I began to run instead, fleeing in the opposite direction, towards the hedge-maze. Perhaps I had visions of drawing the killers away from Alethea – of fulfilling for one last time the task for which I was hired. Had it not been my rash flight from London that brought them to Pontifex Hall in the first place? It was a foolish, fantastic notion: I with my crippled foot and wheezing lungs was no match for either of my pursuers, the second of whom I saw was Sir Richard Overstreet. But as I approached the maze I risked a second glance over my shoulder and saw a deep furrow open in the ground behind me, a long trench running across the park, from the cress-pond towards the coach-and-four.

In retrospect the crevice seems a cataclysm of near biblical dimensions, perhaps even a miracle, if miracles can be so reckless and tragic. The rear wheels of the coach were swallowed first. The ground trembling beneath them crumbled and the coach tipped backwards before heeling in the trough, which had widened to more than six feet and filled with water as the subterranean current burst to the surface. The horses' hind-quarters shimmied for a second and then disappeared. The first of my pursuers, the man in black, stopped short at the brink and stumbled. He stared across at me, aghast and amazed, as the reddish earth collapsed and the chasm yawned ever wider. Then he, too, disappeared into the gaping jaws.

I whirled and kept running. The air was tart with privet and hedge-mustard, whose overgrown branches clawed at my cheeks and shoulders as I dived into the maze and swung left into an even thicker gauntlet of wet branches and sharp holly leaves. Puddles splashed underfoot. Through a small gap in the hedge I glimpsed Sir Richard, his pistol in hand as he dashed towards the entrance to the maze. Another fork. I turned right, then left, threading my way inside the sinuous passages. At one point I tripped on a root and, raising myself, discovered a pair of hedge-clippers abandoned in the undergrowth. I picked them up – the blades were rusty but still sharp – and again took to my heels.

It must have been another minute or two before I heard the scream. By this point I had reached the centre of the labyrinth, a small, scrubby patch of ground on which had been placed a wooden bench, rotted by the elements. I could hear Sir Richard crashing along the paths and realised he must be following my footprints through the mud. Yet another trail that had betrayed me. He would soon catch me – if the hedge-maze wasn't swallowed first, for the ground was trembling and shaking like a stonemason's yard. When the shriek broke the air I was gripping the handle of the clippers and backing into the pruned branches, preparing for a passage of arms. Looking up I glimpsed, above the parapets of box and hornbeam, a lone figure poised in a first-floor window.

Alethea had reached the laboratory after all. I climbed on to the bench's cracked seat and saw her throw the casement wide and gesture wildly. I glimpsed her for only a second, because no sooner had the panes flashed in the sunlight –

for the sun, incredibly, had now appeared – than the south wing of the house began crumbling into the trench. Timbers warped and snapped, then came the landslide of ashlar and stone that exposed the library through a haze of plaster dust before its timbers likewise buckled, shedding scores of books into the great chasm. The first floor overhung the cavity for a few seconds before it began its own ponderous slide. A section of the roof lurched forward, shedding tiles; then the corbels shattered and the last of the roof spilled into the river surging through the foundations.

I was still perched on the bench, frozen with fear as the dreadful spectacle unfolded before me. I heard another scream as the east elevation fissured and collapsed like a rockface, raising clouds of dust that billowed and swirled like cannon-smoke. The magnificent structure with its exposed compartments – each with its furniture and wallpaper – now looked no more than a doll's house or an architect's model. I could even see the laboratory with its telescope and the shelves of shattered vials. But there was no sign of Alethea, not there or anywhere else. I had leapt from the bench and was moving back through the maze when the floor of the atrium disintegrated and the doll's house crumpled inward, its floors collapsing together with a rumble I could feel in my diaphragm. I thought I heard yet another scream, but I must have been mistaken: it was only the sound of tortured iron and splintering beams, the last fragments of Pontifex Hall tumbling into the voracious water.

Epilogue

C losing-time. Darkness has gathered in the windows and fallen over the broad sea-reach of the Thames. The girders of the ancient drawbridge groan as they rise to admit a final passage to the tanned sails of barges and smacks nosing downstream into the grey offing. The last of the afternoon traffic has crunched across the snow-covered carriageway. In a minute there will come a gentle ruffle as the awning is furled, followed by a clapping of shutters. Tom Monk and his three children are astir below, rattling keys and counting coins, while I sit upstairs in my study, here in my last refuge, clasping a goose quill between arthritic fingers and slowly paying out this trail of words behind me. Downstairs the green door opens, and my candle gutters in the breeze. I adjust my spectacles – my eyes have grown even dimmer now – and lean hopefully forward. A lump of coal whistles in the grate. The task, at long last, is almost complete.

There is both much and little left to tell. What happened at Pontifex Hall on that final day I suppose I shall never fully understand, even though I am the only one who lives to tell the story. My survival was a matter of luck or chance, or perhaps the mercy of St John of God, the patron saint of printers and booksellers. I escaped from Sir Richard Overstreet in the end, or, rather, he escaped from me, rushing back through the maze-garden towards the precipice as the house began its collapse. Whether he hoped to save Alethea or salvage the parchment I was not to learn, because he too was consumed by the torrent. I emerged from the labyrinth to see him borne away on the back of the broad serpent as it rushed heedlessly through the park. By this time the house and all its contents had sunk and been swallowed up, save for part of the crypt. Spread before me was a scene of stark and terrible desolation. Even the obelisk had disappeared. Nor was there any sign of Alethea, though I must have spent more than two hours searching for her, overturning pieces of wreckage and even daring to wade hip-deep into the flooded crypt. A dozen times her frantic cry for help echoed in my head. Yet I found nothing more than a few books, which I carefully salvaged as if convinced that these sodden scraps could either atone for her loss or assuage my guilt.

I walked all the way back to Crampton Magna, travelling alongside the torrent of water that coiled through the flooded fields with their small islands of trees and half-submerged shocks of corn. The journey must have taken several hours in all. Among the flotsam of Pontifex Hall drifting past I saw a few more books from the demolished library, most so ruinous I could barely read their covers. These too were retrieved before they could slip away. As darkness was falling I trudged into the Ploughman's Arms with the soggy burden bound in my surcoat, then placed the books, seven in all, to dry beside the fire in my room. For hours I lay sleepless on the bolster, feeling like the survivor of a shipwreck who has washed on to a strand of beach where he will lie still among the driftwood and wrack, taking cautious inventories of his limbs and pockets before rising to his feet and making his first forays into the strange new world into which he is cast.

And the world into which I ventured was a strange one indeed. When I finally reached London, four days later, Nonsuch House looked altered and alien, almost unrecognisable. Everything was in its proper place, including Monk, but the shop seemed subtly transformed as if at some atomic level. Even the old rituals were powerless to counteract the enchantment. I found solace, small as it was, among my books. In those first weeks after my return I used to study the volumes salvaged from Pontifex Hall as if seeking in their blurred and stiffened pages some clue to the tragedy. Their inks had faded and the gilt on their covers eroded; even the ex-libises had peeled away. They still sit together on a shelf above my desk, and of all of the volumes in Nonsuch House, these seven alone are not for sale.

Only one volume is of particular significance. It is a copy of the *Anthologia Graeca* – itself a series of scraps compiled in Constantinople by Cephalas and then discovered, centuries later, among the manuscripts in the Bibliotheca Palatina in Heidelberg. There is no ex-libris, but inscribed on the pastedown are the words 'Emilia Molyneux', and inserted in the centre are a passport and a certificate of health, both in the name of Silas Cobb, both stamped in Prague and dated 1620. None of the names was visible at first. Only with time did they reappear as some mysterious chemical reaction – 'ghosting', Alethea had called it – brought the tannins and iron salts leaching back to the surface of the membranes. And it was from these scraps of paper, these few scribbled words in palimpsest, that I began a patient reconstruction of events.

Some parts of the puzzle were more easily assembled than others. There was, after all, a mention of the affair in most of the newssheets, which reported the death of Sir Richard Overstreet, a prominent diplomat and landowner who had recently returned from exile in France. His body was recovered three days later, some five miles from Pontifex Hall. But there was no mention either of Alethea or of the three Spaniards. Their bodies, I assume, were never found; nor was the palimpsest or, for all I know, Sir Ambrose's thousands of volumes.

And of course Sir Ambrose himself remains as great a mystery to me as ever. I have often wondered, since, why he should have betrayed his allies and hidden the palimpsest in Pontifex Hall. But he was an idealist; he believed in the Reformation and the spread of knowledge, in a community of scholars like that described by the Rosicrucians in their manifestos or by Francis Bacon in *The New Atlantis*, which tells how the natural sciences will return the world to its Golden Age, to that perfect state before the Fall of Man in Eden. On his return to England Sir Ambrose must have been sorely disillusioned. What he discovered among the denizens of the War Party were not enlightened scholars like those in Plato's Academy or Aristotle's Lyceum, but rather thieves and murderers as ignorant and evil as any found in Rome or

Madrid. With Europe poised on the brink of the abyss, the study of Nature and the pursuit of Truth had been replaced by a vulgar contest in which Protestants and Catholics each tried to bend the other to their will. Learning was no longer being used for the improvement of the world: it had become instead the handmaid of prejudice and orthodoxy, and prejudice and orthodoxy the handmaids of slaughter. Sir Ambrose would have wanted no part of it. The island and its riches, if they existed, were best left undiscovered, he must have decided, until the day when the world would be worthy of such treasures.

Yet it was not Sir Ambrose and his books – and not even *The Labyrinth of the World* – that I thought about most of all in those days. For it was Alethea whom I found myself mourning. At times I allowed myself to believe that somehow she had survived the wreck. In later years I would often glimpse through the window of Nonsuch Books a woman with a familiar gait or carriage, or a certain profile or gesture, and suffer for a second an exquisite shock – and then, inevitably, disappointment and regret. Alethea, like Arabella, would retreat once more into the shades of memory, becoming as distant and as much a figment as those lost islands of the Pacific that even now, in the Year of Our Lord 1700, no one has rediscovered. In time even those fleeting remnants vanished from my window, and I see her now, if ever, only in my dreams.